Jonathan Blanchard

Revised Odd-Fellowship Illustrated

22nd Edition

Jonathan Blanchard

Revised Odd-Fellowship Illustrated
22nd Edition

ISBN/EAN: 9783337333461

Printed in Europe, USA, Canada, Australia, Japan

Cover: Foto ©Andreas Hilbeck / pixelio.de

More available books at **www.hansebooks.com**

REVISED

ODD-FELLOWSHIP ILLUSTRATED:

THE COMPLETE

REVISED RITUAL

OF THE

Lodge, Encampment, Patriarchs Militant,

AND THE

REBEKAH DEGREES

THE AMENDED WORK

PROFUSELY ILLUSTRATED,

By a PAST GRAND PATRIARCH.

WITH AN HISTORICAL SKETCH OF THE ORDER, AND AN INTRODUC-
TION AND CRITICAL ANALYSIS OF THE CHAR-
ACTER OF EACH DEGREE BY

PRES'T. J. BLANCHARD OF WHEATON COLLEGE,

AND FOOT NOTE QUOTATIONS FROM STANDARD AUTHORITIES
OF THE ORDER, SHOWING ITS CHARACTER
AND TEACHINGS.

TWENTY SECOND EDITION.

CHICAGO, ILLINOIS.

EZRA A. COOK, PUBLISHER.

1893.

Is this ritual accurate and the analysis of it fair and candid? is doubtless the question which interests the reader most.

That the Sovereign Grand Lodge changed the ritual of the Order mainly because of the extensive circulation of our published ritual entitled " Odd-fellowship Illustrated," is conclusively proved by the statements, both verbal and written, of many members of the Order, besides admissions in the public prints, which announced that the Revised Ritual would be furnished to the lodges and Encampments in January, 1881.

Before that date we had propositions to furnish the new ritual as soon as it was issued. One of these propositions was accepted with an agreement that ample proof of the accuracy of the ritual should accompany or follow the copy.

The signs, grips, passwords, etc., which are known as the secret or unwritten work of the Order, were given to the lodges and Encampments orally, but all of the rest of the ritual was furnished them *printed* in what are called " Charge Books." The three " Charge Books " containing the ritual of the lodge and Encampment were furnished us, and every line of the ritual was carefully corrected thereby.

The secret work had been taken down in short-hand. and even the description of the signs, grips, etc., is given in the very words prescribed by the Sovereign Grand Lodge.

As to the fairness and candor of the Analysis of the ritual, each reader must judge. It seems to us that the statements made are all conclusively proved by quotations from standard and acknowledged authorities, and that the conclusions drawn are perfectly logical. Not the enemies, but the friends, founders and exponents of the Order are cited as witnesses.

This volume is on the same plan as "Freemasonry Illustrated" and "Knight Templarism Illustrated," which are acknowledged to be the most comprehensive and valuable works on the subject in the market.

In the preface of "Odd-fellowship Illustrated," first issued in 1874, we remarked that "careful observation shows that very few honest men care to pay for being put through ridiculous boys'-play ceremonies, even with solemn charges sandwiched in between, *especially if they know what they are beforehand.*" We are most thoroughly confirmed in the opinion just quoted. The official statistics of the Order quoted on pages 25 and 26 of this volume show that not only has the growth of the Order been stopped, but its membership redaced; and we think this is largely due to the wide circulation of our former ritual of the Order. As the present ritual is a great improvement on the other, in that it contains most valuable information in reference to the origin, history and character of the Order, we are encouraged to hope and pray that its circulation may be still more potent, both in keeping men out of the lodge and leading others, especially Christians, to see that Odd-fellowship is a false religion and therefore utterly at variance with the religion of the Bible.

THE PUBLISHER.

CONTENTS.

INTRODUCTION.

CHAPTER I.—HISTORICAL SKETCH.

CHAPTER II.—CHARACTER OF ODD-FELLOWSHIP.

CHAPTER III.—INITIATORY DEGREE.
OPENING CEREMONIES.

[A star (*) denotes that the topic will be found in a foot-note.]

CHAPTER IV.—INITIATORY DEGREE. INITIATION.

CONTENTS. 7

CHAPTER V.—INITIATORY DEGREE.
CLOSING CEREMONIES AND ANALYSIS.

CHAPTER VI.—DEGREE OF FRIENDSHIP.
GENERAL REGULATIONS AND OPENING CEREMONIES.

CHAPTER VII.—DEGREE OF FRIENDSHIP. INITIATION.

CHAPTER VIII.—DEGREE OF FRIENDSHIP.
CLOSING CEREMONIES AND ANALYSIS.

CHAPTER IX.—DEGREE OF BROTHERLY LOVE.
INITIATION AND ANALYSIS.

CHAPTER X.—DEGREE OF TRUTH. INITIATION.

CONTENTS. 9

CHAPTER XV.—Closing Ceremonies and Analysis.

CHAPTER XVI.—Rebekah, or Ladies' Degree.

CHAPTER XVII.—Rebekah Opening Ceremonies.

CHAPTER XVIII.—Rebekah Degree; Initiation.

CHAPTER XIX.—Rebekah Degree.
CLOSING CEREMONIES AND ANALYSIS.

CHAPTER XX.—Secret Work.

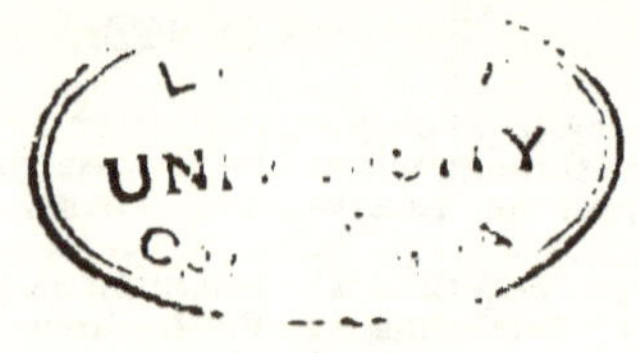

INTRODUCTION.

Satan the God of This World—Secret Orders the Modern Form of his Ancient Idolatrous Worship—Grosh claims for Odd-fellowship Kin with All Other Secret Associations—Initiation to the Odd-fellow what Regeneration is to the Christian—Worship Paid to Devils—The Ancient Mysteries—The Devil's Caricature of Salvation by Christ—Christian *vs.* Odd-fellow Joy—Odd-fellows' Millennium Without Christ—How men can Practice Fellowship with Demons—The "Irrepressible Conflict" of the Ages—Cudworth on Ignorant Paganism as Devil-Worship—Wresting the Scriptures and Scripture Symbols—Odd-fellowship promises Rest to the Soul.

When Satan asked Christ to worship him he asked to be recognized as the "god of this world;" for the god of its worships is the god of the world. Moses, Deut. 32:17; and David, Ps. 106:37; and Paul, 1 Cor. 10:20; and John the Divine, Rev. 9:20 and 16:14, speak familiarly of false worships as paid to devils, or evil demons. These demons are represented, throughout the Scriptures, as fallen angels and spirits of the wicked dead.

The deluge of secret orders, Odd-fellowship among them, are the modern forms of these old idolatries, which sunk the lost nations, from Egypt down. The proof of this is abundant.

In *Grosh*, p. 91, the highest Odd-fellow authority, we read:

"Among all the Mysteries of the Ancients, those celebrated at the city of Eleusis, hence called the Eleusinian Mysteries, are best known. These were copied from the Egyptian, and bore a correspondence to all similar institutions, and hence an account of one is, in the main, an account of all the others."

On the preceding page (90), Grosh explicitly shows these heathen worships to have been counterfeits of Bible religion, thus: " What regeneration by the word of truth is in religion, initiation is in Odd-fellowship. In this, as in many other particulars, our institution has instinctively, as it were, copied after nearly all secret associations of a religious and moral character. In Egypt, the most ancient among the ancient kingdoms, an institution of this kind existed from the earliest period." Again (page 92): " ' From the earliest ages to the present day, there have been similar associations, founded upon the same general principles, with similar rites and ceremonies.' " Again, same page: " *These rites and ceremonies were originally of a religious character*, COPIED * * FROM A DIVINE INSTITUTION."(!)

If the object of this fundamental authority in Odd-fellowship (Grosh) had been to declare the secret worships to be counterfeits of the religion of the Bible he could not have spoken more clearly. And if so, every ceremony and prayer in Odd-fellowship is worship paid to devils.

But he is more explicit still. Thus (page 91): " ' It was a leading characteristic of all the ancient rites, that they began in sorrow and gloom, but ended in light and joy; they were all calculated to remind men of their weakness, their ignorance, their helplessness, and their sinfulness of character; * * and the rising of the just to life eternal and immortal." (!) If this language does not describe a counterfeit repentance and soul-sorrow for sin, leading to " the joys of salvation," then it is impossible for words to describe such counterfeit.

The learned Scotch Presbyterian Macknight, in his " Preface to the Ephesians," collects from Bishop War-burton and old Roman and Greek writers the same account of these old mysteries given by the Odd-fellow Grosh. The following are extracts from Macknight:

"Each of the heathen gods, beside the worship paid to him in public, had a secret worship to which none were admitted but those who were prepared by previous ceremonies;" that is, each pagan shrine or temple was a lodge. These worships were paid, in Egypt, to Isis and Osiris; in Asia, to Mithras; in Samothrace, to the Mother of the gods; in Boeotia, to Bacchus; in Cyprus, to Venus; in Crete, to Jupiter; in Athens, to Ceres and Proserpine; and in other places, to an incredible number. "For," as Zozimus tells us, "These most holy rites were so extensive as to take in the whole race of mankind."

Another old writer, Proclus, describing these mysteries gives, as will be seen in this volume, an exact description of the rites of Odd-fellowship. Thus: "In the most holy mysteries there is a terror diffused into the minds of the initiated." And, " In the lesser mysteries matters were so contrived that the person to be initiated, at his entrance, was filled with inexpressible horror." And, "It seems, darkness was dispelled by the sudden flashing of light," etc.

Thus the Freemason is horrified by being led, stripped and blindfolded, by a rope about his neck, till knocked down as Hiram Abiff. The Odd-fellow is led blindfold in chains, the hoodwink is dropped, and he confronted with a grinning human skeleton. The same terrorism is practiced by other scenic methods in the Mormon Endowment House, and the same effects are produced in a small way in every little temperance lodge, by the night-mystery and mock solemn lectures and obligations.

Thus says Odd-fellow Grosh: " All the ancient rites began in sorrow and gloom, but ended in light and joy." This is the devil's caricature of salvation by Christ through repentance and faith: leading through sorrow for sin to *"joy in the Holy Ghost."* Indeed, this is that " Divine institution " which Grosh says Odd-fellowship was "copied from " (page 92). And in its nature and effects it resembles salvation as whoredom resembles marriage—one leading to hell, the other to heaven. Hence idolatry is branded as soul-adultery throughout the Bible. Christ is the bridegroom in the Scriptures, the devil in the lodge. Christians, in worship, are sanctified by the Holy Ghost; lodge-men are mesmerized by demons.

Both systems lead through sorrow to joy—Christ's to *"joy unspeakable and full of glory"* (1 Pet. 1: 8); the lodge's to the joy of a frolic. The Hebrews, on the great day of Atonement, " afflicted their souls," while Christ was offered in symbol to cleanse them from their sins " before the Lord " (Lev. 16:29); and they were led to " rejoice in the Lord" and "joy in the God of their salvation " (Hab. 3:13), while idolatrous Hebrews were led to an Odd-fellows' dance around a golden calf. Christian joy is holy and therefore eternal: lodge joy is jollification and therefore empty and evanescent. The Christian sings:

> "And every power find sweet employ
> In that eternal world of joy."—*Watts.*

The Odd-fellow sings:

"O, what pleasure 'tis to meet
With friends so blithe and jolly."
—*Odd-fellows' Minstrel, p.* 85.

Any who will patiently consult these quoted authori-ties will find proof abundant and superabundant that Odd-fellowship is part and parcel of the false worships devised by Satan to mislead men, by turning them, through worship of himself,from finding their way to God through Christ; that initiation is counterfeit regeneration; and Satanic mesmerism, of sanctification by the Holy Ghost.

And, like Christianity, the lodge proceeds from particulars to generals; from false salvation of persons to a false millennium for the race. Grosh, amid a multitude of like promises of an Odd-fellows' millennium without Christ, on page 141 says, if men should become imbued with the principles of the Fourth Degree, "happier families and more loving nations would banish clashing interests, discordant feelings, hoary prejudices and wrongs from our earth, and make the world a Paradise."

And this "Fatherhood of God and Brotherhood of Man" is to be produced by Odd-fellowship,—a society whose name is a burlesque; whose origin a dramshop; its ritual devil worship, and its membership open only to "free white males of 21 years," excluding, by book, "Chinese, Polynesians, Indians, half-breeds and mixed bloods" (Donaldson, page 321), and shutting out all women into a contemptible Rebekah's Degree! A universal brotherhood and millennium excluding at least nineteen-twentieths of mankind!

But as the thousands of Odd-fellows are our neighbors and enlightened Americans, how can it be, one asks, that they practice that *"fellowship with devils,"* which Paul denounces (1 Cor. 10:20), and which has universally cursed and degraded mankind? The answer is: Satan, the god of this world *charms* them, as other serpents charm their victims. But if these secret orders are Gentile worships paid to demons, why have not good men found it out long since and warned their fellow-men of the horrible fact?

The answer is: the Bible is replete with warnings, as also the writings of eminent Christian scholars, down to the present Sadducean age of materialistic unbelief.

Take the following extended extracts from Cudworth's " *True Intellectual System of the Universe,*" published first in London, 1678, and again issued at Andover, Massachusetts, in 1837, with repeated intervening editions, thus endorsed by the piety and learning of Europe and America for more than a century and a half. This great and learned writer says:

" There is a perpetual warfare betwixt two polities or kingdoms in the world; the one of light, the other of darkness: and our Savior, Christ, is appointed head or Chieftain of the heavenly militia, or the forces of the kingdom of light. There will be, at length, a palpable and signal overthrow of the Satanical power and the whole kingdom of darkness."—*True Intellectual System of the Universe, Vol. 1, p. 263.*

This leadership of Christ against Satan runs through the whole Bible. Thus, in the Garden, he appears as the " serpent-bruiser to come;" in Moses, as the Paschal Lamb, whose blood shelters and saves; in Joshua, as " Captain of the Lord's host;" in the prophets, as the suffering Conqueror; in the Gospels, as " the Son of God;" in the Acts and Epistles, as the one Mediator and only " way " to God; and in the Apocalypse he appears " the Lamb in the midst of the throne," " slain from the foundation of the world;" and the Drama of Time closes with "the battle of God Almighty," between the hosts of Satan and of Christ.

Such was the universal belief of Christians before Satan had chloroformed the churches by false worships. It is still the belief of honest receivers of the Bible.

In the fourth chapter of his wonderful book, Cudworth teaches—

"That the pagans were devil worshipers, not as though they intended all their worship to evil demons or devils as such, but because their polytheism and idolatry, unacceptable to God and good spirits, was promoted by evil spirits; that others besides pagans worshiped devils, as proved by their bloody and obscene rites and mysteries, especially man-sacrifices, which the God of Israel neither required nor accepted; and that their religion, unsound in its foundation, was more corrupted and depraved by four things, viz.: The ignorance and superstition of the vulgar; licentious figments of poets and fable-mongers; the craft of priests and politicians, and lastly the imposture of demons or devils."

Now pages might be filled with quotations from Masonic and Odd-fellowship authorities declaring the identity of their orders with those ancient mysteries condemned by Paul as too vile for description. Their identity consists in their human origin, their deception, their lying legends and high-sounding professions.

They infest Christian lands to find members who " have visible means of support," and so can pay "dues," yet boast universal fellowship with heathen tribes who have no " visible means of support;" and the legion of temperance and other inferior orders needs no proof of its identity with Masonry and Oddfellowship but the closeness of their imitation, and their swindling and imposing on mankind in the name of one popular virtue and another.

And they light on the Christian Scriptures as nightbugs on green trees, devouring their leaves and robbing them of their glory. They appropriate everything in the Bible but Christ, who is the substance of the Book. They seize on the Scripture narratives, symbols and morals (cutting out the name of Christ where it occurs), to give dignity to their frivolity and vulgarity and cover their robbery of the money and religion of the people, as pirates run up the flags of the vessels which they board, rob and scuttle. These accursed pests have scuttled nations, from Egypt down.

Turn over their Manuals and look at their pictures. The Holy (metallic) Bible; the mimic Ark of the Covenant; the Brazen Serpent, representing Christ's sin-offering, whom they cast from their prayers; the Stone Tables of the Law; the Dove of the retiring deluge, and the rainbow-pledge that it is not to return. What are these but emblems filched from the Bible to give seeming sanctity to an opposition religion, and cover the corruption of a mutual aid society which takes three dollars in dues and pays back one in benefits! (*See Sovereign Grand Lodge Rep., 1880.*)

This might be borne, or charged to the account current of human folly, but that Odd-fellowship, as the following pages will show, is part of a conspiracy to subvert the true religion and destroy our race, promising men "*rest to their souls*" by the Royal Purple Degree, and all the benefits of Christ's peaceful reign, while rejecting Christ himself." *(See Grosh, page 285 and pages 95, 292-3).*

This book is intended as a complete remedy for Oddfellowship, as " Freemasonry Illustrated " is for that order. Its ritual is given with the latest changes made by the Sovereign Grand Lodge in 1880 to defeat former exposures of its secrets, confirmed by its own authority in the notes, and its nature dissected by a thorough analysis.

CHAPTER I.

"The institution of Odd-fellowship originated in Manchester, England, in 1812, although isolated lodges existed in various parts of the country for some time previously. * * * On its institution in Manchester [England], the main purpose of Odd-fellowship was declared by its laws to be to render assistance to every brother who may apply, through sickness, distress or otherwise, if he be well attached to the Queen and government and faithful to the order."—*Chambers' Encyclopedia, Art. Odd-fellows.*

Odd-fellowship was organized in North America in 1819.

"Thos. Wildey and four others organized Washington Lodge No. 1, in Baltimore, Maryland, April 26, 1819, to work according to the usages of the London or Union order. A lodge was organized in Boston March 26, 1820, and one in Philadelphia December 26, 1821, both of which received grand charters from Baltimore in June, 1823. At the same time a grand charter was granted to the Past Grands in New York."—*American Encyclopedia, Art. Odd-fellowship.*

Some writers have claimed great antiquity for Odd-fellowship. Of this claim Rev. A. B. Grosh, a Past Grand and Past Chief Patriarch, states that well-meaning members of the order, "confounding principles with the institutions embodying them, have claimed equal antiquity for both." * * * That "the greatest exertion of tradition was to make our great forefather,

Adam, the founder of the order."   *   *   *   "Grand Sire Wildey, during his visit to England in 1826, procured from one of the lodges there an emblem representing Adam laying the foundation stone of the order, which emblem he presented to the Grand Lodge of the United States."—*Grosh's Manual, pp. 17, 18.*

Odd-fellowship made very little progress during the first ten years of its history. "Its founder and members were comparatively obscure men. Its name excited prejudices which their convivial practices confirmed and thus obscured its merits from the more strict and respectable class of humane men."—*Grosh's Manual, p. 29.*

Like Freemasonry and kindred secret orders, Odd-fellowship requires belief in a deity, and has, in connection with its ritual, religious ceremonies and prayers, and has also a prescribed burial service. On this point the history of the order is interesting. Its enthusiastic votary and historian states that—

"The order as founded by Brother Wildey was simply a humane institution—its *main* objects were to relieve the brethren, bury the dead and care for the widow and orphan. But gradually," he continues, "there was infused into its lectures and charges much moral and (unsectarian) religious instruction; and at each revision these principles were increased, and deepened and strengthened, until its beneficial and relief measures, from being ends, have become means to a higher and greater end—to improve and elevate the character of man; to imbue him with conceptions of his capability for good; to enlighten his mind; to enlarge the sphere of his affections, and thus to lead him to the cultivation of the true fraternal relations designed by the Great Author of his being! _Brother Wildey planted the seed and cultivated the tree. It bore fruit richer and better than he had anticipated. 'He builded better than he knew.' But as Founder and Architect he dwelt in the temple which he had reared for more limited objects. His cherished aims and details were all retained, but directed beyond the merely social and physical to the moral and spiritual—to lift its members up to their proper position—to hold man to a strict standard of duty—to impress him with the value of character among his fellows, and lead him to a true appreciation of his whole duty, whether to God, himself, or to his brother man."—*Grosh's Manual, p. 34.*

Odd-fellows exclude from their order all women, the totally deaf, dumb and blind, men with chronic diseases (say consumption), an infirmity which may prevent a man's gaining a livelihood, Indians, half-breeds, negroes, Chinese, Polynesians—all races and colors except the pure white Caucasian are excluded from membership in the order. (See White's Digest Laws, etc., of the Right Worshipful Grand Lodge I. O. O. F. of the United. States, sections 1101, 195, 1097, 1099, 1090). Thirty or forty dollars is the customary price of initiation. Three black balls exclude a candidate.

"The Grand Lodge of the United States, organized January 15, 1825, held its first annual communication February 22d following, but immediately adjourned to March 30th following, when its officers were installed and reports received showing four grand and nine subordinate lodges in connection."—*Grosh's Manual, p. 35.*

Until 1829, degrees were conferred in the lodge-room on Sundays. (See Grosh's Manual, p. 36.)

In 1842 the Grand Lodge of the United States unanimously severed its connection with the Manchester Unity, and, says Rev. A. B. Grosh, "in view of the fact that the Unity had altered the ancient landmarks, violated the principles and changed the work of the order, and attempted to invade our chartered rights, the Grand Lodge of the United States declared itself the only fountain and depository of Independent Odd-fellowship on the globe."

"The Manchester Unity, in accordance with its frequent threats, subsequently attempted to establish lodges in this country, but failed. Our National Grand Lodge attempted establishing lodges in Great Britain, but failed also."—*Grosh's Manual, p. 40.*

In 1844 five *Past Grand* officers revised the entire ritual of Odd-fellowship.

In 1843 or 1844 a movement commenced to change the basis of representation in Grand Lodges and Grand Encampments, which representation had become very unwieldy.

"The election of grand officers being held only *in* grand bodies, few beside the nearest resident Past Grands and Past Chief Patriarchs could participate therein. All this centralization of absolute power became more and more grievous as the order increased, until a general demand was made for a limited representation by annual elections in the subordinate, and for the election of grand officers by voting in the subordinates. Such a great change was naturally resisted as an invasion of 'vested rights,' and dangerous to the stability of the institution."—*Grosh's Manual, p. 42.*

From 1847 to 1851 the agitation of this question caused a prolonged storm, which threatened permanently to divide the brotherhood. At length, however, a satisfactory adjustment of difficulties was made.

In 1851 Schuyler Colfax, of Indiana, " reported the ' Degree of Rebecca ' for the wives of Scarlet Degree members."—*Grosh's Manual, p. 44.*

In 1852 the " London order of Odd-fellows " (England), numbering 233,000 members, proposed a union with the order in America, which was declined.

In 1853, Grand Lodges of Odd-fellows existed in all the States and some of the Territories.

The annual celebration of the anniversary of Odd-fellowship (April 26, 1819) commenced in 1859.

In 1863 the order was prospering in the Sandwich Islands and " in danger of dying out " in Vermont.

In 1867 the Grand Lodge of the United States decidedly refused to make alterations in its ritual or *secret* work.

Grosh claims that Odd-fellowship has " moulded into a kindred likeness of benevolence not a few institutions nearly as powerful for good as itself."—*Grosh's Manual, p. 49.*

During the Centennial year, 1876, the Grand Lodge met in Philadelphia. From the statistics there reported we quote the following:

Number Grand Lodges.............................48
Number Subordinate Lodges 6395
Number Grand Encampments......................39
Number Subordinate Encampments..............1756
Number Lodge Members...................... 454,689
Number Encampment Members.............. 87,450
Total Relief............................$1,698,868.92
Total Revenue...........................$4,714,241.70

From report of Grand Sire M. J. Durham, Philadelphia, Pa. G. L. U. S. Proceedings (1876), p. 6748.

September 20, 1880, the Grand Lodge met at Toronto, Canada, and changed its title to the "Sovereign Grand Lodge," as the body had jurisdiction over Switzerland, British Columbia, Chili, and the Lower Provinces of British North America, Ontario and Quebec.

On page 8209 of the published proceedings, the Grand Sire gives the following statistics for 1879:

Number Grand Lodges 50
Number Subordinate Lodges......................6,975
Number Subordinate Encampments.............1842
Number Lodge Members 440,783
Number Encampment Members 79,511
Total Revenue.........................$4,391,215.35

It would be a serious error to add together the number of lodge and encampment members, for probably fully nine-tenths of the encampment members hold lodge membership also, and are included in the lodge statistics.

It will be observed that in the space of four years this order has lost 13,906 lodge members and 7,939 encampment members.

Some of the "general correspondence" connected with reports from Grand Lodges is interesting. On page 8,228, the report from Iowa gives 10 new lodges, two "reclaimed" and one "surrendered," with a net loss in membership of 122. On same page Kentucky reports two new lodges and six surrendered, with a loss of 250 in membership during the year. On page 8,233, Ohio reports a loss of 1,030 lodge members and 240 encampment members, and Ontario of 163 lodge members. On page 8,234, Pennsylvania reports a loss of 3,749 lodge members and 1,434 encampment members. On the same page Rhode Island reports a loss of 213 lodge members. None of the States show large gains, and on page 8,236 L. B. Hills, Grand Secretary and Grand Scribe of Wisconsin, says: "I regret to say that our encampments are in a chronic decline."

During the Anti-masonic excitement which followed
the abduction and murder of Captain William Morgan,
Odd-fellowship properly suffered with Freemasonry.
"In Massachusetts the order died away. In Rhode
Island * * * it took no root. In New York all
growth was stopped. Almost everywhere the excite-
ment lessened the numbers or prevented increase."—
Grosh's Manual, pp 36, 37.

In 1868 the National Christian Association, opposed
to all organized secret societies, was formed in Pittsburgh, Pennsylvania, and in the name and strength of
the triune God lifted up the standard of supreme love
to God and equal love to man, in opposition to these
secret, counterfeit brotherhoods. Soon afterward this
Association began the publication of a semi-monthly
paper, the *Christian Cynosure*, which later became
weekly. Additions now began to be frequently made
to the scanty library of anti-secret literature. In 1874
a correct exposition of the ritual of Odd-fellowship was
published. There was a good demand for the book and
overwhelming proof as to its authenticity was from
time to time received from members of the order. In
1880 this work had reached its tenth edition of 2,000
volumes each. Some colored men, among others, obtained the book, organized lodges, and took out a charter for a Grand Lodge of I. O. O. F. A. D. (The Independent Order of Odd-fellows of African Descent).

The Grand Secretary of this brotherhood wrote to
Ezra A. Cook, under date of January 31, 1881, as follows:

"*Dear Sir*—Having obtained a few copies of your
Odd-fellowship Illustrated, Exposition of all the Degrees
of the Lodge and Encampment, and the Rebekah or
Ladies' Degree, *eighth edition, revised,* about **two years**

ago, fifteen of us, who at that time had just withdrawn from the Manchester Unity, on receiving your books at ——, opened a lodge in ——, and called it ' Key of the West.' * * * We tried the work and found that quite a number of Odd-fellows recognized the work as being genuine. * * * We then sought admission into a legally organized lodge, but we being men of African descent (negroes) could not be admitted. Then we formed a Grand Lodge and sent a petition to Springfield and were incorporated." * * *

One may readily see many reasons why any prosperous institution would dislike to make frequent changes. The unanimous vote of the Grand Lodge in 1867 against alterations in the ritual, as well as the following from their laws, shows Odd-fellowship to be no exception to this general rule.

Section 35 of the laws of Odd-fellowship is as follows:

" The unwritten work of the order shall in nowise be altered or amended, except by a unanimous vote of this Grand Lodge; nor shall the written work of the order be in anywise altered or amended, except with the concurrence of four-fifths of the members of this Grand Lodge."—*White's Digest Laws, etc., R. W. G. L. U. S.*

In September, 1880, the Sovereign Grand Lodge of the world met in Toronto, Canada, and altered its secret ritual and written work, and adopted the following resolutions:

" *Resolved*, That the revised Initiatory, Degree and Encampment work. as adopted at this session, shall go into operation on the first day of January, 1881, and from the time it takes effect be the only lawful work, and any other or different work, declared illegal and void.

" *Resolved*, That Grand Secretaries and Grand Scribes in the distribution of the revised work be charged with the collection of the Charge-books containing the old work, and that said officers be authorized and directed to burn or destroy the same and make report of the result to the Sovereign Grand Lodge."

From the foregoing sketch of Odd-fellowship, the facts of which have been taken from writers approved by the highest authority of the order, we learn that the order is of English origin. That it was formed by humble, improvident laborers for the relief of those whom their own prodigality combined with the crushing burdens imposed on laborers by the aristocracy of a dissipated, semi-despotic government, left in a destitute condition. That after being imported to America it gradually assumed as its chief work the divine task of leading man " to a true appreciation of his whole duty, whether to God, himself, or to his brother man." (Grosh's Manual, p. 35). That the order puts beyond the reach of its charities, remarkable instructions and other privileges, all who are in apparent danger of needing charitable assistance. That although only about sixty-two years old it has several times altered its so-called secret ritual, and uses great care to prevent those which it excludes from its temporal and financial benefits from enjoying its moral and spiritual admonitions, lectures and advantages also.

Odd-fellowship during the last fifty years has become strong numerically and financially, but if it is founded upon the sand, " great will be the fall of it."

CHAPTER II.

The main object of English Odd-fellowship seems from its own history to have been conviviality and sensual gratification.

Its founder in America seems to have had a little higher aim, and these convivial proclivities being excluded, his professed object was to develop the humane traits of caring for the sick, the widow and the orphan. While intoxicating beverages are forbidden in the lodge-room, much to the credit of the order, Odd-fellowship is far from being a temperance organization, or even an aid to the temperance cause. Though wine, beer and whiskey may not be served in the lodge (though a flask of liquor from some intemperate member's pocket is occasionally passed round in committee-room), at the close of each meeting it is a general custom for members to adjourn to saloons; and Grosh's description of an early meeting of the order gives us a fair picture of such a saloon gathering of the Odd-fellows of to-day. He says:

"The beer-mug, the pipe and the toast circulated freely, as the song and jest excited their mirth and hilarity, until by frequent repetition, calling for increased indulgence, it is no wonder that the noble objects of their meetings were too frequently made secondary to mere sensual gratifications."—*Grosh's Manual, p. 23.*

A Christian gentleman of this city tells us that before his conversion he attended the meetings of the order; and his lodge, which was and is one of the aristocratic lodges of Chicago, after adjournment used to go to a saloon and there indulge in smoking, drinking, card-playing, jesting and filthy conversation, the members often entertaining each other by rehearsing the false stories about important lodge work, etc., which they were accustomed to tell their wives in order to account for not returning home until one or two o'clock in the morning following lodge night.

The ninth section of the United States Constitution contains the following clause: " No title of nobility shall be granted by the United States." This clause was not inserted without good reason, and Odd-fellowship by educating half a million American voters to use and love such titles shows itself an enemy of American civilization. It calls its collective bodies Grand Lodge, Supreme Grand Lodge, Grand Encampment, etc., and the officers, even of the subordinate lodge, assume the titles of Noble Grand, Past Grand and Vice Grand, and in the Encampment we have a Chief Patriarch, High Priest, etc. The ordinary history in some parts is so interlarded with grandiloquent titles as to nauseate a refined and sensitive taste.

A comparison of some of the pompous assertions of this order with certain of its laws, rules, etc., shows its character to be hypocritical and false.

On page 99 of Grosh's Manual it is stated that " Odd-fellowship is a miniature representation among a chosen few of that fraternity which God has instituted among men. Few as are those who would represent it, the great principle is wide enough for all. On the broad platform of brotherhood all nations, parties and sects can meet and freely mingle in offices of needed kindness and mutual well-doing. Fraternity, therefore, is the corner-stone on which our forefathers based our order. Fraternity in the family of mankind illustrated in our family, the lodge and the order. As all men have God for their father, all are brethren."

With the above or similar statements which abound in Grosh's Manual, compare sections 195, 1090, 1097 and 1101 of White's Digest of Laws, Decisions, etc.

These and others show that Odd-fellowship, the so-called illustration of the fraternity of mankind, excludes from its fellowship the defenseless, the poor, the weak and afflicted:

1st. All women.

2d. All colored men, Polynesians, negroes, Chinese, Indians and half-breeds—all persons except free white Caucasian males; and of these it excludes

3d. All afflicted with chronic diseases, such as consumption; also the deaf, dumb and blind.

4th. All others who, on account of poverty, are unable to pay their dues, or on account of three enemies in the lodge are unable to secure a clear ballot.

While persons who have to struggle against the disadvantages of an unpopular color, infirmity, disease or poverty need, if there is to be any discrimination, the favorable consideration of the strong, it is evident that Odd-fellowship is a menace against that fundamental principle of our civil government that all men are created free and equal.

The professed benevolence of the order is thus seen to be a sham and pretense. At best it is but a mutual insurance society, and a fourth-class one at that, for much more is expended on regalia and other lodge expenses than is paid out in "benefits."

The attempted defense of such a waste of money is on a par with the most popular line of defense of the liquor traffic, as the following quotation shows:

"The cost of our decorations has been employed in giving needed labor (and *by* that labor honorable subsistence) to hundreds and thousands of industrious men, women and children. So far, then, it has not been expended in vain."—*Grosh's Manual, p. 56.*

It is thus admitted that thousands are employed in the manufacture of the emblems, jewels and regalia in which Odd-fellows deck themselves in the name of benevolence.

As to the valuable educational influence of these trinkets, gewgaws and "horse collars," let us hear the testimony of Mr. Grosh:

"When the humble and grateful Mary (Mark 14: 3-9, and John 12: 3-8) took a pound of spikenard, *very costly,* and anointed the head and feet of Jesus, there was complaint that the expensive article had not been sold for the benefit of the poor. *But Jesus declared that the act had a utility worthy of its cost,* and reminded them that the poor could be remembered at any other time and in some other manner. So, if our regalia and emblems tend to *increase* our benevolence and stimulate us to *greater* activity in well-doing, then is their manufacture no idle work, their cost no useless expense. The food or raiment that money would have purchased would, in a few months, have been consumed or worn out."—*Grosh's Manual, p. 56.*

To compare the waste of money for lodge regalia and cheap jewelry with the loving tribute of a forgiven

sinner for her Divine Savior is little short of blasphe-
mous, and the attempt to prove that the cultivation of
a love for gaudy display tends to increased benevolence
will certainly amuse if it does not disgust every candid
person.

That there is no benevolence in the payment of the
benefits of the order is further shown by two brief quotations from *page 64 of Grosh's Manual:* "That we require
the poorest applicant to contribute as much as the wealthiest, is true." "We pay the rich member, when sick
the same amount per week that we pay to our poorer
brethren." This ought to forever settle the question
of the " benevolence " of the order.

Odd-fellowship not only maintains a most clannish
and partial brotherhood of selfishness, but encourages
hypocrisy. On *page 97 of Grosh's Manual*, we read:
"The world may move in a vain show, each man striving to disguise himself from others, often even from
himself, but in our lodge-room we expect brethren to
lay aside the deceitful mask, and look each other
lovingly in the eyes, knowing and known of each other
as they are."

A devil's brotherhood indeed! Such a morality would
befit a gang of thieves. "Lay aside the deceitful
mask" when you are with the gang, your brethren, is
the teaching of this " noble order."

But the crowning objection to this order, and the one
beside which all others pale into insignificance, is the
fact that

ODD-FELLOWSHIP IS A CHRISTLESS RELIGION.

In Grosh's Manual, page 181, is found a Christless

prayer, and on the previous page the following explanatory note, which we copy in full, italicizing the same words that are italicized in the Manual, and which show the evident intention to exclude Christ.

The note is as follows:

" Adopted by the Grand Lodge of the United States, to exclude prayers offensive to members of the order in many of our lodges. It also ordered that on all occasions of the order, ' the *same spirit* as observed in the foregoing, shall be *strictly* followed by the officiating clergyman or chaplain.' "

" It is desirable and eminently proper that all lodges should open and close with prayer. Each subordinate may determine for itself upon opening and closing its session with prayer, and may determine upon the form to be used."—*Digest G. L. U. S., p. 123.*

On this point we have the most unequivocal declarations. On *page 90 of Grosh's Manual,* we read: " What regeneration by the word of truth is in religion, initiation is in Odd-fellowship." On *page 98,* same book, we read: " May your initiation and consequent practice aid in releasing you from all blindness of moral vision, set you free from the fetters of ignorance and error, and bring you from a death in selfishness into a life of active benevolence and virtue."

It is doubtless true that very few Odd-fellows realize fully this Christless yet professedly soul-saving character of the order, for it does not carry on an open war against Christianity. On this point we quote from page 174 of a valuable work by Rev. J. H. Brockman, entitled, *Odd-fellowship Judged by its Own Utterances:*

" The lodge also suffers no new-comers to look into its secret designs and plans, but uses them, unconscious to themselves, as tools, and only by degrees instils its false doctrines into them. Their eyes are darkened, they are gradually, without observing it, turned off from the word of God and the church, become more indifferent to the preaching and the sacraments; the panegyrics and boasting of the many good works are sweet music to the natural heart, and the doctrine of being made good by our own virtues pleases more than repentance and faith, and so they are gradually, without knowing it, converted to the doctrine of the order. The forbidden communion with unbelievers exercises a fearful influence, and that is the reason why so few who have joined with the intention of investigating the subject, come to a perception of the false doctrines and withdraw from the lodge."

Though the entire ritual, signs, grips, passwords and other secrets of the order are published to the world,

ODD-FELLOWSHIP IS A SECRET ORDER.

The work of the order is done in a guarded lodge-room, and no " book Odd-fellow," if an honorable man, will enter an Odd-fellows' lodge pretending that he has paid his fees and is a loyal member of the order.

It is also true that no real Christian, having seen the true character of the order, can innocently remain a member; nor, having seen its anti-Christian character, can he innocently refuse to lift a warning voice against the institution, notwithstanding the fact that former lodge brethren will denounce him and endeavor to injure his character for so doing. While good men differ as to the duty of disclosing the so-called secret work or ritual of the order, the Word of God seems plain. It is doubtless safe to assume that no Christian knowing the obligations and teachings of the order would ever join, and therefore such *ignorantly* fall into sin. Indeed it is clear from Leviticus 5: **4, 5,** that even if the lodge obligation proved to be only a promise to do good, guilt would be incurred and *confession* must follow.

He must help fulfill the declaration of Christ, "There is nothing hidden that shall not be revealed." He must show others the character of the order, and he can not do this fully without forever renouncing his lodge allegiance and revealing the secrets of the institution.

A clear-minded, wise student of the history and character of Odd-fellowship will see that the only hope for the real and permanent change of the order from Deism to Christianity is, first, to receive Christ as the only Redeemer from sin of every kind and the source of all real friendship, love and truth. By thus letting in the "light of the world" all its organized secret ways will be abolished. Its clannishness, putting men into layers, each upper one pledged to concealment from all below, will be changed. Its grand titles will vanish. Its exclusion of all except "free white males" will cease. Supreme love to God and equal love to man will change the name and nature of this foe of the home, of our simple and sublime American principles, and the pure Christian church, into a Sabbath-keeping, Bible-obeying Christianity.

CHAPTER III.

INITIATORY DEGREE.[2]

OPENING CEREMONIES.

Th* following are the ceremonies and ritual prescribed by the Sovereign Grand Lodge I. O. O. F , session of 1880, at Toronto, Canada, *as amended at the next session of the Sovereign Grand Lodge.*

Noble Grand (one rap)—Officers, take your respective stations; Guardians, secure the doors.

After the Guardians have closed the doors, no one shall be admitted into the lodge-room until it is regularly opened.

Noble Grand—Warden, examine the brethren in the lodge-room.

It is the duty of the Warden to receive the password of the current term and the password of the third degree from every member before the lodge is opened   He is not required to respond with any part of the passwords   If any one is present without the password of the current term or the password of the third degree the Warden shall so report to the Noble Grand.

NOTE 1.—"There has been much speculation as to the origin of the institution of Odd-fellowship.   Some have dated it as far back as Adam, who was said to have laid the foundation-stone of the order."—*Donaldson's Pocket Companion, p. 14.*

NOTE 2.—"Upon the petition of five brothers of the Order, in good standing, praying for a Charter to open a Subordinate Lodge, or of seven Patriarchs for one to open a Subordinate Encampment in a State, District or Territory where a Grand Lodge or Grand Encampment has *not* been established, the Grand Lodge of the United States, will grant the same.   Such Lodge or Encampment will be organized by a Past Grand or a Past Chief Patriarch, by authority from the Grand Sire.   Such petition, accompanied by the charter fee (thirty dollars,) must be forwarded to the Grand Secretary of the Grand Lodge of the United States, at Baltimore, Maryland.   The form of the petition is similar to that submitted to a State Grand Lodge."—*Donaldson's Pocket Companion, p. 20.*

Warden (having completed the examination)—All is right, Noble Grand.

Noble Grand—Vice Grand, what is your duty in the lodge?

Vice Grand—To act in conjunction with you in maintaining order; to require brethren to be decorous during lodge hours; to enforce, in your absence, a due observance of the laws; and to assist you in the performance of your duties.

Noble Grand—Vice Grand, examine your supporters.

Vice Grand—Right Supporter, what is your duty?

Right Supporter—To observe that brothers give the signs correctly and behave properly; to report to you the names of such brothers as do not conduct themselves according to the regulations of the order,[3] and to occupy yonr chair temporarily, when vacated by you during lodge hours.

Vice Grand—Left Supporter, what is your duty?

Left Supporter—To act in conjunction with your Right Supporter, and to officiate for him in his absence.

Vice Grand—My officers are correct, Noble Grand.

Noble Grand—Secretary, what is your duty?

Secretary—To keep accurate minutes of the transactions of this lodge. [When the duties are divided between a Recording and a Permanent Secretary the answer of the Recording Secretary ends here, and the Permanent Secretary gives the remainder.] To keep correctly the accounts between this lodge and its members, without prejudice or partiality; to receive all

---

NOTE 3.—"Grand Sire Wildey, during his visit to England, in 1826, procured from one of the lodges there an emblem representing Adam laying the foundation-stone of the order, which emblem he presented to the Grand Lodge of the United States."—*Grosh's Manual, p. 17.*

moneys[4] due this lodge, and pay the same to the Treasurer.

Noble Grand—Warden, what is your duty?

Warden—To examine the brethren with circumspection before the lodge is opened; to give the charge of office at the initiation of a candidate; to perform such other duties as may be required of me in conferring the degrees; to place and replace the regalia in a careful way and to report to you any damages it may have received.

Noble Grand—Right Supporter, what is your duty?

Right Supporter—To support you in keeping order; to execute your commands; to assist at the initiation of a candidate; to open and close the lodge in due form, and to see that the signs are given correctly.

Noble Grand—Left Supporter, what is your duty?

Left Supporter—To see that brothers who enter the room are in proper regalia, and give the signs correctly; to officiate for your Right Supporter in his absence, and to assist at the initiation of a candidate.

Noble Grand—Outside Guardian, what is your duty?

Outside Guardian—When candidates are to be initiated, or brothers admitted, to see that they are orderly and qualified according to lodge rules; to examine and reject any one I suspect, until your opinion is taken; to

Note 4 —"That we require the poorest applicant to contribute as much as the wealthiest, is true, as it is a matter of necessity. Equality in payments is essential not only to equality in benefits but also in feelings. We aim to abolish all considerations of wealth or poverty in our fraternity; to make all feel that as Odd-fellows, at least, they are not only brethren, but equals. He who did not pay an equivalent would feel degraded at receiving benefits; would feel that they were not his just due, but alms. Under this feeling of dependence on his wealthier brethren, he would not feel free to act and speak in opposition to their wishes—would not feel that he had an equal right to direct the expenditure of our funds, or the affairs of the order. Hence we pay the rich member, when sick, the same amount per week that we pay to our poorer brethren. We would conserve the independence of the latter, and exclude all feeling of moneyed superiority from the former. They must not only be *told* that all are equal, but they must be made to *know*, to REALIZE it in every possible way, that they may freely *act* on it under all circumstanes.' '—*Grosh's Manual, p. 64.*

receive the password previously to admission, and to guard the lodge against improper intrusion. To prevent the admittance of any one during a making or at other times, when so directed; to prevent any person from listening to acquire a knowledge of what is going on in the lodge, and to act in conjunction with the Supporters and the Inside Guardian in the execution of your commands.

[The Outside Guardian cannot admit a brother into the ante-room without the password of the current term unless directed by the Noble Grand, although he may be satisfied that the brother is a member of the lodge, and he is not required to respond with any part of the passwords.]

Noble Grand—Inside Guardian, what is your duty?

Inside Guardian—To act in conjunction with the Outside Guardian; to receive the password of the degree in which the lodge is open, during his absence to officiate for him, and obey your commands.

Noble Grand—Officers and brothers, I hope and expect each officer will do his duty, and that brothers will be orderly and attentive to the business of the evening, so that we may not be under the necessity of *enforcing* the restrictive laws or fines. It is a duty incumbent on the Noble Grand to judge impartially of every transaction, and to admit no brother (except a member of this lodge) who has not received the password of the current term* and the password of the degreee in which the lodge is open. I, therefore, trust that all will act with prudence, zeal and integrity, as on the exercise of these virtues depends our happiness and comfort; keeping in view that philanthropic principle by which we

----

*Note.—This is not to be so construed as to confl'ct with the duty to admit strangers having legal cards in their possession or as otherwise specially provided for by the General Laws of the Sovereign Grand Lodge.

hail each other as brothers[5]—regarding our lodge as our family; and whose actions, if founded on that grand principle, are calculated to make men social and humane.

Officers and brothers, I will thank you to be standing and assist my Right Supporter in opening the lodge.

SONG.

Brethren of our friendly order,
　Honor here asserts her sway;
All within our sacred border
　Must her high commands obey.
Join Odd-fellowship of brothers,
　In the song of Truth and Love;
Leave disputes and strife to others,
　We in harmony must move.

Honor to her courts invites us;
　Worthy subjects let us prove;
Strong the chain that here unites us,
　Linked with Friendship, Truth and Love.
In our hearts, enshrined and cherished,
　May these feelings ever bloom—
Failing not when life has perished,
　Living still beyond the tomb.

Noble Grand—Officers and brothers advance the sign of the third degree.

Right Supporter—Proclaim this lodge opened.

Right Supporter—By direction of our Noble Grand, I proclaim this lodge duly opened, for the transaction of such business as may be lawfully brought before it, and for the diffusion of the principles of benevolence and charity.

Noble Grand—During which time we admit of no

NOTE 5.—"No church in its present state is extensive enough in its fellowship to embrace many good men who need the ministration of kindred spirits, nor far reaching enough to reach even its own members when distant from it, and needing aid and protection. But if an Odd-fellow, far away from kindred and home, falls down by the wayside, penniless and faint, he has but to inform the nearest lodge, and hands are reached out to provide, and watchers are at his side to uphold his drooping frame. Or, if he falls under the cold suspicions of an unfriendly world, and is cast unmeritedly into a felon's cell, brothers are active around him with counsel, and labor to remove the dark web of circumstances that becloud his fame or endanger his life, to secure him a fair trial, and, if just proper acquittal and a safe return to society and friends."—*Grosh's Manual, p. 84.*

political, sectarian or other improper debate, under
penalty.

The lodge, at its option, may open and close with prayer, if the Chaplain be
present.

OPENING PRAYER.[6]

"Thou King eternal, immortal, and invisible! the only
wise God, our Saviour! Thou art the Sovereign of
universal nature, the only true object of our best and
holiest affections. We render Thee hearty thanks for
that kind providence which has preserved us during the
past week, protecting us from the perils and dangers of
this life; and for permitting us now to assemble in Thy
name for the transaction of business.

We humbly beseech Thee, our Heavenly Father, to
preside over our assembly, to breathe into our hearts
the spirit of love and of a sound mind; and may each
and all be governed by an anxious desire to advance Thy
glory and ameliorate the condition of mankind.

Let Thy blessing rest upon our order, upon all the
lodges, Grand and subordinate, belonging to our entire
family of brothers. Let Friendship, Love and Truth
prevail, until the last tear of distress be wiped away,
and the lodge below be absolved by the glory and
grandeur of the Grand Lodge above. This we ask in
humble dependence upon, and in most solemn adoration
of thy One mysterious and glorious Name. Amen."—
Grosh's Manual, p. 181.

NOTE 6.—"Adopted by the Grand Lodge of the United States, to exclude
prayers offensive to members of the order in many of our lodges. It is also
ordered that on all occasions of the order, ' the *same spirit* as observed in the
foregoing, shall be *strictly* follo*ed by the officiating clergyman or chaplain.'"—
Grosh's Manual, p. 180.

ORDER OF BUSINESS.

In the Subordinate Lodge (unlike Freemasonry), the business of each degree has been transacted in that degree, and even Initiatory members are entitled to pecuniary benefits' while in good standing, but in one of these two points the two orders have been rendered alike by the following amended resolution of the Sovereign Grand Lodge, session of 1881:

Resolved, That, in the judgment of the Sovereign Grand Lodge, the business of Subordinate Lodges should be transacted in the Third Degree.

Resolved, That on and after July 1st, 1882, all the business of the Subordinate Lodge shall be transacted in the Third Degree, or the Degree of Truth. The lodge shall open in each degree for the purpose of conferring the degrees, and each degree shall be conferred when it is opened in that degree.

Respectfully submitted:

J. W. Stebbins, Geo. B. Boyles, Henry F. Garey, Fred Carleton, Geo. II. Bigelow, Albert M. Harris. Jos. II. Sloss, J. B. Goodwin.

GENERAL INSTRUCTIONS.

When a candidate is to be initiated, after he has been elected, and it has been announced to the Noble Grand that he is in waiting, it will be the duty of that officer to appoint a Past Grand or the Vice Grand to act as Outside Conductor, who will retire to the ante or preparation-room, receive the candidate, propound to him the questions laid down in the Charge-Book, record the answers received (which must be signed by the candidate and attested by the Outside Conductor), and require of him the *primary obligation* necessary for all persons to take prior to initiation. (Page 48).

While this is being done, the *Warden*, by direction

Note 7.—"Even when extraordinary events render it necessary to give extra aid to an unfortunate brother, it still comes from a fund he aided to create for such purposes, and to which even his wealthiest brother *may* be reduced to apply. His relief comes not, therefore. even then, from one or a few *individuals*, but from *all*."—*Grosh's Manual*, p. 65.

of the Noble Grand, will prepare the lodge-room for the initiation. The officers shall clothe[8] themselves appropriately, and the members shall each be furnished with a mask or covering for the face, not of a ludicrous nature. During an initiation the Noble Grand shall wear a scarlet robe; the Vice Grand a blue robe; the Warden and Conductor each a black robe, and the Scene Supporters each a white robe; and all of said officers shall wear caps color of their robes. No other officer or member shall wear caps or robes. The Conductor and Scene Supporters shall, during an initiation, bear wands color of their robes; the Supporters of the Noble Grand and Vice Grand shall bear wands color of the robes of the officers they support, and the Warden shall bear a staff.

When the Outside Conductor has performed his duty, he will report to the Noble Grand.

If the answers are unsatisfactory, the Outside Conductor shall receive directions as to further proceedings.

When everything is ready in the lodge, the Noble Grand will request the Outside Conductor to retire, prepare and introduce the candidate. The Noble Grand will then place the lodge under the charge of the Vice Grand, while he (the Noble Grand) retires behind, or the curtain is dropped before him, in accordance with the work.

Note 8.—"If our regalia and emblems tend to *increase* our benevolence, and stimulate us to *greater* activity in well-doing, then is their manufacture no idle work, their cost no useless expense." *Grosh's Manual.* p 56.

PLAN OF SUBORDINATE LODGE-ROOM.

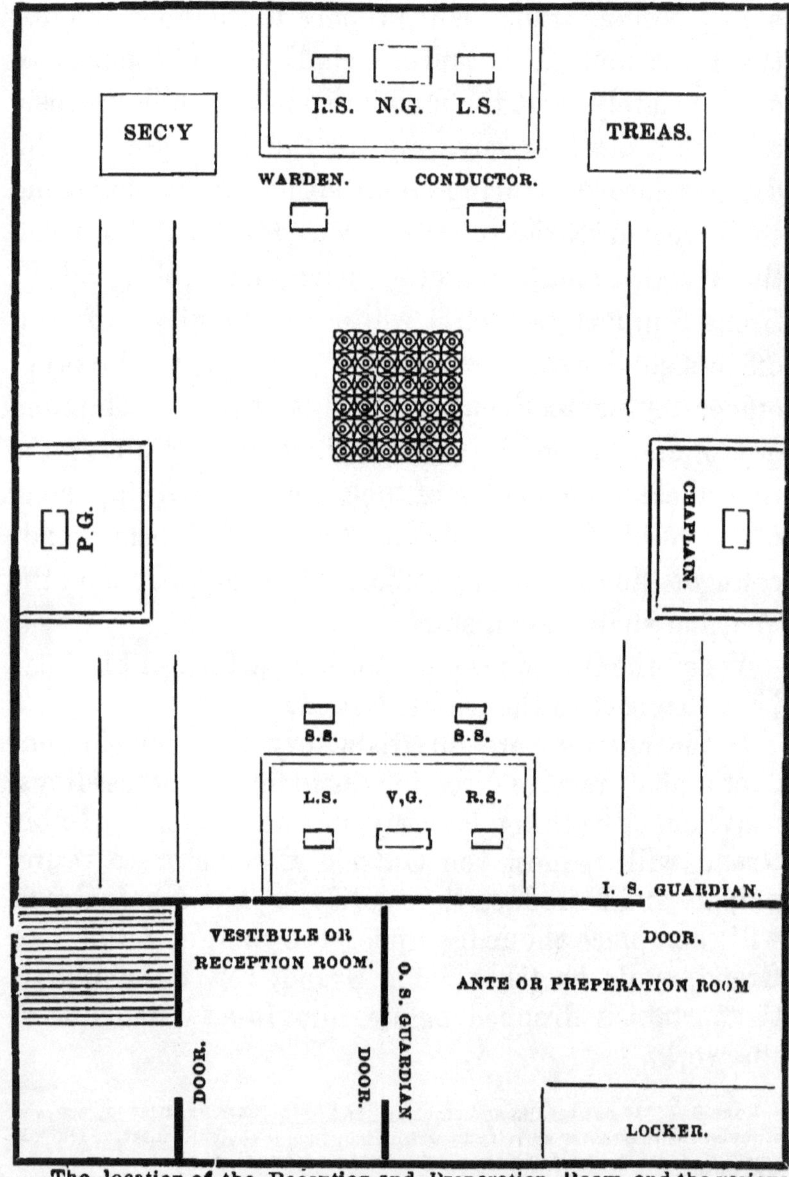

The location of the Reception and Preparation Room and the various doors are of course different in different lodges. The above diagram shows the position of the various officers of a Subordinate Lodge, but the place of the Treasurer and Secretary are interchangeable and the Past Grand sometimes occupies the opposite side of the room, but the Chaplain, *if there is one*, should sit opposite the Past Grand.

CHAPTER IV.

Initiatory Degree.

INITIATION.[9]

This Ritual conforms strictly to the Revised Form of the Initiatory Charge-Book I. O. O. F., as adopted at the Annual Session of the Right Worthy Sovereign Grand Lodge of the Independent Order of Odd-fellows, held at Toronto, Dominion of Canada, on the twenty-second day of September, *Anno Domini* 1880, and the year of the Order the sixty-second.

EXAMINATION.[10]

The candidate having been accepted by vote of the brothers, is taken into the ante-room of the lodge and catechized in the following manner by the Vice Grand or a Past Grand especially deputed, the answers being recorded in a book with printed questions and a blank for answers.

1. What is your name?
2. Where do you reside?
3. What is your occupation?
4. How old are you?
5. Do you hold membership in or are you suspended or expelled from any Lodge of this Order?
6. Are you, so far as you know, in sound health?

Note 9.—"A thoughtful man's first entrance into a lodge, unknowing what is to be transacted there, is a serious event."—*Grosh's Manual, p.* 93.

Note 10.—"The manner of introducing candidates is as follows: A brother of the lodge proposes his friend, whom he must be willing to recommend. On the reception of the proposition a committee is at once appointed, whose business it is to ascertain the character, age, condition of health and standing of the applicant. If this committee, after due investigation, report that they believe him worthy, he is, on the week following such report, balloted for, and if three *black balls* appear against him, he is rejected; if not, he is elected. [In some States *two black balls* are sufficient]. He may then be initiated to membership in the lodge."—*Donaldson's Pocket Companion, p.* 21.

7. Do you believe in the existence of a Supreme, Intelligent Being," the Creator and preserver of the Universe?

The candidate signs his name to the answers given and his examiner attests the signature with his own name below. Should the candidate give an unsatisfactory answer to any of the questions, he is dismissed from the room and the case is reported to the lodge. Should all prove satisfactory, the examiner asks the candidate: "Are you willing to enter into an obligation to keep secret all that may transpire during your initiation?" If this is answered in the affirmative, the candidate repeats after the examiner the following

PLEDGE :

"I hereby pledge my sacred honor that I will keep secret[12] whatever may transpire during my initiation."

While the Outside Conductor is with the candidate in the ante-room the officers and members inside the lodge are making active preparations for the initiation. A curtain of scarlet color is drawn in front of the Noble Grand's chair, hiding that officer from view. The Venerable Warden provides himself with a *long gray beard, long gray wig,* a long black robe tied closely about the neck and waist, and reaching to his feet, everything being done to give him the appearance of a very old man. The Right and Left *Scene Supporters* are clothed in white robes; the Conductor is also clothed in a long black robe similar to that of the Warden, while all the other members wear semi-masks over their faces, the upper part of the mask reaching to about the middle of the forehead and the lower part covering the mouth. A coffin containing skeleton imitation, usually kept under the *dais* on which stands the chair of the Noble Grand, is now brought out and placed in the center of the lodge-room and the *Right and Left Scene Supporters* provide themselves with two flambeaus which they light when the proper time comes.

The examiner, termed the Outside Conductor, now blindfolds the candidate, leads him to the door of the lodge and gives the usual alarm or entersign: three raps on lodge-room door. . . . .

Inside Guardian—Who comes there?

Outside Conductor—The Outside Conductor, with a

———

NOTE 11.—"Excepting in regard to your religious faith in God, and your relations to the Order, the questions are merely such as a health or life insurance company require to be answered in good faith."—*Grosh's Manual, p.* 87.

NOTE 12.—"Our institution has instinctively, as it were, copied after nearly all secret associations of a religious and moral character. In Egypt, the most ancient among the ancient nations, an institution of this kind existed from the earliest period. Of the nature of that institution we know very little. History informs us that many benefits were supposed to be derived from a participation in the secrets of the society; that those secrets were revealed only to the initiated, and that the mode of initiation was well calculated to make a serious and abiding impression on the mind of the recipient."—*Grosh's Manual, p.* 90

ṣtranger who desires to be initiated[13] into the Indepenâent Order of Oddfellows.[14]

The Inside Guardian reports this to Vice Grand, on whose command the door is opened and the candidate is led into the lodge-room, where he is received by the proper Conductor attended by the Supporters.

CONDUCTOR'S CHARGE.

You are now within a lodge of Odd-fellows[15]—here the world is shut out—you are separated from its cares and distinctions, its dissensions and its vices. Here Friendship and Love assert their mild dominion, while Faith and Charity combine to bless the mind with peace and soften the heart with sympathy. Those who surround you have all assumed the obligations and endeavor to cherish the sentiments peculiar to Odd-fellowship;[16] but before you can unite with them you must pass through an initiatory ceremony, which will ultimately lead you

---

NOTE 13.—"The qualifications required are that the candidate must be a free, white man, twenty-one years of age, of good moral character and sound health, and a believer in the Supreme Being, the Maker and Ruler of the Universe."—*Donaldson's Pocket Companion, p.* 19.

NOTE 14.—"Says Brother Ridgely, in his 'Eulogy on the Life and Character of Thomas Wildey:' 'Odd-fellowship was organized in 1819. During its first decade it made but little progress. . . . . Since 1829 [to 1862 only] it has gathered within its folds, by initiation, 426,963 members. Its revenue, derived from weekly contributions (varying from six to twelve cents) from these members, has amounted to $20,368,057. Of these receipts (after disbursements for ordinary expenses amounting to $5,092,000) it has applied, for the relief of the sick, the burial of the dead, and the education of the orphan, the sum of $8,-804,000, leaving a balance of $6.472,000 for the same objects. These funds, thus employed, have relieved 558,068 members, and 37,567 widowed families.'"—*Grosh's Manual, p.* 49.

NOTE 15.—"*As it now is*, it is really an institution of American growth, and exists nowhere else on earth except where it has been planted and nurtured by the Grand Lodge of the United States."—*Donaldson's Pocket Companion, p.* 15.

NOTE 16.—"For several years the order made but little progress. Its founder and members were comparatively obscure men. Its name excited prejudices, which their convivial practices confirmed, and thus obscured its merits from the more strict and respectable class of humane men."—*Grosh's Manual, p.* 29.

to primary truth."

Conductor—Are you willing to proceed?

Candidate answers.

Conductor—Be patient, therefore, and firm.

Conductor—Brothers, the stranger now awaits oui mystic rites.

Right Scene Supporter—Then at once the chains prepare!

Left Scene Supporter—They are here! entwine their links about him! [The chain is put across his shoulders, brought around under his arms and tied behind].

Left Scene Supporter—Now! bind him to the stake!

Conductor—Hold! Brothers! Shall we proceed with these, our mystic rites, or shall we mercy show?

Vice Grand and brothers (slowly and in a low tone of voice)—Mercy—mercy show!

Conductor—Then mercy I will show, but will first a solemn warning give.

A procession may be formed as follows:
Conductor.
Scene, supported by four brothers, with or without black gowns.
Scene Supporters with lighted candles.
Two or more brothers, with or without black gowns.
Outside Conductor, escorting candidate.
A gong may be slowly and lightly sounded, a bell be tolled, or an organ be played while the procession is moving around the room.

Conductor to Supporters—Lead on our friend. [They pass slowly around the room].

Conductor—Man in darkness and in chains![18] How mournful the spectacle! Yet it is but the condition of millions of our race, who are void of wisdom, though they know it not. We have a lesson to impart to him —one of great moment and deep solemnity; a faithful exhibition of the vanity of worldly things—of the in-

---

NOTE 17.—"What regeneration by the word of truth is in religion, initiation is in Odd-fellowship."—*Grosh's Manual, p.* 90.

NOTE 18.—"Bound by his ignorance and fears in the indurating fetters of self-ishness, he knows not that any have more light and freedom than are his; and yet, not fully realizing his own need of both, he may marvel if told that nearly all mankind are in darkness and chains which they neither behold nor feel. It is not until some voice greets his ear with a promise of instruction, that he begins to conceive that the chaos around him *may* be resolved into order, the discord to harmony. This conception leads him to desire that wisdom which shall shed light upon his darkness, and unravel the perplexities which bewilder his soul."—*Grosh's Manual, p.* 94.

stability of wealth and power—of the certain decay of all earthly greatness.

The Conductor is careful to take a route and gait that will occupy the time while the Conductor's Charge is being given. They halt before a coffined corpse *or an imitation* already alluded to; the Right and Left Scene Supporters now light their torches and place themselves one at each end of the coffin; the Conductor begins to take off the blindfold and says to the candidate:

Conductor—Be serious, for our lesson is as melancholy as it is truthful. [Blinds[19] are now off]. Behold a representation of the effect of death. That silent yet impressive lecturer—to vice, confusion, but to virtue, peace—is all that remains on earth of one who was born as you were born, who lived as you now live, who for many days enjoyed his possessions, his power and his pleasures. But now, alas! nothing is left of him save that sad memorial of man's mortality.[20] The warm heart that throbbed for others' woes, or the cold one which held no sympathy, has mouldered away and joined its kindred dust. Contemplate the scene! [A solemn dirge may be sung or played]. Should it not humble human pride? Should it not awake the soul to a just sense of responsibility to its God—of duty to itself? And in view of this, the common lot of all, should it not enlist the tenderest of human sympathies? My friend, that gloomy monitor is but an emblem of what you are sure to be, and what you may soon become. Seriously meditate the solemn admonition it affords; ponder it well, and see that your own heart fosters not evil—the bane of society, the fountain of all wrong, the progenitor of crime, hatred and violence, whose consequences must continue to afflict mankind until that period to which Hope looks forward with ardent joy, when one law shall bind all nations, tongues and

NOTE 19.—"The first ray of light will but increase the apparent gloom; for it will exhibit more strongly the vanity of human pursuits and possessions, the brevity of life and the certainty of death, and all life's evils fearfully aggravated and increased by the strifes, discords and dissensions which flow from human ignorance and folly, and end at last in death itself."—*Grosh's Manual, p.* 95.

NOTE 20.—"As he thus realizes his own mortality, its possible nearness, and his own dependence and helplessness, he will the more willingly ponder the ties that bind him to the woes and sufferings of all around him, and joyously look forward to that bright era when all these woes and pains shall be banished by the prevalence of benevolence and peace, by the reign of brotherhood and love."—*Grosh's Manual. p.* 95.

kindreds of the earth; and that law will be the law of Universal Brotherhood.

Right Scene Supporter—I have seen the rose in its beauty spread its leaves to the morning sun. I returned, and behold! it was dying upon the stalk. Its grace and form were gone; its loveliness was vanished away; its leaves were scattered to the ground, and no one gathered them again. I have seen man in the pride of his strength; his cheeks glowed with beauty; his limbs were full of activity; he walked, he ran, he leaped, he rejoiced in that he was more excellent than the rose. I returned, and behold! life was departed from him, and the breath from out of his nostrils. Death is in the world and the spoiler is among the works of the Almighty. All that is born must die.

Left Scene Supporter—I have seen the leaves fall and lie thick upon the ground; I have heard the wintry blasts sing sad requiems over their decay; and yet spring came; the soft zephyrs played among the branches, they budded forth again, and in the place of death there was life, beauty and joy. [Candidate is again blindfolded].

Conductor—You may think it strange, my friend, that we thus blindfold" you; its symbolic purpose will, in due time, be fully explained. [Candidate is led to the Warden, where the blinds are removed].

Conductor—This, my friend, is our Venerable Warden; he has a charge to deliver to you; listen attentively to what he may say. Assist him to rise.

Warden—Stand! presumptuous mortal! How old art thou?

Note 21.—"*It was a leading characteristic of all the ancient rites, that they began in sorrow and gloom, but ended in light and joy; they were all calculated to remind men of their weakness, their ignorance, their helplessness and their sinfulness of character; of the shortness and uncertainty of life, and of the ills which flesh is heir to; of the punishment of guilt, the reward of virtue, and the rising of the just to life eternal and immortal.* In all, too, *the mode of initiation was calculated to make a deep and lasting impression upon the mind of the candidate.* For these purposes, striking exhibitions of the consequences of sin, and the pleasures of virtue, were presented for consideration, in sudden and striking contrast, and everything was designed to impress the candidate with a lively sense of what was thus represented."— *Grosh's Manual, p. 92.*

Candidate answers.
Warden—What trade, profession or calling hast thou?
Candidate answers.
Warden—Canst thou keep a secret?
Candidate answers.
Warden—Ah! but wilt thou?
Candidate answers.
Warden—Be serious, then, while I address you as a man. Listen to the voice of wisdom speaking from age and experience, and let it sink deep into your heart. These trembling limbs and this wrinkled brow betoken that the weight of years is upon me. I have indeed seen many years, and many solemn changes have passed before me. A wise man has said: "I have been young but now am old, yet have I not seen the righteous forsaken or his seed begging bread." I would impress this upon your mind, and add another maxim, which I pray you also heed and be wise. It is this: that in the practice of Friendship, Love and Truth will be found the best safeguard against the ills of life. Forget it not; forget it not.

Warden to Conductor—Brother Conductor, you will now present the stranger to the Vice Grand.

Candidate is again blindfolded and taken to the Vice Grand. Right and Left Supporters cross their wands over head of Vice Grand, and the Scene Supporters cross theirs over the head of the candidate.

Conductor—You are now at the chair of our Worthy Vice Grand.

VICE GRAND'S CHARGE.

Vice Grand—Stranger, having entered within these walls, you are never to make known the secrets of this Order, or make any discovery to any person or persons upon any pretense or for any purpose. Will you comply with these rules?
Candidate—I will.
Vice Grand to Conductor—Restore him to light and liberty. [Lights are turned up, blindfold is taken off, and the chains also].
Vice Grand to Candidate—Stranger, it is my duty to

administer to you a solemn and binding obligation—one which we have all taken, but which will not conflict with any of those exalted duties you owe to your God, your country, your family or yourself. With this assurance, are you willing to take such an obligation?

Candidate—I am.

Vice Grand—Place your right hand on your left breast, and repeat after me the following

OBLIGATION.

Vice Grand—(three raps, all rise).

I, —— ——, in the presence of the brothers of the Order now assembled, do solemnly promise that I will never communicate to any one, unless directed to do so by a legal lodge, the signs, tokens or grips, the term, traveling or other passwords belonging to the Independent Order of Odd-fellows. Nor will I expose or lend any of the books or papers relating to the records or secret work of the Order to any person or persons, except to one specially authorized to receive them. That I will never reveal any private business which may be transacted in my presence in this or any other lodge. I also promise that I will abide by the laws, rules and regulations of this lodge, of the Grand Lodge of the Independent Order of Odd-fellows of (here name the State) or any other Grand or working lodge to which I may be attached.

I further promise that I will never wrong a Subordinate or Grand Lodge to the value of anything. Nor will I take part or share, directly or indirectly, in any illegal distribution of the funds or other property of the lodge; but will, to the best of my ability, endeavor to prevent the same. Nor will I wrong a brother or see him wronged without apprising him of approaching danger, if in my power so to do. Should I be expelled or voluntarily leave the Order, I will consider this promise as binding out of it as in it. To the faithful performance of all which I pledge my sacred honor.

Vice Grand—(one rap, all are seated.)

Vice Grand to Candidate—Stranger(s), you have now entered into a society that is far more important than you may at first imagine. It conforms to law, religion, and sound morality, and does not permit anything contrary to the allegiance we owe to our country, or the duty we owe to ourselves. Let good conduct procure you the esteem of your family and friends. Let strict caution guard you against making any improper discoveries to the uninformed, so that by your example you may convince the world that good faith and virtue are the peculiar characteristics of a true Odd-fellow; for according to our laws we can be Odd-fellows only while we act like honest men. I will now recommend you to the Noble Grand, who will further instruct you, and I hope your deportment will be such after your initiation as to give us no cause to regret that we have accepted you as a brother.

Vice Grand to Conductor—Proceed with our friend to the principal chair, there to be introduced to the Noble Grand.

Vice Grand—(three raps, all rise).

INITIATION ODE.

The following words are sung as the candidate goes around the room to the chair of the Noble Grand.

> Stranger(s), you've nought to fear,
> For Honor's court is here,
> Love, Peace and Joy.
> Here in good faith we meet;
> Here friends and brothers greet,
> And in communion sweet
> The hours employ.
>
> Stranger(s), amid a band
> Of brothers here you stand,
> Firm, tried and true;
> Here Friendship's power is shown;
> Here Love and Truth are known;
> And here before their throne
> We welcome you.

Arriving at the Noble Grand's chair as the last line is being sung, the Noble Grand being behind the curtain, the Conductor addresses his Right Supporter.

Conductor—Brother Right Supporter, is the Noble Grand engaged?

Right Supporter—He is, my brother.

Conductor—Business of importance demands his attention. A stranger desires to be introduced to him.

Right Supporter—Then he may be disturbed. [Right Supporter passes behind the curtain and holds the following dialogue with the Noble Grand].

Right Supporter—Noble Grand!

Noble Grand—Well, my brother.

Right Supporter—A stranger stands before you.

Noble Grand—A stranger stands before me? How gained that stranger admittance within these walls?

Right Supporter—By the recommendation of worthy brothers and the permission of the Vice Grand.

Noble Grand—Has he taken upon himself that serious, solemn and binding obligation?

Right Supporter—He has, Noble Grand.

Noble Grand—Then let him be introduced to me.

Curtain is thrown back and Noble Grand rises.

Noble Grand—(one rap, seating the lodge).

Officers now take off their robes and the members their masks.

Conductor—Noble Grand, by direction of the Vice Grand, I present to you a stranger for instruction in the mysteries of our Order.

The Supporters of the Noble Grand cross their wands over Noble Grand's head, holding them there till he gets to the secret work.

NOBLE GRAND'S CHARGE.

Noble Grand—My friend, I welcome you among the fraternity of Odd-fellows, with whose customs I trust you will soon become better acquainted. Under our disguise I have no doubt you took us for odd fellows" indeed. Learn from this that men are not always to be taken for what they appear.[23] Some may have a rough and unseemly exterior, but a good, true heart within, while others possessing a captivating person and manners, may be destitute of all genuine principle. I hope

---

NOTE 22.—"The singularity of its name, and humility of its origin, needed not these convivial practices to bring the institution into suspicion and disrepute, nor a defective organization to involve it in trouble and internal dissensions."— *Grosh's Manual*, p. 24.

NOTE 23.—"The forms through which you have passed are not what they seem to many. Under each act and emblem there is deep significance. So in life. Apply your instructions there, and everything becomes vocal with wisdom. The eyes blinded by the darkness of a dungeon are nought to the blindness of the moral sense obscured by indulgence in selfishness and sensuality."—*Grosh's Manual*, p. 96.

you will pardon us the innocent deception and make a proper application of the moral it is designed to convey.

We will now proceed to instruct you in the mysteries of the initiatory degree of this order, they are:

First—The entersign.

Second—The countersign.

Third—The password of the Initiatory degree.

Fourth—The password of the current term, which is changed each term and will be given to you privately in the course of the evening by the Noble Grand, who alone is authorized to communicate it or cause it to be communicated to members.

Fifth—The grip.

THE ENTERSIGN consists of one rap, or one pull of the bell if there be one, at the outer door, and three raps at the inner door.

THE COUNTERSIGN

has three motions: *First*, with the thumb of the right hand in the palm thereof, place the four fingers perpendicularly across the mouth, the back of the hand outward. *Second*, close the last three fingers upon the thumb in the palm of the hand, the index or fore finger being extended; carry it to the

outer corner of the right eye, the back of the hand being outward, forming a right angle with the nose. *Third*, let the hand drop toward the ground, open and palm outward, the thumb to be nearly parallel with the fingers and the hand about six inches from the body.

Explanation of the Counter Sign—The first motion signifies silence, and reminds us that we are bound to keep inviolate the secrets of the Order. The second motion signifies Omniscience, and reminds us that the all-seeing eye of God is continually watching over our actions. The third motion signifies fraternity, and reminds us that the hand of an Odd-fellow should always be open to a brother. The password is *Fides* to be lettered at all times when used for working purposes, working into a lodge or in examination prior to opening. In communicating this word either to the Inside Guardian or to the Warden the brother must give the letters F. I. and if required by the Inside Guardian or the Warden, he must give the remainder of the word, D. E. S., lettered as before. The Inside Guardian and the Warden must be satisfied.

INITIATORY GRIP.

With the first two fingers of the right hand seize and link with the first two fingers of the brother's right hand; with the thumb (your own) touch each of the two fingers (your own) and thus form the link. No shaking hands in making the grip.

Noble Grand—This Grip has never been broken by any good Odd-fellow, and we hope and trust that it never will be by you.

INSTRUCTIONS TO CANDIDATE.

Noble Grand—In all lodges there is an outer and an inner door, and between them what is termed an ante-room. At the outer door there is stationed an officer called the Outside Guardian, and at the inner door an officer called the Inside Guardian.

Wishing to visit a lodge which is open in the initiatory degree, you will announce your presence at the outer door by giving one rap, or one pull of the bell, if there be one; but any alarm will be attended to.

The Outside Guardian will open the wicket, and require from you the Password of the current term, which must be given in full. If given correctly you will be admitted to the ante-room. You will then clothe yourself in the regalia appropriate to your rank and station in the lodge, which for the present will be a plain white collar; advance to the inner door and give three raps.

The Inside Guardian will announce to the proper officer (either the Noble Grand or Vice Grand of the lodge, as the rules of the lodge shall have prescribed), that there is an alarm at the door. The Inside Guardian is directed by such officer to inquire the cause—whereupon the Inside Guardian will open the wicket, and obtain from you your name, rank, and the number of the lodge to which you belong.

The Inside Guardian will close the wicket and inform the proper officer, who, if he is satisfied, will direct the Inside Guardian to admit you, if correct. The Inside Guardian re-opens the wicket, and you must give him the Password of the initiatory degree. If correct the Inside Guardian will admit you, when you will advance to the center of the room and address the Noble Grand with the Countersign, who will acknowledge you as a brother by giving the same Countersign. You will then turn and address the Vice Grand with the Countersign, who will acknowledge you as a brother with the same Countersign. You will then be seated.

Wishing to leave the lodge before it is closed, you will make the same Countersign to the Noble Grand which will be answered by him.

If you are visiting your own lodge when it is open in the Initiatory degree and are without either the Password of the current term or the Password of this degree, the proper officer of the lodge (the Noble Grand) being so informed asks the Secretary as to your standing in the lodge. If the Secretary reports favorably, directions will be given to admit you, but if the report is unfavorable you are so informed by the Outside Guardian and you cannot be admitted.

Without these signs[24] you cannot gain admittance into this or any other lodge of the Independent Order of Odd-fellows. Be observant, therefore, that you may acquire them, and be careful that you do not improperly reveal them. Remember, also, that you have given us your pledge of honor—a pledge which is the most binding of any that can be given or received. We feel confident that you will keep it inviolate. You have been admitted by certain forms of initiation, in which there is deep significance. You were blindfolded to represent to you the darkness and doubt through which man gropes his way to a knowledge of himself, his duty, and his destiny; a darkness not only of reason, but of the moral nature. And you were bound with chains, to illustrate that slavery of soul[25] to sense—that subjection to things outward and perishable, into which man is brought by his own passions. You were then led to a scene where an emblem of mortality was exhibited, to represent to you the end of this servitude, to remind you of the insignificant and perishable nature of all those outward objects that so often excite men's passionate ambition. After this representation, intended to reach your conscience and touch your heart, you have been restored to light and liberty. One of these acts is emblematical of that liberty which the virtuous enjoy when conscious of being disenthralled from sensuality and passion; the

---

Note 24.—"Keep in remembrance the signs and words imparted to you, to enable you to enter these courts, and to recognize and be recognized of your brethren. Trifling as they may seem to some, they are the key to our treasures and our mysteries. And in their use, remember that they are pledges of secrecy to the brotherhood from you, and to you from us."—*Grosh's Manual, p.* 98.

Note 25.—"He who practices this charity and teaches it to others, shall be crowned with honor and come down to the grave in peace, with the full assurance of a blessed future."—*Donaldson's Pocket Companion, p.* 41.

other is emblematical of the light of that truth which reveals to us Love as the grand remedy for all social evils, as it is indeed the foundation of all good towards God or man. In this light we trust you will ever walk; this liberty we hope you will ever maintain. It will be our duty—it is one of the great ends of our institution —to aid you in so doing. We claim the privilege, therefore, of watching over your conduct, not only in the lodge-room, but in your intercourse with the world at large.

Noble Grand—The Conductor will introduce the candidate to the acting Past Grand. [Noble Grand disrobes.]

Conductor—Worthy Past Grand, by direction of the Noble Grand I present to you this candidate for further instruction.

PAST GRAND'S CHARGE.

My friend: You are now initiated[26] into and made acquainted with the organization and work of a lodge of the Independent Order of Odd-fellows, and are recognized as a member. The institution of Odd-fellowship is progressive in its character. You have passed its threshold, and, after a reasonable probation, may ad-

---

NOTE 26.—"The selection of a few individuals out of the mass to unite them in associated efforts for the diffusion of important principles, and to exercise them in the practice thereof, that they may become the teachers of others, appears to be the method of Divine Providence itself.

"When God determined to institute among men a pure worship of himself as 'God of the whole earth,' he called Abram, of Ur, in Chaldea, to be his 'friend' and agent in the work. Revealing himself to the patriarch, he constituted him the progenitor of that 'chosen people' who were to be the depository of Divine truth until *the world* should be prepared to receive and practice the mysteries of human redemption. Every precaution was taken to make these *selected pupils of God* 'a peculiar people.' They were to be 'Odd-fellows' among the nations around them, not only by hereditary descent, but also by a singular form of government, a singular code of laws, and a singular ritual of worship, *all* adapted to keep them from mingling with other nations and adopting their idolatries. The decorations of their temple and tabernacle, the regalia of their priesthood, the emblems for their instruction, were all prescribed for them, even to form, color and material. The mode for initiating proselytes from other nations was clearly defined. and certain physical defects and conditions of health were made causes of perpetual exclusion from 'the congregation of Israel.'"—*Grosh's Manual, p.* 61.

vance step by step, through all its gradations until you shall have fully attained a knowledge of its intrinsic excellencies, its adaptation for the promotion of good-will among men, and its fitness as a minister to the trials and adversities which are inseparable from human life.

We have at this time a few general lessons to inculcate, which, in addition to those you have received in your progress to this chair, will serve to give you proper views as to the character and true objects of Odd-fellowship.

Odd-fellowship is founded upon that eternal principle which, recognizing man as a constituent of one universal brotherhood, teaches him that as he came from the hands of a common Parent he is bound to cherish and to protect[27] his fellow man. It thus presents a broad platform upon which mankind may unite in offices of human benefaction. Under its comprehensive influences, all the nations of the earth may concentrate their energies for the good of the common race. Based upon certain truths which are like axioms among all nations, tongues and creeds, its sacred tolerance presents a nucleus which, by its gentle influence, gathers within its orbit antagonistic natures, controls the elements of discord, stills the storm and soothes the spirit of passion, and directs in harmony man's united efforts to fraternize the world. This is the great first principle of our fellowship, which we denominate fraternity; a universal fraternity in the family of man. Our forefathers have wisely made this principle the corner-stone

---

Note 27.—"In all the circumstances of life in which a brother may be placed, he is to receive the aid, the counsel, or the protection of his fellow-member, *not as a favor merely, but as a right.*"—*Donaldson's Pocket Companion,* p. 13.

of Odd-fellowship.[28] Upon its solid basis the whole superstructure has securely rested, and, as we believe, is destined immovably to repose until time shall be no more.

From this principle we learn to regard the Great Author of our existence as our Father,[29] " in whom alone we live and move and have our being;" to recognize each other as alike the offspring of the same Parent, as the master-piece of his handiwork, and designed as such to reflect in our nature and relations the image of Him after whose likeness man was formed. We are, therefore, brothers; and in all our intercourse we illustrate the truthfulness of this profession by reciprocal relief and kindly offices to one another in the day of trial. With the divisions and classifications of human society our Order holds no fellowship. While it inculcates a veneration for religion and subordination to civil government and its laws, it studiously avoids all affinity with systems of faith or sects, whether religious or political.

In becoming an Odd-fellow no sacrifice of your opinions, no change of your relations to the State, no loosening of the obligations which, as a good citizen, you owe to the laws and institutions under which you live, is required.

Note 28.—"FRATERNITY! this is our corner-stone. Upon its solid basis rests our superstructure. It teaches us to regard the great family of mankind as our brethren, children of one Heavenly Father, the Great Author of our existence, ' in whom we live, and move, and have our being'; and that we should, in our conduct, reflect the image of that Father, after whose likeness man was formed."—*Donaldson's Pocket Companion, p.* 33.

Note 29.—"'The Fatherhood of God and the Brotherhood of man, then, are the great principles of our Order, embodied in the mottoes thereof, 'In God we trust,' and 'Friendship, Love and Truth.' To illustrate these principles on the limited scale prescribed by human abilities and our pecuniary resources, we have united in lodges, each of which is a mutual improvement and mutual aid association."—*Grosh's Manual, p.* 78.

On the contrary, learn now and forever, that you cannot become an Odd-fellow, in spirit and truth, unless you are grateful to your Creator, faithful to your country and fraternal to your fellow man. Within the walls of a lodge-room we meet for mutual counsel, the relief of distress, and the elevation[30] of human character. With pure hearts and clean hands must we come to such offices. Strife and discord, party and sect, which create heart-burnings and divisions among men, are banished by our laws without this counsel; and if, perchance, some thoughtless brother should so far wander from this injunction as to permit evil influences to control his actions, he must atone to the offended law. We war against vice in all its forms. Friendship toward man prompts the contest; the gentle influences of Love supply the weapons; Truth consecrates the effort and leads to victory.

Such, my friend, are among the first principles of Odd-fellowship; its objects you will more clearly understand as you advance in the order. If you have become initiated into this institution from the influence of a too common error, namely, that Odd-fellowship is a mere beneficial society, having for its single purpose the relief[31] of its members in the struggle incident to human life—if you have united yourself with this great brother-

---

NOTE 30.—"The great duties of our order, by and through which we aim to improve and exalt the character of our members, are few in number:—1. To visit the sick. 2. To relieve the distressed. 3. To bury the dead. 4. To educate the orphan. To these we have added, by charges and obligations, two others, viz., to aid the widow, and to exercise over each other fraternal watch-care and moral discipline."—*Grosh's Manual, p.* 83.

NOTE 31.—"Fraternity, therefore, is the corner-stone on which our forefathers based our order; fraternity in the family of mankind, illustrated in our family. the lodge and the order. As all men have God for their Father, all are brethren; and we would illustrate this great fact in all our offices of mutual aid, relief, sympathy and benevolence."—*Grosh's Manual, p.* 99.

hood from the promptings of idle curiosity, be at once undeceived. Mutual relief, it is true, is a leading office in our affiliation. To visit the sick, relieve the distressed, to bury the dead and educate the orphan, is the command of our laws, and an imperative duty which Odd-fellowship enjoins. But these, although its frequent and almost daily ministrations, are but a tithe of the intrinsic virtues of our beloved order. We seek to improve and elevate the character of man—to imbue him with proper conceptions of his capabilities for good; to enlighten[32] his mind—to enlarge the sphere of his affections—in a word, our aim is to lead man to the cultivation of the true fraternal relation designed by the Great Author of his being. Brother, for by that endearing name you are now privileged to be hailed, I greet you as an Odd-fellow of the Independent Order, and welcome you as a member of —————— Lodge No. —, under the jurisdiction of the Grand Lodge of —————. May you ever be animated by the pure principles of Odd-fellowship, and may your life and conduct[33] afford

———

NOTE 32.—''The order as founded by Brother Wildey, was simply a *humane* institution—its *main* objects were to relieve brethren, bury the dead and care for the widow and orphan. But gradually there were infused into its lectures and charges much moral and (unsectarian) religious instruction; and at each revision these principles were increased, and deepened, and strengthened, until its beneficial and relief measures, from being *ends*, have become *means* to a higher and greater end—'to improve and elevate the character of man; to imbue him with conceptions of his capability for good; to enlighten his mind; to enlarge the sphere of his affections, and thus to lead him to the cultivation of the true fraternal relations designed by the Great Author of his being.' Brother Wildey planted the seed and cultivated the tree. It bore fruit richer and better than he had anticipated. 'He builded better than he knew;' but as Founder and Architect he dwelt in the Temple which he had reared for more limited objects.'' — *Grosh's Manual, p.* 34.

NOTE 33.—'' May your initiation and consequent practice aid in releasing you from all blindness of moral vision, set you free from the fetters of ignorance and error, and bring you from a death in selfishness into a life of active benevolence and virtue.''—*Grosh's Manual, p.* 98.

no reproach to the new character which you have this night voluntarily assumed.

Noble Grand to Conductor—Conduct the candidate to the Secretary, where he will sign the Constitution.

After this the candidate is led by the Conductor to the left-hand side of the Noble Grand's chair, and is by him privately instructed in the Password of the term and its Explanation.

He is then given in charge of the Warden, with whom he will retire to the ante-room, without giving the Countersign, and be clothed with a white apron, the proper regalia of an initiatory member.

The Warden will then enter and await the candidate, who will work his way in by giving the Alarm and the Explanation of the Password.

On arriving at the center of the room, he will, with the Warden, address the Noble Grand with the Countersign, who will answer with the same sign; turning to the Vice Grand, he will address him with the Countersign, who will also answer with the same sign.

The Warden will then lead him to the chair of the Noble Grand, who will greet him as a brother.

Noble Grand—Brother, I congratulate you upon having worked your way into a lodge of our Order. I will now proceed to give you further instruction.

SIGN OF DISTRESS.

Place the open right hand palm downward on the top of the head, raise the hand upward about nine inches;

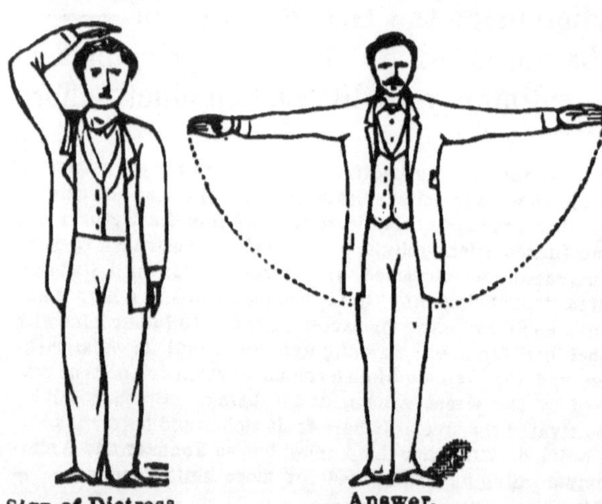

Sign of Distress.   Answer.

drop the hand to the head; this do three times; the hand after being placed on the head is to be raised and replaced on the head three times; then drop the hand to the side. *Answer*—extend the hands at arm's length off from the sides and at right angles to the body, palms outward; pause a moment and drop the hands to the side; this is not repeated.

Explanation—The Sign of Distress gives information to a brother at a distance that a brother of the Order is in want of assistance. The answer is given by a brother who shall observe and recognize the Sign and denotes a readiness to give the requisite assistance. When this Sign cannot be observed the brother in distress may use the words "*Give ear, O ye Heavens!*" which words must be pronounced in full and not the initials thereof.

THE SIGN OF RECOGNITION.

Sign of Recognition.   Answer.

First—When a brother shall desire to be recognized as an Odd-fellow by a member of the Order, he shall grasp with his right hand the lapel of his coat, the hand being placed over the right nipple, the thumb extended upward *Second*—An Odd-fellow observing this Sign shall recognize and answer the same by taking hold of the right lapel of his coat with his left hand, the same being also placed over the right nipple, thumb concealed beneath the coat *Third*—When the brother who made the Sign shall observe the answer he shall advance to the person making the answer and extend to him his right hand, which the person (if he be an Odd-fellow) shall accept and shake with his right hand and at the same time shall ask, Are you looking for me? when the other shall respond, For you.

If either of the brothers should be at the time without a coat he shall place his hand on his person in the same position, the challenging brother with his fingers turned under, the brother answering with his thumb concealed in the palm of his hand.

VOTING SIGN—The right hand uplifted.

Noble Grand—In the use of the gavel, one blow (Noble Grand gives one rap) calls the lodge to order, or seats it when standing; three blows (gives them) call up the lodge. The candidate is made to face the Vice Grand.

Noble Grand—Officers and brothers, I now introduce to you brother........ and commend him to your friendship and protection.

CHAPTER V.

Initiatory Degree.

Closing Ceremonies.

Noble Grand (three raps, all rise)—Officers and brothers, I will thank you to rise and assist me in closing the lodge.

SONG.

Brothers, we thank you all
For this your friendly call
　Our hearts to cheer;
May Peace her influence shed,
And heaven its wing outspread,
To guard each brother's head
　From pain and fear.

Good-night! and as you go,
Bear hence, and fully show
　Stamped on your breasts,
The seal of Friendship pure,
And Love through life t' endure,
And Truth, which still secure
　With honor rests.

Noble Grand—Vice Grand, I will thank you to perform the last duty of your station.

Vice Grand—Brethren, we thank you for your attendance this evening, and invite the company of as many of you as can make it convenient to attend at any future meeting.

Noble Grand—Warden, what is the last duty of your station?

Warden—It is to collect the regalia and deposit it in its proper place.

Noble Grand—Guardian, what is the last duty of your station?

Guardian—It is to open the door, that the brothers may depart in peace.

Noble Grand—I will thank you to do that duty as soon as the lodge is closed.

Guardian—I will.

Noble Grand—Right Supporter, I will thank you to perform the last duty of your station.

Right Supporter—By desire of our Noble Grand, I proclaim this lodge closed until next lodge night, at —— o'clock, when it will be re-opened for the transaction of such business as may be lawfully brought before the lodge, and for the diffusion of the principles of benevolence and charity.

Noble Grand (one rap, repeated by Vice Grand)—I, therefore, declare this lodge closed.

ANALYSIS INITIATORY DEGREE.

TAMERLANE had three arts by which he subdued and subjugated mankind: bribing, dividing, and amusing. Odd-fellowship *bribes* men by the hope of benefits; *divides* its members from outsiders and those of one degree from another by secrecy, and *amuses* them by ceremonies.

What redeems these *opening ceremonies* from wearisome stupidity, is their religious character. All beyond the Outside Guardian, hoodwink and pledge of secrecy is worship, and puts and holds the mind in a posture for receiving the mesmeric or spiritual influence of the system and of the spirits who inhabit and wield it. They, also, in apparently harmless and unimportant particulars, commence the perpetual lodge lesson of submission and obedience to superiors. This is calculated, by degrees, to wean the mind of the initiate from the open and free subordination to law, government, and the religion of Christ, by a weekly night-drill in obedience to another system, unknown to the true God, —the secret empire of " the god of this world."

Walking, as a visitor, through the Gray Nunnery at Montreal, and a convent at Quebec, I saw beautiful young females busy at their devotions in inaccessible galleries in sight from the chapel floor. In a long hall or corridor I saw pale, wan women in a row on one side, working with their needles under the eye of a lady superior, like convicts under keepers; and, on the other side of the apartment, a row of ninety cots, beside each of which, sitting or kneeling, were extremely aged people whose lips moved in silence as they counted their beads. The Papacy keeps its votaries *submissive* and *busy*. Odd-fellowship, like every false system of religion, must do the same; and these "*opening ceremonies*," which cover six or seven pages in describing them, —though a single paragraph might answer the ends of opening the lodge—are an initiatory drill of subjection, copied, in some parts, nearly verbatim from the opening of a Masonic lodge. Every such initiation is a mental debauch, operating on mind like tricks, sorcery and fortune telling.

But the chief power of this fool's-play of despotism is in the robes of the officers—scarlet, blue, black and white, with caps the color of their robes, while the members' faces are all covered with masks. This scene, in a lighted hall, at night, guarded by sentinels, and all under such balderdash names as " Odd-fellow," " Noble Grand," and the like, forms a hocus-pocus invented in sport by ignorant English operatives in 1812, to give zest to their idle hours and relish to their cups. The trick took like Aaron's calf-worship. The cunning have joined it for the sake of its funds; the ambitious, for its votes, and " behold, the world is gone after it."

And this is Odd-fellowship! which numbers its mem-bers by hundred thousands, and reckons its revenues by millions! What is it? Where is " the hiding of its power?" To one class of thinking minds, the greatest mystery of the lodge is that sensible, fair-minded men can repeat its twaddle, wear its gew-gaw finery, and obey its puerile regulations. *Dr. Leonard Bacon* has said of the Masonic institution: " It seems to me one stupendous mass of dreary nonsense." And yet Presidents of this Republic have been Masons and Odd-fellows, and to say they have joined the lodges for popularity is to confess their power over civilized mind in the leading nations of the earth.

A handful of neighbors in a hall, at night, get another neighbor as a candidate for initiation. He is taken into an ante-room. asked his name, residence,

occupation, age, lodge relations, health, and belief in a
" Supreme Intelligent Being." His answers are taken
down and signed by his name. He then begins to be
pledged to conceal what is to happen to him in the
lodge, which gives a devil's dignity to the unknown
trifles before him. He is blindfolded and led in, lectured,
chained, and threatened with binding " to the stake."
In this plight he is led around, his blind taken off, and
he confronted with a grinning human skeleton, with
flaming torches held each side. His captors then repeat some school-boy lessons on death. Hoodwinked
again, he is led to one officer after another, his blinder
being put on and off, till the Vice Grand orders the
chains off and re-pledges him, with his hand on his
heart, to conceal the whole work of the lodge, and not
to wrong it. He is then further lectured, twaddled,
charged, told the falsehood that " Odd-fellowship presents a broad platform upon which mankind may unite,"
when he is just now pledged, and afterward sworn, to
conceal the whole thing called Odd-fellowship from
that very " *mankind* " who are to unite on its platform.
He is now hailed as a brother, and told that Odd-fellowship is not " a mere beneficial society;" that its aim is
" to elevate man," and " lead him to cultivate the true
fraternal relations designed by the Great Author of his
being " *(See the degree);* that, in short, it is a religion:
that it will bring men out of the blindness of error and

the chains of sin, into the liberty of the sons of God. And this contemptible farce is preceded by a solemn prayer to the god of the lodge, and closed with an ode on friendship, love and truth. This is Odd-fellowship, and the whole of it, the further degrees being but repetitions of similar doses.

There is but one possible explanation of the fact that hundreds of thousands of grown, rational men repeat this farrago weekly, and from year to year. It is that Satan is its god, and that he imposes these and other pagan puerilities on man, made in the image of God and redeemed by Christ, to avenge himself on the God whom he hates for casting him and his angels out of heaven; to travesty the Christian religion and shut the only door of hope for man through Christ, by opening false doors leading to himself. To treat such a system as frivolous " nonsense " is to commit a dreadful mistake. If " the heavens and earth " were now in flames —as they one day will be *(2 Pet. 3: 7)*—if one only bridge of escape, built by Christ, could give safety to those fleeing from the conflagration of the world, and a revolted angel should set open false doors, promising to lead to Paradise, but actually leading to hell, " where their worm dieth not and their fire is not quenched," —such is the door of every secret lodge. Every pagan shrine, or temple, or man-made religion, is such a gateway of perdition, no matter what the worships are made of, or what frivolities are practiced within them. Legions of devils give them their mesmeric power over mind; and while the motives of the worshipers are as various as their callings and hopes, "their way is as darkness; they know not at what they stumble."—*Prov. 4:19.*

CHAPTER VI.

FIRST, OR DEGREE OF FRIENDSHIP."

GENERAL REGULATIONS.

Adopted by the Sovereign Grand Lodge, I. O. O. F., Session of 1880.

When subordinate lodges open in the degrees for the purpose of balloting for or conferring the degrees, the titles of the officers shall be the same as in the Initiatory Degree; and the officers shall, respectively, occupy the same chairs as in the Initiatory Degree.

No officer or member can enter a lodge open and working in the degrees, without addressing the presiding officer, except the Conductor when he enters or retires with a candidate; nor can any officer or member retire without addressing the presiding officer with the proper sign. All voting is by the voting sign, unless otherwise provided.

Working Lodges must close in the Initiatory Degree before opening in the higher degrees.

In voting to advance brethren to the degrees, when the balloting takes place, the lodge must be opened in the particular degree applied for, and when balloting, the ballot-box shall be placed on a pedestal near the center of the room, and the Noble Grand shall supervise the balloting.

NOTE 34.—"The chief attributes of our fraternity are Benevolence, Brotherly Love and Charity."—*Grosh's Manual, p.* 109.

The right of a lodge to grant two or more degrees to
.4 brother at the same time is left for local legislation.

A lodge can confer the degrees upon a member of
another lodge, provided he presents a certificate of his
lodge that they have been voted him and paid for, with
a request that they be conferred.

In all the degrees three raps call up the lodge and
one rap seats the lodge.

The dramatic parts of the degrees should be acted
quite slowly. Proper pauses should occur between each
event in the drama, so that the candidate may be duly
impressed with each incident.

The work in the degrees must be done in regular
numerical sequence, closing in one degree and opening
in another, according to the number of the degrees.

Any number of candidates may receive the First
Degree at the same time, and in the Second Part, when
David and Jonathan kneel, members should be assigned,
one to each of the other candidates, who shall kneel
with him and clasp hands in proper form and unite in
the covenant. Such members may be styled Assistant
Outside Conductors.

Upon closing a Subordinate Lodge in the Initiatory
Degree, the lodge must open in the Third Degree, and
in that degree the minutes must be read and acted upon;
then, after balloting in or conferring the First or Second degrees, the lodge must re-open in and close from
the Third Degree.

DEGREE LODGES.[35]

In a regularly-constituted Degree Lodge, the titles of

NOTE 35.—" Degree Lodges were established in 1829, by the Grand Lodge of
Pennsylvania. Prior to this, degrees were conferred in the lodge-room on Sundays."—*Grosh's Manual, p. 36.*

the officers shall be Degree Master (who occupies the principal chair), Deputy Degree Master (who occupies the chair of Vice Grand), First, Second, Third and Fourth Assistant Degree Masters, whose stations are to the right and left of the Degree Master and the Deputy Degree Master; Past Grand, Warden, Conductor, Secretary, Treasurer, Outside Guardian and Inside Guardian, whose positions are the same as in the Subordinate Lodge.

Where the title of Noble Grand is used in a Subordinate Lodge, that of Degree Master is to be substituted in a Degree Lodge.

A Degree Lodge shall also have such other officers as the degrees may require.

In all other respects a Degree Lodge may do anything which a Subordinate Lodge may do when working in the degrees, for the purpose of conferring them in a proper manner.

OPENING CEREMONIES.

The Opening Ceremonies are the same in the First, Second and Third Degrees, with very slight variations.

As stated on page 76, the officers of a "Subordinate Lodge," when conferring the "degrees," retain the same titles as in the Initiatory Degree; but as stated above, in a regular "Degree Lodge," the Noble Grand is termed "Degree Master," Vice Grand, "Deputy Degree Master," etc.; hence the two titles given in this chapter.

At the time appointed for opening a Degree Lodge in the degrees, the proper officer shall take the chair, and, after calling to order, with one rap, will proceed to open the lodge as follows:

Noble Grand (or Degree Master)—Officers and brothers, we are about to open the lodge in the First Degree for the transaction of business. If any one present is not qualified to sit with us in this Degree, he will please retire.

Noble Grand (*or Degree Master*)—The Inside Guardian will close the door, and the brethren will please clothe themselves in appropriate regalia.[36] No one will be admitted during the opening ceremony.

Inside Guardian—Noble Grand (or Degree Master), the door is secured.

Noble Grand (*or Degree Master*)—Warden, examine the brothers in the lodge-room in the password of the First Degree, and in the password and explanation of the current term. [It is not required of the Warden or either of the Guardians to respond to brothers by giving any portion of the password].

Warden—Noble Grand (or Degree Master), I have examined the brothers and find them all correct and duly qualified to sit with us in this degree.

Noble Grand (*or Degree Master*)—Vice Grand (or Deputy Degree Master), what is your duty in the lodge?

Vice Grand (*or Deputy Degree Master*)—To assist you according to my office in any work which may lawfully come before the lodge, and to aid you in preserving order.

Noble Grand (*or Degree Master*)—Secretary, what is your duty?

Secretary—To keep accurate minutes of the proceedings of this lodge; to receive all moneys due the lodge, and pay the same to the Treasurer. [Proceedings of lodges, when opened in particular degrees for the purpose of conferring degrees or for balloting for degrees,

---

Note 36.—"One of our uses of regalia, is to teach us to beware how we judge men by mere *appearances.*"—*Grosh's Manual, p.* 53.

are recorded in a distinct minute or record book.]

Noble Grand (or *Degree Master*) (rising)—Officers and brothers, we have met for the purpose of transacting business in the degrees, in which I trust I shall receive your fraternal assistance and cordial co-operation. The interest of the Degree Lodge depends greatly upon the prompt attendance, strict attention and gentlemanly deportment of the members. It is your duty to remain until the work for which we have assembled shall have been completed, and to aid me with your presence and support. It is my duty to preserve order and to see that our work conforms to the laws and regulations of the Sovereign Grand Lodge of the Independent Order of Odd fellows; but I feel confident that I shall not be under the necessity of exercising any restraining authority on the present occasion.

Noble Grand (or *Degree Master*) (three raps)–Brothers, rise and advance the sign of the First Degree.

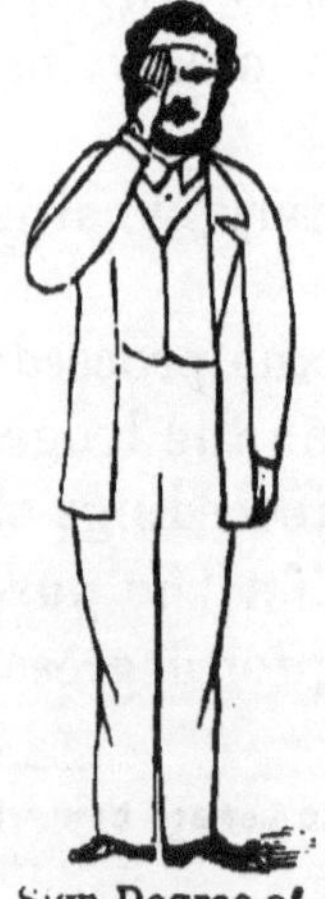

Sign Degree of Friendship.

SIGN.

The Sign is made as follows—extend the fingers of the right hand; place the thumb inside of, and parallel with, the first finger; carry the hand to the brow, with the thumb resting on the left temple; draw a line across the forehead (fingers touching) until the end of the thumb reaches the right temple describing a bow, then drop the hand.

Noble Grand (*or Degree Master*)—Warden, declare the lodge opened.

Warden—By direction of the Noble Grand (or Degree Master), I declare this lodge duly opened in the First Degree, for the transaction of such business as may be lawfully brought before it.

Noble Grand (*or Degree Master*)—Officers and brothers, so be it.

All " So be it."

Noble Grand—(one rap, seating the lodge.)

RAISING OR REDUCING THE LODGE.

When it is necessary to close the Degree Lodge in any of the degrees, with the intention of opening in another degree, it is done as follows:

Noble Grand (three raps, all rise)—Brothers, we are about to close the lodge in the ——— Degree, to be re-opened in the ——— Degree, for the purpose of conferring the same (*or* to ballot for the degree).

Noble Grand (*or Degree Master*)—Warden, declare the lodge closed accordingly.

Warden—By direction of the Noble Grand (or Degree Master), I declare the lodge closed in the ——— Degree, to re-open in the ——— Degree.

Noble Grand (*or Degree Master*)—Officers and brothers, so be it.

All—" So be it."

Noble Grand—(one rap, seating the lodge).

Should it become necessary to open the Degree Lodge in any other degree during the meeting, it shall be done as follows; or when a Subordinate Lodge has closed in the Initiatory to open in the degrees, the following form shall be used:

Noble Grand (*or Degree Master*)—Brothers, we are

about to open the lodge in the —— Degree. The Warden will examine in the password of the degree. [The order is obeyed.]

Warden—Noble Grand (or Degree Master), I have examined the brothers and find them correct.

Noble Grand (three raps)—The brethren will rise and advance the sign of the —— Degree. Warden, declare the lodge duly opened in this degree.

Warden—By direction of the Noble Grand (or Degree Master), I proclaim this lodge duly opened in the —— Degree, for the transaction of such business as may be lawfully brought before it.

Noble Grand (*or Degree Master*)—Officers and brothers, so be it.

All—" So be it."

Noble Grand—(one rap, seating the lodge.)

CHAPTER VII.

FIRST, OR DEGREE OF FRIENDSHIP."

INITIATION.³⁸

PART I.

In connection with the opening ceremonies, page 78, attention was called to
the fact that in "Degree Lodges" the titles assumed by the officers are different
from those used in the Subordinate Lodge.   We here use the Subordinate Lodge
titles entirely.

The Noble Grand having appointed an Outside Conductor, directs him to retire
to the ante-room, receive and introduce the candidate without blindfolding him.
As the Outside Conductor retires, he must salute "the chair" (Noble Grand)
with the sign of the degree, when he proceeds at once to the ante-room and comes
to the inside door of the lodge-room.

Outside Conductor—(with candidate; three raps on
door).

Inside Guardian—Noble Grand, there is an alarm at
the door.

Noble Grand—Attend to the alarm.

NOTE 37.—"The *First Degree* teaches the loveliness of charity, as manifested
by a benevolent heart, feeling good-will to all, and warm sympathy for the afflicted.   The *Second Degree* teaches the devotion of fraternal love in a covenant for
mutual relief.   The *Third Degree* exhibits the same friendship, not as expecting
mutuality of benefits, but self-sacrificing, tested by adversity, exercised toward
brethren who may be strangers, though members of the great family of Odd-
fellowship."—*Grosh's Manual, p.* 131.

NOTE 38.—"By the most beautiful lessons, we instruct him in those great
principles which will not only inform his own mind and render more susceptible
to goodness his own heart, but will enable him, if he so wills, to become an apt
teacher and ready example to others, in all those virtues that adorn and bless
humanity "—*Grosh's Manual, p.* 85.

Inside Guardian (opening the wicket)—Who comes there?

Outside Conductor—A brother who, having been initiated, now seeks to obtain the mysteries" of the First Degree of Odd-fellowship.

Inside Guardian (closing the wicket)—Noble Grand, a brother, having been initiated, now seeks to obtain the mysteries of the First Degree of Odd-fellowship.

Noble Grand—Why does he seek to obtain these mysteries?

Inside Guardian (opening the wicket)—Why does he seek to obtain the mysteries?

Outside Conductor—Because he wishes to be more fraternal."

Inside Guardian (closing the wicket)—Because he wishes to be more fraternal.

Noble Grand—Admit him, then, in friendship, which is the bond of fraternity." [Candidate is admitted and conducted before the Noble Grand].

Outside Conductor—Noble Grand, I present to you (give the candidate's name), a worthy brother, who, having been duly elected, seeks to obtain the mysteries of this degree.

Noble Grand (rising)—Brother, in presenting yourself for advancement in our order, it becomes my duty to remind you of the importance of the step you pro-

———

NOTE 39.—"The solemnities of initiation may be novel, even startling by their novelty."—*Grosh's Manual, p.* 88.

NOTE 40.—"All our operations are designed to lead each other to the knowledge and practice of the true brotherhood of man."—*Grosh's Manual, p.* 100.

NOTE 41.—"Odd-fellowship is a miniature representation, among a chosen few, of that fraternity which God has instituted among men."—*Grosh's Manual, p.* 99.

pose to take, and to caution you against making engagements that you may be unwilling to fulfill, or, for the gratification of idle curiosity, taking upon yourself obligations which may hereafter prove burdensome. It will be necessary before you receive this degree for you to take a solemn obligation, pledging yourself not to disclose any of its mysteries to persons whom you do not know to be lawfully in possession of them, and binding yourself to the performance of the duties prescribed in this degree, so far as it may be in your power to perform them. Have you duly considered the subject, and are you now prepared to advance? [If candidate answers in the affirmative, the Noble Grand continues]:

Noble Grand—Then place yourself in the attitude in which you were initiated into this order, and repeat after me (Noble Grand calls up the lodge by three raps):

OBLIGATION, DEGREE OF FRIENDSHIP.

I, —— ——, in the presence of the covenanted brothers of the Degree of Friendship here assembled, do solemnly promise, that I will never improperly divulge the secrets of the degree about to be intrusted to my keeping; and I hereby pledge myself to help and support my afflicted and persecuted brother, and warn him of approaching danger, whether it be from his own imprudence or from the evil designs of others, or from some accidental cause. I will point out his advantage" and interest, where they do not conflict with the rights

---

Note 42.—"Remember that when on the surging waters of human life, far from haven and from home, you may summon any brother to your aid. But forget not, also, that the obligation is mutual. When you are summoned, you also are bound to fly and save your perishing brother from sinking in despair."—*Grosh's Manual, p.* 100.

of others, if it should be in my power so to do. I will protect his property, assist his family, defend his character and save his life and limb, should opportunity offer. To the faithful performance of all which I pledge my sacred honor.

Noble Grand—(one rap, seating the lodge).

Noble Grand (to candidate)—Are you willing to submit to the ordeal by which you may become a brother of this degree?

Candidate answers.

Noble Grand (to the Outside Conductor)—Let the brother be taken to the ante-room, that he may re-enter and take his next step in fraternity. [Outside Conductor, without stopping to salute the " chair " with the sign, conducts candidate to the ante-room, when he blindfolds him and comes with him to the door].

Part II.

Outside Conductor—(three raps on inside door).

Inside Guardian—Noble Grand, there is an alarm at the door.

Noble Grand—Attend to the alarm.

Inside Guardian (opening the wicket)—Who comes there?

Outside Conductor—A brother who is ready to receive the mysteries of this degree.

Note 43.—"Let him not wonder that he is yet unable to behold steadily this light through surrounding darkness. Man advances gradually in light and knowledge. But how can he apply these principles of fraternity so as to enlighten and liberate his own soul, then enlighten the darkness and break the bonds of others, and so hasten the coming of that age when this Aceldama shall be a blossoming Paradise, and clashing interests and jarring strifes give place to a universal union of all energies for the general good, to a community of happiness and peace!"—*Grosh's Manual, p.* 96.

Inside Guardian (closing the wicket)—Noble Grand, a brother is ready to receive the mysteries of this degree.

Noble Grand—What is his name?

Inside Guardian (opening the wicket)—What is his name?

Outside Conductor—David, the son of Jesse.

Inside Guardian (closing the wicket)—David, the son of Jesse.

Noble Grand—Why comes he here?

Inside Guardian (opening the wicket)—Why comes he here?

Outside Conductor—To visit Saul, king of Israel.

Inside Guardian (closing the wicket)—To visit Saul, king of Israel.

Noble Grand—Admit him to the presence of the king.

Noble Grand—(three raps, all rise).

The Outside Conductor enters with the candidate, and conducts him to the middle of the room, facing the Noble Grand. After a pause, he exclaims *reverently:*

Outside Conductor—Hail to the king!

Noble Grand (as king)—Welcome, son of Jesse! Thou hast smitten mine enemies and brought me the spoils of victory.

The Lodge (led by Warden)—Saul has slain his thousands, and David his tens of thousands!

Noble Grand (as king)—This is treason to the king! Ho! my guards! I will smite him with the sword!

Here a sword or some heavy substance is thrown down by the side of the candidate

The Lodge (led by Warden)—Fly!—Away!—He will kill thee! Away! Away!

The Outside Conductor hurries the candidate entirely around the lodge-room; then walking slowly, he is met near the Vice Grand's chair by the Inside Conductor, who represents Jonathan.

Inside Conductor (laying his hand upon the shoulder of the candidate)—David, I am thy friend; my father seeketh to kill[44] thee; now, therefore, take heed and abide here. I will go and stand by my father, and what I see I will tell thee. Hide thyself by the stone Ezel: I will shoot three arrows on its side as though I shot at a mark. And will send a lad, saying, " Go, find the arrows." If I say to him, " Behold, the arrows are on this side of thee," then come thou, for there is peace to thee, and no hurt; but if I say to the lad, " Behold, the arrows are beyond thee," go thy way.

Noble Grand—(one rap, seating the lodge).

The Inside Conductor, as Jonathan, goes away, and the Outside Conductor leads the candidate once entirely around the lodge-room, halting at the side of and near the middle of the room, where something representing the stone Ezel is placed.

Outside Conductor—Let us hide by this rock.

Inside Conductor (as Jonathan, from opposite side of the room, after a pause, loudly)—Here, lad, find out the arrows that I shoot. [Twangs his bow loudly several times, then shoots three blunt arrows].

Right Scene Supporter (as lad, standing between David and Jonathan, loudly)—Where are they?

NOTE 44.—"1 Samuel xix: 1-7: And Saul spake to Jonathan his son, and to all his servants, that they should kill David. But Jonathan, Saul's son, delighted much in David; and Jonathan told David, saying, Saul, my father, seeketh to kill thee. Now, therefore, I pray thee, take heed to thyself until the morning, and abide in a secret place, and hide thyself: and I will go out and stand beside my father in the field where thou art, and I will commune with my father of thee; and what I see, that I will tell thee. And Jonathan spake good of David unto Saul his father, and said unto him, Let not the king sin against his servant, against David: because he hath not sinned against thee, and because his works have been to thee-ward very good. For he did put his life in his hand, and slew the Philistine, and the LORD wrought a great salvation for all Israel: thou sawest it, and didst rejoice; wherefore, then, wilt thou sin against innocent blood to slay David without a cause? And Saul hearkened unto the voice of Jonathan, and Saul sware, As the LORD liveth he shall not be slain. And Jonathan called David, and Jonathan showed him all those things, and Jonathan brought David to Saul, and he was in his presence as in times past."—*Grosh's Manual, p.* 117.

Inside Conductor—Are not the arrows beyond thee? Make haste! speed! stay not!

Inside Conductor (after waiting for lad to run and get the arrows)—Here, lad, take this bow and arrows; go, carry them to the city.

Right Scene Supporter (as lad, near the inside door of the lodge-room)—I go, my noble prince.

After a lengthy pause, the Outside Conductor leads the candidate around the room, and halts near the middle of the lodge-room, where they are met by the Inside Conductor as Jonathan.

Inside Conductor (as Jonathan, laying his hand upon the shoulder of the candidate)—David, son of Jesse, behold my father would kill[45] thee, and yet I love thee as my own soul. Let us swear the one to the other in friendship forever.

The Inside Conductor (as Jonathan) kneels down upon his right knee, and the Outside Conductor causes the candidate also to kneel in the same manner, with his face to the Inside Conductor, their left knees touching, and their right hands clasped.

The Inside Conductor (as Jonathan), and the Outside Conductor for the candidate, slowly, solemnly and together utter the following:

The Lord be between me and thee, and between my seed and thy seed forever.

The candidate and the Inside Conductor continue kneeling, the lodge is called up, and being led by the Chaplain or Warden, repeat this covenant slowly as follows:

The Lodge—The Lord be between me and thee, and between thy seed and my seed forever.

The Inside Conductor and the candidate arise and the Inside Conductor retires. The candidate is then faced towards the Vice Grand.

Vice Grand—Hail to the covenant of friendship![46]

NOTE 45.—"But soon the evil spirit again came upon Saul, and his attempts on David's life compelled the young man to flee to Samuel in Ramah."—*Grosh's Manual, p.* 118.

NOTE 46.—"This teacher of past ages also says that Friendship, Love and Truth are not only a safeguard, but a remedy for all the social and moral evils that afflict our race."—*Grosh's Manual, p.* 96.

Candidate is made to face the Past Grand.

Past Grand—Hail to the covenant of friendship!

Candidate is made to face the Noble Grand.

The Lodge (led by the Warden)–Hail to the covenant of friendship!

Noble Grand to Outside Conductor (after a pause)—Conductor, restore our brother to light.

The Outside Conductor removes the blindfold, the lodge is seated, and the candidate is lead to the Noble Grand's chair.

Noble Grand—My brother, I will now instruct you in the mysteries of this degree.

In this degree there is an alarm at the inner door, a Password and Explanation of the Password, a Countersign an answer to the Countersign, a Sign, an answer to the Sign, a Memento, the Warning Sign, the Sign of Safety, the Sign of Danger, a Grip and a Token.

THE ALARM at the inner door is three raps.

THE PASSWORD is QUIVER to be lettered at all times when used for working purposes, working into a lodge or in examination prior to opening. In communicating this word, either to the Inside Guardian or to the Warden the brother must give the letters Q-U-I, and if required by the Inside Guardian or Warden, he must give the remainder of the word V-E-R—lettered as before. The Inside Guardian and Warden must be satisfied.

Sign Degree of Friendship.

Explanation-That from which Jonathan drew his arrows, given in full but not used for working purposes.

SIGN.

The Sign is made as follows—extend the fingers of the right hand; place the thumb inside of, and parallel with, the first finger; carry the hand to the brow, with the thumb resting on the left temple; draw a line across the forehead (fingers touching) until the end of the thumb reaches the right temple describing a bow, then drop the hand.

Answer.

ANSWER.

Grasp the root of the left ear with the fore finger and thumb of the right hand, fingers below, thumb above the root of the ear.

THE MEMENTO

Is a bundle of sticks, to represent the strength of union; united cannot be broken; a single stick to represent that separated each may be easily broken.

Memento Degree of Friendship.

Warning Sign.

WARNING SIGN.

Close the fingers of each hand, with the thumb in front of the first finger; place each elbow by the side of the body; extend each arm and closed hand horizontally.

Sign of Safety.

SIGN OF SAFETY.

The hands and arms being in the same position as in the Warning Sign, extend the index finger of the right hand, with which point to and just touch the second or knuckle joint of the thumb of the left hand.

Sign of Danger.

SIGN OF DANGER.

Elbows same as before described, place the wrist of the right hand on the second or knuckle joint of the thumb of the left hand; extend the index finger and point towards the ground.

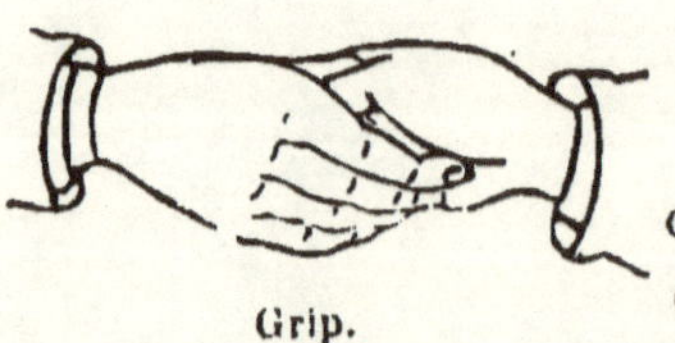

Grip.

GRIP.

Form a link with the thumbs of the right hand; clasp hands, enclosing it, (link of thumbs.)

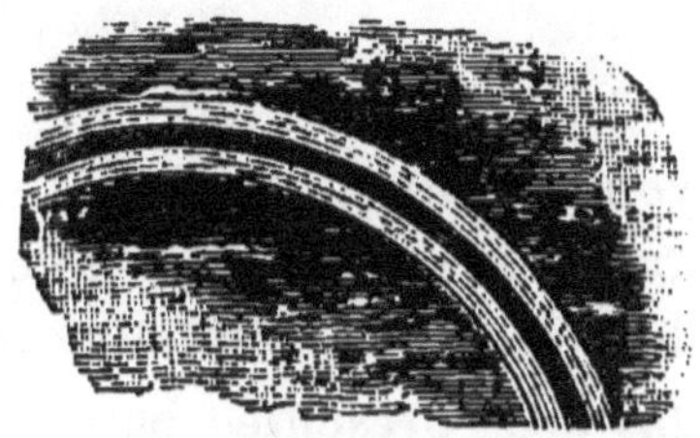

Token—The rainbow. 

SPECIAL INSTRUCTIONS.

Instructions for working into a Degree Lodge, or a Subordinate Lodge, opened in the degrees, for the purpose of conferring degrees, balloting for degrees, or for any other purpose.   These instructions should be given to every candidate receiving degrees, immediately after he has been instructed in the secret work.

Noble Grand to Candidate—Wishing to visit a Degree Lodge, or a Subordinate Lodge opened in the first degree, you will announce your presence by an alarm at the outside door (the alarm at the outside door is the same as in the Initiatory—*one rap,*) when the Outside Guardian will open the wicket and require from you the Password of the current term.   If correct, you will be admitted to the ante-room.   After clothing yourself in appropriate regalia (having ascertained from the Outside Guardian that the lodge is open in the first degree) you will give three raps at the inside door.   The Inside Guardian will open the wicket and obtain from you your name, rank and the number of the lodge to which you belong.   The Inside Guardian will close the wicket and inform the proper officer who, if he is satisfied, will direct the Inside Guardian to admit you if correct.   The Ins'de Guardian re-opens the wicket and you must give him the Password of the first degree.   If correct the Inside Guardian will admit you, when you will advance to the centre of the room and address the Noble Grand with the Countersign, who will acknowledge you as a brother by giving the same Countersign.   You will then turn and address the Vice Grand with the Countersign who will acknowledge you as a brother by giving the same Countersign.   You will then again turn to the Noble Grand and address him with the sign of the first degree.   The Noble Grand will give the proper answer to the sign.   You will then be seated.   Wishing to leave the lodge before it is closed in the first degree you will address the presiding officer only with the sign of the first degree and that officer will answer you with the proper sign.   The Inside Guardian will then allow you to depart.   If you are visiting your own lodge and are without either the Password of the current term or the Password of this degree, the Noble Grand being so informed asks the Secretary as to your standing in the lodge.   If the Secretary reports favorably, directions will be given to admit you.   But if the report is unfavorable you are so informed by the proper guardian and you cannot be admitted.   [The Noble Grand should carefully instruct the brother in the method of using the Passwords in working into a Lodge and in examination prior to opening].

CONCLUDING CHARGE.

Noble Grand (standing)—Brother, by the consent of your brethren, you have been advanced to a position of great responsibility. The most ancient as well as the most true and beautiful example of earthly friendship has been presented before you, and you have in your own person illustrated a noble history. In that touching drama you stood in the presence of royalty and listened to the voice of praise, but your merit provoked enmity, and you were hunted down as a traitor, when you were full of truth and honor. You have thus enacted a part of the common life. Envy is the malicious foe of virtue, and is ever ready to destroy what it can not imitate or surpass; it is the vice of the weak and the vain and the weapon of an ignoble mind. In suffering its persecution you have learned a lesson never to be forgotten. Man is prone to selfishness and thus to live for himself alone; in this isolation he has but little sympathy with his fellow-man. In such a mind envy takes possession and hatred follows with its horrid brood. But there is also a divinity[47] in man which weds him to lofty motives and honorable actions. The good have an affinity for each other which grows up into confidence and affection. Generous deeds and unselfish purposes are the strongest bonds of union—in his high estate, no man liveth to himself. You have acted a

Note 47.—"He will find in these instructions the voice of Wisdom and Truth; and he will see that whoever shall hear and obey them must be respected by the wise and good. They teach him his duty to his God, his country, his neighbor, his family and himself; they show him how he may live in the enjoyment of a peaceful, contented mind."—*Donaldson's Pocket Companion, p.* 24.

part where all was oppression upon the one hand, and all was love and protection upon the other. Thus you have seen the picture upon both sides. It is possible that men should combine for the common good; hence we have societies communities, states and nations united by a compact which protects their members. But the bond is stronger when individuals are united by personal contact and held together by a personal covenant. Such a covenant we have all entered into, and you have been solemnly added to our fraternal union. By such a tie has God bound himself to his creatures on the scroll of heaven, with the rainbow as his seal. Such obligations have come down to us from every age and country; by these, the mystic rights of all nations have been protected, and men everywhere brought into fellowship. By your solemn pledge you are now entitled to give and receive the tokens of a deathless friendship.[48] Every Odd-fellow[49] is your brother, and his family the sacred object of your fraternal care. You have become one of a vast brotherhood[50] which extends to many lands, and in their assemblies you will always be welcome. The mysteries you have learned will insure you an honorable reception in strange cities and distant states,

NOTE 48.—"The Fatherhood of God and the Brotherhood of man, then, are the great principles of our Order, embodied in the mottoes thereof, 'In God we trust,' and 'Friendship, Love, and Truth.' To illustrate these principles on the limited scale prescribed by human abilities and our pecuniary resources, we have united in lodges, each of which is a mutual improvement and mutual aid association. And further to extend our operations and increase our advantages and usefulness together, we have united all these lodges in a general Order, which we desire to render universal as the family of man on earth."—*Grosh's Manual,* p. 78.

NOTE 49.—"The earth is our country, and the human race our nation."—*Grosh's Manual,* p. 45.

NOTE 50.—"As the largest secret association of the age, it has accomplished more good, and dispensed more real blessings among men. than any similar society."—*Donaldson's Pocket Companion,* p. 12.

where you will be the subject of tender attentions [51] because you are an Odd-fellow.

Brother (naming the candidate), such is the nature and effect of the covenant you have taken; the emblematic color of this degree is pink.

I now welcome you as a brother of the Degree of Friendship.[52]

Note 52.—"This internal, truly living spirit of Love and of universal fraternity, pervading all our rituals and ceremonies; recognized in emblems, colors and regalia; using every adjunct for strengthening its influence on the soul; speaking to ear and eye in every lecture, charge, sign and token, and to the touch in grip and pressure; and manifesting itself (silently, like rain, and sunshine, and electricity) in beneficent organizations and institutions; this soul of all its teachings and workings is Odd-fellowship, the hidden name in the white stone, which he knoweth best who most truly possesses it."—*Grosh's Manual, p.* 78.

Note 51.—"In a perfect financial system of dues and benefits, there is no place for charity; and every dollar taken from the sick-fund for mere charity is robbery of that fund."—*Jour. Proc. Supreme Grand Lodge, Session of* 1880, *p.* 8213.

CHAPTER VIII.

First, or Degree of Friendship.

Closing Ceremonies.

Noble Grand (or Degree Master)—Brothers, having concluded our business for the evening, you will please rise (*three raps*) while we proceed to close the lodge. We thank you for your presence, and wish your attendance at our future meetings. You will now advance the sign of the Third Degree. Warden, proclaim the lodge duly closed.

Warden—By direction of the Noble Grand (or Degree Master) I proclaim the lodge duly closed.

Noble Grand (or Degree Master)—(one rap).

ANALYSIS DEGREE OF FRIENDSHIP.

Shakspeare's Portrait of Odd-fellowism—The Degrees Invented and Added for Purposes of Greed or Ambition—Ex-Vice-President Colfax and the Rebekah Degree a Case in Point—Sacrilegious Use of the Narrative of David and Jonathan in This Degree—How Initiates Feel—"Is This Real Masonry or Have They Been Fooling Me?"—Repetition the Cure for Disgust at the Ceremonies—A Deceived Man in the Initiation, but a Devil-Worshiper in the Degrees—The Body Profaned and the Will Subdued and Fascinated, he Delights in the Moral Uncleanness of False Worship—The Only Remedy— The Diversity of Form Conceals the Unity in Essence of the Secret Worships—A Shame even to Speak of them in Paul's Time—Orders Never Grow Rapidly until they Begin to Worship—Effect of Religious Rites without Religion—Nurses of Nihilism.

> 'But then I sigh and, with a piece of Scripture,
> Tell them—that God bids us do good for evil:
> And thus I clothe my naked villainy
> With old, odd ends stolen forth of Holy Writ,
> And seem a saint when most I play the devil."
>
> —*Richard III.*

The " many simple gulls " of Shakspeare's day are not all dead yet. Who could imagine, were there not facts to prove it, that grown men of ordinary sense and capacity could act over, year after year, weekly, the puerilities of this " Friendship Degree " in Odd-fellowship! All of this " ORDER," beyond initiation, which was at first a drinking-bout in an ale-house, as Grosh confesses *(Manual, p. 23)*, and which still retains a tinge from the complexion of its origin, has been invented and added by designing men for the purposes of greed or ambition. What else ever moved *Schuyler Colfax* to invent an outside degree for women? The fame which moved the hunchback politician, Richard, to smile and quote Scripture moved Colfax. Richard wanted a crown, and he got it. Colfax wanted office, which he gained by the same "old, odd ends stolen forth of Holy Writ," and seeming saintship.

This story of David and Jonathan, beautiful as a sacred historic fact, acted over in a lodge, at night, by a promiscuous body of men selected for their "sound health" and capacity to pay dues, is literally "stolen" for selfish ends, and becomes an affront and a sacrilege. Its use in Odd-fellowship, like that of all the "degrees," is that of splints to a weak back. Thousands of initiates, when put through the initiation, feel as did Hon. Samuel D. Greene, after being made an Entered Apprentice, and sitting down beside the Senior Deacon, who was also deacon in Greene's church. He turned and pleadingly asked his Christian brother in a whisper: " Deacon, won't you tell me if this is real Masonry, or have they been fooling me?"

. The cure for this rational, natural disgust at being hoodwinked, handled and profaned, is repetition. Now, the initiate knows the fool's play as he did not at first. And the first time a man imposes on me, the fault is his; the second time, the fault is my own. The three knocks of the entersign, the hollow rattle of the gavel strokes, the mock-solemn wording and mouthing of the lecture and the charge, all leading to the practical realities, degree fees and obligations of concealment, enlarged and deepened by repetition, and all canonized by prayer and song; when all this is gone over with the second time in this "friendship degree," the dupe becomes a voluntary devil-worshiper. The sacredness of his body gone by handling, his will habituated to yielding without a reason, and he practicing religious worship in what he now knows to be a farce—a change slowly comes over him. He becomes possessed, and he goes forward under an impulse like that which takes the charmed bird or frog into the snake's mouth! His virgin disgust is now gone, and he delights in the lodge as prostitutes delight in a brothel; and when once Satan has thus infected his moral nature with his sorcery, nothing but the blood of Christ can ever take it out of him.

The endless diversity in the forms of false worships conceals from the worshiper the fact that a supernatural power is evermore present in them. And the rank and file of Masonry and Odd-fellowship are filled up by young men artizans, students and shopmen, whose occupation or frolic, or both, prevents comparison and generalization; and hence the dupe of one lodge imagines that his is the only thing of its kind, little dreaming that, as Grosh says, "one lodge is a moral copy of another," from the Pyramids and the "rite of Mizraim" down to a juggling spirit-circle or a village lodge. So that while the poor deluded soul supposes he is favored above and beyond the rest of mankind he is only being put through bodily and mental processes identical with the experience of the myriads of false worshipers over the whole earth.

The heathen god Proteus was said to escape detection by changing his shapes—now a tiger, a lion, a flame of fire, a whirlwind or a rushing stream. So Satan shifts the forms of his worships to hide his hateful presence, the meanness of their moral nature and their disastrous effects. It was " a shame even to speak " of the filthy abominations covered by these pretentious and lofty "mysteries" in the days of the Apostle Paul. They were suppressed at Rome. As soon as Christianity became popular they shifted their shapes into the knight-hoods of the Temple and St. John; and, like Aaron and Jeroboam, added a heathen ritual to an orthodox creed. They swindled, strutted, strumpeted, prayed and grew rich, till the maddened multitude whom they had imposed upon and whose money they had absorbed suppressed their lodges and executed them by hundreds in a day. (See any authentic history of medieval Europe.)

The explanation of this rapid and fearful degenerating process in all false worships is that Satan is their god—the deity of all the worships on earth which leave out Christ. And Satan is an unclean spirit, a " liar," " murderer," and, as Judas was after he entered him, a " thief."

And a careful inspection, comparison and pondering of these dark orders will show that they never grow and spread rapidly till they begin to worship—that is, till Satan enters them and receives what he asked of Christ—WORSHIP. Masonic and Odd-fellows' lodges were but semi-occasional drinking frolics till they ceased to be trades-unions and set up worship. Then they grew. And as nothing hardens like religious rites practiced without religion, their leaders turned to stone. Their secrets were revealed and they murdered the re-vealers. And though they cease to murder where they lose more than they gain by it, they are still nurses of Nihilism, whose creed is nothing but blood!

CHAPTER IX.

Second,[53] or Degree of Brotherly Love.

INITIATION.

GENERAL INSTRUCTIONS.

The Conductor, in conferring this degree, will proceed very deliberately. In the dramatic parts he should, after saying, ''A priest is passing,'' appear to wait until the priest has time to come up. So when he says, ''But passes by on the other side,'' he should pause to allow him to go away. The same should occur in the case of the Levite. A sufficient time should be allowed for the Samaritan to come, after he speaks of him, and before he calls upon him for help.

He will particularly note the various pauses required in delivering his part, and avoid all appearance of haste, so as to produce a solemn effect. The same directions will apply to the part of the Warden.

Appropriate scenery, costumes and furniture may be used in this as well as in the preceding degree, the same being left, within reasonable limits, to the option of the lodge; but in no case must such additions be allowed to conflict with, or modify either the form or language of the written work.

Any number of candidates may receive the First Part of the Second Degree, or the whole of the Third Degree at the same time.

There will be no objection to having members to personate the priest and the Levite in the Second Degree; if done, it should be in suitable costume, and the priest and the Levite should come and go as required by the written work. In no event shall they be permitted to speak or take any part which will make them known to the candidate, or change any part of the work as now written.

NOTE 53.—''WHEREAS, The work of the Order has been revised at this session, therefore

Resolved, That all the members of the Order who have heretofore received the First and Second degrees under the old work, shall be entitled to rank as members of the *First* Degree of the revised work. All members who have received the Third and Fourth degrees of the old work, shall be entitled to rank as members of the *Second* Degree of the revised work, and all members who have received the Fifth Degree of the old work, shall be entitled to rank as members of the *Third* Degree of the revised work without charge.''—*Journal of Proceedings Supreme Grand Lodge, Session of* 1880, *p.* 8412.

Part I.

Noble Grand—Conductor, you will retire to the anteroom, receive and introduce the candidate.

Conductor "addresses the chair" with the sign of the degree, retires to anteroom, conducts the candidate (not blindfolded) to the inside door and gives the alarm—three raps.

Inside Guardian—Vice Grand, there is an alarm at the door.

Vice Grand—Attend to the alarm.

Inside Guardian (opening the wicket)—Who comes there?

Conductor—A brother who has taken the covenant of the order, and now seeks to advance further into our mysteries.

Inside Guardian (closing the wicket)—A brother has taken the covenant of the order and now seeks to advance further into our mysteries.

Vice Grand—Why does he seek to advance?

Inside Guardian (opening the wicket)—Why does he seek to advance?

Conductor—Because he would learn how to discharge his obligation.

Inside Guardian (closing the wicket)—Because he would learn how to discharge his obligation.

Vice Grand—Admit him, that he may be instructed in the divine lesson of humanity. [Conductor enters and proceeds with candidate to chair of Vice Grand.]

Conductor—Vice Grand, I present to you for instruction in the Degree of Brotherly Love, our worthy brother, —— ——, who has been duly elected thereto.

Vice Grand (to candidate)—Before you receive the mysteries of this degree, are you willing to enter into a solemn obligation to retain its secrets, and to perform all the lawful duties which it may enjoin? [If the candidate answers in the affirmative, the Vice Grand continues]: Then place yourself in the attitude in which you were initiated into this order and repeat after me.

Noble Grand—(three raps, all rise).

OBLIGATION DEGREE OF BROTHERLY LOVE.

I, —— ——, in the presence of the brethren of the Degree of Brotherly Love now assembled, do solemnly promise that I will never reveal the signs, secrets or mysteries of the Degree of Brotherly Love, to any person, unless by the laws and usages of this order he is entitled to receive such information; but will guard them with jealous care from all persons who have not lawfully obtained the same. To the faithful performance of all which I pledge my sacred honor.

Noble Grand—(one rap, seating the lodge).

Vice Grand (to the candidate)—Are you willing to submit to the ordeal by which you may become a brother of this degree?

Candidate answers.

Vice Grand (to Conductor)—Let the brother be taken to the ante-room, that he may re-enter and take another step in fraternity.

The Conductor, without ''addressing the chair,'' will retire with the candidate to the ante-room, where he places a short cloak on him, blindfolds him, and conducts him to the inside door.

PART II.

Conductor (three raps on inside door).

Inside Guardian—Noble Grand, there is an alarm at the door.

Noble Grand—Attend to the alarm.

Inside Guardian (opening the wicket)—Who comes there?

Conductor—A brother who is ready to receive the mysteries of this degree.

Inside Guardian (closing the wicket)—Noble Grand, a brother is ready to receive the mysteries of this degree.

Noble Grand—Whence comes he?

Inside Guardian (opening the wicket)—Whence comes he?

Conductor—From Jerusalem, and is traveling to Jericho on a mission of humanity.

Inside Guardian (closing the wicket)—From Jerusalem, and is traveling to Jericho on a mission of humanity.

Noble Grand—Admit him in the name of that humanity which he invokes. [The Conductor enters with the candidate and conducts him to the chair of the Noble Grand].

Conductor—Noble Grand, a stranger is passing this way.

Noble Grand—Traveler, whither art thou journeying?

Conductor (for the candidate)—To Jericho.

Noble Grand—Let the traveler go down to Jericho, and may no danger meet him by the way. [The Conductor walks around the room with the candidate, addressing him as follows]:

Conductor—The day is fine; the way is pleasant, and let us hope that the journey will be safe. How those pines cluster on the mountain side, and in the distance the sea is so calm and beautiful! That row of green trees marks the course of Jordan, the sacred river of the chosen people. But see, we are entering a narrow defile of the hills.

Several members as robbers surround them in the middle of the lodge-room crying out, "Stand and deliver!"   "Strike!"   "Lay on!"   "Death!" and such like exclamations.

During the confusion *no person but the Conductor shall be permitted to touch the candidate*. The Conductor shall strike the candidate on the shoulder with his open hand, and cause him to lie down. When the candidate is lying down, the thieves run away, taking away the cloak of the candidate.

A low bench, box or lounge may be provided as part of the furniture, upon which the candidate may be laid.   No rough usage to be allowed.

The candidate continues lying down and after a pause of a moment, the Conductor, speaking for the candidate, exclaims:

Conductor (speaking slowly and painfully to himself)—Alas! alas! I am stripped of my raiment and wounded and left for dead.

Conductor (calling a little louder)—Help! Help!

Conductor (again speaking to himself)—Ah! a priest is passing.

Conductor (after a pause, then calling a little louder)—Help! holy servant of the Temple, I am robbed and wounded.

Conductor (pausing, then speaking to himself)—But no, he will not look upon me, but passes by on the other side.

Conductor (calling a little louder)—Help! Help!

Conductor (to himself)—God of Israel, help me—he is gone! Must I linger here and die? No! behold, a Levite—he stops—he comes this way—he is here.

Conductor (calling a little louder)—O son of Levi, servant of the altar, help me! I am robbed and wounded.

Conductor (pausing, then speaking to himself)—But no, he looks upon me and has no pity. He also passes by on the other side.

Conductor (calling a little louder)—Help! Help! Son of Levi, help!

Conductor (to himself)—He also has forsaken me. But who comes this way? It is a hated Samaritan, an enemy of my people.

Conductor pausing, then calling a little louder)—Help! man of Samaria—I am wounded and dying!

The Warden slowly approaches the candidate, and as he approaches says:

Warden (as Samaritan)—What have we here? an Israelite wounded and bleeding by the wayside! the poor man is about to perish. Is he not after all my brother?

He advances to the candidate.

Warden (taking hold of him)—Ah, my friend, you shall not perish.

Warden—Take this garment for your protection. [Assisted by the Conductor he puts a cloak upon him.]

Warden—Arise and lean upon me.

[Lifts him up.]

Warden—Come, cheer up and take heart, and we will find a place of safety.

The Warden leads the candidate around the lodge-room, and then to the side facing the Past Grand.

Warden (to the traveler)—Here is an inn—a place of refuge. (Calling a little louder)—Ho, there! ho! open, landlord!

[Warden knocks loudly on a table or pedestal.]

Past Grand (as host, after a pause)—The door is open; enter, travelers.

[The candidate is led near to the Past Grand and seated.]

Warden—Here, host, is a wounded man, who fell

among thieves; give him attention, for he has been robbed and left for dead. Take this money and provide for him.

[Shakes some small coins in his hand.]

Warden—Whatsoever thou spendest more, when I come again, 1 will repay thee.

Past Grand (as host)—He shall be cared for, good Samaritan.

After a pause, the candidate will be assisted to rise and be taken twice slowly around the lodge-room by the Conductor, and be led to the chair of the Noble Grand.

Conductor—Noble Grand, the traveler has returned.

Noble Grand—Traveler, thou hast been robbed and left for dead; a priest has seen thee, and a Levite has looked upon thee. A Samaritan, an enemy of thy people, came where thou wast. The priest and the Levite were thy brothers of the seed of Abraham. Which of these was thy true brother" and friend?

Conductor (for the traveler)—He was my brother and friend who had mercy on me.

Noble Grand—Go thou, O traveler, and do likewise; and know that the true priest is not of the Temple, nor the true Levite of the altar, but he alone is the servant

Note 54.—"Singular as that name is—yea, odious as it may sound to some—it has been rendered dear to our hearts by the glorious deeds of benevolence and philanthropy performed under it, and by the great moral and religious principles associated with it, until its singularity is lost in its moral value and beauty. To us, *Odd-fellow* is an honorable name. We love to wear it, and to bear its reproach we deem an honor."—*Grosh's Manual, p*. 52.

of God and thy brother who delivers the needy when he crieth, the poor also, and him that hath no helper.

Noble Grand—(three raps, calling up the lodge).

Noble Grand (to the lodge)—Brothers, what think you of that which you have witnessed?

The Lodge (led by the Warden)—He is my brother and friend who had mercy on me.

[This is repeated.]

Noble Grand (to Conductor)—Let the eyes of the brother be opened, that he may see a lodge of Brotherly Love.[55]

[Blindfold is removed.]

Noble Grand—(one rap, seating the lodge).

Noble Grand—My brother, I will now instruct you in the mysteries of this degree.

In this degree there is an Alarm at the inner door, a Password, a Countersign, an answer to the Countersign, a Sign, an answer to the Sign, a Grip and a Token. The alarm at the inner door is three raps.

The Password is Moses, to be lettered at all times when used for working purposes; working into a lodge or in examination prior to opening.

In communicating this word either to the Inside Guardian or to the Warden; the brother must give the letters M O, and if required by the Inside Guardian or Warden, he must give the remainder of the word, S E S, lettered as before. The Inside Guardian and Warden must be satisfied.

NOTE 55.—"It is unfortunate for our Order. and for not a few of its members, that too much prominence has been generally given to its feature of *pecuniary* benefits in seasons of sickness and death, and *pecuniary* aid in circumstances of want and distress. This, though a laudable and useful trait in our operations, is hardly a tithe of our aims and objects. By this undue prominence of the pecuniary relief afforded even our own members have had their attention and efforts greatly withdrawn from the moral and social influences which the Order is so eminently calculated to promote."— *Grosh's Manual, p. 76.*

The countersign and answer are made the same as in the preceding degrees.

Sign 2d Degree.

SIGN.

The right hand is placed across the left hand, palms touching; clasp the hands both by fingers and thumbs, thumbs meeting. The answer is the same as the sign.

TOKEN—The Token is Moses' Rod.

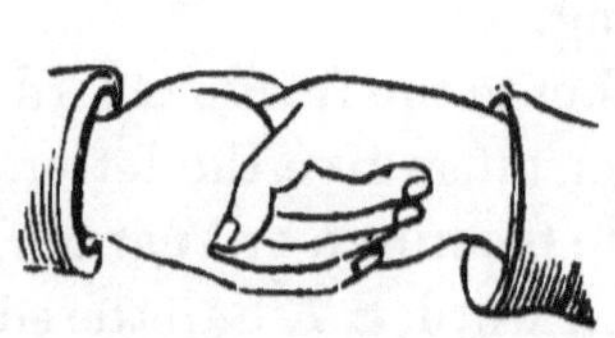

GRIP.

Clasp the right hands with the thumbs pressing the third or knuckle joint of the second finger. No shaking hands in making the Grip.

LECTURE OF THE DEGREE OF BROTHERLY LOVE.

Noble Grand—My brother, in the Degree of Friendship you assumed an obligation which changed your relations to a vast number of persons. You can never forget the hour when you were the object of envy and hatred, and were cheered by a spectacle of confidence and devotion. It was a moment of heart-felt enjoyment when your hand was grasped in friendship, and a voice full of sympathy gave you encouragement. It was then that two hearts melted into one in a solemn league and fraternal covenant."⁶ By that engagement you were bound to perform the offices of Brotherly Love. Heaven has witnessed your vow, and the Common Father has smiled on that compact. All Odd-fellows are now your comrades, your advisers and your friends. A solemn duty has been devolved upon you, and you have been taught how it ought to be performed. The central link in the chain of Odd-fellowship is " mutual assistance."⁵⁷ Fraternity, unless embodied in acts of humanity, is but an empty name. If a brother be naked and destitute of daily food, and one of you say unto him, " Depart in peace, be ye warmed and filled!" notwithstanding ye give him not those things which are needful for the body, what doth it profit? The answer is obvious: he who witnesses suffering and does not hasten to relieve it, is ignorant of the lesson that it is more blessed to give than to receive. He is an enemy of his race who does not care for its welfare, and is wedded to selfishness and greed. Friendship leads to Brotherly Love, which

----

Note 56.—"He, therefore, who assails a brother's rights, attacks our own: an invasion of his welfare is an aggression on ours; for our rights are the same, and our happiness is increased by the enjoyments of those who surround us. It is our recognition of this great principle that leads us to *claim* and to *grant* sympathy in suffering, unity in work, freedom in thought and worship, and to resist the force that would invade the natural rights of the human soul."—*Grosh's Manual, p.* 273.

Note 57.—" The aid we give is received with a proper dignity and self-respect, so that when ability returns the family resume their usual avocations, blessing the Order which sustained and aided it without bestowing *alms!*"—*Grosh's Manual. p* 67.

makes the strong to support the weak, the young to reverence the old, the rich to help the poor, the educated to instruct the ignorant, the well to nurse the sick, and makes all good men seek to imitate the goodness of the Father of all men.

My brother, in the Degree of Brotherly Love you have acted a part in a famous drama, which has received the plaudits of the world for many generations. You were assaulted and robbed, wounded, and left upon the highway to perish.[58] A priest of the Temple journeyed that way and saw your condition; his office required that he should have pity, but he passed on and left you to die by the wayside. A Levite, who swung the golden censers in the holy place and served at the consecrated altar, also saw you, and approached and looked upon you; but he, like the robbers and the priest, abandoned you to your fate. But wonderful to relate, an enemy on his journey came that way and found you bleeding and suffering. Although he knew that you were not of his religion, nor of his people, and that you were not his friend; though he had no fortune and no tithes with which to pay for your nursing and support, yet his bowels of compassion were moved; he stopped—he ran to your relief.[59] How tenderly he raised your stricken

Note 58.—"Though a storm more fearful than any thou hast yet encountered—that of physical death—shall soon burst upon thee, the hand of God almighty, which has sustained thee thus far, will protect thee amid that storm, and thou shalt come up through it with joy and gladness to the land of eternal delight."—*Donaldson's Pocket Companion, p.* 138.

Note 59.—"It is not to be wondered at, then, that so many, even among Odd-fellows, have overlooked, or at times forgotten, the most important uses and aims of Odd-fellowship to be, the imbuing of the minds of our brethren with proper conceptions of their powers and capacities, giving them just and practical views of their duties and responsibilities, exhibiting their dependence upon God, and bringing them to a knowledge and practice of the true fraternal relations between man and man."—*Grosh's Manual, p.* 80

oody and poured balm into your wounds, and how gently he brought you to life by words of pity and encouragement! You can never forget that he exposed himself to the keen mountain winds when he took off his cloak and wrapped it around you. How carefully he led you to the inn, and with what liberality he gave the money that assured you of shelter and safety. Such is the story of the good Samaritan. All Odd-fellows, so far as they have the ability, seek to imitate this memorable example. Learn from this history that he only is an Odd-fellow who has pity and mercy, and who hastens to the relief[60] of a brother in distress. Membership in a lodge is nothing, the obligation of friendship is nothing, the assertion of our principles less than nothing[61] unless we have Brotherly Love,[62] which is the bond of unity. Of all historical men, Moses exhibited the most self-denial and fraternal affection. He represents an ideal of unselfishness without a parallel. A man of rare learning, he cast his lot among a multi-

---

NOTE 60.—"Let us, then, persist in the glorious work we have commenced, with vigor and unflinching stability; let our bark, while sailing on the extensive ocean of Fellowship, be guided by the compass of justice; and, if we may continue the metaphor, let us perseveringly pursue the track its needle indicates; that, when arrived at our destined haven, we may with a pure consciousness of having supported to the utmost our purpose of benevolence and charity, securely recline our heads on the satisfactory pillow of contentment, and indulge in the aspiring hope that when summoned from this sublunary sphere we may meet with an eternal welcome in that 'angel-land' where 'sorrow intrudes not,' where 'the wicked cease from troubling and the weary are at rest.'"—*Donaldson's Pocket Companion, p.* 182.

NOTE 61.—"A brother of noble character and long years of service, suspended because of absolute inability to pay his dues, is classed with the rich bad men who won't pay them. We apply the law when the dues are not paid, *assuming* there is no cause for the failure. This is not charity."—*Journal of Proceedings Sovereign Grand Lodge, Session of* 1880, *p.* 8213.

NOTE 62.—"This Order can never be made a merely beneficial institution. It is more than that: it is as lofty as human thought and aspiration."—*Journal of Proceedings Sovereign Grand Lodge, Session of* 1880, *p.* 8213.

tude of uncultured slaves; the adopted son of royalty, he laid down his rank and riches, and became an out-cast for defending one of his lowly people. It was enough for him that they were poor and afflicted. For them he left a royal court and became an exile in the wilderness; and, having led them to national greatness, he meekly died in sight of that inheritance which, denied to him, became the portion of his ungrateful" brethren. Such are the examples which compose the instruction in this degree, whose emblematic color is blue. And now, by authority of the Independent Order of Odd-fellows, I declare you a brother of the Royal Blue, or Degree of Brotherly Love

NOTE 63.—"OLD ODD-FELLOWS. These brothers are subjected to one wrong. On changing residence they take a withdrawal-card and seek to join a lodge at their new home; but they are rejected because of age. The old lodge frequently declines to take them back, and they are turned out to die."—*Journal of Proceedings Sovereign Grand Lodge, Session of* 1880, *p.* 8212.

ANALYSIS DEGREE OF BROTHERLY LOVE.

Christ's Parables in a Satan's Lodge Theatre with the Name of their Author Suppressed—Why do Masonry and Odd-fellowship take their Moral Lessons from the Christian Bible instead of from the Koran?—Why is there no Odd-fellow Brotherly Love in UnChristian Lands?—The Lodges Depend Upon Christ, Whom they Exclude and Reject, for their Ideas of Brotherly Love —Yet They Claim the Credit of Originating the Virtues Stolen from Christ— The Lodge is Thus Deism and Infidelity—Claims Superiority to Christianity— It Cannot Promote Brotherly Love—A Practical Illustration of Odd-fellow "Brotherly Love," given by the Lodge at Galesburg, Illinois—A Masonic and Odd-fellow Pastor's Verdict on the Two Institutions—True Love and Lodge Love Contrasted—This degree a Counterfeit of the Friendship of Christ.

This degree is Christ's parable of the Good Samaritan, dramatized by, and acted in, a lodge which excludes Christ! The lecture calls it "a famous drama, which has received the plaudits of the world," *but suppresses the name of its Author!* thus, literally,

> * * * stealing the livery of the Court of Heaven
> To serve the devil in."

Why do Masonry and Odd-fellowship take their sacred lessons from the Christian Bible? Why not from the Koran or the Book of Mormon? And why are there no "degrees" of brotherly love taught by Odd-fellows in the kingdom of Dahomey or the Cannibal Islands? The answer is, the lodges depend on Christ for their ideas of virtue. Christ has come, has "elevated" mankind by his teachings, sufferings, death, and by sending his Holy Spirit on Christians; and these Satanic lodges impudently put his Bible on a level with the false revelations, which they never quote. And when Christianity has civilized a land, these lodges stand by and seize on the Christian virtues as their capital stock and claim the merit of originating the virtues thus stolen from Christ! And in this Degree of Brotherly Love they dramatize Christ's wonderful parable, while they treat its Author with silent contempt! The lodge is thus deism and infidelity. If it were not, deists and infidels would not love it as they now do. And, with an amazing effrontery which sinks below shame, they claim superiority for the lodge as a worldwide religion, for casting out Christ, whose Scriptures give them their ideas of virtue, and whose civilization furnishes them members, degree fees and dues!

The idea that "Brotherly Love" can be promoted by such a concern is simply preposterous.

A Colonel, now in our regular army, and who fought at the head of a regiment of volunteers in the horrible battles of James River, joined the Odd-fellows in Galesburgh, Illinois, while he was a member of my Senior Class in Knox College. He was an amiable young man, and made a brave and capable officer. I remonstrated with him and he left the lodge. He afterwards told me that, after all their " brotherly love " professions, the night on which he took, as he had a right by their rules to take, his withdrawal card, the tone, looks and demeanor of his lodge brethren was such that *he should have feared to be alone with them that night in the woods!* A respected pastor of the Congregational church in Sandwich, Illinois, who had been both Mason and Odd-fellow, said to me: "It is devil-worship, as you say."

"Why, brother," said I, "you never belonged to them, did you?"

"Yes," he replied, "when clerk in a business house in New York I joined both lodges; and as I look back over the nights I spent in those lodges, and see, at this distance, the faces and mien of the members, the whole thing seems to me simply diabolical."

There is but one person in the Universe who can overthrow this system of lodges. That person is the " Stronger than the strong man armed."

The direst of all hatred is counterfeit love. It is the best thing corrupted into the worst: *corruptio optimi, pessima!* It is, indeed, the kiss of Judas Iscariot. Such is the "Brotherly Love" of Odd-fellowship.

True love is natural; that of the lodge, artificial. Bible love "worketh no ill to his neighbor:" lodge love worketh no good. Its very favor is "for value received,' and dies a certain number of weeks after its victim stops paying dues. John Randolph said his philosopher's stone was "Pay as you go." Grosh says that of Odd-fellowship is " Pay in advance " the dues of the lodge.—*Odd-fellows' Manual, pp. 192–3.*

And, curiously enough, a member in the Encampment must still keep paying in the lodge below, whether he attends there or not. *"In fact, good standing in the Subordinate Lodge, which signifies freedom from disability by non-payment of dues, is essential to good standing everywhere else in the Order."—Grosh's Manual, p. 255.*

To call such a thing "Friendship " is treason to human language! Paying for and entering higher degrees does not exonerate from steady payment in the lower degrees. So that, as the Odd-fellow goes on from one degree to another in this temple of mock friendship, he increases his taxes, and so he literally " *drags at each remove a lengthened chain.*" The love of husband, wife, parents, children, brothers, friends, wells up in the human heart at the mandate of nature. The artificial love of the lodge is pledged to strangers, and springs from grips, signs, oaths and obligations. It is not even that love of humanity which led the Roman poet to exclaim: *" I am a man, and what concerns man concerns me!" For Odd-fellowship excludes humanity from its portals by denying its instructions to nineteen-twentieths of the race; and, like all other mystic secret orders, feeds the religious cravings of man on the ashes and chaff of its ritual; excites his veneration by scenic mystery and show; pays back a fraction of its " dues " in benefits to the sick—to rich and poor alike—provided they are not too poor or unfortunate to be able to pay the dues, and calls this swindling imposture " Brotherly Love!"

But all its manifold mischiefs center in and subserve this one grand purpose. It is a *counterfeit* or mimicry of the friendship of Jesus Christ. The New Testament teaching is that God sends '' the Spirit of his Son," the Holy Ghost, into a soul, and he immediately calls God his " Father," and Christ becomes his Elder Brother and " Friend."—*Jno. 15: 15.* He not only called his disciples '' friends," but they are called '' his brethren." —*Heb. 2: 17.* This stupendous endearment, essentially sublime and magnificent in the very theory and thought of it, is met and counterfeited by Satan in the lodge, by putting HIS spirit on the members, leading them to worship him and calling them "brothers," and all outside of the lodges " Gentiles " and " profane!" Thus the infinite and infinitely glorious friendship and brotherhood with the eternal God through Jesus Christ is counterfeited, caricatured and counteracted by Satan by means of his degrees of " Friendship " and " Brotherly Love!"

_____

Homo sum, et nihil humanum a me alienum puto.

CHAPTER X.

THIRD, OR DEGREE OF TRUTH.[64]

ORDER OF BUSINESS.

By reference to page 44 it will be seen that previous to July, 1881, the business of each degree was transacted in that degree.

The Noble Grand will proceed to business by giving one rap with his gavel, which is repeated by the Vice Grand, for silence and order, immediately after opening the lodge.

1. *Noble Grand*—Brother Secretary, I will thank you to call the roll of officers, and read the proceedings of last lodge night.

2. Does any brother know of a sick brother, or brother in distress?

3. Consideration of previous proposal for membership.

4 Candidates admitted.

5. Has any brother a friend to propose to become a member of this lodge?

6. Unfinished business appearing on the minutes to be attended to.

7. Has any brother anything to offer for the good of this order?

The lodge may proceed to close after the necessary business is transacted.

INITIATION.

GENERAL INSTRUCTIONS.

In conferring this degree, the candidate shall not be blindfolded, but the following shall be observed:

The Noble Grand will direct the Conductor to retire to the ante-room, receive and introduce the candidate.

When the Conductor retires he shall address the chair

The Conductor, having examined the candidate in the First and Second Degrees, will approach the inside door with the candidate and give the alarm.

NOTE 64.—"Having been duly prepared to receive this highest degree of our Subordinate Lodges, by a diligent acquaintance with those which have preceded it, and a proficiency in their duties and workings, the candidate will do well to give earnest heed to the instructions he will receive from those who confer this degree on him."—*Grosh's Manual, p.* 153.

Part I.

Inside Guardian—Noble Grand, there is an alarm at the door.

Noble Grand—Attend to the alarm.

Inside Guardian (opening the wicket)—Who comes there?

Conductor—A brother, who, having taken the covenant of the Order, has learned the divine lesson of humanity, and now seeks to obtain the Degree of Truth.

Inside Guardian (closing the wicket)—Noble Grand. a brother, having taken the covenant of the Order, has learned the divine lesson of humanity, and now seeks to obtain the Degree of Truth.

Noble Grand—Why does he seek to obtain this degree?

Inside Guardian (opening the wicket)—Why does he seek to obtain this degree?

Conductor—Because, Truth is the Imperial* virtue.

Inside Guardian (closing the wicket) Because Truth is the Imperial virtue.

Noble Grand—What does he expect from the Truth?

Inside Guardian (opening the wicket)—What does he expect from the Truth?

Conductor—That it will teach him his duty to God and his fellow-man.

Inside Guardian (closing the wicket)—That it will teach him his duty to God and his fellow-man.

Noble Grand—Admit the brother to the mysteries of the Degree of Truth.

Being admitted, the Conductor will proceed with the candidate to the chair of the Vice Grand, and introduce him as follows:

———

NOTE 65.—"As the Imperial virtue, Truth appropriates to this degree all preceding colors and emblems. *White* represents its purity, *Pink* its steadiness of purpose or irrefrangibility, *Blue* its persistence in right speech and action, *Green* its perpetual freshness and eternity; and, as the cardinal virtue, it appropriates to itself the *Scarlet* badge, and sways a sceptre of dominion over the rest. He, therefore, who has this virtue enthroned in his soul, is priest and monarch of himself and all around him; for its power gives him ministry and dominion. This is why the brother of this degree finds all stations of the lodge open to him, and is enabled to speak as by authority concerning the laws of our Order."—*Grosh's Manual, p.* 154.

Conductor—Vice Grand, I present to you —— ——, a worthy brother, who having been duly elected, seeks to obtain the mysteries of this degree.

Vice Grand (standing)—Has he been found worthy in the degrees he has already received, and is he one who is likely to perform with fidelity the obligations of an Odd-fellow?

Conductor—He seems in all respects worthy of our confidence.

Vice Grand—Have you carefully examined the brother in the preceding degrees?

Conductor—I have, and find him correct.

VICE GRAND'S CHARGE.

Vice Grand—Brother, you are now entering upon the last degree of a Subordinate Lodge—that which crowns the fabric; and we devote it to the principle of truth,[66] which is appropriately introduced in this portion of our work; for it follows close after Love, and has an intimate connection with it. It is the spontaneous result of genuine and constant Love. If you are faithful to the duties enjoined in the last degree, Truth will appear in all you say and do, as an intrinsic ornament of your character. If Love is the fundamental element of all morality, Truth is the Imperial virtue. It is the treasure for which the candid mind ever seeks, the consummation for which we apply in all our investigations. It is the sanction of every appeal that is made for the good and the right. It condemns the wrongs, the sins,

NOTE 66.—"The former degrees have been devoted to the development and applications of LOVE; this has for its great theme, TRUTH as a principle of sentiment and of action. Love in the heart, and Truth in the understanding are closely related. Both issue in the words of the mouth and the actions of the life; and are unitedly, therefore, the foundation of moral duty. Love is the motive power prompting to right action—Truth the guiding light to direct it. Truth is therefore the crowning virtue. It is the great good sought by candor; the great object of all our researches. Every appeal for righteousness and virtue rests on it; for it is opposed to all iniquity and wrong, all error and ignorance. To dwellers in time it may seem tedious in its progress, and hopelessly to struggle for conquest; but eternity will prove it omnipotent, and show it to be the victor at last."—*Grosh's Manual, p.* 153.

and the falsehoods of the world. It may be long in achieving its victory, but it is omnipotent, and must triumph at last. The man of Truth is the best and the strongest man; his soul, like a spring of clear water, reflects the light of heaven and is full of life. His speech and his actions are always just—he wins involuntary respect—he blesses and purifies all around him. He is a solid landmark amid the waves of faction, the storms of passion, and the conflicts of error.

Vice Grand (to Conductor)—Conduct the brother to our Noble Grand. [Vice Grand resumes his seat].

The Conductor leads the candidate to the chair of the Noble Grand.

Conductor—Noble Grand, by order of the Vice Grand, I present to you this brother for obligation.

Noble Grand (standing)—Brother, in view of what has been intimated in this degree by our worthy Vice Grand, are you willing to enter into an obligation with us?

If the candidate replies in the affirmative, the Noble Grand will call the lodge up, and continue:

Noble Grand—Place your right hand on your left breast and repeat after me:

OBLIGATION DEGREE OF TRUTH.

I, —— ——, in the presence of the members of the Degree of Truth now assembled, do solemnly promise, that I will conceal and never reveal the signs, secrets, and mysteries of this degree, unless it be to a brother Odd-fellow of this degree in good standing, or in a lawful lodge of brothers who shall be legally authorized to receive the same. And, furthermore, I promise to be faithful to my former obligations in this Order to the extent of my power so to do. To the faithful perform-ance of all which I pledge my sacred honor.

The Noble Grand gives one rap, seating the lodge.

Noble Grand—Brother, are you willing to advance, that you may become a brother of this degree?

If the candidate answers in the affirmative, Noble Grand addresses the Con-ductor:

Noble Grand—Brother Conductor, let the brother be taken to the ante-room, that he may re-enter and be instructed in the Degree of Truth.

The Conductor, without " addressing the chair " with the sign, will retire with the candidate to the ante-room.

PART II.

The candidate in this part will be attired in a white robe.

The Noble Grand will be attired in a scarlet robe and cap, and he may wear a wig and beard.

A chart containing the emblems of the degrees will be placed near the "prin-cipal chair" (Noble Grand's), and the Conductor (with a wand or sword) will point out to the candidate each emblem as it is being described by the proper officer.

The Priests, in describing the meaning of the emblems must remain at their respective stations, and speak therefrom.

All being ready, the Conductor will advance to the inside door with the can-lidate, and give the alarm; three raps.

Inside Guardian—Vice Grand, there is an alarm at the door.

Vice Grand—Attend to the alarm.

Inside Guardian (opening the wicket)—Who comes there?

Conductor—A brother who is ready to receive the mysteries of this degree.

Inside Guardian (closing the wicket)—A brother is ready to receive the mysteries of this degree.

Vice Grand—Admit him.

Being admitted, the Conductor will proceed with the candidate to the Vice Grand, and introduce him as follows:

Conductor—Vice Grand, I have the pleasure of presenting to you for instruction Brother ——— ———, who is a probationer, has served his time as such, and has proved to be obedient and willing to do his duty in conformity with his obligations.

Vice Grand—Brother ——— ———, I welcome you, and commend your zeal for promotion in our Order, fully believing that you have an ambition to do good. Before you can be advanced to the full enjoyment of this degree it is necessary that you give acceptable answers to the following questions in presence of the brothers here assembled:

Several brothers draw near, so as to nearly surround the candidate. The Vice Grand proceeds.

Vice Grand—Do you know of any reason why we should not intrust to you the mysteries of this degree?

Candidate answers.

Vice Grand—Is it your desire to receive the Scarlet[67] Degree, for the purpose of promoting your moral[68] and intellectual welfare?

Candidate answers.

Vice Grand—Brethren of the Priestly[69] Order, are you satisfied with the answers?

NOTE 67.—"Scarlet vestments, as allusive to the glory, dignity, and excellence of the sacerdotal office, are given to the Fifth, or Degree of the Priestly Order. God said to Moses, 'Thou shalt make holy garments for Aaron, thy brother, for glory and for beauty.' (Exod. xxviii: 2). In the several specifications which follow the Divine charge, we find that *scarlet* was ordained to be a constituent part of the robe, the ephod, the curious girdle of the ephod, and of the breast-plate of judgment."—*Grosh's Manual, p.* 155.

NOTE 68.—"Prayer is not part of the work at initiations in a Subordinate Lodge and therefore not admissible."—*Journal of Proceedings Sovereign Grand Lodge. Session of* 1880, *p.* 8209.

NOTE 69.—"It is optional with a lodge whether to appoint a Chaplain or not. His duty is to open and close the meetings with prayer (using none other than the prescribed form), to attend at funerals of deceased brothers, and to officiate on all public occasions where the lodge may require his attendance. It is scarcely necessary to add that the Chaplain should be a man of good moral character."—*Donaldson's Pocket Companion, p.* 166.

If satisfied with the answers, each member says, I am.
The brothers surrounding the candidate retire.

Vice Grand—Conductor, you will introduce the brother to the High Priest of this degree.

The Conductor leads the candidate near the principal chair.

Conductor—High Priest Aaron, I present to you Brother —— ——, a probationer, who is qualified to receive the Scarlet Degree or Priestly Order.

Noble Grand (as High Priest)—My brother, you will take your position in charge of the Conductor, and be attentive to the instruction you are about to receive.

The candidate may here be seated until the symbols have all been described and shown to him.

Noble Grand—Brother Warden, what are the symbols of the Initiatory Degree?

Warden—The All-Seeing Eye,[70] the Three Links, the Skull and Cross-Bones, and the Scythe.

Noble Grand (as High Priest)—Priest of the Initiatory Degree, what do these symbols teach?

NOTE 70.—''THE ALL-SEEING EYE.—*Emblem of Omniscience.* The *special* emblem of the Initiate.

'' 'Enveloped in a blaze of light and glory, it reminds us that the scrutinizing gaze of Our Father is ever upon us,' beholding our actions and even our thoughts; for He 'searcheth the heart and trieth the reins.'

''On entering or leaving a lodge, we note it as a reminder of the instructions at our initiation, and it serves to keep us steadfast in our integrity. Although, to mortal vision, 'clouds and darkness are round about' the Invisible One, yet we know that 'judgment and justice are the foundations of His throne,' and that 'He dwelleth in light,' and 'in Him is no darkness at all.' 'If I say, Surely the darkness shall cover me—even the night shall be light about me. Yea, the darkness hideth not from thee; but the night shineth as the day: the darkness and the light are both alike to thee.'

''But this emblem also teaches us the soul-cheering truth that God looketh *kindly* and *pityingly* upon us; for 'He remembereth that we are dust ;'—and that He provideth for all our wants, and is so minute in His paternal care, that even the hairs of our heads are numbered.

''Let us, then, gratefully, as well as reverently, so live under His all-seeing eye, that we may thank Him for the past, rejoice before him in the present, and cherish an humble hope in Him for the future—thus fulfilling the great motto of our Order: 'IN GOD WE TRUST.'''—*Grosh's Manual, p.* 101.

Left Supporter of the Vice Grand (as **Priest of the Initiatory Degree)—**

THE ALL-SEEING EYE

Enveloped in a blaze of light and glory, reminds us that the scrutinizing eye of Omnipotence is ever upon us; that all our thoughts, words and actions are open to his view. The light of morning and the darkness of night are alike to him; and he trieth the reins and searcheth the hearts of the children of men. Yet, at the same time it illustrates that sleepless goodness which looks down in mercy upon our frailties, and kindly ministers to our ever returning wants.

THE THREE LINKS[71]

Represent the grand motto of our Order: Friendship, Love, and Truth. They belong to that long chain of moral principles that bind us together as a fraternity. They are welded in the fires of purity by the sacred hands 

Note 71.—"The Three Links.—*Emblem of F. L. & T.* It represents the all-encircling chain of sympathy that unites us as one in our aims, labors, and abundant rewards; and reminds us that we are thus bound for our own and each each other's welfare. And it teaches us (as we have learned from the lips of Antiquity), that the best safeguard against the ills of life will be found in the practice of Friendship, Love, and Truth.—' Forget it not.'"—*Grosh's Manual, p.* 103.

of Jehovah. Thus bound with the **chain** of sincere friendship, unfeigned love, and simple truth, we may live in the bonds of peace, and harmoniously pursue our labors for the amelioration of our race.

THE SKULL AND CROSS-BONES[72]

Are to remind us of the consuming process of nature. To-day we are in the full realization of health, and

enjoyment of the pleasures of this world. In a little while, the ever-burning furnace of time will consume to ashes all that hath life and vigor in this terrestial sphere. They most forcibly remind us that we are bound by solemn engagements to give to the mortal remains of a departed brother decent sepulture; and, while we lay his body in

---

NOTE 72.—''THE SKULL AND CROSSED BONES.—*Emblem of Mortality.* It reminds us, not merely that 'dust we are, and unto dust we must return,' but also, 'that we are solemnly bound to commit the mortal remains of a departed brother carefully and lovingly to the tomb, to cherish a lively recollection of his many virtues, and to bury his imperfections with his body beneath the clods of the valley.'

"It also teaches us the vanity of worldly things—the instability of wealth and power, and the certain passing away of all earthly greatness. This lesson, as melancholy as it is truthful, humbles pride, awakens compassion for others, rouses the soul to a proper sense of responsibility to God, and of duty to our fellow-men; and creates a deep abhorrence of SIN—that greatest of all evils—that bane of human happiness and peace which has bathed the world in tears and deluged it in blood. Thus it inspires us to labor for the spread of that great law of human brotherhood, which shall yet bind all nations, kindreds, tongues, and peoples, in the bonds of benevolence and peace."—*Grosh's Manual, p.* 102.

the tomb, to cherish a lively recollection of his virtues, and bury all his imperfections beneath the clod that rests upon his bosom.

THE SCYTHE,[73]

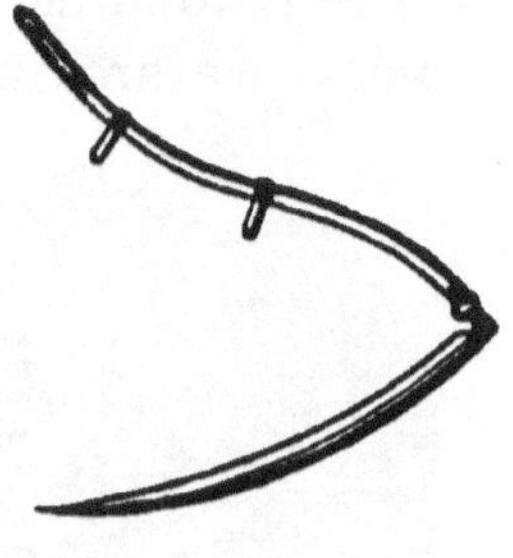

The universal emblem of time, is to us the symbol of death. As the grass falls before the mower's scythe, so man, like the flower and grass of the field, must wither beneath the touch of Time, and fall before the scythe of the King of Terrors.

Noble Grand (as High Priest)—Warden, what are the symbols belonging to the First Degree, or the Degree of Friendship?

Warden—The Bow and Arrows, the Quiver,[74] and the Bundle of Sticks.

Noble Grand (as High Priest)—Priest of the First Degree, what do these symbols teach?

Note 73.—"The scythe 'reminds us of the solemn truth, that as the grass falls before the mower's scythe, so man, being as the grass and flower of the field, must wither before the touch of Time, and fall before the King of Terrors. Both teach us, that it is only through Time that we can reach Eternity—only through Mortality that we can attain Immortality—only through death to sin that we can enter into eternal life."—*Grosh's Manual, p.* 292.

Note 74.—"The Quiver and the Bow.—*Emblem of Preparation.* 'In peace prepare for war.' Truly, the bow is unstrung, the quiver unslung, the arrows undrawn—but all are *ready!* They remind us of the ancient mode of warfare, and of the manifestations of devoted friendship between Jonathan and David.

"The unstrung bow teaches the benefit of relaxation from undue tension of mind or body, when recreation can be safely sought—and the full quiver as impressively teaches the importance of preparation for action, even in our hours of ease and enjoyment.

"The true Odd-fellow will always have ready his quiver and his bow to guard a brother from danger, or to promote his welfare—a brother, ever, in war as in peace."—*Grosh's Manual, p.* 127.

Right Supporter of the Vice Grand (as Priest of the First Degree)—

THE BOW, ARROWS, AND QUIVER,

Are to remind us of the covenant between Jonathan

and David, and by them we are taught to put forth every laudable effort to save a brother from the wrath of an enemy. They also remind us that we should always be ready to do battle in the cause of truth and justice.

THE BUNDLE OF STICKS[76]

Is a beautiful emblem of union, and teaches us the importance of that virtue in our benevolent enterprise. Separate the sticks, and the strength of a child may destroy them; but while united a giant's power might be exerted in vain to break them. Separated, we should be speedily broken and destroyed by the accumulating tide of worldly selfishness; but united as brothers we bid defiance to all opposition, and triumph over the greatest difficulties.

NOTE 76.—"THE BUNDLE OF RODS.—*Emblem of Strength in Union.* The *peculiar* emblem of the Covenant Degree.

"This memento of a dying father, to teach his children the value of union, speaks no less impressively to our larger brotherhood. It reminds us of the power of each member to sustain, and be sustained by, the others, when all are bound into one bundle by the bands of F, L. & T.—making the interests and labors of all the common property of each. In Odd-fellowship, union is strength indeed. One rod, separated from the rest, can easily be broken—one brother, isolated by selfishness, may be disheartened and destroyed—but in the firmly bound bundle each brother can easily resist evil and accomplish good. Each strengthens the others against unhallowed opposition, and all stand firm and unmoved in the mighty power of our Fellowship."—*Grosh's Manual, p.* 126.

Noble Grand (as High Priest)—Warden, what are the symbols belonging to the Second Degree, or the Degree of Brotherly Love?

Warden—The Axe," the Heart and Hand," the Globe, the Ark and the Serpent.

Noble Grand (as High Priest)—Priest of the Second Degree, what do these symbols teach?

Left Supporter of the Noble Grand (as Priest of the Second Degree)—

THE AXE

Is an ancient implement of the artisan. It is an emblem of progress, as by it the pioneer makes advancement through the forest for the spread of civilization.

Note 76.—"The Axe.—*Emblem of Pioneering.* It reminds us that as the trees of the wilderness must fall before the axe, ere the sunlight can disperse its gloom and the land become a fruitful field, so must Divine Truth be applied to every cumbering tree and poisonous vine within us, before we can realize the genial glow and fully profit by the influences of Fraternity in our lodge, our Order, and in the family of man. It thus teaches us to clear away every blinding prejudice and passion—'every tree that bringeth not forth good fruit'—and cast them into the consuming and purifying fires.

"[In many lodges it is customary to collect donations for the needy and distressed on the Warden's axe, which has painted on the side presented for the donation the expressive *Heart in Hand*]."—*Grosh's Manual, p.* 104.

Note 77.—"The Heart in Hand.—*Emblem of Sincerity.* And, included in this, Candor and Frankness. Though the insignia of the Past Grand, yet it is an emblem of the initiate, to remind him of the Past Grand's charge—that 'basis or substratum of our Moral Temple,' which our feet press at our entrance, and whose lessons, opening as we advance, precede us through all the degrees and offices of the Order.

"It reminds us that there should be no improper concealment of feelings and purposes among brethren—that our greetings should be of the heart as well as of the hand—'that what the one in love dictates, the other in alacrity should perform.' And it teaches us that when distress and suffering call, the hand should be 'open as day to melting charity,' and the heart warm as mother-love to sympathy and relief, remembering that 'the Lord loveth the *cheerful* giver.' And it also teaches us, not only sincerity in affection and frankness and candor in expression, but that 'with pure hearts and clean hands' must we come to perform the mission of an Order dedicated to Trust in God, and to 'Friendship, Love and Truth.'"—*Grosh's Manual, p.* 104.

THE HEART AND HAND

Imply, that when we greet our brethren, it should be with that sincerity and affection which p r o c e e d s from the heart. This emblem, also, reminds us of that constant and uniform desire for the welfare of our brothers, which should impel us to action in the furtherance of those plans that will most promote their happiness.

THE GLOBE[78]

Represents the extensive field of our labors. It not

NOTE 78.—"THE GLOBE IN CLOUDS.—*Emblem of the World of Mankind.* The *special* emblem of the First Degree. It represents the earthly home of man —the field of our life-efforts and labors—the nursery of immortality. It reminds us that the world in which we have now advanced, as it were, one step, and put forth our hand anew for greeting and labor, is still partly in clouds; and therefore there is much to learn and to teach in this great field, over which our brethren are so widely scattered; and it teaches us that as light is dispersing those clouds, so may our light aid in dissipating the ignorance which yet obscures those true relations that bind man to his Creator and to his fellow-man. It thus incites us to meet together as brethren, and apply the light and warmth augmented and strengthened by our union wherever ignorance needs the one, or want and woe the other. We thereby quicken our sympathies—become 'more helpful to the distressed—more regularly thoughtful of the happiness of others'—until, by increasing faith and hope, we have a prelibation of that grand period when the whole world shall bask in the light of God's Fatherhood, and all its vast fraternity reflect to heaven, in gratitude and praise, the radiance of 'His glory."— *Grosh's Mannal, p.* 113.

"THE GLOBE IN FULL LIGHT.—*Emblem of the Regenerated World.* It represents 'the world, and they that dwell therein,' as beheld in its Creator's purpose, when 'God saw everything that He had made, and, behold, it was very good!'—as seen by the heavenly host in visioned future, when 'the morning stars sang together and all the sons of God shouted for joy'—and as it will be seen in *reality*, when purified from selfishness and sin, by the Spirit of the Most High breathing over and into it the sanctifying influences of Friendship, Love and Truth, and of Faith, Hope and Charity.

"By contrast with the world in clouds, it reminds us of the world *as it is*, with the world *as it should be*, and of our solemn duty to '*go on*,' and still 'onward,' under such guidance as will bring us through all darkness, temptation and trial, to light, and virtue, and victory, at last."—*Grosh's Manual, p.* 202.

only teaches that we are to move onward in our work

until misfortune has no want to relieve and sorrow no tears to dry; but. also, that from whatever nation our brethren may come, they are not to be sent empty away.

THE ARK[79]

Reminds us of the receptacle of the two tables of stone upon which the Ten Commandments were written; and

---

NOTE 79.—"THE ARK OF THE COVENANT.—*Emblem of the Presence of the Most High God, Our Heavenly Father.* This is the *special* emblem of this most solemn, sublime and exalted degree—the last, highest, greatest of our Ritual.

"The Ark of the Covenant was placed in the Holy of Holies; that is, within the second vail of the Tabernacle, and in the innermost part of the Temple. It contained the golden pot of manna, Aaron's rod that budded, and the tables of the Law. *On* it was the Mercy-Seat, overshadowed by the wings of the Cherubim, between which the SHEKINAH (Cloud of Glory), denoting the Presence of the Holy One, appeared to the High Priest. All these were made after the Pattern which God shewed unto Moses in the Mount. (Exodus xxv: 40). That Ark with its contents, and the Cherubim with the SHEKINAH, links together the remembrance of all sacred things with the Presence of God, and the hope of heaven. It is therefore a most solemn emblem, suggestive of all things most sacred—of the Holy of Holies, that type of heaven itself, and of the very presence of 'the Lord—the Lord God, merciful and gracious, long-suffering and abundant in goodness and truth, keeping mercy for thousands, and forgiving iniquity, transgression, and sin, and that will by no means clear the guilty.'

"And it teaches us, that 'as the prosperity of ancient Israel depended on the respect, devotion, and obedience paid by them to the Ark of the Covenant and its sacred deposits, so will our purity, peace, and prosperity' be commensurate with our obedience to, and communion with, the Most High and Holy One, our ever-present Heavenly Father."—*Grosh's Manual, p.* 294.

as the prosperity of the ancient Israelites depended upon their observance of that law deposited in the Ark of the Covenant, so will our happiness be promoted by an observance of our good and wholesome laws.

THE SERPENT[80]

Is an emblem of wisdom, and is placed among our symbols to indicate the necessity of a wise caution, which will protect our mysteries from improper disclosure, and guide us in the proper regulation of life and conduct.

Noble Grand (as High Priest)—Warden, what are the symbols belonging to the Third Degree, or the Degree of Truth?[81]

NOTE 80.—"THE SERPENT.—*Emblem of Wisdom.* It represents 'the brazen serpent erected by Moses, according to God's direction, to heal the Israelites when bitten by the fiery serpents sent among them to chastise them for their sins.' In the infancy of nations, wisdom included every degree of knowledge, and especially its applications for healing, which, again, was synonymous with salvation."—*Grosh's Manual,* p. 137.

NOTE 81.—"All the emblems heretofore explained belong to this degree, for in their true symbolic meanings they all teach *truth.* Truth in the abstract— pure truth, freed from the attributes of materiality—cannot be as easily received and understood by man in the flesh, as when presented in a material garb. Hence parables and apologues, which are but word-emblems, are so acceptable among all nations; and this, too, is why, in all ages, the various objects in nature have been used as symbols. Humanity seems to require such representations. They are found in use as far as history reaches among the mists of the past. Their language seems the only one that escaped and survives the confusion of Babel." —*Grosh's Manual, p. 156.*

Warden—The Scales and Sword, the Bible, the Hour-Glass, and the Coffin.

Noble Grand (as High Priest)—Priest of the Third Degree, what do these symbols teach?

Right Supporter of the Noble Grand (as Priest of the Third Degree)—

THE SCALES AND SWORD[82]

Are emblematical of justice, which judges with candor and rewards with impartiality. Among Odd-fellows, both justice and mercy are administered without regard to the false distinctions of society. In the lodge-room the high and low, the rich and the poor, the learned and the unlearned,

NOTE 82.—"THE SCALES.—*Emblem of Equity*. It represents the weighing of evidence and opinions, to determine their true values and relations; and reminds us that though the love of family and country are natural, and may be made useful, yet we must not stop with these, nor array them in conflict with our more comprehensive duties to mankind and to God. It thus teaches us 'that mankind is our family—our country, the earth—our nation, the human race—that all men are one—from the monarch on his throne to the beggar in his rags, all have one nature, all are immortal,' and God is the equal Father of all.

"THE SWORD.—*Emblem of Justice*. It represents the defending and enforcing power of Righteousness—and reminds us that God requires us to decide justly, after weighing equitably; and to defend the right even (if need be) unto death. In this contest the sword is ever drawn, and therefore needs no scabbard.

These united emblems admonish us to 'judge not according to the appearance, but to judge righteous judgment'—and teach us that 'however much of partiality may exist in the world, yet among Odd-fellows both justice and mercy are administered without regard to the artificial distinctions of society. In the lodge, rich and poor, high and low, learned and unlearned, meet as *brethren*, and unitedly engage in the work of benevolence and charity."—*Grosh's Manual*, p. 147.

meet as brothers, and unitedly engage in the promotion of benevolence and truth.

THE BIBLE[83]

Is an exhaustless fountain of Truth, the store-house from which all our principles are derived. Guided by

its instructions, we may approximate that golden age when the fetters of prejudice will be broken, the shackles of mental and moral bondage fall off, and man, redeemed and disenthralled from the slavish life of the passions, will assert his high birthright, and own the ties which bind him in universal consanguinity with his brother man.

THE HOUR-GLASS[84]

Indicates the march of time, and tells us of the frailty

of human life. Like the sands of the glass, we are passing away. How important that we improve our fleeting hours, in order that we may meet our end with peace!

"NOTE 83.—THE BIBLE.—*Emblem of Revealed (Spiritual) Truth.* The re-creative, only real and enduring Truth. 'For the things which are seen are temporal; but the things which are not seen are eternal.' The Bible is therefore 'placed among our emblems, because it is the fountain whence we draw instruction, the storehouse whence our precepts are derived, and most of our emblems are found in its pages.' No lodge can be held without it.

"Its teachings of God, and His Fatherhood—of man, and human brotherhood—as well as 'the first and great command,' and 'the second commandment which is like unto it,' on which 'two commandments hang all the Law and the Prophets'—give this emblem peculiar value to all Odd-fellows of every sect and every creed. And in view of our certain mortality, all need its teachings of a future life. Assured that man must die, we desire to be assured that the ever-living God is our Father, and will make us the sharers of His immortality and eternal life, as revealed in that Book of Books."—*Grosh's Manual, p.* 161.

NOTE 84.—"The world, at its brightest and best, is of Time—subject to all Time's chances and changes—and this emblem reminds us that all the goodliness and fashion thereof is but as the grass that withereth and the flower that fadeth. The Hour-Glass 'admonishes us to improve the moments as they fly, in a manner that shall redound to the glory of God, and our own and our neighbor's good. It also brings before us the great contrast between Time and Eternity."—*Grosh's Manual, p.* 292.

THE COFFIN[85]

Points to the last home of man. How great or small,
high or low, all must meet on this common level—all
must submit to the
dominion of death.
How cheerless the
home of the dead un- 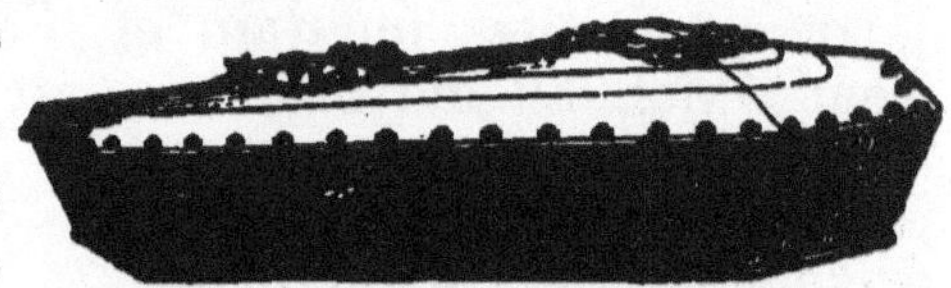
relieved by the prospect of immortal life! But hope
bends over man's last resting-place a bow bright with
immortality, which, based upon earth, extends far into
the sacred realms of eternity.

If the candidate has been seated he must now rise.

CONCLUDING CHARGE.

Noble Grand (as High Priest)—My brother, you are
now admitted to the Third Degree, known also as the
Priestly Order. You have already been informed that
it is dedicated to the principle of truth. You were prepared for admission by having placed on you a white
robe. This was intended to represent the purity of
truth. But the emblematic color of this degree is
Scarlet, implying that truth is an Imperial virtue. The
pure white robe is an external symbol, representing
that your lips should speak the truth, and at all times
be ready to administer[86] words of affection to a brother

NOTE 85.—''THE COFFIN.—*Emblem of Certain Truth.* It represents that
most certain but too little heeded truth, that the honors of the world, the ap-
plause of men, the distinctions of birth, wealth, fame, *all* end in that 'narrow
house.'"—*Grosh's Manual, p.* 159.

NOTE 86.—'' Let us not forget that, while we cultivate the perfection of our
fraternal duties, we shall improve in the knowledge of Deity, of our duty to
Him, to our neighbor, and to ourselves : *Friendship* will bind us together,
Truth will direct us, and *Love* will make our labors easy; so that, at the last,
when we are summoned from the terrestial lodges to the Grand Lodge Celestial,
we may leave form and ceremony behind, find our work approved, and, as the
mysteries of heaven are unveiled to our admiring vision, we may arrive at its
perfection, and enjoy its *benefit* throughout ages eternal. Even so may it be!
Amen."—*Grosh's Manual, p.* 187.

requiring consolation. You are now placed in a position among us to gain rank, the highest in a lodge. It, therefore, becomes your duty to enforce by example,[87] as well as by precept, the tenets of our Order. Its mysteries are confided to your charge; you are to preserve them inviolate; duty and honor, your own solemn vows, all require that you be faithful, and that you also guard your brethren against any breach of fidelity. Be true and steadfast in this as well as in all things, and thus demonstrate that merit[88] constitutes the great title to our privileges, and that on you they have not been undeservedly conferred.

Noble Grand (three raps, all rise)—Members of the Priestly Order, are you willing for Brother —— —— to receive the decoration of the Third Degree or Priestly Order?

The Lodge answers.

Noble Grand—(one rap, seating the lodge.)

Noble Grand (as High Priest)—Conductor and Warden, you will now disrobe the brother. [They take off

---

NOTE 87.—"To prepare the Odd-fellow for these daily duties and privileges of life, and to direct him in their proper performance and use, is the great end and aim of the weekly meeting in the lodge-room. The work of the Lodge being but a school to exercise him in his proper work of Odd-fellowship in his own heart, in his family, and in the world at large. The tokens and emblems of the one are designed to direct his mind to the sun, the moon, the stars, the light-woven bow on the cloud, the open hand, and all the other visible and invisible objects in the other, which speak of God's goodness, and man's duties, and nature's blessedness, and make them incitements to the pursuit of knowledge and virtue."—*Grosh's Manual, p.* 188.

NOTE 88.—"Careless, indolent, or ill-instructed, therefore, must he be, who rests satisfied with a mere attendance on lodge-meetings, and whose mind and heart reach not beyond the mere routine of its workings, the letter of its lectures and charges, or the outward appearance of its forms, emblems, and allegorized representations. The true Odd-fellow, using these but as an outline map, will study them that he may fill up their vacancies, understandingly mark out his journey in the world, and pursue his life-pilgrimage, 'knowing whence he cometh, whither he goeth, and what he doeth."—*Grosh's Manual, p.* 188.

his robe].   My brother, I present to you this collar; it indicates your rank.   We trust that your zeal for the promotion of the principles of the Order will be ardent and pure.   I will now instruct you in the mysteries of this degree.

In this degree there is an Alarm, at the inner door, a Pass Word, a Counter Sign, an Answer to the Counter Sign, a Working Sign and Answer, an Explanation of the Working Sign and Answer, a Principal Sign, a Grip, a Voting Sign, and the Honors of the Order.

The Alarm at the inner door is three raps.

PASSWORD—The Password is AARON to be lettered at all times when used for working purposes; working into a lodge or in examination prior to opening.   In communicating this word either to the Inside Guardian or to the Warden the brother must give the letters A-A and if required by the Inside Guardian or Warden he must give the remainder of the word, R-O-N, lettered as before.   The Inside Guardian and Warden must be satisfied.

WORKING SIGN.

The sign is made as follows: Close the right hand except the index finger which is extended, thumb over fingers; press the centre of the forehead with the point of the index finger.

ANSWER.

Place the open right hand over the mouth, the fingers to conform to the face, looking the brother addressing earnestly in the face.

Explanation—Think before you speak.

Working Sign.   Answer.

Principal Sign.

PRINCIPAL SIGN.

Place the thumb of the right hand on the right nipple, using it as a pivot; make a span down with the little finger, then make a span across the breast with the forefinger.

GRIP.

Clasp the right hands; with the thumbs press hard on the third or knuckle joint of the third finger. No shaking hands in making the Grip.

VOTING SIGN—The Voting Sign is the right hand uplifted.

HONORS.

Honors.

The Honors of the Order are given as follows; Officers and Brothers standing, the Warden standing in front of the chair of the Noble Grand, the members looking to and following his motions which are: Place the open right hand across the left hand palms touching; clap the hands three times, full blows, pause a moment and repeat, pause again and repeat.

Wishing to visit a Degree Lodge or a Subordinate Lodge open in the third degree, you will announce your-presence by an alarm at the outside door, [the alarm at the outside door is the same as in the Initiatory,] when the Outside Guardian will open the wicket and require from you the password of the current term. If correct you will be admitted to the ante-room. After clothing your-self in appropriate regalia [having ascertained from the Outside Guardian that the lodge is open in the third degree] you will give three raps at the inside door. The Inside Guardian will open the wicket and obtain from you your name, rank and the number of the lodge to which you belong. The Inside Guardian will close the wicket and inform the proper officer, who, if he is satisfied, will direct the Inside Guardian to admit you if correct. The Inside Guardian re-opens the wicket and you must give him the password of the third degree. If correct the Inside Guardian will admit you, when you will advance to the centre of the room and address the Noble Grand with the Countersign who will acknowledge you as a brother by giv-ing the same Countersign. You will then turn and address the Vice Grand who will acknowledge you as a brother with the same Countersign. You will then again turn to the Noble Grand and address him with the Sign of the third degree. The Noble Grand will give the proper answer to the Sign. You will then be seated. Wishing to leave the lodge before it is closed you will address the presiding officer with the sign of the third degree and that officer will answer you with the proper sign; you will then receive from the Vice Grand the password of the evening which you must give to the Inside Guardian before you will be allowed to depart. Should you wish to re-enter the lodge on the same evening you may use the Vice Grand's password or the password of the third degree at the inner door for that purpose. The Vice Grand's retiring password is only used in this degree. If you are visiting your own lodge and are without the password of the current term or the password of this degree, the Noble Grand, being so informed, asks the Secretary as to your standing in the lodge. If the Secretary reports favorably, directions will be given to admit you, but if the report is unfavorable you are so informed by the proper Guardian and you can not be admitted. (The Noble Grand should carefully instruct the brother in the method of using the passwords in working into a lodge and in examination prior to opening.) After which the Noble Grand will call up the lodge and instruct the brother in the Honors of the order and to whom they are to be given, requiring the brother to face the Warden, and to participate with the members in the performance of the ceremony, according to the work; the candidate taking position to the left of the conductor. [After the performance of this ceremony and the candidate has been placed facing the Vice Grand—]

Noble Grand—(to the Conductor)—Conductor, you will proceed with the closing ceremony.

Noble Grand—(one rap, calling up the lodge).

[The Conductor proceeds with the candidate to the centre of the room, and turning faces the Past Grand.]

Past Grand (advancing to the candidate)—By this grip [he gives the grip of the First Degree as on page 92] I greet you in Friendship, as one who has attained to the First Degree.

[The Conductor turns the candidate to face the Vice Grand.]

Vice Grand (advancing to the candidate)—By this grip [he gives the grip of the Second Degree as on page 110] I greet you in Brotherly Love, as a member of the Second Degree.

[The Conductor turns the candidate to face the Noble Grand.]

Noble Grand (advancing to the candidate)—Brother, I welcome you in Truth, and urge you to attend our meetings, that you may assist your brethren and promote your own happiness by acts of mutual assistance. By this grip [he gives the grip of the Third Degree as described] I greet you as a brother of the Degree of Truth, and I now declare you fully entitled to all the rights and privileges of the three degrees of Odd-fellowship.

[The Noble Grand resumes his station.]

Noble Grand—Brothers, I now introduce to you Brother —— ——, who has been advanced[89] to the Degree of Truth. You will welcome him as a brother of this degree.

The Lodge--Welcome, Brother.

Noble Grand—(one rap, seating the lodge).

NOTE. 89.—"The three degrees received have put you in possession of peculiar means for conferring and receiving benefits for and from your brethren in the Order, even when they are utter strangers to you, and you to them. But forget not that every privilege has attached to it a corresponding obligation resting on you to make it a privilege to your brother also, when he requires it. If he is bound to give you timely warning of danger, to caution you against your own imprudence or the evil designs of others, or to risk his property, life, or reputation in a lawful effort to rescue yours, you are no less bound to him, to render like offices in the day of trial, need and peril. That demand may never be made; but *when* made, may it not find you faithless to obligation and recreant to duty!"—*Grosh's Manual, p. 138.*

ANALYSIS DEGREE OF TRUTH.

This is a " Degree of Truth " in which no particular truth is taught: like the conclusion of Johnson's Rasselas, in which nothing is concluded. It is decidedly insipid, even beyond the others, and bears the marks of exhausted invention like poetry written without inspiration.

The friendship of David and Jonathan, and the neighborly kindness of the Good Samaritan, are not spoiled by repetition or shorn of their power and beauty even when filched from the simple, sacred narrative and woven into a Christless worship. Indeed, their ceaseless repetitions, as dramatized and acted over and over, might be of some real benefit to the actors if they

were not made part of a system of social swindling
in which men's hopes of heaven itself are used as means
and motives to get money and votes. So this last and
crowning " degree " of a Subordinate Lodge is a hodge-
podge of heathenism made up of the symbols of pagan
and Jewish worship; as " The All-seeing Eye," " The
Skull and Crossed-Bones," " Scythe of Time," " Arrows
and Quiver," " Axe," " Heart in Hand," "Globe," and
other pictures whose explanation constitutes the degree;
and which taste, after the stories of David and Jonathan
and the Good Samaritan, like a dish of hash-victuals
after a feast of lamb. Indeed, if the ritual had gone
on quoting the Bible much farther, Odd-fellows would
have thought the joke carried too far, and considered it
about as bad as religion. So the contrivers turned from
Scripture narratives to the above symbols and others, as
the serpent on a pole, which the Lecture explains, with
the pagans, to mean " wisdom," while the notes say
(note 80), " It represents the brazen serpent raised by
Moses," to show Christ as made sin for the people, the
sight of which healed them. But still, these wicked
inventors cannot get on without Christ's Scriptures,
but put into this hodge-podge degree, in addition to the
above, a little metallic *Bible*, an *Ark of the Covenant*,
and a Globe in Light, as " the field of our [their] labors," to copy Christ's saying: " The field is the world,"
to sanctify the absurd mass; and a pictured coffin is
thrown in at the end to solemnize the play.

And this devil's compound, seasoned with pagan, prayer, is called "*The Degree of Truth*," practiced, sanctioned and taught by Schuyler Colfax and Rutherford B. Hayes, once Vice-President and President of the United States! And the duped initiate is told by the Conductor that this strange medley, which does not leave one sound, substantial idea in his mind, " WILL TEACH HIM HIS DUTY TO GOD AND HIS FELLOW-MAN!" *(See Ritual, p. 120.)*

Of course, after receiving this "*Degree* of Truth," he needs neither Moses nor prophets, Christ nor apostles, the Bible nor the Holy Ghost, to teach him his whole duty and the way of life. He has graduated; taken his degree from the Subordinate Lodge, and is assured of "a happy resurrection to a glorious immortality." *(See the Grand Sire's Address Consecrating the Odd-fellows' Burying Ground, Chicago.)*

But are not Schuyler Colfax, R. B. Hayes, and a host of such men, Americans and patriots? If this analysis be true, why are such men in Odd-fellowship?

The answer is: The same cause that took "Aaron the Saint of the Lord," into that calf-worship and jollification at Sinai. The explanation which he gave to Moses was popular: "Thou knowest the people that they are set on mischief." The motive in both cases is popular favor: "*For they loved the praise of men more than the praise of God.*"—*John 12: 43.*

And we read in the Ritual (p. 136), " The emblematic color of this degree is SCARLET;" a color prominent in Odd-fellowship regalia, as in the Apocalypse.

" And there came one of the seven angels, which had the seven vials, and talked with me, saying unto me: Come hither, and I will shew thee the judgment of the great whore that sitteth on many waters;

" With whom the kings of the earth have committed fornication, and the inhabitants of the earth have been made drunk with the wine of her fornication.

" So he carried me away in the Spirit into the wilderness *(of America?)* and I saw the woman sit upon a scarlet-colored beast, full of names of blasphemy, having seven heads and ten horns.

" And the woman was arrayed in purple and scarlet color, and decked with gold and precious stones and pearls, having a golden cup in her hand full of abominations and filthiness of her fornication."

" These shall make war with the Lamb, and the Lamb shall overcome them; for he is Lord of lords, and King of kings: and they that are with him are called, and chosen, and faithful."

" And he saith unto me, The waters which thou sawest, where the whore sitteth, are peoples, and multitudes, and nations, and tongues."

" And the woman which thou sawest is that great city, which reigneth over the kings of the earth."—*Rev. 17: 1–4, 14, 15, 18.*

This is God's photograph of false worships showed to John in Patmos.

False worship debauches the soul, whose worship, like fealty in woman, is for one. The scarlet woman on the seven-headed beast is Rome on her seven hills, "that great city which reigneth over the kings of the earth;" but she is the "mother of harlots and [all spiritual] abominations of the earth." That is, all the elements of all false religions and religious worships are in her, those of Freemasonry and Odd-fellowship included. And every false worship on earth is a despotism, ruling rulers and people.

·False worshipers are "drunk." Their heads swim. "The god of this world" hath BLINDED their MINDS. "These make war with the Lamb," cut his name out of his Bible, cast his Bible out of schools and his atonement out of their prayers, or make him as the Papacy does, a mere tool of incantation in the hands of priests, owning him in words, but denying him in works.

All moral and spiritual filthinesses are combined and concentrated in false worship. Like fornication it destroys shame, and confounds all moral and spiritual ideas. Freemasons and Odd-fellows who have drunk this filthiness tell the truth when they say they can not see aught in the lodge inconsistent with Christianity. They can not. Their minds, as their eyes were, are blinded. And unless they escape by Christ, for them "is reserved the blackness of darkness forever."

No Scripture, least of all Scripture prophecy, is of any local or particular interpretation. ROME is not alone on the Tiber. She is everywhere where her rites are. For in them is " the hiding of her power." And " the great whore, sitting on many waters," which are the tongues, peoples and nations who have been made drunk, with her filthiness and false worships, is the spiritual photograph of false worships to-day, as it was when John was " in Patmos for the word of God and the testimony of Jesus Christ."

These now, as then, " make war with the Lamb." Certain " United Brethren," falsely so-called, denounce their brethren who resist the moral filthiness of the false worships, because they make their church unpopular, especially in the cities, which are almost " wholly given to idolatry," as in the days of Paul.

But if the world hateth them, we know that it hated Christ before it hated them. " If," says Christ, " ye were of the world, the world would love his own; but because ye are not of the world, but I have chosen you out of the world, therefore the world hateth you."— *John 15: 18, 19.*

The world does not hate Bishops Glosbrenner and Weaver, and Agent Shuey, and their helpers in the church of the United Brethren in Christ. But it hates all those who, by prayer and testimony, are seeking the overthrow of the lodge. Though if Otterbein, and

Boehm, and Newcomer, Guething and the sainted dead who founded that church were now here, every well-informed member of it knows they would be among the sternest abhorrers of the lodge. And, till lately, those who would have stood by those founders, in the whole membership of one hundred and fifty-nine thousand, would have been more than one hundred to one.

The coincidence in hue between the scarlet woman and her scarlet-colored beast filled with the names of blasphemy, and the scarlet caps, robes and degree of Odd-fellowship, and the same color also prominent in the regalia of Rome, may be thought incidental. But there is no mistaking the identity of their nature. The filthiness of false worship is the same in all three. And their moral effect is the same. The people are drunk with it.

There are now about one hundred secret orders, working nightly, outside and inside of our courts, legislatures, schools, colleges and churches; and every such order, little or large, is an apocalyptic Beast or image of a Beast; each one is a living embodiment of an anti-Christian force, and each lifts the same serpent head which appeared in Eden to estrange man from his Maker; each swears or pledges its votaries to conceal they know not what, and each subjugates them for life to unseen and unknown superiors. Nor is their poison restricted to their own membership. The outside world

" wonder after the Beast, saying: Who is able to make war with him?"—*Rev. 13:3, 4.*

These all make war upon the Lamb; but, blessed be God, " the Lamb shall overcome them."

Plan of Encampment Room.

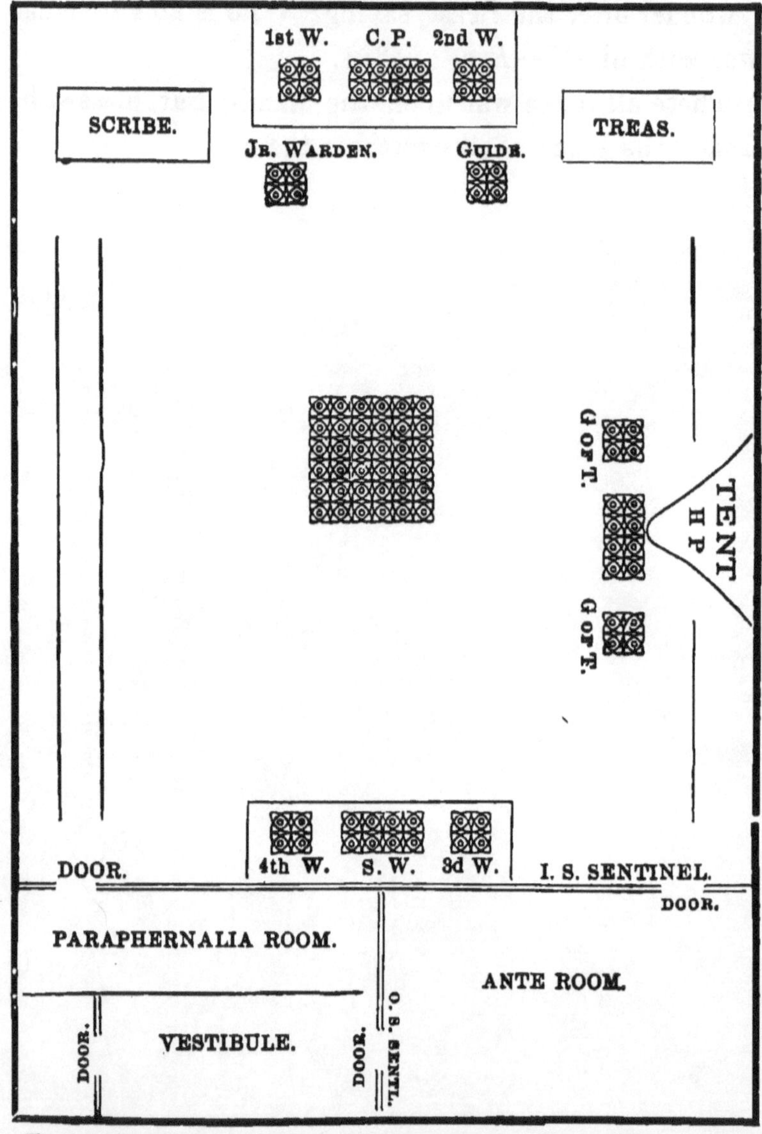

The location of the doors, either to the encampment room or the ante-room, or from outside to the vestibule, cannot be determined, and it is not proposed to fix definitely which side of the Chief Patriarch the Scribe and Treasurer shall sit, nor on which side of the room the Tent shall be.

CHAPTER XI.

The Encampment[90] Degrees.

The ceremonies and ritual here given conform exactly to the Subordinate Encampment Charge-Book furnished by the Sovereign Grand Lodge, I. O. O. F., adopted at the session of 1880, at Toronto, Canada.

BY-LAW OF THE SOVEREIGN[91] GRAND LODGE I. O. O. F.

"All State, District or Territorial Grand Lodges and Grand Encampments shall enforce upon their Subordinates[92] a strict adherence to the Work[93] of the Order,

---

NOTE 90.—"Though teaching peaceful lessons, the Encampment assumes military forms. The candidate is therefore met with a more rigid scrutiny and in a sterner manner than on his entrance into the Subordinate Lodge. He need not wonder, then, at the strict watch which will be kept over him, nor the restraints that will be imposed on him until he has passed the ordeal, and proved himself to be no enemy in disguise, but a true Odd-fellow. Let him rely on the kindness of his guardian to sustain and defend him until justice awards him release, and the benevolence of the Patriarchs greets him with hospitality and fraternal welcomes."—*Grosh's Manual*, p. 263.

NOTE 91.—"While the Sovereign Grand Lodge has granted State Grand Lodges large powers of supervision over their Subordinates, it has not surrendered its own inherent right to interfere in the financial concerns of individual lodges whenever necessary for the furtherance of the principles of the Order."—*Journal of Proceedings Sovereign Grand Lodge, Session of* 1880, *p.* 8452.

NOTE 92.—"The powers of Subordinate Lodges are extremely limited. They are 'restricted to the exercise of powers conferred by their charters and the laws of the several Grand Lodges under which they exist' (1014); they may make by-laws for their own internal government, but these by-laws must not conflict with the laws and decisions of their State Grand Lodge (1019)."—*Journal of Proceedings Sovereign Grand Lodge, Session of* 1880, *p.* 8452.

NOTE 93.—"Subordinate Lodges are termed 'working lodges,' (in distinction from Grand Lodges, which are legislative bodies), because in them candidates are initiated, moral and social instructions given, and provision *directly* made for performing the active works of Odd-fellowship."—*Grosh's Manual*, *p.* 182.

according to the forms furnished by the Sovereign[94] Grand Lodge, I. O. O. F., and shall be held responsible for any irregularities that they may allow under their jurisdiction. They shall neither adopt nor use, or suffer to be adopted or used, in their jurisdiction, any other Charges, Lectures, Degrees, Ceremonies,[95] Forms of Installation, or Regalia, than those prescribed by the Sovereign Grand Lodge, I. O. O. F."

ENCAMPMENT[96] OPENING CEREMONIES.

These ceremonies are the regular opening exercises of the Encampment and for convenience are given introductory to the first Encampment degree; but, as will be observed, the Encampment is opened in the Royal Purple Degree and all the business of the Encampment must be transacted in that Degree.

Chief Patriarch (one rap, calling to order)—Junior Warden, see that all present are Patriarchs, that the Sentinels are at their stations, and the password of the evening is given.

In this examination the Junior Warden must obtain from each member the Check Password (in full), and the password of the Royal Purple Degree (lettered), but neither the Sentinels nor Junior Warden are required to respond to members by giving any portion of the passwords. The Junior Warden must see that every officer, including the Sentinels, Guide, Watches and the Guards of the

-----

NOTE 94.—"SECTION 5, ARTICLE I., OF CONSTITUTION SOVEREIGN GRAND LODGE. To this Grand Lodge belongs the power to regulate and control the unwritten work of the Order, and to fix and determine the customs and usages in regard to all things which appertain thereto; and to it alone belongs the power to provide and establish suitable lectures and other written work therefor. But the unwritten work of the Order shall in no wise be altered or amended, except by a four-fifths vote of the members of this Grand Lodge, nor shall the written work of the Order be in anywise altered or amended, except with the concurrence of two-thirds of the members of this Grand Lodge."—*Journal of Proceedings Sovereign Grand Lodge, Session of* 1880, *p.* 8323.

NOTE 95.—"*Resolved,* That the revised Initiatory, Degree and Encampment Work, as adopted at this session, shall go into operation on the first day of January, 1881, and that to this end the Grand Secretary is directed to have the same ready for distribution, upon orders of subordinate Grand Secretaries and Grand Scribes, by that time."—*Journal of Proceedings Sovereign Grand Lodge, Session of* 1880, *p.* 8455.

NOTE 96.—"While the military forms are observed in its opening and closing, the business is transacted as in the Subordinate Lodge, the officers recite their duties at opening, and it is always opened and closed with prayer by the proper officer."—*Grosh's Manual, p.* 256.

Tent, is at his post, and it is also his duty to ascertain whether the password of the evening has been given by the Senior Warden to the Inside Sentinel; but the Junior Warden neither gives nor receives the password of the evening from officers or members.

Junior Warden—Chief Patriarch, all present are Patriarchs, the Sentinels are at their stations, and the password of the evening is given.

Chief Patriarch—Has the High Priest assumed his station?

Junior Warden—(answers accordingly).

Chief Patriarch (two raps, all rise)—The officers and Patriarchs will rise while the Junior Warden assists me in opening the Encampment in the Royal Purple Degree.

Junior Warden—By direction of the Chief Patriarch, I proclaim this Encampment open in the Royal Purple Degree.

Chief Patriarch—Senior Warden, what is your duty in the Encampment?

Senior Warden—It is my duty to perform the ceremonies intrusted to me, and to support the Chief Patriarch and the High Priest in the discharge of their duties.

Chief Patriarch—Junior Warden, what is your duty?

Junior Warden—To examine the Patriarchs prior to opening; to assist the Chief Patriarch and High Priest according to my office, and to see that the signs are given correctly.

Chief Patriarch—Scribe, explain your duty.

Scribe—It is my duty to record all proceedings of this Encampment [*when the duties are divided between a Recording and a Financial Scribe, the answer of the Recording Scribe ends here, and the Financial Scribe gives the remainder*]: to keep accurate accounts between this Encampment and its members; to receive all its moneys[97] and pay them to the Treasurer, taking his receipt for the same.

Chief Patriarch—Outside Sentinel, explain your duty.

Outside Sentinel—It is my duty to take charge of the ante-room, and to admit no Patriarch [*except a Patriarch with a card*] without the Chief Password of the term, unless directed by the Chief Patriarch so to do.

Chief Patriarch—Inside Sentinel, explain your duty.

Inside Sentinel—It is my duty to prove every Patriarch before he is admitted; to report his name to the Chief Patriarch, upon whose direction to obtain the password of the degree in which the encampment is opened, and, when the Encampment is open in the Royal Purple Degree, to suffer none to retire without the password of the evening, or to return without that password or the password of the degree.

A password of the evening is used in the Encampment when open in the Royal Purple Degree, and it is determined upon by the Senior Warden, who communicates it to the Inside Sentinel, and to members retiring, who must give it to the Inside Sentinel before they depart.

Chief Patriarch—Most Excellent High Priest, explain the duties of your office.

High Priest—It is my duty to counsel the members of the encampment to improve themselves in the Lectures and Charges, as well as in the practice of their doctrines; to conform to the General Regulations, and thus preserve the uniform mode of working in this En-

---

Note 97.—"Each lodge is not only a Beneficial, or Mutual Aid Society, but also an Association for mental and moral improvement, whose meetings and operations are designed to improve and elevate the characters of its members."—*Grosh's Manual, p.* 80.

campment; and to give such instructions to newly initiated members as the good of the fraternity may require.

Chief Patriarch—Patriarchs, my office gives me charge of this Encampment, and requires me to see that the respective officers and brethren perform their duties in a proper manner. It is unnecessary now to recapitulate those duties, or to enlarge upon the relations which we all bear to each other. Our own experience has established the value of our laws and regulations, and we are pledged strenuously to support them, and be ready at all times to aid in their execution. We are not to palliate or aggravate the offenses of our brethren, but in the decision of every trespass we should judge with candor, admonish with friendship, and reprehend with justice. Such is the nature of the engagements which we are bound by the most sacred ties to perform.

An ode may now be sung.

Chief Patriarch—Officers and Patriarchs, be attentive while the Most Excellent High Priest offers a prayer.

PRAYER BY THE HIGH PRIEST.

Heavenly Father, we pray thee to look with favor upon this meeting. Guide us in our efforts to improve the time before us; let thy care and the good we receive at thy hands instruct us in our duties toward each other; and so direct all our acts that thy name may be magnified now and forever. Amen.

Chief Patriarch—(one rap, all are seated).

ORDER OF BUSINESS.

One rap calls to order, two raps call up the Encampment and one rap seats it.

1. *Chief Patriarch*—Scribe, you will call the roll of officers, and read the proceedings of our last meeting.

2. Does any brother know of a Patriarch who is entitled to our aid or sympathy?""

3. Previous proposals for admission to membership will now be considered.

4. Candidates admitted and degrees conferred.

5. Proposals for membership received and referred.

6. Unfinished business.

7. New business.

8. Has any Patriarch anything to offer for the good of the order?

9. Closing.

GENERAL REGULATIONS

Adopted by the Sovereign Grand Lodge, Session of 1880.

VOTING AND ADVANCEMENT.

The voting in an Encampment, unless otherwise provided by ballot or ticket, is by yea and nay; but if a division is asked for, all who vote in the affirmative are required to rise and stand until counted—those voting in the negative rise and stand until counted. If the Junior Warden counts (by direction of the Chief Patriarch of course), he will inform the Chief Patriarch of the number of votes for and against the proposition, and the Chief Patriarch announces the result. When balloting in a Subordinate Encampment, the ballot-box shall be placed on a pedestal near the center of the room, and the Chief Patriarch shall supervise the balloting.

NOTE 98.—"John Randolph professed to have found that the philosopher's stone consisted simply in these four words—'*Pay as you go*.' But an Odd-fellow will more surely find it in the *three* words—'*Pay in advance*.'"—*Grosh's Manual, p.* 192.

When a brother is initiated into the Encampment it shall be called admitted.

When the Golden Rule Degree is conferred, it shall be called advanced.

When the Royal Purple Degree is conferred, it shall be called exalted; to-wit:

Admitted to the Patriarchal Degree.

Advanced to the Golden Rule Degree.

Exalted to the Royal Purple Degree.

MISCELLANEOUS.

The Check Password is determined upon by the Grand Patriarch of the State, District or Territorial Grand Encampment. It is communicated to the Chief Patriarch and Senior Warden of each Subordinate Encampment at the installation of its officers, each term. After his installation the Chief Patriarch shall himself, or by the Junior Warden or other member of the Encampment, give the Check Password, privately, to each member of the Encampment who shall be present and entitled to receive it.

The Check Password shall be given to proper officers of Encampments immediately subordinate to the Sovereign Grand Lodge of the Independent Order of Oddfellows, by the District Deputy Grand Sire of the jurisdiction.

The Chief Patriarch, or in his absence the Senior Warden, can alone give (or cause to be given) the Check Password to members entitled thereto.

No officer, nor, of course, member, can enter or retire from an Encampment when open and working as such, without the proper sign, etc. (addressing the chairs), except the Junior Warden in charge of a candidate.

The law in regard to the Honors of the Order refers to Subordinate Encampments as well as to Subordinate Lodges.

The Holy Bible[99] is an integral part of Odd-fellowship, and it is necessary that it should be present in every Encampment while open for business.

QUALIFICATIONS[100] FOR MEMBERSHIP.

Brothers in good standing in lodges under the jurisdiction of the Sovereign Grand Lodge of the Independent Order of Odd-fellows, and who have attained the Degree of Truth, may be admitted to and retain membership in an Encampment of Patriarchs, subject to the regulations applicable to this branch of the Order.

The High Priest of an Encampment shall, when conferring any of the degrees, wear a robe[101] made of royal purple fabric, trimmed with ermine or white fabric, with a white surplice of muslin, linen or silk, together with a mitre and breastplate.

Note 99.—"The Christianity which is lawful on one side of a mountain, or stream, or even an imaginary line, is punished with confiscation, imprisonment, or death, on the other side. Does God require this at the hands of one portion of his children toward the other portion, their brethren? Has he instituted such laws: does he inflict such penalties for differences of opinion? Then, if we take into consideration *all* the religions in the world, how much greater the intolerance! Not only between the North and the South of Europe, but the European, living amid the refinements of art and science, is but little in advance of the Asiatic, who, though living in the land of Adam, of Noah, of Abraham, and other Bible worthies, rejects that Book and clings to the Shaster or the Koran, and calls all infidels who acknowledge not the authority of Confucius, or Mahomet, or Brahma."—*Grosh's Manual*, p. 271.

Note 100.—"The descendants of Abraham, the diverse followers of Jesus, the Pariahs of the stricter sects, here gather around the same altar, as one family, manifesting no differences of creed or worship, and discord and contention are forgotten in works of humanity and peace."—*Grosh's Manual*, p. 277.

Note 101.—"The cost of our decorations has been employed in giving needed labor (and *by* that labor, honorable subsistence) to hundreds and thousands of industrious men, women, and children. So far then, it has not been expended in vain."—*Grosh's Manual*, p. 56.

The guards of the tent shall, during the conferring of degrees, be clothed with a pilgrim's blouse and cap, bearing each a spear and shield.

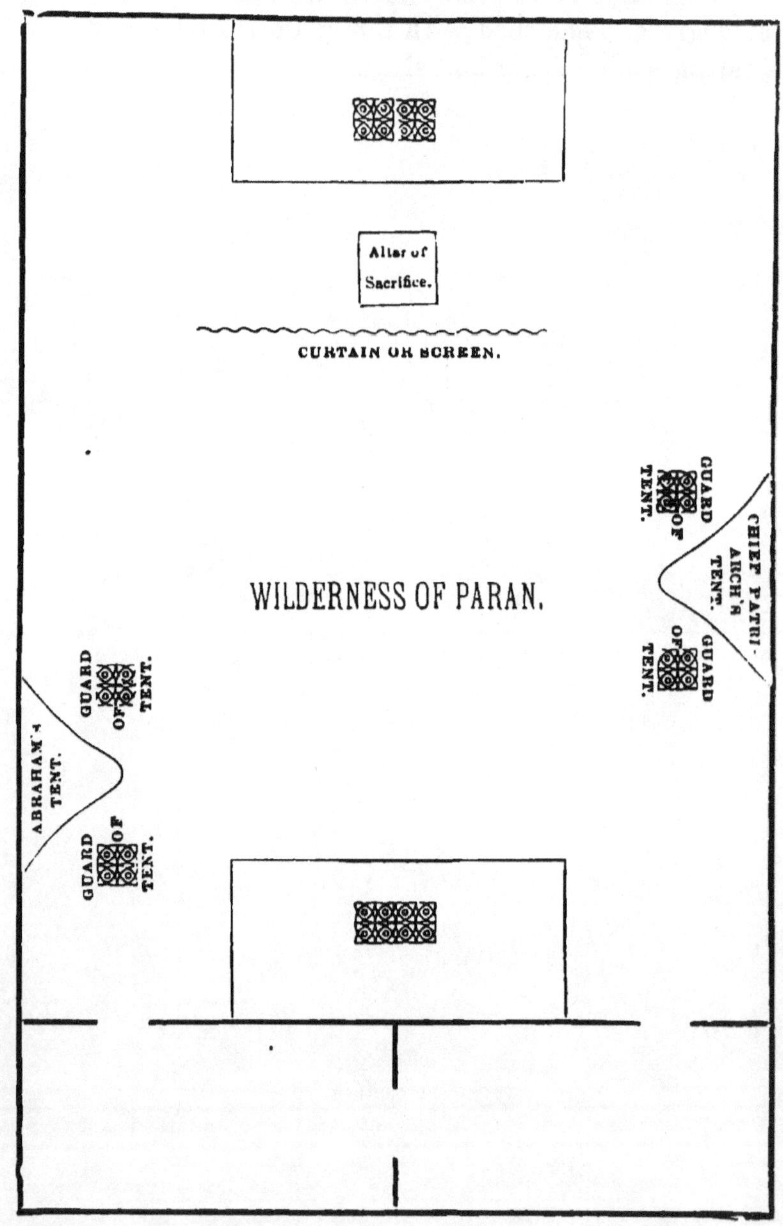

Altar of Sacrifice.
CURTAIN OR SCREEN.
WILDERNESS OF PARAN.
GUARD OF TENT.
CHIEF PATRI-ARCH'S TENT.
GUARD OF TENT.
GUARD OF TENT.
ABRAHAM'S TENT.
GUARD OF TENT.

CHAPTER XII.

PATRIARCHAL,[102] OR FIRST ENCAMPMENT DEGREE.

INITIATION.

Clothing[103] *of Members and Officers.*

CHIEF PATRIARCH.

Purple gown, yellow belt; turban with black band and yellow top; crook.

SENIOR WARDEN.

Purple gown, yellow belt; turban with black band and yellow top.

JUNIOR WARDEN.

Purple gown, yellow belt; turban same as Senior Warden.

SUBORDINATE OFFICERS.

Purple gowns, yellow belts, black turbans.

NOTE 102.—"The patriarchal branch of the Order is, in the estimation of many, far more desirable than the initiatory branch. Every Odd-fellow should make it his aim to reach the 'topmost round of the ladder of Odd-fellowship,' the Royal Purple Degree."—*Donaldson's Pocket Companion, p.* 197.

NOTE 103.—"Such our decorations, emblems, and forms are to us. The light shed on their meaning, as we advance in Odd-fellowship, and their novel applications to impress on our minds important principles and precepts, render them peculiarly pleasing and highly useful. The thoughtful Odd-fellow is continually reminded by them of important duties to God and man."—*Grosh's Manual, p.* 54.

MEMBERS GENERALLY.

Purple gowns and belts.

The High Priest acts as "Abraham" in this degree, and occupies a tent, which should be of the ridge-pole style. His dress should be like the Chief Patriarch's, and he should have a very heavy white beard and wig —no turban.

In parts I and II the official stations are vacated excepting Senior Warden's, and that officer has charge of the Encampment.

The Chief Patriarch occupies a tent in part I of this degree.

The Junior Warden acts as a companion candidate in parts I and II.

PART I.

PREPARATION OF CANDIDATE.

The Junior Warden proceeds to the ante-room and dresses the candidate as himself, in a common light brown gown, with a rope around the waist for a girdle, a brown turban and a staff to carry. The candidate is blindfolded and sometimes has a sack on his back and sandals upon his feet. There is a dim light in the Encampment room. A curtain or screen is so arranged as to conceal the altar. The Watches act as "Wilderness Sentinels," and also as Torch Bearers. All rough usage when conferring this degree is strictly forbidden.

Junior Warden (entering Encampment door, which is left a little ajar, with candidate)—Halloo! Halloo!

Members rise as if unprepared for an intrusion.

Inside Sentinel—The camp is assailed.

Others—The camp is assailed!

Junior Warden—Hold! we are not enemies,[104] we are brothers and friends. We desire to see the Chief Patriarch and be instructed, that we may become herdsmen, and at the proper time Patriarchs.

First Sentinel (with spear elevated to the breast of candidate)—You cannot pass except as captives. Bring forth the chains. [They are brought.] Now bind the prisoners. [Candidate is bound and blindfolded.]

Senior Warden—(one rap, seating the Encampment).

Junior Warden—Bind us as you will, but true friendship will ultimately sustain us in all our trials. And remember, though prejudice impose bonds and fetters, that justice will award the greetings of a brother.

First Sentinel—Captives, you have permission to approach the Chief Patriarch with a Guide.

Guide (taking him in charge)—Captives, come this way. If you are friends he will give you welcome, but you must prove to him that you are not impostors.

The trial to which you are to be subjected will serve to test your faith and sincerity. Be not weary in well-doing, for in due season you shall reap if you faint not. You are as one entering a pathless forest, relying on patience and perseverance for his guides. But all cause for gloom and doubt will soon be dispelled.

Hark! I hear the tramping of feet. What can it mean? Oh, I see; it is the Patriarchs returning from their visit to the venerable Abraham at Beersheba. It is their custom to visit him and do him honor at certain

---

Note 104.—"Depend upon it, that if a public excitement is ever got up against our Order, the improper modes of performing our work pursued by some Encampments will be the fuel to feed its destroying flames."—*Grosh's Manual, p.* 253.

feasts, and receive his blessing. [They pause, and a procession passes near the candidate. Sometimes there is music and singing.] They are traveling in the direction of Mt. Horeb, and we will follow them. We are still crossing the wilderness of Paran, the mountains are near, and our journey will soon be at an end. Ah, here are the inner sentinels, and we shall have to stop.

Third Sentinel—Who comes there?

Guide—Friends from Mt. Hor, traveling, by permission, to see the Chief Patriarch, desiring to get employment as herdsmen.

Fourth Sentinel—Friends, you look fatigued. Pass and rest with the Chief Patriarch.

Guide—That sentinel was very kind. He has had experience as an old Patriarch, and he has sympathy for you. Ah! here is the tent.

First Guard to Tent—Who comes there?

Guide—Travelers from Mt. Hor, who desire to see the Chief Patriarch. They have passed the sentinels and desire food and rest.

First Guard to Tent—Wait, and I will report their presence.

First Guard to Tent—Chief Patriarch, there are travelers without who need food and rest, and wish employment that they may become herdsmen.

Chief Patriarch—Whence came they, and did they properly pass the sentinels?

First Guard to Tent—They are from Mt. Hor, and have crossed the plains of Paran. The outer sentinels passed them as captives, and gave them a guide.

Chief Patriarch (seated)—Let the strangers enter and provide them with seats. [They enter the tent or are seated at the door.] Take off the bandage and **remove**

those chains. [The bandage and chains are removed.]
Travelers, I welcome you. The door of a Patriarch's
tent is never closed against any one in distress. Guard,
bring forth refreshments, that we may give food to the
strangers, for they must be hungry and thirsty, after
having crossed the wilderness. [He brings bread, salt
and water, placing them on a small table in or before
the tent.]

Chief. Patriarch (seated)—Strangers, partake with me
of some bread and salt, and drink of this pure water.
I have but little, but that little I cheerfully share with
you. Hospitality to the stranger is a solemn duty,
acknowledged and practiced among the Patriarchs.
The God whom we worship is the Father of all men; he
sends his rain and his sunshine alike upon the evil and
the good. The ties of a common humanity unite us
with every creature, and stamp the character of brothers upon the whole intelligent creation. But while
this is our duty and should ever be our practice, it is
equally imperative upon us to admit no traitor or spy
into our camp to mar our happiness or disturb our
peace. It is necessary, therefore, having relieved your
present wants, that you should now undergo a strict
examination, to prove that you are not enemies in disguise, but true and honest men. Strangers, are you
willing to prove, by an examination, that you are friends
and not spies?

Junior Warden—We are.

Chief Patriarch—Give me the Password of the Degree
of Friendship. [Candidate gives it.]

Chief Patriarch—Give me the Grip of the Degree of
Brotherly Love. [Candidate gives it.]

Chief Patriarch—Give me the Password and Grip of the Degree of Truth.   [Candidate gives them].

Chief Patriarch—I am satisfied with your proficiency and greet you as Odd-fellows. Ever remember that you must be hailed and recognized as the representatives of the Oracle of Truth, and that it behooves you to form your characters by that expressive symbol which has been selected as the basis of the Scarlet Degree. And now, my brethren, what is it that you desire?   .

Junior Warden (for candidate)—To be admitted as novitiates of the Patriarchal Degree, that we may obtain employment as herdsmen.

Chief Patriarch—That being your wish, and being Odd-fellows, I have confidence in your fidelity, and you have now my permission to become novitiate Patriarchs. Guide, conduct the brothers to the Senior Warden, with my request to administer to them the Patriarchal obligation. [The candidate is led to the chair of the Senior Warden].

Guide—Senior Warden, I am instructed by the Chief Patriarch to request you to administer to these brethren the Patriarchal obligation.

Senior Warden—My brethren, it being your wish to take the obligation of the Patriarchal Degree, you will place yourselves in the attitude in which you were initiated into Odd-fellowship and repeat after me the following:

Senior Warden—(two raps, calling up the Encampment).

OBLIGATION.

I, —— ——, do solemnly promise never to reveal the secrets, signs, passwords or grips of the Patriarchal

Order to any person or persons, except to a legal Patri-arch, or within a legal Encampment of Patriarchs. I will never reveal, directly or indirectly, any transaction of this or of any other Encampment, which, by the regulations of the Order, should be kept secret. And if I know that a brother has violated this duty, I will report him at the first meeting of the Encampment thereafter. To the keeping and performance of all this, I pledge my sacred honor.

Senior Warden—(one rap, seating the Encampment).

Senior Warden—Brothers, having taken the obliga-tion of the Patriarchal Degree, you are now qualified to enter upon your course of life as shepherds. As herdsmen, watch well your flocks; see that none perish for want of attention. It is your duty to be good and faithful to all that may be placed in your charge. Brothers, you will now have three days for preparing yourselves for service as herdsmen. You will then report to me for employment.

Junior Warden (for Isaac, the candidate)—I am the son of Abraham who is at Beersheba. Before I enter with my friend upon my duties as herdsman, I desire to make obedience to my father, that I may receive his blessing.

Senior Warden—I commend your zeal and filial af-fection. Go to your father; and that you may travel safely across the wilderness of Paran, I will give to you the wilderness pass, which will insure your safety—advance and receive it. [Junior Warden and candidate advance close to the Senior Warden].

Senior Warden—The pass is " Chosen Friends." You may now proceed on your journey.

Junior Warden and candidate retire to the ante-room, where the candidate is blindfolded, and when the Encampment is prepared he is conducted to the door, which is left ajar, and they enter without ceremony.

PART II.

The High Priest, as Abraham, is seated at the entrance to the tent. A curtain or screen is arranged so as to conceal the Altar of Sacrifice. But one candidate can proceed with the Junior Warden in this part.

First Sentinel (stopping Junior Warden and candidate who have just entered the room)—Who comes there, and where are you going?

Junior Warden—We are novitiate Patriarchs, traveling to Beersheba.

First Sentinel—Have you the pass?

Junior Warden—We have.

First Sentinel—What is it?

Junior Warden—" Chosen Friends."

First Sentinel—The pass is correct. Proceed, and be careful not to aggravate by arrogance or otherwise, for you may find that many are stronger than a few. [They pass on.]

Junior Warden—We will be careful, for we are but two, and we may find, when too late, that many are stronger than a few. [They proceed around the room until they meet the Second Sentinel.]

Second Sentinel—Who comes there, and where are you going?

Junior Warden—Travelers, going to Beersheba.

Second Sentinel—Give me the wilderness pass.

Junior Warden—" Chosen Friends."

Second Sentinel—The pass is correct. Should you meet with difficulties on your journey from quarrelsome men, remember that a soft answer turneth away wrath, but grievous words stir up strife. [They pass on.]

Junior Warden—We have nearly completed our journey. I see the walls of Beersheba. There we shall have rest. Our sandals are worn out, and our feet are bleeding. Ah, here we are at the Third Sentinel.

Third Sentinel—Who comes there, and where are you going?

Junior Warden—We are travelers, and wish to enter through the gates of Beersheba.

Third Sentinel—Give me the pass.

Junior Warden—" Chosen Friends."

Third Sentinel—The pass is correct. Whom do you desire to see in Beersheba?

Junior Warden—Abraham, the promised father of nations.

Third Sentinel—You will find his tent within the walls of the city. You have my permission to pass through the gates. My words of exhortation are, A wise son maketh a glad father.

Junior Warden—We are now passing through the walls of the city.

They pass on as through the gates and the Fourth Sentinel stops them.

Fourth Sentinel—Who comes there, and where are you going?

Junior Warden—We are herdsmen, traveling to see the venerable father Abraham.

Fourth Sentinel—There is his tent and he sits at the door. Listen to wisdom. The glory of young men is their strength, and the beauty of old men is the gray head.

Junior Warden—The glory of young men is their strength: and the beauty of old men is the gray head.

They proceed, and on arriving at the tent the blindfold is removed by the Junior Warden. Abraham rises and recognizes the candidate as Isaac.

Abraham—Isaac! my son! I welcome you. Sit down with your friend. You must be hungry and weary. Guard, bring refreshments, that we may extend hospitality to the travelers. [The Guard brings bread, salt and water and they partake as in Part I.]

Abraham—Tell me, my son, if you saw the Chief Patriarch at Horeb, and did he accept of your offer to be a herdsman?

Junior Warden (for Isaac)—He received me with great kindness; conferred upon me the rank of a noviatiate Patriarch, and I can now take charge of a flock.

Abraham—You give me great joy, my son. Your footsteps have been led to Beersheba by the finger of the Lord. He has commanded me to make a three days' journey to the land of Moriah and there offer up to him a sacrifice.

Junior Warden (for Isaac)—Let obedience crown your head. Honor the Lord's behests, and make no delay in fulfilling them.

Abraham—My son, you speak wisely, and we will proceed on the three days' journey.

A procession is formed, headed by the High Priest as Abraham and the candidate as Isaac, the latter being blindfolded and carrying a bundle of sticks. A psalm or ode may be sung. The altar is placed to suit. On arriving at the place for the altar the blindfold is removed.

Abraham—Here, my son, we will erect an altar, for this is Mount Moriah.

Junior Warden (for Isaac)—What shall we do for a sacrifice?

Abraham—Be patient, my son, and the Lord will provide one.

The altar being in readiness, the Watches (one or more) stand near, holding torches.

Abraham—We have been blessed hitherto, and we

must hasten to serve the Lord, for his will must be done, that we may realize honor and glory. His command that I, Abraham, shall make this sacrifice, is not for an idle purpose, but that it may serve as an illustrious example to generations unborn, to show that God ever blesses the obedient, and accords to them prosperity. My son Isaac, be not surprised; it is God's order that you shall be the sacrifice. The angel of the Lord shall gather and keep your ashes sacred in a golden urn as a memorial of your submissive obedience, and of my faith in God.

A bowl of water and a towel are provided.

Abraham—Patriarchs, let us place the fagots upon the altar. Isaac, wash your hands with me in this bowl which contains pure water. With this white linen dry your hands. [They wash and wipe their hands].

Abraham—Patriarchs, place Isaac upon the altar.

The candidate, as Isaac, is blindfolded and caused to kneel on the altar.

Abraham—Let us unite in praise to God.

Patriarchs surround the altar. Lights are turned low. Torches are lighted, ready to fire the altar. The High Priest, as Abraham, stands with his left hand on Isaac, right hand elevated, and recites the first four verses of Psalm XXIII, as follows:

Abraham—The Lord is my shepherd: I shall not want.

He maketh me to lie down in green pastures: he leadeth me beside the still waters.

He restoreth my soul: he leadeth me in the paths of righteousness for his name's sake.

Yea, though I walk through the valley of the shadow of death, I will fear no evil: for thou art with me; thy rod and thy staff they comfort me.

The above may also be chanted.   A short pause.

Abraham—Now, let the torch be applied!

At a distance from the altar, the muffled gong is struck three times.   A short pause.

Abraham—Let the fagots be fired.

Imitation thunder.
The muffled gong is struck three times, followed by a short pause.

Abraham—Isaac is not to be sacrificed.   Let him be removed from the altar and restored to light, and become a member of the Patriarchal family, and I will return and dwell at Beersheba.

Blindfold is removed.
A psalm or ode may be sung, and a procession may move around the room, the Junior Warden and candidate in the rear.   At the conclusion of the last verse they retire, and re-enter when order has been restored.

PART III.

The officers having resumed their stations, and order being restored, the door being opened, the Junior Warden and candidate or candidates re-enter.

Junior Warden—Chief Patriarch, I present to you Brother —— ——, who has been duly qualified and instructed as a novitiate Patriarch, and now desires to be admitted to the rank of a Patriarch.

Chief Patriarch—My brother, I will proceed to instruct you in the mysteries of this degree.

In this Degree there is an Alarm at the inner door or Entersign. A Check Sign and Answer, a Sign and Answer, and a Grip.

The Alarm at the inner door is two raps; the Password is *Adam* (Ad–am), to be divided at all times when used for working purposes; working into an Encampment, or in examination prior to opening.   In communicating the Password either to the Inside Sentinel or Junior Warden the Patriarch must give the syllable " *Ad*," pronounced; and if required by the Inside Sentinel or Junior Warden, the rest of the word, " *am*," pronounced; the Inside Sentinel and Junior Warden must be satisfied.

1st Position.

2nd Position.

CHECK SIGN.

Place the right hand, open, on the left breast, thumb parallel with the fingers; withdraw the hand and extend it nearly to a line off from the side, palm outward and the thumb parallel with the fingers; let the arm drop to the side. The Answer is the same with the left hand.

SIGN.

Place the fingers of the right hand in and across the left hand, palm upward; grasp the fingers of the right hand with the last three fingers of the left hand; elevate the two thumbs and the index finger of the left hand so as to form three pillars. The Answer is the same as the Sign.

Sign of Patri-
archal Degree.

GRIP.

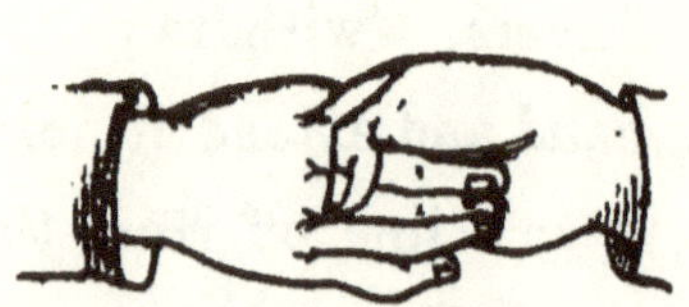

Grasp the fingers of the Patriarch's right hand with your right hand; press the same with the thumb, which must be across the fingers below the knuckle joint. No shaking hands in making the Grip.

INSTRUCTIONS TO CANDIDATE.

Chief Patriarch (to candidate)—Desirous of being admitted to an Encampment, you will give at the outer door the same alarm as in the Subordinate Lodge. The

Outside Sentinel will open the wicket, and require of you the Check Password of the term, which is given in full. If correct, he will admit you to the ante-room. You will then clothe yourself in regalia appropriate to your rank and station, and, after ascertaining from the Outside Sentinel that the Encampment is open in the Patriarchal Degree, you will give three raps at the inner door, when the Inside Sentinel will open the wicket, and obtain from you your name, rank, and the number of the Encampment to which you belong, which he will report to the Chief Patriarch, who will instruct him to admit you if correct. The wicket is again opened, when you will be required to give the Password of the Patriarchal Degree (divided). If correct, you will be admitted, and will advance to the centre of the room and address the Chief Patriarch with the Check Sign. The Chief Patriarch will acknowledge you as a Patriarch with the answer to the Check Sign. You will then turn and address the Senior Warden with the Check Sign, who will also acknowledge you as a Patriarch with the answer to the Check Sign. You will again turn to the Chief Patriarch and address him with the Sign of the Patriarchal Degree. The Chief Patriarch will give the proper answer to the sign. On leaving the Encampment, before it is closed, you will address the Chief Patriarch only, with the Sign of the Patriarchal Degree, and that officer will answer you with the appropriate sign.

The Chief Patriarch should carefully instruct the candidate in the method of using the Password in working into an Encampment, and in examination prior to opening.

Chief Patriarch—My brother, I now present to you this black apron. It indicates that you have served as a novitiate Patriarch. You have sought employment to qualify yourself to assume the high duties of manhood. You have traveled across the wilderness to reach the Chief Patriarch's tent, and, on your arrival, a welcome was given you. You have been obligated, that you might become a shepherd in the fields, on the mountains and in the valleys, preparatory to full recognition as a Patriarch. You assisted in the exemplification of Abraham's faith in God. You have toiled ardently in the pursuit of truth, a cardinal virtue of Odd-fellowship, and you have been instructed in the unerring law by which you are to be governed. VIRTUE should be the great aim of your life—that virtue which gives whatever is great and good in man. Honor, Fidelity, Friendship, social and domestic happiness, are but empty sounds in the mouth of any but a virtuous man. Virtue gives joy which vice with all her flattering promises never pretends to offer, and bestows a zest upon those joys that are common to all which they can never have without it. Its influence spreads through life, diverges in every direction, and penetrates every condition. It is the guardian of youth, the honor of manhood, the crown of age, the shield of prosperity, the prop of affliction, our guide in active life, and our solace in retirement. It holds the keys of life, and will finally open to us the gates of immortality. My brother, it is proper that you be prepared to test the presence of an intruder, in case he should invade our camp.

How shall I distinguish a Patriarch of this degree?

Junior Warden—By the signs and tokens of the Patriarchal rank.

Chief Patriarch—Advance the Patriarchal Sign. [Candidate gives sign].

Chief Patriarch—What does it represent?

Junior Warden (for candidate)—The three pillars of the Order—Faith, Hope and Charity.

Chief Patriarch—What else does it represent?

Junior Warden (for candidate)—The motto of our Order—Friendship, Love and Truth.

Chief Patriarch—Have you a Password?

Junior Warden (for candidate)—We have. *Ad-am.*

Chief Patriarch—My brother, I commend your skill, and trust that the remembrance of these symbols and the virtues which they imply will never fade from your mind. Our institution is a science of symbols, conveying by striking emblems the most interesting and exalted truths. There are moments in the experience of the most virtuous life when incentives are needed to dispel the lethargy of the soul and excite it to action.

I now present to you a crook, an implement of your vocation as a Patriarchal herdsman. It was used by the Patriarchs of old, and strikingly reminds us of the simplicity of their lives and the purity of their faith. They dwelt in tents, and, surrounded by their flocks and herds, spent their lives in the inculcation of the most exalted social virtues. The onward march of civilization, and the advance of human society, have deprived the world of much of that simplicity and virtue which gave its richest charm to the Patriarchal life. Here, in this sacred retreat, we would revive that simplicity and inculcate that purity. Here we would lay the broad foundation of that universal brotherhood, which shall link in the golden chain of our ever ex panding sympathy, heart with heart, man to man, until the vices which defile and the passions and prejudices which separate the children of a common Father shall be extirpated from earth, and the abodes of sorrow and suffering be lighted with the benignant beams of peace and love.

The following in brackets may be omitted.

[To effect the great moral and social revolution, individual action must be combined with associated effort. Each should believe that his individual duty is essential to the integrity of the whole. Ever let that principle of generous beneficence dwell in your heart which, silently and unseen, like the dew of heaven, blesses and refreshes with the gentle droppings of its bounty. Cherish the beautiful teachings of our Order, which, falling upon the heart like rays of light, give color to every affection of our nature, and dictate every act of our lives. Succor the stranger in distress; give him food and rest when he is hungry and weary, without inquiring his country or creed, by whatsoever misfortune he may have fallen, by what destiny he may be controlled. With your brother shepherd, guard against jealousy and strife. Remember that he is your brother. If, under the influence of imperfection, the common lot of mortals, he wrongs you, go to him, and in the language of affection tell him his fault between him and you. If he repent, forgive him; enter no harsh judgment against him. Conscious of your own frailty, remember that to err is human, to forgive divine. These, my brother, are the principles we should ever practice. A man may enter our camp and dwell beneath our tent; mistaken confidence may invest him with our mysteries, and clothe him with the badges of our Order; he may be exalted to official station among us; but all this does not make him an Odd-fellow, unless he behaves and acts as becomes an Odd-fellow].

Chief Patriarch—Brother —— ——, you have passed through the several degrees of the Order to reach the distinction of Patriarchal fellowship. You are solemnly pledged to practice the virtues which, in your progress here, have been illustrated.

They teach sentiments that you will find useful to cultivate through life. They will give tone and honor to your manhood.

And now, in the name and by authority of the Independent Order of Odd-fellows, I declare you duly admitted to the Patriarchal Degree.

The Encampment must always be closed in the Royal Purple, or highest degree, as given in chapter XV.

ANALYSIS PATRIARCHAL DEGREE.

The history of Odd-fellowship is the history of a fog. It is a moral miasm rising from a human morass, and its analysis is as difficult as its history. I have seen respectable-looking English women, wives of mechanics and laborers, sitting in rows on benches in a tap-house, some with babies in their arms, waiting wishfully for some one to give them a glass of beer, while, farther in, their husbands sat guzzling at their mugs around dirty tables in rooms filled with tobacco smoke. Such an ale-house was the birthplace of Odd-fellowship, both in England and in this country.

Their standard historian, Grosh (*p. 23; see also note 22*), says: "Meeting, as they did, in public houses of not the most select character, the beer mug, the pipe and the toast circulated freely." And on the same page (23d) of his volume Grosh gives the following chorus, sung till their tongues became too heavy·

"Then let us be social, be generous, be kind;
Let each take his glass and be mellow—
Then we'll join heart and hand, leave dissension behind,
And we'll each prove a hearty Odd-fellow."

Seeing what could be made of it, cunning men turned this social row into a rowdy religion, gave the lodge a devil's constitution by packing it in degrees pledged to secrecy from the world and each other—a secrecy growing dense to the top. Then they gave it a creed of one article, which is belief in the god of this world, with Christ left out in compliment to Jews and deists. They named its degrees "Friendship," "Love" and "Truth," held up their fingers, when not too drunk, to signify "Faith," "Hope" and "Charity;" and as more money can be got by secret societies than by anything else except Popery, they put on masks and red, blue, white, purple, yellow and black robes, and Odd-fellowship flourished!

But there came to be too many at the top of the lodge, and an upper side-show called "Encampment" was invented, with Patriarchal, Golden Rule and Royal Purple degrees. This Encampment answered a double purpose. It brought more degree fees, and, by long lectures which none but men of strong memories and much leisure could commit, it increased the funds and diminished the leaders among whom, after paying small benefits, the money was to be, and is, divided. Thus Odd-fellowship, like Masonry, became a model for Mormonism.

There is a true old pagan proverb which says, "*Man is a worshiping animal.*" When the plough was introduced to Asiatics, and the pedlar's back was turned. it is said they painted it red, set it up on end and worshiped it. This explains the success of Odd-fellowship, when turned from a drinking-bout into a religion.

This First Encampment or Patriarchal Degree is saved from insipidity by theft from the Bible, like the first two degrees of the lodge. It is to make Odd-fellows *Patriarchs* by playing Abraham's sacrifice of Isaac, but says nothing about Abraham's faith in the promise of God that Christ, the Messiah, should come through his posterity. The sublime part of Abraham's trial was his belief that Christ should come through the posterity of Isaac, whom he was about to kill, " accounting that God was able to raise Isaac from the dead."—*Heb. 11: 19.* Of this the inventors of the Patriarchal Degree either knew nothing or cared nothing, or both. They had no occasion for Christ. He is to Odd-fellowship a sectary, a."stone of stumbling and rock of offense." They were inventing a system of salvation without Him; a system in which Odd-fellows should lift themselves to heaven, as it were, by their own boot-straps— save themselves by symbols and ceremonies and

"Old, odd ends stolen forth of Holy Writ,"

without atonement, without the Holy Spirit, the purchase of Christ's blood, and in contempt of that very Savior who was symbolized by Abraham's offering of his son which they are playing, and the sheep which suffered in his (Isaac's) stead. So they make balderdash of the Scripture. And as the future Messiah is the end and substance of Abraham's faith and trial, this Patriarchal Degree is like the poor strollers' " play of *Hamlet* with the part of *Hamlet* left out;" while the whole significance of the thing is, that the lodge leaders get their money and Satan gets his worship.

> " Thus he supports his cruel throne
> By mischief and deceit;
> And drags the sons of Adam down
> To darkness and the pit."

And, be it remembered, this extemporized, got-up religion is, by its own authorities, declared to be the chief end of Odd-fellowship.

An excellent little book by a Lutheran pastor—Rev. J. H. Brockman, which every one should read, gives abounding proof from the utterances of the Order itself that it does not claim to be a charitable society, but pays the weekly allowance to rich and poor alike. Hence, as rich and idle men are quite as apt to be sick and die as the poor and industrious, it may happen, in a given lodge, that the poor pay in all the money and the rich get all the benefits!

Rev. Mr. Brockman gives from Grand Lodge minutes —year and page given—the case of Henry L. Gunther, who mailed five dollars to pay his lodge dues on the fourth day of October. The money was received, credited, paid all his dues and left a balance in his favor. Meantime (October eleventh) Gunther's wife died, while the money was on the road. The letter was registered and the money belonged to the lodge when it left Gunther's hands, yet the State Grand Lodge of Pennsylvania allowed his local lodge to keep his money, but refused the funeral benefit for his dead wife.

The same Grand Lodge minutes, 1871, p. 486, give the case of Jacob Daumb, Chambersburg (Pennsylvania) lodge. He sent five dollars from Ft. Wayne, whither he had removed. The money paid up his dues and left a balance of seventy-five cents in his favor. Daumb died while his money was on the road, and his wife was refused the constitutional funeral benefit. Those men may have paid dues regularly for twenty-five or thirty years, and drawn out nothing; but dying five cents in debt, after paying hundreds of dollars, would deprive them of the funeral benefit! And as the poor and unfortunate Odd-fellows are the ones most likely to fail to keep up their dues, the rich and well-to-do members are the ones likely to receive the benefits. These are but specimens of a multitude of similar cases reported in the minutes of the lodges. For such an order to sing in their odes of " drying the widow's tears," etc., etc., is a mockery and profanation, as all sensible Odd-fellows would see if Satan did not blind their minds by his false worships.

DIAGRAM FOR GOLDEN RULE DEGREE.

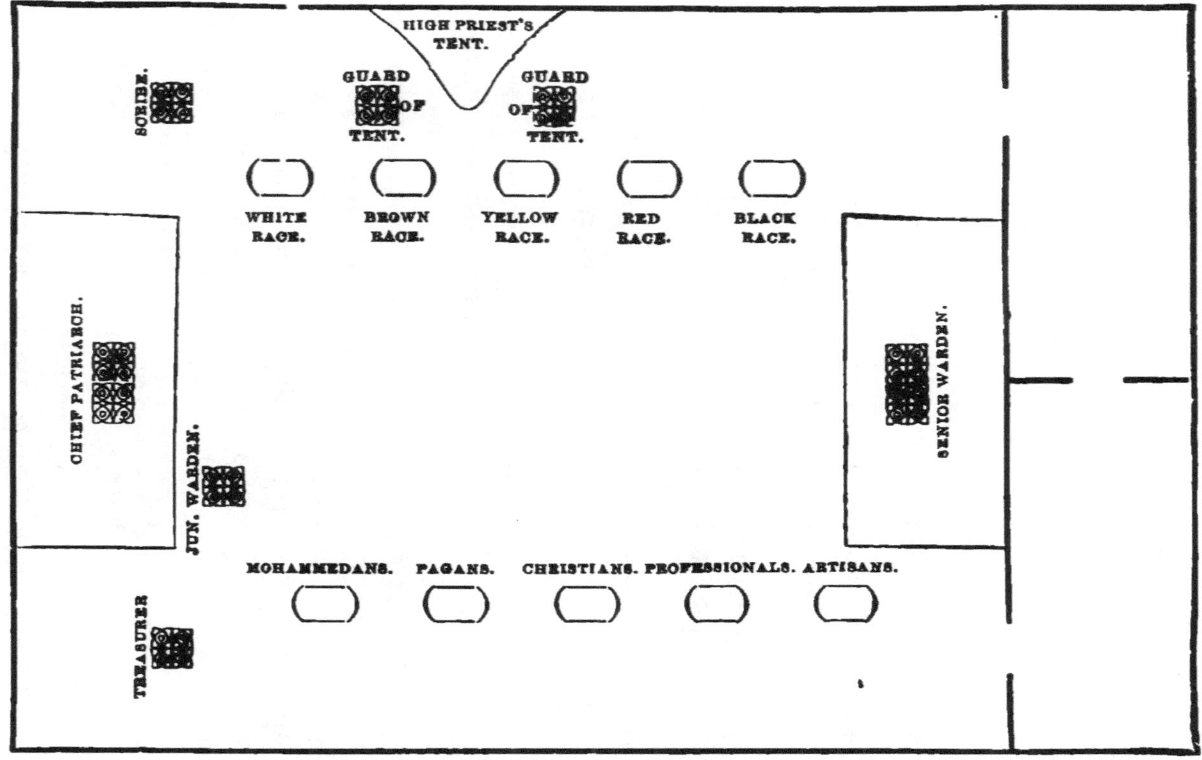

CHAPTER XIII.

Golden Rule, or Second Encampment Degree.

INITIATION.

Any number of candidates may be conducted through all the Parts of this degree. When more than one is initiated the officers will use the plural number instead of the singular of the text.

Junior Warden—[Having retired to the ante-room addresses the candidate there as follows:] You are now to be advanced to the Degree of the Golden Rule. There is a solemn and impressive ceremony through which you must pass. Be candid and firm, and answer truly and without hesitation such questions as may be put to you.

Junior Warden—(three raps).

Inside Sentinel—Who comes there?

Junior Warden—A Patriarch who wishes to be instructed in the Golden Rule.

Inside Sentinel—Is he prepared to learn the mysteries and practice the duties of this degree?

Junior Warden—He has hitherto proved himself a faithful and true man, and I have no doubt he is worthy of further confidence.

Inside Sentinel—He has permission to enter.

The door is opened and the Junior Warden conducts the candidate to the Chief Patriarch.

Junior Warden—Chief Patriarch, I present to you

Patriarch —— ——, who has faithfully served his time
as a herdsman in the field, and has been admitted to the
rank of a Patriarch. He has been instructed to bestow
upon those in want a generous hospitality, and he now
wishes to be taught the principle of TOLERATION.

Chief Patriarch—Patriarch, I congratulate you on
having a desire to comprehend the cardinal virtue of
Odd-fellowship. Practical toleration is one of the
noblest of human actions. The authority of conscience
should be respected in all the relations of life; and our
Order teaches that there should be no discrimination in
the exercise of this right.

Chief Patriarch—Junior Warden, present the Patriarch to the Senior Warden for obligation.

Junior Warden—Senior Warden, by direction of the
Chief Patriarch, I present to you Patriarch —— ——,
who desires to take the obligation of the Golden Rule
Degree.

Senior Warden—Patriarch —— ——, the lesson of
this degree is toleration. It permits others to think
and act according to their convictions of duty. If you
are willing to recognize this principle of action, you
will place yourself in the attitude in which you were
initiated into this Order, and repeat after me the following:

Senior Warden—(two raps, calling up the Encampment).

OBLIGATION.

I, —— ——, do sincerely promise, that I will never
reveal the secrets of the Degree of the Golden Rule to
any one not legally authorized to receive them. And I
do further promise on my sacred honor, that I will truly

endeavor to practice the principles of this **degree.**

Senior Warden—(one rap, seating the Encampment).

Senior Warden—Junior Warden, you will present the Patriarch to the Most Excellent High Priest for further instruction.

Junior Warden—Most Excellent High Priest, I present to you Patriarch —— ——, who has taken the obligation of this degree.

High Priest—Patriarch, you have been taught to recognize as a cardinal virtue the golden rule, which commands us to do unto others as we would have them do unto us. Here we endeavor to inculcate a just observance of those high moral affections and duties for the enforcement of which society can enact no code.

Here no artificial distinctions of nation, sect or tribe are recognized. All stand upon one common level, and are alike entitled to that consideration and regard which each claims for himself. The rule by which we walk is founded upon the immutable truth that all men are brethren: but the code of society regulates the degree of association. From one common source the existence of all is derived, and we are bound to each other by common ties. A nerve of the same life runs through the human race and gives to each an interest in the welfare of all that live. Recognizing as we do this bond of union, the evils that afflict our brother-man become in a measure our own; his misfortunes are our misfortunes, and his sufferings do but increase the pains that shoot through our systems, and render life so feverish and fitful. If we smite him we smite a member of our own body; and if we strike for his blood, our own flesh shall feel the wound. From all this must brotherhood we claim sympathy in distress, truth in intercourse, and full and free toleration. As we claim these for ourselves, and yield them up at the mandate of none, so we are bound freely and fully to accord them to others.

High Priest—Junior Warden, you will retire with the candidate.

Junior Warden and candidate retire to the ante-room, where the candidate is blindfolded, and when the encampment is prepared he is conducted to the door, which is left ajar, and they enter without ceremony.

PART II.

The Patriarchs representing the different races and characters in this degree must dress and act as will truthfully represent the people referred to. They may employ various emblems representing their manners, customs, government, religion, etc.

The Encampment-room may be arranged according to diagram and instructions.

The lights are turned low and the blindfold is removed from candidate.

The First and Second Watches assume the character of Mohammedans, who assault the candidate; and the Third and Fourth Watches represent persons of the candidate's faith, and endeavor to rescue him. In the confusion these four only are to handle the candidate.

SUGGESTED COSTUMES.

The WHITE race: may wear the usual dress.

The BROWN race: a single-breasted frock coat, or a gown of black material, extending below the knees. The dress may be ornamented or plain. Turban of red, or of India-shawl material.

The YELLOW race: the Chinese or other Mongolian dress.

The RED race: the dress of the North American Indian.

The BLACK race: can wear the Nubian or other African dress.

The PAGANS may wear the Chinese, but different from the race costume.

The MOHAMMEDANS can dress as Turks, Arabs or Persians, wearing white turbans or other appropriate covering for the head.

If not convenient, the artisan and professional characters in the diagram, and text explaining them, may be omitted.

Junior Warden (to candidate)—You see before you representatives of the different peoples of the earth.

There is the WHITE RACE, now scattered throughout the world. Its origin was in ancient Asia, the region once occupied by Adam, Noah and Abraham, but now overrun by semi-barbarous hordes as different in religious faith as in manners. Many of them still cling to the ancient worship of Judaism, some to the Crescent and some to the Cross. The religion of the Cross prevails where civilization exists, and yet its devotees are divided into sects as antagonistic in creed as though they were dissimilar in origin.

The BROWN RACE inhabits parts of southern Asia. It is far advanced in the arts and sciences. Its temples of worship are of great splendor, and exhibit architectural skill equaling that of any other people. Its religion is Paganistic; and its social habits are defined by strict and rigid caste.

The YELLOW RACE, consisting of the Mongolians of Asia, are votaries of Pagan rites, according to the teachings of Confucius. For centuries they have given practical evidence of advanced mental power, by the production of handiwork whose mysteries have remained unfathomed by other races.

The RED RACE consists of unlettered savages, roaming through the pathless wilderness, chasing the fleet deer with the quiver and bow. The sun, moon, and the myriads of stars receive their profound adoration as symbols of an eternal Great Spirit.

And there you behold the BLACK RACE. It inhabits, as hordes, the wilds of Africa. In general they are barbarians and monsters in the practice of the most dire rapine; yet some of them are more gentle—as the Nubians, who dwell upon the burning sands of the Equator and dance to the music of a reed beneath the spreading palm.

If the artisan and professional characters are omitted, the following in brackets may be omitted.

[These races are employed to some extent, as artisans, by whose hands are constructed palaces, temples, and all the implements required for man's convenience and mental culture. Some are devoted to the pursuit of letters or the sciences, such as chemistry, geography and astronomy. By their genius and mental power, man is educated and advanced to a higher and better condition.]

In recognition of the Benign Power that created all things, man seeks to honor the Creator by ceremonies of adoration. That group embraces men of different creeds, who are followers of the Christian religion, and there is the Pagan, a worshiper of idols, or of the elements of fire.

And here are the intolerant and persecuting Mohammedans, who are ever ready to immolate the man of another creed upon the altar of their own peculiar faith.

Mohammedan—Of what country are you?

Candidate answers.

Mohammedan—What is your religion?

Candidate answers.

Mohammedans (all hurriedly rise and exclaim)—Seize him! Bind him in chains! Cast him into prison! Put him to the sword! [Or exclamations of similar character].

The Mohammedans all rush to the candidate, and a like number of the candidate's faith rush to defend him—a general confusion ensues. No rough usage to be allowed. He is bound with chains.

Chief Patriarch (one rap, calling to order)—Silence! What means this uproar and confusion?

Instantly each one stands motionless until the Chief Patriarch gives another command.

Junior Warden—The Patriarch having declared that he is ——— and ———,they have seized and bound him.

Chief Patriarch—Junior Warden, bring hither the disturbers of the peace; also the Patriarch.

Junior Warden—Let us proceed to the presence of the Chief Patriarch.

The Mohammedans follow the Junior Warden and candidate, and form a semi-circle in front of the chair of the Chief Patriarch, who rises to his feet.

Chief Patriarch (to the Junior Warden)—Remove the chains which have been imposed by the intolerance of man, and let our brother feel that a code prevails here which tramples on human prejudices,[105] and asserts the high birthright of humanity.

Chief Patriarch (to the candidate)—My friend, be always just and fear not. You have not hesitated when occasion demanded, though surrounded with danger, to avow your principles. This is the solemn duty of every honest man.

Chief Patriarch—Warden, you will proceed in the duties of your office. [Chief Patriarch resumes his seat].

The candidate is again blindfolded and conducted slowly around the room, during which time the representatives of the different races and pursuits of the earth seat themselves among the Patriarchs. The room is again fully lighted.

Junior Warden (on arriving at the chair of the Chief Patriarch)—Chief Patriarch, I present Patriarch ——— —— to you for further instruction.

Chief Patriarch (standing)—Restore him to light. [It is done.]

Chief Patriarch—Patriarch, look around you. Be-

NOTE 105.--"Chinese, Polynesians, Indians, Half-breeds or mixed bloods are not eligible to membership."—*Donaldson's Pocket Companion, p.* 320.

hold the change a few moments have wrought! emblematic of that change which shall occur when the Golden Rule shall have asserted its power and obtained its dominion over the world. The high and impassable barriers that separate man from his fellow-man are broken down. All sit together as brothers in harmony and love. The descendants of Abraham and the followers of the Crescent are commingled with those of the Cross as one happy family,[106] knowing no diversity[107] of faith or creed, and a calm repose has come upon the elements of strife. The spear of the warrior is broken and the sword of the conqueror lies rusting in the scabbard, and discord and contention shall be known no more.

If the following be not sung, the High Priest shall read it:

ODE.

No more shall nation against nation rise,
Nor ardent warriors meet with hateful eyes,
Nor fields with gleaming steel be covered o'er,
The brazen trumpets kindle rage no more,
But useless lances into scythes shall bend,
And the broad falchion in a ploughshare end;
No sigh, no murmur, the wide world shall hear,
From every face be wiped off every tear;
All crimes shall cease, and ancient fraud shall fall,
Returning Justice lift aloft her scale;
Peace o'er the world her olive wand extend,
And white-robed Innocence from heaven descend.

If the preceding be read, then another ode may be sung. During the singing a procession may be formed, including the representatives of the different races, creeds and pursuits of the earth, and pass slowly around the room, the Junior Warden and candidate in the rear. When the last verse of the ode is being

---

Note 106.—" A Lodge or Encampment sometimes presents, in its assemblage of persons of various nations and creeds, a beautiful illustration of the excellency of toleration, and of the possibility of a ' unity of the spirit in the bond of peace' amid a diversity of faith."—*Grosh's Manual, p.* 275.

Note 107.—"Jew or Gentile, Catholic or Protestant, is, as such, welcome to our lodges and our hearts."—*Donaldson's Pocket Companion, p.* 291.

sung, the Junior Warden and candidate retire to the ante-room, where the candidate is blindfolded, and when the Encampment is prepared he is conducted to the door, which is open, and they enter without ceremony.

PART III.

After the candidate has retired, order is restored. All wear the usual regalia. Officers resume their stations.

Junior Warden (proceeding with the candidate to the chair of the Chief Patriarch)—I present to you Patriarch —— ——, who desires final instructions in the Golden Rule

Chief Patriarch—Patriarch, it is now my duty to instruct you in the mysteries of this degree.

In this degree there is an Alarm at the inner door, or Entersign, a Password and Explanation of the Password, a Sign and Answer to the Sign, a Check Sign and Answer and a Grip.

THE ALARM at the inner door is two raps

THE PASSWORD is A. M., to be lettered at all times when used for working purposes; working into an En-

Sign of Golden
Rule Degree.

campment or in examination prior to opening. In communicating this password either to the Inside Sentinel or Junior Warden the Patriarch must give the letter A, and if required by the Inside Sentinel or Junior Warden, he must give the remaining letter M. The Inside Sentinel and Junior Warden must be satisfied. The Explanation of the Password is, Gold a Metal, given in full, but not used for working purposes.

The CHECK SIGN and Answer are made the same as in the Patriarchal Degree.

SIGN.

Press the elbow of the right arm to the side, close the right hand, thumb over fingers; extend the index finger; when extended raise the arm from the elbow in a perpendicular direction; drop the arm in front, the index finger pointing to the ground. The Answer is the same as the Sign.

GRIP.

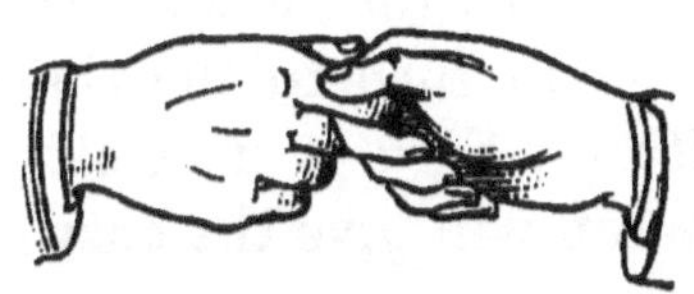

With the index finger of the right hand form a link at the second joint, and with the ball of the thumb press the back of the index finger of the Patriarch forming the link with you, between the knuckle and second joint. No shaking hands in making the Grip.

INSTRUCTIONS TO CANDIDATE.

Chief Patriarch (to candidate)—Desirous of being admitted to an Encampment, you will give at the outer door the same alarm as in the Subordinate Lodge. [One rap, or one pull of the bell, if there is one]. The Outside Sentinel will open the wicket, and require of you the Check Password of the term [which is given in full]. If correct, he will admit you to the ante-room. You will then clothe yourself in regalia appropriate to your rank and station, and, after ascertaining from the Outside Sentinel that the Encampment is open in the Golden Rule Degree, you will give two raps at the inner door, when the Inside Sentinel will open the wicket, and obtain from you your name, rank, and the number of the Encampment to which you belong, which he will report to the Chief Patriarch, who will instruct him to admit you, if correct. The wicket is again opened, when you will be required to give the Password of the Golden Rule Degree [lettered]. If correct you will be admitted, and will advance to the center of the room, and address the Chief Patriarch with the Check Sign. The Chief Patriarch will acknowledge you as a Patriarch with the Answer to the Check Sign. You will then turn and address the Senior Warden with the Check Sign, who will acknowledge you as a Patriarch with the answer to the Check Sign. You will again turn to the Chief Patriarch and address him with the Sign of the Golden Rule Degree; the Chief Patriarch will give the answer to the sign.

On leaving the Encampment before it is closed, you will address the Chief Patriarch only, with the Sign of the Golden Rule Degree, and that officer will answer you with the appropriate sign.

The Chief Patriarch should carefully instruct the candidate in the method of using the password, in working into an Encampment, and in examination prior to opening.

Chief Patriarch—Junior Warden, you will now present the Patriarch to the Most Execllent High Priest for further instruction.

Junior Warden—Most Excellent High Priest, by direction of the Chief Patriarch, I present to you Patriarch —— ——, for further instruction in this degree.

High Priest—Patriarch, the scene that has been presented to you illustrates an era[108] for which kings and patriarchs waited and sought, but never found. We trust that the lessons of this occasion will be deeply engraven on your heart. The ceremonies you have witnessed are especially designed to impress you with the great principle of Toleration. In the present condition of mankind, owing to the prejudices of education or habit, it cannot be expected that men should think alike. This is philosophically impossible. But,

---

Note 108.—''The authority of conscience in religion must be paramount. Those high moral affections and duties which have the Creator as their object, no human legislation can or should restrain or suppress. In our Tents no sectarian or national distinctions are recognized.''—*Grosh's Manual*, ` 272.

honest in our own opinions, we should accord the same honesty to others; and, while we should in no instance tolerate licentiousness or vice, we should overlook all differences of a minor nature which may divide us from our brethren, and cordially unite with the virtuous and good, irrespective of country, religion[109] or politics, in the discharge of those duties which all agree to be paramount. As a brother of this sublime degree, it is expected that you will always act upon the Golden Rule, doing unto others as you would have them under similar circumstances do unto you. Thus will you co-operate with the great mission of Odd-fellowship and hasten the period when man shall hail his brother-man with fraternal greetings; when falsehood shall be driven from the earth, and the race of man form a universal family acknowledging the God of the Universe as Father, and every child of man as a brother.

High Priest—Junior Warden, you will present the Patriarch to the Chief Patriarch.

An ode may be sung and a procession formed, to move around the room during the singing.

After the ode the Junior Warden presents the candidate before the Chief Patriarch.

Junior Warden—Chief Patriarch, by direction of the High Priest, I present to you Patriarch ———— ————.

Chief Patriarch—Recognizing you as a Patriarch of the Golden Rule, the Junior Warden will invest you with a black apron trimmed with yellow, emblematical of this degree. [An apron is placed upon the candi-

---

Note 109.—"During the years 1877, 1878 and 1879, we have lost from our fold 15,342 members, reducing the grand aggregate from 456,125 active Odd-fellows in 1876, to 440,783 in 1879, yet there is no cause for despondency, our annual loss from 8106 in 1877 having been reduced to 1508 in 1879."—*Journal of Proceedings Sovereign Grand Lodge, Session of* 1880, *p.* 8260.

date]. Patriarch —— ——, in the name and by the authority of the Independent Order of Odd-fellows, I declare you duly advanced as a Patriarch of the Golden Rule Degree.

ANALYSIS GOLDEN RULE DEGREE.

The Real and Professed Object of this Degree—The Unity of Christianity Mocked—Union of Idolatrous Religions in Malice Against Christ—Bald Hypocrisy—Excluding Nineteen-twentieths of the Race and then Pretending to Unify Mankind—Teaches that '' All Mankind are Brethren,'' while Admitting only White Men of Sound Health, Able-Bodied and Between Certain Ages—The Lie Acted Out in the Lodge—Intolerance—Christianity having Secured Toleration, Odd-fellowship Claims the Glory of it—The Success of such Swindling Pretenses Explained—Little Orders Short Lived—The Falsehood and Frivolity of Odd-fellowship its Protection—The Ancient Oracles—The Philosophy of the Power of Secretism—The Religion of Odd-fellowship the Religion of Masonry—Denies the Distinction Between the Righteous and the Wicked—The Bible Quoted in Confutation of Itself.

The professed object of this degree is to teach " *the principle of* TOLERATION." *(See ritual, p. 187.)* The *real* object, as of Odd-fellowship throughout, is to hold up Christ's religion to contempt, by concealing its unity and exposing its dissensions and divisions, and claiming superiority for the motley and many-hued religions of Satan over that of Christ.

The object and end of Christianity as taught by Christ himself is, " That they all may be one: as thou, Father, art in me, and I in thee; that they also may be one in us."—*John 17 : 21.*

To checkmate and foil this magnificently sublime picture of the spiritual oneness of all God's children, through " one Mediator " and " one Spirit," with the infinite God himself—and thus counteract the moral effect, on the intellects of other worlds gazing on God's redemption in this, of a cone of spiritual oneness, based on regenerated souls and hiding its apex in the infinity

which veils God's throne, the lodge religions, various
as the dress of Otway's " Old Woman "—

" Whose patchwork robe but shows variety of wretchedness,"

must needs have a mock unity of their own.

And yet their unity, like the vaunted unity of
drunkards in their cups, is all the time ending in
brawls. They are truly one only in their malice against
Christ: and their malice is excelled by their bald hypocrisy. Take this Golden Rule Degree as a specimen. They
meet as a sect or lodge which excludes more than nineteen-twentieths of mankind. They admit only " free
white males " over twenty-one and under sixty, and
those only when hale and able-bodied; and with this
badgered, blindfolded and bewildered handful of humanity they set themselves to unify mankind. They cant
and deplore over the sects of Christianity, and teach
their own little sect, divided from other secret sects
and the outside world by walls of secrecy, and excluding
all who inherit the least tinge of brown or yellow in
their complexion, they boast *(see note 105, p. 192.)*:
" Here no artificial distinctions of nation, sect, or tribe
are known! "

To utter such lofty falsehoods must require the brazen tongue and brow of the hypocrite. Yet they
insist, " The rule by which we walk is founded upon the
immutable truth that all mankind are brethren." *(Ritual, p. 188.)* And this fearful untruth is uttered of an
order where, on the face of it, the single word " free,"
defining its membership, excludes millions of unhappy
slaves.

The degree then proceeds to *act* the lie which it had
uttered. To do this they dress up some members of
their lodge as Turks, and when the blindfolded candidate
answers that he is not a Mohammedan, but of another

creed, then the turbaned Turks seize and chain him. *The Chief Patriarch* (that is to say, Odd-fellowship), then loftily commands: " Remove the chains which have been imposed by the intolerance of man ."—*Ritual*, *p. 192.*

Now this play is a slander on the Turks. There are now Armenian students in Wheaton College whose Turkish rulers and neighbors *tolerated* them at home even after they became Christians in the American sense. So so our missionaries are tolerated by the Asiatic and African races.

Thus when the benign hand of Christianity has pulled down the Chinese walls of intolerance; while Fanny Wright, Victoria Woodhull, and the Ingersolls and even Mormons are tolerated, while they abstain from the crimes of polygamy and assassinations which they teach, forth steps this spruce Order of Odd-fellowship, and, excluding from its " brotherhood " nineteen-twentieths of the human race, proclaims that all "mankind are brethren;" sneers at Christianity as intolerant, and invites to its religious brotherhood all who can pay their dues, and keeps them in its world-wide fellowship until poverty or misfortune has made them no longer able to keep them paid.

" Oh, what authority and show of truth
Can cunning sin cover itself withal."—*Shakespeare.*

The success of such swindling pretenses—so thin and self-contradictory throughout—is owing to one single fact, viz., the toiling masses of Papists, Mormons and members of secret orders read little and reason less. There are probably not one hundred Odd-fellows of the hundred thousands who can, to-day, repeat without prompting the whole of their ritual of near two-hundred pages. The little secret orders are short-lived. The permanent ones are those enlarged by additions at the top, until the honest and industrious who " have visible means of support" can not learn the rituals; and the lodges are thus managed by depraved and hardened men, who make secret orders their trade.

The falsehood and frivolity of Odd-fellowship are its protection.   Sensible people cannot believe a system so shallow and self-contradictory can be very dangerous. The leading Roman and Greek oracles were equally puerile and contemptible.   Cicero said he could not see how one augur or priest of the mysteries could meet another in the street " without laughing each other in the face."   Some of the most popular Grecian oracles " owed their celebrity to exhilarating or stupefying gases issuing from subterranean caverns."   Yet the wealth which they accumulated was, like the funds of Odd-fellowship, fabulous.   " One hundred and seventeen tiles of gold were presented to one of these oracles by a single man.—*Stowe's Int., p. 177.*

The philosophy of their power over mind is in the fact that they are each *a counterfeit salvation.*   The prayer at the dedication of a cemetery asks the lodge god to " purify our hearts, elevate our desires, and fit us for thy service."   And the Grand Master assures the Odd-fellows that over their " departed dwells ever the bright halo of the hope of a glorious resurrection."— *Grosh, pp. 374, 375.*

And this Golden Rule Degree assures the brethren that " Confessions of faith " are mere " differences of opinion."   *"Followers of different teachers, ye are worshipers of one God, who is Father of all, and therefore ye are brethren."*

That is, theirs is the Masonic religion, in which all mankind agree :   and every reflecting child must understand that the god of this religion is the god and " prince of this world."   Each new degree is but a new modification and statement of this religion.

CHAPTER XIV.

Royal Purple, or Third Encampment Degree.

Part I.

INSTRUCTIONS.

Chief Patriarch, should have a purple gown, yellow belt, yellow and black turban and a crook.

High Priest, should wear a robe made of royal purple fabric, a white surplice of muslin, linen or silk, together with a mitre and breastplate.

SPECIALS.

1. Every fixture should have in view its use, so as not to injure or be offensive to the candidate.

2. All fast walking, rushing or rough usage of the candidate is forbidden.

3. The bridge should be at least two feet wide, with rough poles as railings, and it should be level with the roadway or floor.

4. Rough road to be of stone, pieces of wood, stumps, limbs of trees or brushwood.

5. A railing may be used to guide the candidate over the rough road. The guide in advance, seemingly passes over it.

Any number of candidates may be conducted through parts I and III of this degree. When more than one, the officers will add the plural number to the text.

Junior Warden—(with the candidate—two raps on inside door.)

Inside Sentinel—Who comes there?

Junior Warden—The Junior Warden, with a Patriarch who has served as a herdsman on the mountains of Horeb and in the wilderness of Paran, has suffered persecution by the prejudices of selfish and bigoted men, and now seeks further instruction, teaching him the good and evil that beset the pathway of life.

Inside Sentinel—Enter. Your appeal shall not be in vain.

The Junior Warden leads the candidate around the room, and they finally reach the Senior Warden's chair. While passing around the Junior Warden says:

Junior Warden—Patriarch, you are now about to receive the last degree of Patriarchal Odd-fellowship. Thus far in your progress through the Order, each degree has illustrated morals that will, if observed by you, give ultimate rest. Here is the Senior Warden, let us seek his advice.

Junior Warden—Senior Warden, I present to you Patriarch —— ——, who has served as a novitiate on the mountains and in the wilderness with the herds, has been assailed and has suffered for his religious faith, and he now hopes among the Patriarchs to find rest.

Senior Warden—Rest? Knows he not there is no rest but one? That once launched on life's broad wilderness, thenceforward all is turmoil even from the cradle to the grave? Rest cannot be found on earth. Behold the joyous child basking in affection's sun, its careless hours are each beguiled with some new hope or beauty. See, next, the gladsome youth—his ardent heart, deep filled with young ambition's fires, is ever mounting to some new achievement. Then view manhood's loftier state, and mark through what immensity of danger, toil and strife he struggles on to reach some wished-for, though imaginary, goal. Thus it is ever. Proud aspiration and never-ending hope lure on man's restless spirit, until exhausted nature sinks, and the weary body finds repose beneath its kindred earth.

Junior Warden—Nay, but my friend is sound of body and of mind. The world is before him, tempting his stern energy; and he has confidence to stem its wild and reckless torrent, shunning the rocks and whirlpools which have proved the wreck of others' hopes.

Senior Warden—I am glad to hear of his laudable ambition to enter upon the career of life, with a determination to avoid the errors that have destroyed the hopes and usefulness of others. Animated by such a sentiment he will ever have the encouragement of good men, and the commendation of his God. What assistance, Junior Warden, can we give the brother?

Junior Warden—The protection of the Patriarchs of the Royal Purple Degree.

Senior Warden—That being your wish, my brother, I will administer to you the obligation of this, the highest degree of Patriarchal Odd-fellowship. You will place yourself in the attitude in which you were initiated, and repeat after me the following obligation.

Senior Warden—(two raps, calling up the Encampment).

OBLIGATION.

I, ——— ———, do solemnly promise, in the presence of

the witnesses here assembled, that I will never improperly disclose or make known to any person, by any means whatever, any of the signs, passwords or mysteries of the Royal Purple Degree, or those of any other of the Patriarchal degrees of the Independent Order of Odd-fellows. I also promise to obey all legal summonses that may be issued by authority of any Encampment to which I may belong. I also promise that I will not write, print or indite, in any manner or for any purpose, any of the written or unwritten work or mysteries of this degree, or of any other degree which I have received in this Order. For the faithful performance of all which, I pledge my sacred honor.

Senior Warden—(one rap, seating the Encampment).

Senior Warden—You are now an obligated Royal Purple Degree member of this Order. I need not add more than to call your attention to the moral teachings of the preceding degrees.

Senior Warden—Junior Warden. you will retire with the candidate to the ante-room, and prepare him for further instructions.

Junior Warden and candidate retire to the ante-room, where the candidate is blindfolded and a short dark gown placed upon him.

PART II.

In part II the official stations may be vacated, excepting the Senior Warden's, and that officer can have charge of the Encampment.
Encampment-room is prepared, darkened, and order restored.

Junior Warden—(with candidate at inside door—two raps).

But one candidate at a time can proceed through part II.

Inside Sentinel—Who comes there?

Junior Warden—The Junior Warden, with a friend

who wishes to make the journey to the Most Excellent High Priest.

Inside Sentinel—He may enter, but he must beware of pretended friends. [Candidate is conducted to chair of Senior Warden].

Junior Warden—Senior Warden, I present to you a brother Odd-fellow, who has become an obligated Patriarch. He wishes to make the journey to the Most Excellent High Priest.

Senior Warden—Is he aware of the difficulties he will meet in the journey before him?

Junior Warden—He is not; but he is prepared to meet them, and he has faith in his ultimate success.

Senior Warden—Then let him onward. *Go on!* Be that the word—even the countersign. Go on! But give him safe guidance and the best protection. I should think, Junior Warden, that you are too inexperienced to conduct the brother along the difficult pathway of life.

Junior Warden—There is a Guide near by, who is by good habits well qualified to conduct the brother, so as to shun all places of vice and men of evil habits. This Guide has been a sinful man, but now he is willing by industry and example, to make atonement for the errors of his past life.

Senior Warden—Place him in charge then, and remember the word—Go on.

Junior Warden—Halloo! Halloo! Guide of the wilderness!

Guide—Who comes there?

Junior Warden—A pilgrim awaits you.

Guide approaches the Senior Warden's cha''.

Junior Warden (to Senior Warden)—Here comes the Guide, who will conduct the brother safely through the wilderness.

Senior Warden—Guide, in taking care of this brother you assume a great responsibility. Be sure that you warn him of all dangerous places, so that he will be benefited by the light of your experience.

Guide—I will prove to him a faithful companion. Intrusted to me I will conduct him safely. But is he prepared for the hard, uncertain fare that awaits him by the way?

Junior Warden—No, except through mere intimation; but you can advise him as you proceed.

Guide—Well, be it so. We must take our leave, for we have a long and toilsome journey to perform.

Junior Warden—My friend, give me your hand. Here we part, and may never meet again. You have, as through life, a rugged journey before you. It is beset with difficulties; you must meet them with confidence and courage. Be not too hasty in forming opinions against the one having you in charge. Farewell, my brother. [They bid adieu.]

Guide—You are safe with me, my friend, though if you hear me spoken of, no terms of flattery will be used, as you will find. Be cautious now—we are near the First Watch, an unerring indication of our onward progress.

First Watch—Hold! How entered you the wilderness?

Guide—Lawfully.

First Watch—Have you the countersign?

Guide—Yes, or rather my pilgrim has.

First Watch—Your pilgrim! Who intrusted him to you?

Guide—His friend, and he did well.

First Watch—I have seen such as you before, and know you think so; yet many have been led astray on this route. But now to talk is profitless. Stranger, give me the word.

Candidate—Go on.

First Watch—Ay, go on—and beware how you tread. The way is encompassed with difficulties. On the one hand is a straight and narrow path, presenting a toilsome and laborious progress; while on the other your safety is hourly endangered in a broad and expansive plain, beautiful to the sight, but abounding with infections the most poisonous and destructive to human happiness. Death, in its most frightful shapes, lurks constantly by the wayside. May heaven grant you safe deliverance.

Guide—Come, my pilgrim, you must have confidence; be not alarmed by the words of that man. Here the pathway is narrow.

Make this pathway by two poles about waist high, but not close enough to make the walk between them unpleasant.

Guide—We here meet an impediment such as too often discourages a timorous spirit. But press on, be not dismayed. And now [entering the woods] we seem encircled by a wild and dismal thicket. The living here is very bad, for the traveler is often in want of water as well as bread. But here is the Second Watch, another index of our progress.

Second Watch—Stand! What is your object in entering this wilderness?

Guide—It is decreed that we shall travel through it.

Second Watch—Have you passed the First Watch?

Guide—Yes, he directed us to go on.

Second Watch—Then I will not detain you, except merely to admonish the pilgrim that, as the road grows rougher, he be not tempted to seek momentary ease at the expense of future pain and sorrow. A single aberration may tarnish and forever overcast a rash though well-meaning spirit. One false step may cost a limb, or even life itself. Beware, then, that you plunge not down some dark and deep abyss, involving disaster the most sad and irreparable. Beware how you proceed.

Guide—Come, let us go. We can make our way. [Pausing.] Yet, how strangely varied are the paths before us. [Merriment, seeming to be distant.] Hark! Heard you the voice of mirth and revelry? How fascinating, how easy of access is the path that leads that way. Yet it is beset with dangers. Lust, intemperance, sensuality—vice, in all its odious forms and all its horrors, lies deep concealed beneath tempting blandishments. We must not be deceived. [The clash of arms heard at a distance.] There, again! from a different direction come the clang of arms and sounds of deadly strife—a sad display of worldly glory, where cruel war tramples meek humanity in the dust. It is the stern warrior's sport to gratify the statesman's proud ambition. Fame would tempt us on, but we must keep aloof, lest we be slain, or, surviving, imbibe the same fell spirit of destruction. No, we will not turn aside, either for fleeting pleasures or the soldier's honors. They who till the soil or ply the loom and hammer are far more happy. There surely is some good in store for us. We will cross this rugged path and see what lies beyond. [Passing the ruins or other rough place]. Ah! what is this? It is the ruins of an old castle where pomp and vanity once held sway. Can we already have come so far? How quick time flies! I see by the waning light through the dense forest before us that our course lies around a steep declivity, beyond which will terminate our pilgrimage. Be careful, and not too hasty.

Third Watch—Stand! Whence come you?

Guide—Through the wilderness.

Third Watch—And passed the Watches?

Guide—Yes. Informed of our purpose, they bade us go on.

Third Watch—You have done well in arriving at this Watch, for ere they get thus far on their journey, many sink by the wayside, overcome with difficulties which they cannot surmount. You are now far advanced, though some troubles, such as you have passed, still appear in the distance. There is yet another Watch, whom many have tried in vain to reach. You must be careful when you get to the river Jordan. The recent rains have raised the water almost to the bridge, and you may not be able to cross. The stream there is very deep and rapid; be careful, therefore, and follow your Guide. While his reputation is said by some to be bad, he was never known to be unfaithful to a pilgrim placed in his care. Go on—my best wishes attend you.

Guide—Yes, we will go from such a comforter as this; but so it is all along this road, and no one can ever judge of his treatment till he reach its end, and then, alas! it is too late. Our progress, however, should be more calm, much less exciting, and with our present experience, more free from danger. Your eyes are covered for your good; all who travel here are blinded; they neither see nor know what may befall them. A sudden change has come upon the air, indicative of an approaching storm. [Thunders.] It is near us, but we have naught to fear. Let us pause beneath this oak tree until the rain is over. How strangely significant, for the oak is the symbol of hospitality! [Pause.] We will now proceed, for I see in the heavens the bright rainbow of promise, reminding us that we are under the protection of a covenant-keeping Father, whose goodness is effectual to dispel the wretchedness of man.

But here we are at the river. It is very high and muddy. I am afraid we cannot cross, and it is dangerous for us to stay here at night, as beasts of prey infest these woodlands. We must venture to cross on this bridge. I will go before you. Hold to the side supports, and be careful. Fear not! [They cross the bridge.] We are now over the worst of our journey. But here is the Fourth Watch.

Fourth Watch—Hold! How far have you come?

Guide—Through the wilderness, traveling by night as well as by day.

Fourth Watch—Pilgrim, I congratulate you on having journeyed so far with such a Guide.

Guide—He that has experienced my care is best qualified to judge of me. Good or bad, few would desire to try the journey over again, even could they endure its fatigue.

Fourth Watch—I merely apprised the pilgrim of the

company he is in. I am rejoiced at his arrival, and, if admitted to the society of just men, he will find the way more pleasant, and the paths more smooth.

Guide—I suppose, pilgrim, you think it very strange that all these Watches tell you of my bad character. You will see that it is prejudice. If a man commits an error, some people ean neither forgive nor forget it, nor consider the beam in their own eyes. This last Watch has given me the credit of not neglecting a pilgrim placed in my charge, and that is all that you require.

We must pass on, for night is approaching.

After walking a few moments, music is heard in the distance and continues to be heard until it dies away to the ear. This music may be instrumental or vocal. It should be dignified.

Guide—Hark! I hear music. How sweet those notes! They soothe the heart and fill it with aspirations for the eternal home. Let us pause for a while, and learn the cause for such a charm in these solitudes. Oh! I see people full of joy coming this way. They are harvesters. They have finished their work, and are now keeping their annual festival. We have passed all danger, and soon shall be at the end of our journey. You have escaped bad company and journeyed safely through dangerous places. Ho! here we are at the High Priest's tent, and we are safe.

Guide—Guards of the Tent, I have a pilgrim, who desires to see the high Priest.

First Guard—Most Excellent High Priest, a pilgrim has arrived, and desires your blessing.

High Priest—Present the pilgrim. [He is presented.] Restore him to light. [Blindfold is removed.]

If there be other candidates, the candidate may be seated until the last one shall have reached this point; then all will be presented to the High Priest, when he will proceed.

High Priest—Patriarch, I welcome you to this temple of our Order. Your progress hither may have appeared tedious, but we trust that the lessons you have gathered by the way will prove profitable. All human excellence is the reward of perseverance, toil, and danger, such as we have endeavored to picture to the imagination in the mimic journey of life through which you have been conducted—a scene that has not been rehearsed for idle amusement, but to awaken rational meditation in a mind as mature as yours. The uncertainties of life are ever present to the understanding of considerate men. Literally blindfold, and beset on every side with danger and temptation, we struggle through this earthly pilgrimage. With desires never gratified, we are the subjects of endless toil and care, of never-ceasing hope and never-ending disappointment. The false and flattering charms, which in the distance so attract our admiration, disappear the moment they are placed within our reach. Frail mortals that we are, we know not what a day or an hour may bring forth. Encompassed with peril on every side, with the seeds of disease implanted in our nature, and the very air we breathe impregnated with death, all the promises of life are but dust. They fade as a leaf, and pass as the shadow that fleeth away. How essential, then, that we should understand our true position, and keep constantly in view the realities that surround us! How essential that we should learn to practice those living and immortal virtues, which, while they secure ultimate happiness, contribute so largely to smooth the troubles and soften the asperities of life!

High Priest—Junior Warden, you will retire with

candidate, and, after having prepared him, re-enter and present him to the Chief Patriarch for further instructions.

They retire. The room is restored to order, and the officers, in proper costume or regalia, resume their respective stations.

If there be more than one candidate, each, after receiving part II, may remain in the room until the last shall have passed through that part, and then retire to re-enter with the last candidate for instruction in part III.

PART III.

The door being open, the Junior Warden re-enters with the candidate and proceeds to the chair of the Chief Patriarch.

Junior Warden—By direction of the Most Excellent High Priest, I present to you Patriarch —— —— for further instruction.

Chief Patriarch—Patriarch, in congratulating you on your elevation to the highest rank in this Order, it would be useless for me to attempt to add a word to the moral instruction which has been already bestowed upon you. If this instruction shall have served to impress your mind with a train of moral thought, founded in principles the most pure and exalted, our labor will not have been in vain, your time will not have been wasted, and neither you nor your brethren will have cause to regret your connection with our fraternity. We earnestly hope that such may be the case, and that, as your mind shall advance in the progress of calm investigation, it may be continually blessed with a brighter and yet stronger light, until it realizes the fruition of all its earthly desires, and the care-worn man shall have bowed him down before his God.

Patriarch, it is now my duty to instruct you in the mysteries of this degree.

In this degree there is an Alarm at the inner door, or Entersign, a Password, an Explanation of the Password and Interpretation of the Password, a Check Sign and Answer to the Check Sign, and a Grip.

THE ALARM at the inner door is two raps.

THE PASSWORD is M. K., to be lettered at all times when used for working purposes; working into an Encampment or in examination prior to opening. In communicating this password either to the Inside Sentinel or Junior Warden, the Patriarch must give the letter M, and if required by the Inside Sentinel or Junior Warden he must give the remaining letter K. The Inside Sentinel and Junior Warden must be satisfied. The Explanation of the Password is K. S. The Interpretation is Melchizedek, King of Salem, both given in full, but not used for working purposes.

The CHECK SIGN and Answer are made the same as in the former Encampment degrees.

SIGN.

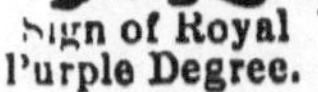

Sign of Royal Purple Degree.

Conceal the last two fingers of the right hand in the palm thereof; place the first two fingers and thumb together, ends touching, and with them trace a line from the left side of the brow to the centre of the forehead; then drop the hand to the side.

Answer.—With the left hand arranged as in Sign, trace a similar line from the right side of the brow to the centre of the forehead, then drop the hand to the side.

GRIP.

Each Patriarch will grasp the index finger of the other's right hand, with the ball of the thumb across the knuckle joint on the back of the hand. No shaking hands in making the Grip.

Chief Patriarch (to candidate)—Desirous of being

admitted to an Encampment, you will give at the outer door the same Alarm as in the Subordinate Lodge. [One rap or ring of the bell]. The Outside Sentinel will open the wicket and require of you the Check Password of the term [which is given in full]. If correct, he will admit you to the ante-room. You will then clothe yourself in regalia appropriate to your rank and station, and, after ascertaining from the Outside Sentinel that the Encampment is open in the Royal Purple Degree, you will give two raps at the inner door, when the Inside Sentinel will open the wicket and obtain from you your name, rank and number of the Encampment to which you belong, which he will report to the Chief Patriarch, who will instruct him to admit you, if correct. The wicket is again opened, when you will be required to give the Password of the Royal Purple Degree [lettered]. If correct you will be admitted, and will advance to the center of the room and address the Chief Patriarch with the Check Sign. The Chief Patriarch will acknowledge you as a Patriarch with the Answer to the Check Sign. You will then turn and address the Senior Warden with the Check Sign, who will also acknowledge you as a Patriarch with the Answer to the Check Sign. You will again turn to the Chief Patriarch and address him with the Sign of the Royal Purple Degree; the Chief Patriarch will give the proper answer to the Sign.

On leaving the Encampment before it is closed, you will address the Chief Patriarch, only, with the Sign of the Royal Purple Degree, and that officer will make the Answer to the Sign. You will then obtain from the Senior Warden the Password of the evening [which is only used in this degree], which must be given to the

Inside Sentinel before he will allow you to depart. Should you wish to re-enter the Encampment the same evening, you may use the Password of the evening, or the Password of this degree, for that purpose.

The Chief Patriarch should carefully instruct the candidate in the method of using the Password in working into an Encampment, and in examination prior to opening.

Chief Patriarch—Junior Warden, conduct the candidate to the Most Excellent High Priest for further instruction.

Junior Warden—Most Excellent High Priest, by direction of the Chief Patriarch I present to you Patriarch —— —— for further instruction.

High Priest—Patriarch, I will now instruct you in the signification of the emblems belonging to the Patriarchal Order.

The candidate may be seated.

A chart containing the emblems is placed near the High Priest, and the Junior Warden will point out to the candidate each emblem as it is being described.

THE THREE PILLARS.[110]

The Three Pillars represent Faith, Hope and Charity; but the greatest of these is Charity. Although we may possess all other virtues, if we are destitute of charity we are but as sounding brass or a tinkling cymbal. As symbols the Three Pillars direct to an enlightened faith in God, the Father of Spirits, the Maker and Preserver of the Universe, and impress upon us the importance of always wearing the mantle of Charity and Brotherly Love.

Note 110.—"The Three Pillars. *Emblems of Faith, Hope, Charity:*— the Wisdom, Strength, and Beauty of Religion, and the supports and ornaments of our Temple of Universal Brotherhood.

"Every time we enter an Encampment they remind us of the Wisdom of humility, the Strength of trust, and the Beauty of kindness which brought us to the emblematic Tent, and before its solemn altar. And they teach us to cherish and cultivate these treasures and virtues of the soul, by an observance of the Great Law of duty to God, duty to our neighbor, and duty to ourselves."— *Grosh's Manual, p. 268.*

THE TENT.[111]

The patriarchs dwelt in tents, and esteemed hospitality as one of the greatest of virtues; to them costly mansions were not necessary to acts of humanity. The sympathizing heart will provide the cooling draught and shelter for the stranger  in the humblest places of abode; without it they cannot be found within palace gates.

THE PILGRIM'S SCRIP, SANDALS ND STAFF.—These emblems symbolize the journey of life. The Scrip to contain the food, the Sandals to protect the feet, and the Staff to support the wearied limbs. How much more important to make provision for a journey which begins in infancy, lasts through life, and ends in death; for all beyond three score years and ten are but labor and sorrow. We soon pass away and are gone; and be your journey long or short, let it be guided by well-

---

NOTE 111.—"THE TENT. *Emblem of Hospitality:*—the *peculiar* emblem of this degree. It is always represented open, to remind us that when we needed hospitality we found it, and should, therefore, be ready to grant it when needed by others. But while it is our duty, and should be our pleasure to 'entertain strangers,' we are admonished that we owe it to ourselves and our families to admit 'no enemy in disguise'—no treacherous or vicious person, to our homes and our bosoms.

"This emblem discourses 'to us of the ancient patriarchs, who abode in tents;' and teaches us, 'that in this world we have no continuing city,' but are 'pilgrims and sojourners' who seek one to come. 'Soon will our earthly tents be struck, and we pass beyond the swelling waters.'

> "'Here, in this body pent,
> Absent from heaven I roam,
> Yet nightly pitch my tent
> A day's march nearer home.'"
> —*Grosh's Manual, p. 257.*

regulated industry, perseverance in all good works and a humble reliance upon God.

THE ALTAR OF SACRIFICE.—The Altar of Sacrifice symbolizes Faith in God, and obedience to his commands, and implies that no sacrifice is too great for the creature to please the Creator. Self-denial and submission are constantly recurring events in a virtuous life, and when called upon you should not hesitate to sacrifice comfort and personal gratification upon the altar of duty.

THE TABLES OF STONE,[112] CRESCENT AND CROSS.

The Tables of Stone. the Crescent and the Cross, are

symbols that signify to an Odd-fellow Universal Toleration. In works of humanity all differences in politics, creeds, or worship should be forgotten. THE TA-

---

NOTE 112.—"THE TABLES OF THE LAW. *Emblem of Divine Government:* —It represents the common basis of the three great religions of the world (Judaism, Christianity, Mohammedanism) which recognize the One, only living and True God—and the foundation of all governments which acknowledge God as the Ruler of nations, and the interests and welfare of the human race as their end and aim. This Law is a constantly operating fact in the progress of religions and of human governments among men, teaching us faith and trust in the Divine Ruler.

" This common basis of religion and of morals teaches Christians that having received so much through the Jew, they may well bear with his supposed deficiency until they can impart to him again—and the Moslem, that the foundation on which he stands is also the common ground of the others—and the Jew, as his Law progresses among the nations, moulding legislation and elevating morality, even while he is without a national home, it instructs in patience and in hope, and to follow with his love wheresoever his Law goes in blessing and in triumph.

" Followers of different Teachers, ye are worshipers of One God, who is Father of all, and *therefore ye are brethren!* As such, Charity, and speaking the truth in love, should prevail among us—*unity* in *good works*, wherein *all* agree; *toleration* in *opinions*, wherein we differ."—*Grosh's Manual, p.* 280.

BLES OF STONE, with the moral law written upon them, present a common basis of worship and pure morality for all mankind. They teach that God is our Father, and we are brethren. Let the Golden Rule prevail, and whatsoever ye would that men should do to you, do ye even so to them.

THE ALTAR OF INCENSE.[113]

The Altar of Incense reminds us of the rude altar of the patriarchs, and of the simplicity of that true worship which the Ruler of the Universe requires of his intelligent creatures: no costly oblation, no rendering of the fruit of the body for the sin of the soul—but to act justly, love mercy, and walk humbly

NOTE 113.—"THE ALTAR OF INCENSE. *Emblem of Worship:*—the *peculiar* emblem of this degree. It represents the universality of the spiritual instinct in men to 'seek the Lord, if haply they might feel after him and find him,' and to worship, whether on an altar of earth or of stone, or of the living heart only. And it reminds us that to this highest interest of man, as to all others, we are to apply the GOLDEN RULE—"*All things whatsoever ye would that men should do unto you, do ye even so unto them.*" And it enjoins this, not to make us indifferent in our religious faith or practice, but to impress upon us the great duty of TOLERATION—not as a policy, but as a principle taught by the Divine Benignity and Compassion. For 'a zeal according to knowledge' makes us compassionate toward those who bow not at our altar, and enjoy not our hopes and consolations; and thus increases our efforts to convert them to our faith.

"And it further instructs us that 'God now requires His people to offer unto Him the incense of Prayer and praise, of gratitude and thanksgiving;' and that among the 'acceptable sacrifices of God, are a broken spirit: a broken and a contrite heart' He will not despise. 'Therefore, if thou bring thy gift to the altar, and there rememberest that thy brother hath aught against thee, leave there thy gift before the altar, and go thy way; *first be reconciled to thy brother, and* THEN *come and offer thy gift.*'—Matt. v. 23, 24."—*Grosh's Manual, p. 279.*

with God. Therefore if thou bring thy gift to the altar, and there rememberest that thy brother hath aught against thee, leave there thy gift before the altar and go thy way; first be reconciled to thy brother, and then come and offer thy gift.

If the candidate has been seated he must now rise.

High Priest—Junior Warden, present the candidate to the Chief Patriarch.

Junior Warden—Chief Patriarch, I present to you Patriarch —— ——.

Chief Patriarch—Patriarch, the Junior Warden will now invest you with a Royal Purple collar, emblematic of this degree.

And now, in the name and by the authority of the Independent Order of Odd-fellows, I declare you duly exalted to the Royal Purple Degree.

The candidate is then placed facing the Senior Warden, and the Encampment is called up by two raps.

Chief Patriarch—Patriarchs, I now introduce and commend to you Patriarch —— —— as a member of the Patriarchal family.

An ode may be sung.

The members may advance and greet the Patriarch, after which the Encampment is seated, and the regular business proceeded with.

NOTE 114.—"The organic law of this body does not contain the seeds of its own dissolution. It has power, if need be, to act directly on individual Odd-fellows in the various States of the Union. It is legally as indestructible as the government of the United States."—*Journal of Proceedings Sovereign Grand Lodge, Session of 1880, p. 8215.*

CHAPTER XV.

Royal Purple, or Third Encampment Degree.

CLOSING CEREMONIES.[115]

The opening and closing ceremonies in the three Encampment Degrees are substantially the same, but the final closing ceremonies of an Encampment must be in this degree.

Chief Patriarch (two raps, all rise)—The officers and Patriarchs will rise while our Junior Warden closes the Encampment in the Royal Purple Degree. Officers and Patriarchs, be attentive while our Most Excellent High Priest offers a prayer.

The Chief Patriarch should remain in his place in closing the Encampment, and the Senior Warden in his place, unless, in consequence of the want of numbers, it is necessary for the Senior Warden to close in. The chain is formed (the link being made with the second finger) by all present, standing, including the Chief Patriarch and Senior Warden: the Junior Warden to the right of the Chief Patriarch, and the High Priest in the center of the ring.

PRAYER.

Father of all mercy, God of love, we beseech thee, of thy great goodness, to defend us from the perils and dangers of this night. Let thy blessing rest upon us;

Note 115.—"The Encampment opens, and closes finally, in its highest degree, as it transacts all its business in that degree only. It opens and closes in each degree (with proper ceremonies) which it confers during each session."—*Grand Lodge, p. 226.*

and may all our works—begun, continued and ended—
redound to thy glory and the happiness of all mankind.
Amen.]

After prayer an ode may be sung

Junior Warden—By order of the Chief Patriarch, I
proclaim this Encampment closed in the Royal Purple
Degree. [The chain is then broken without shaking
arms.]

The same form of proclamation for opening and closing adapted to each degree,
is used in changing from one to another for the purpose of conferring the degrees.

ANALYSIS ROYAL PURPLE DEGREE.

The Stock in Trade of Secret Orders—Toggery of This Degree—Rough Usage of the Candidate—A "Mimic Journey of Life"—The Bible Picture of Life's Journey—Odd-fellowship Mimics it—The Coincidence Between Ancient and Modern Mysteries Not Fortuitous—The Kappa Alpha Society's Murder of Mortimer D. Leggett During Initiation at Cornell University—The Devil's Mill Yet Grinding There—The Puppy Secret Societies at Yale College—Grim Travesties of Real Religious Experiences—How Related to Christianity—Secretism and Christianity Antagonists to the Death—Ancient and Modern Mysteries Claim Identity—They All Celebrated the Death and Resurrection of Some Hero or God—All Promised Salvation—Paul's Intelligent Opinion Concerning Them—Secret Orders Like Polyps—Their Object—Origin of the Oracle of Apollo at Delphi—Inspired by Sulphurous Gas from a Cavern—Satanic Aid Also—Rich Presents the Price of Responses—The Oracle at Trophonius Cave—All Made Subservient to Political Ends, as Now—God's Utterances About Secretism—Some Ignorance or Knavery on the Part of Masonic Authors—No Cheat can be Perpetual.

The secret orders have exhausted the vocabulary of kingcraft and priestcraft, which have scourged our race for six thousand years and still scourge it. And, during all that time, regalia, mock mysteries and sounding titles have been their stock in trade and tools of incantation.

This Royal Purple Degree ends the present sorcery of Odd-fellowship, amid purple gowns, yellow belts, black turbans and white surplices, with mitres and breastplates. *(See ritual, p. 203.)* And in this, as in preceding degrees, "special" warning is given against "rough usage" of the candidate, which shows the whole thing to be a religious horse-play. But one ground idea underlies and runs through the whole. It is a misletoe on the tree of life; a travesty and degrading caricature of God's system and Christ's way to heaven. The professed purpose and intent of this degree, as given by the contrivers *(ritual, p. 214)*, is " a mimic journey of life."

Now the Bible picture of the Christian's life-journey is to " run with patience," " through much tribulation," " looking to Jesus," " by whom we have access " to the infinite and eternal God.

Christ existed " before the foundation of the world," and has, ever since, been the " Way " for a man out of the trouble and guilt of sin into the rest and holiness of heaven. This crowning " royal purple degree " mimics or burlesques this *" way "* in God's eternal system of redemption. Thus: The candidate goes blindfold, looking on nothing, instead of Christ. The " tribulation " is " mimicked " by leading him over " stones, pieces of wood, stumps, limbs of trees or brushwood." *(See ritual, p. 203.)* But the guide of the poor simpleton is forbidden " all fast walking, rushing or rough usage of the candidate." This is the devil's mimicry of Christ's *" strait and thorny road,"* through a world which sin has made one of suffering.

And when the candidate has been badgered and bamboozled over the " stones, brush, stumps," etc., in the night, across a " bridge two feet wide, with rough poles as railings," over a swollen stream, amid home-made " thunder " and other frights, he is brought by the guide into the Odd-fellows' mimic heaven, his ears filled with sweet music, and he is told that he is among " people full of joy!"—*Ritual, p. 213.*

It is not a happen-so that, from the old Egyptian and Greek Mysteries down through Freemasonry and Odd-fellowship to little secret college clubs, this " mimicry " of the struggle with sin and sorrow through to peace with God is kept up. "Our rites," says Grosh, " begin in gloom and end in joy." And in this he says Odd-fellowship is a copy of all secret religious orders.

The students of Cornell University, N. Y., bound young Mortimer D. Leggett's hands behind him, at midnight, and ran him up and down a bluff six miles out of Utica, N. Y., and when wearied and bruised with " rough usage," pulled off his blinder to make him, at midnight, look down the bluff (by measure) forty feet, where they had prepared an artificial hell, whose flames were Chinese lanterns, and its devils students in horned masques! They intended, after giving him a devil's " broken heart," to lead him to " mimic " "joys of salvation " in nightly revelry and debauch; but, being too drunk to carry out the programme, they let him fall down the bluff and broke his neck. And when the poor boy was dying—when the dimness of death was coming over him—he thought they were putting on the hood-wink, and begged piteously, " Don't! Take it off! *Do* take it off !" The coroner's inquest revealed these facts to President White and his Faculty, but the literal mills of hell still grind on in Cornell University, and others. Similar, if not worse, " initiations " are practiced in Yale College. A New Haven daily told the public that, at one of these initiations into a Greek-letter fraternity, one student had his arm broken by " rough usage," and several others were so bruised that they had to be taken home in a carriage after the savage handling and night of debauch.

Now remember that these grim travesties of " sorrow for sin " and " rest to the soul " in Christ all have religious oaths or obligations, and the leading orders have " priests," "altars " and " prayers," and it requires neither profound learning nor philosophy to understand the teachings of the Bible that these devil worships stand related to Christianity exactly as whoredom does to marriage; at once a substitute for, a caricature of, and a contempt for it; and that, in the words of the poet Burns, who knew—

> " Oh, it hardens all within
> And petrifies the feeling!"

The religion of the Bible is a religion that makes men better; that transforms sinners into saints; while its counterfeits, the world over, propose to take unrepentant sinners to heaven; and we find the laws of Odd-fellowship consistent with this fact.

Although Grosh tells us *(Manual, p. 90),* " What regeneration by the word of truth is in religion, initiation is in Odd-fellowship," we find that by the laws of Odd-fellowship infidels cannot be excluded from membership in the Order.   Article 1095, *White's Digest,* reads as follows:

" INFIDELS.—To the question ' Can a State Grand Lodge legally approve a by-law of a Subordinate which provides that " Infidels shall not be proposed as members," ' the Grand Lodge of the United States answers: ' Since no peculiar religious views which do not affect the belief of the person asking admission into the Order ' in a Supreme Being, the Creator and Preserver of the Universe,' can disqualify him for membership, neither can these views be allowed to interfere with the privilege of members in respect to propositions for admission."—*1849, Journal, 1503, 1513.*

Article 1094, same book, is still more conclusive, and covers the whole subject:

"No Peculiarities of Religious Belief or practice are requisite to admission into the Order, and none disqualify."—*1848, Journal, 1198, 1246.*

Nor is the morality enforced by this professedly soul-saving religion any better than its infidel creed. Article 975 of *White's Digest* reads as follows:

"Temperance a Cardinal Principle; Total Abstinence Not Enforced.—Lodges cannot abridge the liberties of the citizen, nor dictate to him *what* he shall *eat* or *what* he shall *drink*. All good Odd-fellows despise as such the *abuse* of intoxicating drinks, and in their 'war against vice' they look upon drunkenness as incompatible with every principle of the Order. But neither will the laws nor the principles of Odd-fellowship descend to the restriction or regulation of the *beverage* of its members.

"While *temperance* is a cardinal principle of the Order and must be observed, they will not attempt to enforce *total abstinence*, a principle never intended by the framers to be ingrafted upon our Order."—*1849, Journal, 1504, 1513.*

The next article (976), same book, is as follows:

"Traffic in Intoxicating Liquors.—On a petition being presented to the Grand Lodge of the United States to enact a law allowing State Grand Bodies to prohibit members of Subordinates under their respective jurisdictions from engaging in the traffic in intoxicating liquors, it was decided that it is 'contrary to the spirit and policy of our institution to pass any law on the subject referred to, creating a new test of membership in the Order."—*1870, Journal, 4836, 4869.*

These last two quotations form also a most conclusive rebuttal of the frequent and loud-mouthed claims of the institution as a "temperance" order.

If the analysis and notes of this volume are carefully and prayerfully read, no honest, intelligent reader will fail to see that, in the words of the learned Cudworth, as before quoted, " there are two kingdoms or polities in this world in perpetual conflict—the kingdoms of light and of darkness"; and that Christ's kingdom of supreme love to God and equal love to man can never come on earth till these accursed dens of organized darkness and deism are disfellowshiped and driven from the Church of the Living God, the pillar and ground of the truth.

Now Mackey and Grosh, the highest living authorities on the point, both boast the moral identity of the old Mysteries with Freemasonry and Odd-fellowship. "They both," says Mackey, "emanated from one common source." *(Lexicon, p. 320.)* Let us see a little what these mysteries were.   And

1st. *They all had a counterfeit of the death and resurrection of Christ.* Says Mackey *(Lexicon, p. 315)* "In all these various mysteries we find a singular unity of design, clearly indicating a common origin." "They celebrated the death and the resurrection of some cherished being, the object of either esteem as a hero, or of devotion as a god." He is speaking of Egyptian, Persian, Greek, Roman, Scandinavian, Druidical, Gothic and Celtic mysteries.

2d. And *they all promised heaven or salvation. (Lexicon, p. 321.)* " Cicero tells us, that in the mysteries of Ceres at Eleusis, the initiated were taught to live happily and to die in the hope of a blessed futurity." The same promises are, over and again, made to Odd-fellows and also to Masons, whose well-known death and resurrection of Hiram Abiff is Satan's caricature of Christ's death and resurrection.

3d. The Apostle Paul, who was well-read in all these Mysteries, denounces them as " unfruitful works of darkness," as " idolatry," and, in his terse and terrible

words, their cup is "the cup of devils," and their table
"the table of devils." *(See I Cor., 10th chap.)* And
he commands Christians to "have no fellowship" with
them. *(Eph. 5: 11, 12.)*

The ancient mysteries, too, like the modern, were all
the time sending off shoots and starting new centers.
And as every slice cut off from the Polyp becomes a
new animal, so of these mysteries, ancient and modern
alike; every offshoot, and even every new degree of an
offshoot, becomes a perfect secret order, putting the initiate through from gloom to gaiety, from fear to fun
and frolic, from awe and terror to joy and jollification.
In short, the object is to produce in the initiate, as
nearly as possible, feelings like those produced by the
Holy Spirit's correction of sin and joys of pardon, and
thus give him a devil's regeneration, in which Satan
officiates as the Holy Ghost.

The oracle of Apollo at Delphi, according to Diodo-
rus Siculus, (B. C. 16) originated thus:

" Upon Mt. Parnassus there was a deep cavern, with
a small, narrow mouth; to which when any goats approached, they began to leap after an unusual and antic
manner, uttering strange and unheard-of sounds."

" The goatherd, observing this, went himself to view
the cavern, whereupon he also was seized with a like fit
of madness, leaping and dancing, and foretelling future
events."

A temple was erected over that jet of exhilarating
gas, and the priestess was inspired by it. " Whoever,"
says Archbishop Potter, " went to consult the oracle
was required to make large presents to the god; whereby
it came to pass that this temple, in riches, splendor and
magnificence, was superior to almost all others in the
world." The priestess, called the Pythoness, like the
damsel in Acts 16: 16 who " brought her masters much

gain by soothsaying," was doubtless aided by the god · of all Gentile worships, to deceive and delude the then most enlightened people on earth. The imposture took, and when its reputation was established kings poured their wealth into its exchequer for the sake of its political influence, and the multitude paid dues for initiation and degrees.

The worshiper at Trophonius Cave went through preparatory ceremonies, lasting several days, offering many sacrifices, which, of course, enriched the shrine; then he was taken out by night and washed in a river, etc., etc. These oracles were made subservient to politics. The Council of the Amphictyons met at Delphi alternately, and its decisions were influenced by the purchased responses of the priestess, as the vote of Masons and Odd-fellows is by the sham religion of the lodge.

It was in abhorrence of this secret cave-worship that God declared "*I have not spoken in secret, in a dark place of the earth.*" *(Isa. 45:19.)* So the words of Christ, "In secret have I said nothing," *(John 18:20)* condemned the mystic religions of his day, whose filthiness, Paul said, was too shameful to be spoken of, and which he commanded Christians to disfellowship. And yet Masonic and Odd-fellowship writers, either in their own ignorance or relying on the ignorance of their members, boast the moral sameness of those ancient abominations with their lodges as if it were an honor!

No cheat can be perpetual. The moral meanness of its results soon condemns it; hence those old mysteries, as ours do, kept shifting their shapes and trundling from one folly and wickedness until they finally sunk with the nations they had debauched.

CHAPTER XVI.

LODGE OF THE DAUGHTERS OF REBEKAH [116]

HISTORY AND REGULATIONS.

This revised work of the Rebekah Lodge was adopted by the Sovereign Grand Lodge at Baltimore, Md,, Sept. 23rd, 1882 and as in the old work was termed the Rebekah Degree, and was conferred in a regular Subordinate Lodge of the order. By order of the Sovereign Grand Lodge, from Jan. 1st. 1893 the word "Degree" is dropped and the ritual is given only in a Rebekah Lodge.

The following instructions of the Sovereign Grand Lodge still remain in force. Foot Note 116 was taken from Grosh's Mannul before it was revised to fit the new work, hence the reference to the Scarlet Degree instead of Degree of Truth.

The Degree of Rebekah is a side degree of the Independent Order of Odd Fellows, or, in other words, an honorary degree, and, as such is conferred on such qualified persons as may desire to receive it.

The Degree of Rebekah is conferred on the wives of members of the Degree of Truth, in good standing, as a matter of course.

NOTE 116,—"The Degree of Rebekah is conferred without charge in a Subordinate Lodge, on the wives of fifth-degree members (and widows whose husbands died in good standing,) in the presence of their husbands or proper guardians. No dues or benefits are attached, but it brings them into closer relations to the Order, and enables them to make themselves known to Scarlet members when needing aid or protection."—*Grosh's Manual, p. 76.*

The degree may also be conferred upon the unmarried daughters of Odd Fellows of the Degree of Truth, who are above the age of eighteen years, when proposed by either parent, or by a guardian, and the same rule applies to unmarr'ed sisters of Odd Fellows of the said degree over eighteen years of age, when proposed by their brother, and an unmarried daughter of an Odd Fellow of the Degree of Truth, who has attained the age of eighteen years, and whose parents are dead, when proposed by the Noble Grand of the Lodge of which her father was a member at the time of his death. It may also be conferred upon widows of Odd Fellows of the Degree of Truth who were in good standing at the time of their death, application for the degree having been made in open Lodge. And it may be conferred on the widow of an Odd Fellow who had not attained the Degree of Truth, but who was in good standing at the time of his death, at the option of the Lodge of which her husband was a member at the time of his death.

The Degree of Rebekah cannot be conferred on any one, male or female, or in the presence of any one who is not qualified to receive it, and who has not previously obligated himself, or herself in due form, not improperly to divulge it.

The degree can be conferred on any convenient number of persons at the same time, but it should in no case be conferred at one and the same time upon both males and females. The sexes should receive it separately. Therefore, when brothers are present who have not received the degree, the obligation should be administered to them before the ladies are admitted to the Lodge-room. They would then be privileged to witness the conferring of the degree, and, hearing the instructions to the ladies, would thus be put in possession of the work of the degree.

After the Lodge has been prepared for the admission of lady candidates, no person shall be admitted unless with the forms hereinafter prescribed.

In the ceremony to be observed by the lady candidates on entering a Lodge-room, they may be accompanied by their husbands or proposers.

When the Degree of Rebekah is to be conferred, it is optional with the officers of the Lodge for the time being, either to preside and officiate in conferring the degree themselves, or to call past officers to the chairs for that purpose.

Degree Lodges of the Daughters of Rebekah may confer the degree on such members of the Degree of Truth and their wives as present certificates from a Subordinate Lodge located in the district designated in the charter of such Degree Lodge, and on widows of Odd Fellows presenting certificates from the Lodges of which their husbands were members at the time of their decease; on unmarried daughters of Odd Fellows of the Degree of Truth, who are above the age of eighteen years, when proposed by either parent, or by a guardian; on unmarried sisters of Odd Fellows of the said degree, over eighteen years of age, when proposed by their brother; on the unmarried daughters of Odd Fellows of the said degree, who have attained the age of eighteen years and whose parents are dead, when proposed by the Noble Grand of the Lodge of which their fathers were members at the time of their death, or by a member of the Degree Lodge of the Daughters of Rebekah, when furnished with certificates from the Subordinate Lodge of which their fathers were members, that they were in good standing at the time of their decease.

Chapter XVII.

Lodge of the Daughters[117] of Rebekah.

OPENING CEREMONIES.

[The Noble Grand takes his position, gives one rap, directs all present to clothe themselves in appropriate regalia, and calls upon the officers to take their stations.]

Noble Grand. [*Standing.*] Officers and Members, we have assembled for the purpose of transacting business in the Degree of Rebekah, and we are enjoined to keep inviolate our secret work and see that no unworthy person is allowed to be present at the performance of our sacred rites. Therefore, those who are not entitled to a seat with us in this degree are kindly requested to retire to the anteroom. The Inside Guardian will close the door, and the Warden will prove those present according to our laws and usages.

[Warden examines and reports.]

[In Lodges of the Daughters of Rebekah, in examination prior to opening, the Warden will examine those present in the Semi-Annual Password of the Degree (given in full), and Permanent Password of the Degree of Rebekah (to be lettered), and that officer is not required to respond by giving any part of either word.]

Note 117.—"*Resolved,* That an unmarried daughter of an Odd-fellow of the Fifth Degree who has attained the age of eighteen years and whose parents are dead, may be admitted to membership in a lodge of the Degree of Rebekah when proposed by the Noble Grand of the lodge of which her father was a member at the time of his death, or by a member of a lodge of the Degree of Rebekah, when furnished with a certificate from the Subordinate Lodge of which the father was a member that he had attained the Scarlet Degree and was in good standing at the time of his death "—*Journal of Proceedings Sovereign Grand Lodge, Session of 1880, p. 8477.*

Noble Grand.   Inside Guardian, what is your duty?

Inside Guardian.   To see that none but the qualified are allowed to enter, and permit all members * to retire unless forbidden by the Noble Grand.

[The Inside Guardian will require from every one seeking admission his or her name (which must be reported to the Vice Grand), and the Permanent Password of the Degree of Rebekah (lettered), and that officer is not required to respond by giving any part of the word.]

Noble Grand.   Conductor, what are the duties of your office?

Conductor.   To conduct candidates through the mysteries of the degree, and to assist the Warden in the duties of his office.

Noble Grand.   Warden, what is your duty?

Warden.   To prove those present at opening, in the passwords; to see that the room is neat, and in order, that members may be comfortable, and spend a pleasant as well as a profitable evening whenever they meet together.

Noble Grand.   Secretary, what is your duty?

Secretary.   To keep accurate minutes of all transactions and business of the Lodge when open in this degree

NOTE * "No business whatever, except that of conferring, can be done in the Degree of Rebekah. The preliminaries must all be settled in the Subordinate Lodge. We particularly make this statement, because an erroneous impression has prevailed that ' women are to be introduced to the lodges!' "—*Donaldson's O.-F. Pocket Text Book, p. 413.*

"The simple truth is this: Woman is not entitled to and seeks not a place among us. Our institution was originally intended and framed exclusively for men, and the various modifications it has undergone have not adapted it to the other sex. They could not, with propriety, in conformity with the usages of the world, take part in our private assemblages, without exposing themselves to the censoriousness of the age,"—*Donaldson's O.-F. Text Book, p. 416.*

Same book, page 418: "*It is a secret society for gentlemen only.*"

Noble Grand.   Vice Grand, what are the duties of your station?

Vice Grand.   To officiate in my station, and, if qualified, for the Noble Grand in his absence, and to give my assistance in the performance of the business of the Lodge.

Noble Grand.   Worthy Chaplain, what are the general duties prescribed for our members?

Chaplain.   To live peaceably, to do good unto all, as we have opportunity, and especially to obey the Golden Rule, "Whatsoever ye would that others should do unto you, do ye even so to them."

Noble Grand.   Such are our duties—see ye that they are duly performed.

[Calls up the Lodge, by giving two raps.]

Noble Grand.   The members will sing the opening ode.

OPENING ODE.

Brethren of our mystic union—
  Sisters of our social band—
Here in peaceful. pure communion,
  We at FRIENDSHIP's altar stand.

LOVE unfurls her banner o'er us—
  TRUTH will guide us on our way—
FAITH illume the path before us—
  HOPE a future bright display.

CHARITY that faileth never,
  Calls to worship at her shrine,
Here we bow and pledge forever,
  Labor in her cause divine.

When the clouds of sin and sadness,
  Shroud in gloom the weary head,
There in peace, and joy, and gladness,
  Shall the light of LOVE be shed.

Noble Grand.   Worthy Chaplain, please invoke the blessings of the Supreme Ruler of the Universe upon our convocation.

[Prayer by the Chaplain.]

[The following may be used,]

Almighty God, our Creator and Preserver, we invoke Thy blessing upon the members of this Lodge and our entire brotherhood. May we be ever faithful to the principles of our beloved Order, so that benevolence and charity may be promoted. Bless the widow and orphan, and all in affliction or distress, and relieve their necessities. "Our Father who art in heaven, hallowed be Thy name: Thy kingdom come: Thy will be done, on earth as it is in heaven: Give us this day our daily bread: Forgive us our trespasses as we forgive those who trespass against us, and lead us not into temptation, but deliver us from evil: For Thine is the kingdom, and the power and the glory, forever. AMEN."

Noble Grand. Warden, you will proclaim this Lodge duly opened.

Warden. By order of the Noble Grand, I proclaim this Lodge of the Daughters of Rebekah, open for the transaction of any business that may be legally brought before it.

Noble Grand. Officers and members, so be it.

Members. So be it.

[The Noble Crand calls down with one rap.]

ORDER OF BUSINESS

IN

LODGES OF THE DAUGHTERS OF REBEKAH.

Noble Grand. The Secretary will call the roll of officers.

II.—The Secretary will read the proceedings of the last meeting.

III.—Reports on applications for Memberships.

IV.—The Degree will be conferred.

V.—Consideration of proposals for membership.

VI.—Report of Sick Committee.

VII.—Reports of Committees by seniority

VIII.—Unfinished Business.

IX.--New Business.

X.—Good and Welfare.

CHAPTER XVIII.
LODGE OF THE DAUGHTERS OF REBEKAH.

INITIATION.

[Application for this degree having been made as prescribed by law, and the Lodge having been regularly opened in this degree, according to the form, and the ladies being announced in waiting in the anteroom, the Noble Grand will direct the Conductor to retire, prepare, and introduce them.]

[The Conductor having required the ladies to remove their bonnets and shawls, will approach the inner door with the ladies and give one rap.]

Inside Guardian.   What do you desire?

Conductor.   To be admitted with a lady (*or* a number of ladies) who desires (*or* desire) to be instructed in this degree.

[The Inside Guardian reports this to the Noble Grand.]

Noble Grand.   Admit them.

[Calling the Lodge up, with two raps, as they enter.]

[Being admitted, the Conductor, with the candidate(s). and their husbands or proposers, if present, two by two (if more than one), shall march around the room while the ode is being sung, and at the conclusion thereof the Conductor shall present them to the Vice Grand.]

ODE.

Welcome, Sisters, to a shrine,
Where the social graces twine,
Hallowed by a work divine,
  Blest in charity!
Seal the promise, fraught with good,
To the gentle sisterhood:
Thus, of old, Rebekah stood,
  Type of constancy.

Here life's purest joy we hail,
Mercy's radiant deeds prevail;
Vainly want and woe assail,
  As we onward move;
Honor binds the triple chain;
Faith shields from a world of pain;
Hope inspires the glad refrain,
  "Friendship, Truth, and Love."

Conductor.   Worthy Vice Grand, I present to you these ladies, who are desirous of obtaining the privi-

,eges and honors of a degree that will enable them *more fully* to co-operate in the work of our beloved Order.

[The members, including the brothers accompanying the ladies, are seated by the Noble Grand, with one rap.]

Vice Grand. Ladies, are you desirous to unite in this degree of Odd Fellowship with those who have devoted themselves through life—in sunshine and in storm—through good or evil report—to visit the sick—relive the distressed—bury the dead—and protect and educate the orphan?

Conductor. We are.

[The ladies also bow assent.]

Vice Grand. Will you devote yourselves to this work in our way? Will you silently do good, as good ought always to be performed; and, in spite of envyings or calumny, keep your charities and your labors of love secret from the selfish world? Will you pursue the thorny pathway that we have trod, where the slanders of prejudice and bigotry assail on every side, still doing good for its own sake—returning kindness for hostility—and ever striving, quietly and unboastingly, to mitigate the vast amount of suffering and pain in our world?

Conductor. We will.

Vice Grand. You *must* be warned before you proceed. We seek to impose on you no obligation that in after life you may regret. No reluctant vows are asked for here. Pause, therefore! for you may not think—you *cannot* realize how difficult is the duty you are, in common with us, about to assume. It is a constant war with selfishness, unaided by even human praise, for which alone so many toils are undertaken. Our law is: "When thou doest alms, let not thy left hand know what thy right hand doeth; that thine alms may be secret; and thy Father, which seeth in secret, himself shall reward thee openly." Behold in that law the only recompense you can hope for—the only praise to which you can aspire. We have none other to offer. Still more: consider the sacrifice implied in that second great commandment—"Thou shalt love thy neighbor as thyself." You are yet free. Pause then, before you consent to take upon yourselves obligations that will bind you, as they have bound us before you, to duties like these. Pause and reflect—for it *may* happen that you will be called upon to give up the pleasures of life to minister at the couch of suffering—you may be summoned from the whirl of gayety to stand, with brethren and with sisters, at a bedside of anguish—you may be asked to forego the pleasures of some social evening circle to watch through the long vigils of night, the struggle between life and death, and to pour oil, if possible, into the expiring lamp of life.

Before imparting the secrets of this degree to you, it is your duty to take a solemn obligation with us, both to impress on your mind and conscience the humane duties of our Order, and to rivet on your remembrance the deep importance of strictly guarding the tests of the degree.

With this explanation of our object in asking you to pledge to us, and to each other, your word of honor, are you willing to enter into an obligation with us?

Candidates. We are.

[The Vice Grand will then call the husbands or proposers of the candidates forward, who, with the ladies, will place their right hands on the Bible, which will be open at the fifteenth chapter of Exodus, and the ladies will each repeat the following obligation.]

[The Noble Grand calls the Lodge up, with two raps.]

OBLIGATION.

I, —— ——, in the presence of the members of the Independent Order of Odd Fellows of——Lodge, No.——,of the State of ——, do most solemnly promise that I will never reveal to any one this degree, or the password, signs, countersign, and token belonging to it, and now about to be intrusted to me, except to a member of this degree, whom I may find, on due trial, to be equally in possession of them, or when in the discharge of official duties within the Lodge; and to all due secrecy in this respect, I hereby pledge my sacred word of honor, without any mental reservation whatever, and with a full determination to preserve my plighted faith inviolate until the end of life.

Vice Grand. Conductor, you will now present these sisters to the Noble Grand for the necessary instructions.

Conductor. I will, worthy Vice Grand.

[The Conductor shall proceed with the ladies, accompanied by their husbands or porposers, around the room, as instructed, during which time the ode shall be sung.]

ODE.

When gathered 'round the altar fair
　Which love and duty meet to bless,
The purest lights which greet us there,
　Are woman's trust and tenderness.

Hail! ye who bear the wine and oil
　To bless the stricken mourner's lot;
Lo! angels smile upon the toil
　Of hearts and hands that weary not.

Conductor. Noble Grand, I have the pleasure of presenting to you these ladies, for further instruc on in the work of this degree. They have passed honorably through all our ordeals, and have pledged to our worthy Vice Grand their sacred honor never to reveal the secrets now about to be intrusted to their keeping.

[The members. including the brothers accompanying the ladies, are seated by the Noble Grand, with one rap.]

Noble Grand. [*Standing.*] Reposing confidence in your plighted faith, I will now proceed to give you such instructions as appertain to this degree, and as will also enable you to know a brother or sister who has received it.

In this degree there is an Alarm at the inner door, a Permanent Password, a Test or Trial sign for a sister and answer, a Countersign for recognizing brothers and answer.

[The Alarm at the inner door is one rap.]

THE PERMANENT PASSWORD of the degree is MIRIAM, to be lettered at all times when used for working purposes: working into a Lodge, or in examination prior to opening. In communicating this word, either to the Inside Guardian or to the Warden. the brother or sister must give the letters M-I-R-, and if required by the Inside Guardian or Warden, he or she must give the remainder of the word I-A-M, lettered as before. The Inside Guardian and Warden must be satisfied.

THE TEST OR TRIAL SIGN for a sister, is made by placing the index or fore finger of the right hand, nail outward, perpendicularly to the right corner of the mouth; that portion of the fore finger beneath the nail resting on the corner indicated, the other three fingers being closed, with the thumb closed over them.

Signification. Are you of the Degree or Rebekah?

Sister's Trial Sign.

THE ANSWER TO THE TEST OR TRIAL SIGN is made by closing the last three fingers and thumb of the right hand as just described and place the fore finger thereof perpendicularly on the chin, resting the end of said finger, with the nail outward, about the center of the chin.

Answer to Trial Sign.

THE COUNTERSIGN for recognizing brothers, is made by placing the first three fingers of the right hand, extended but closely touching each other, (thumb and little finger concealed) on a table, a chair or any other object; or by placing them on a book, recticule, hankerchief, or other object held in the left hand.

THE ANSWER TO THE COUNTERSIGN is made the same as the Trial Sign for a sister.

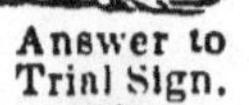

Countersign.

INSTRUCTIONS IN A LODGE OF THE DAUGHTERS OF REBEKAH.

[The Noble Grand having instructed in the secret work, will address the candidates as follows.]

Wishing to visit a Lodge of the Daughters of Rebekah, when open, you will give at the outer door two raps, and the Semi-Annual Password of the degree (in full), which will secure your admission to the anteroom. Clothed with appropriate regalia, you will approach the inner door and give one rap, when the Inside Guardian will open the wicket, and require from you, your name and the number of the Lodge of the Daughters of Rebekah to which you belong, after this has been repeated to the officer in charge you will give the Permanent Password of the degree (lettered). If correct, you will be admitted to the Lodge-room, when you shall advance to the center thereof, and address the Noble Grand with the Test Sign, to which that officer will respond by giving the answer to the Test Sign.

On retiring, while the Lodge is open, you will address the Noble Grand with the Test Sign, to which he will respond with the answer to it.

[There is no retiring password to be used in a Lodge of the Daughters of Rebekah, or a Subordinate Lodge, when open in that degree.]

Let me state to you distinctly and emphatically, that that these signs are never to be used merely for pleasure or curiosity. They are intended for useful purposes only; and though you are at liberty to practice them in the securest privacy, with others whom you may know, OF YOUR OWN KNOWLEDGE, to have received them legally, you are not allowed to use them at home or abroad, without some practical, useful end in view. In times of distress or peril or difficulty, you are not only at liberty to use them, but are also instructed to do so.

The Semi-Annual Password of the present term is ——.

[To be communicated in a whisper.]

This word is intended as a test of good standing in a Lodge of the Daughters of Rebekah, and is only to be used by such Lodges, and in the particular jurisdiction to which it belongs.

The Annual Password of this degree for the present year is ———

This last word is intended as a further proof test of membership in the degree. It is therefore changed annually by the Sovereign Grand Lodge, and goes into operation on the first of January of each year. You will receive all annual passwords from the Noble Grand of the Rebekah Lodge to which you may be attached, who alone can instruct you therein. This annual password is used as a test, thus: *After* having received some sign, which would seem to indicate membership in this degree, you are at liberty to ask her or him for the password, and upon being answered, "Commence yourself," you will commence with the *last* letter of the word. This is replied to by the person you challenge with the *first* letter of the word, and you then respond with the middle or any of the middle letters, to be replied to, "Even so." The password is *never* to be given in full under any circumstances whatever—*never* to be written—*never* even to be spoken as a word, except in giving instructions as in the present case; and especially no experiments, are to be tried with it for the mere sake of experment without some useful or friendly purpose in view.

The annual password is also to be used in conjunction with a card, as a traveling password, when visiting Lodges of the Daughters of Rebekah in other jurisdictions than the one to which the visitor belongs. The Noble Grand of the Lodge will communicate or cause to be communicated to you the annual and semi-annual passwords of the Rebekah Degree.

[The Noble Grand will here practice the ladies in the use of the annual password, and prove them in the signs, &c.]

If you desire to be recognized by one of your own sex, you should give the test or trial sign, to which the lady addressed should respond by giving the answer to it.

If you desire to be recognized by a gentleman, you should give the countersign for recognizing a brother, to which he should respond by giving the test sign.

The countersign is not to be used by a brother at all. A gentleman has no right to challenge a lady under any circumstances, but only to respond when he is challenged, and then it must be with the test sign,

[The Noble Grand may deliver the Past Noble Grand's Charge, in the absence of a competent Past Noble Grand of a Lodge of the Daughters of Rebekah.]

Noble Grand. The Conductor will proceed with the sister(s) to the chair of the Past Noble Grand, there to receive the lecture of the Rebekah Degree,

Conductor. Past Noble Grand, by direction of the Noble Grand, I present to you this (*or* these) sister(s), who has (*or* have) been instructed, and is (*or* are) now prepared to receive the lecture appertaining to this degree.

Past Noble Grand. Our sister(s) will please be seated fronting this chair.

He who reads the page of Holy Writ intelligently, often finds his memory wandering back to those sketches of the women of the Bible, which appear as delightful episodes in the Great History—linking it, by a chain that all can see and feel, with our own realizations of domestic life. And woman needs no higher eulogy than to be judged by those noble specimens of her sex, immortalized by having their names embalmed in the Book of books. What a glorious Galaxy glitters on those sacred pages!

We refer you not alone to the beautiful and graceful REBEKAH, the daughter of Bethuel—who, pointed out by God himself to Eliezer as the fitting wife for Isaac, goes forth from the vale of Haran at that bidding, turning her back upon home, family, and friends, to travel the journey of life with a stranger of a distant land; nor to the MOTHER OF SAMSON, who held discourse, timid yet confiding, with the Angel whose name is Wonderful; or to HANNAH, who dedicated her first-born to that illustrious service of the Almighty, which has linked the name of Samuel to all our brightest recollections of prophecy and priesthood; to DEBORAH, who, as has been so beautifully said, in that era of her widowhood, rose, in times of trouble, like a morning star over the night of Israel's calamities, and at whose word the stars, in their courses, fought aginst Sisera; nor to that unselfish and queenly ESTHER, who promptly risked station and life to shield her people and her race; or to RUTH, whose character is enshrined in the pastoral record that bears her name, and that has handed down to us her fortitude, her affection, and her piety in a simple narrative more thrillingly fascinating than the most highly wrought scenes of fiction. Need we even allude, in passing, to that heroic and well-remembered decision she exhibited in her sad but fearless reply to Naomi, when in spite of the dangers of toil and exposure, of poverty aud trial, of frowning and adverse prospects, she attested her filial piety in that strain of as lofty and impassioned eloquence as ever fell from human lips— "Entreat me not to leave thee, or to return from following after thee; for whither thou goest, I will go; and where thou lodgest, I will lodge; thy people shall be my people, and thy God my God; where thou diest, will I die, and there will I be buried: the Lord do so to me, and more also, if aught but death part thee and me·"

Nor yet alone would we cite you to the history of Sarah, emphatically chief among the Mothers of the Bible—the ancestress of Israel's hosts—the wife of the patriarch of patriarchs— at whose tent the Angels of the Lord sat down at meat—and who was indeed the most specially honored of God.

Nor alone to the vestal prophetess, Miriam, the sister of Moses and Aaron, who stands forth inferior to none in whatever makes a true woman memorable in action or suffering—who in the afflictions of Egypt, in the triumph of the Red Sea, and in the perils of the Wilderness, towers resplendent in her zeal and her devotion. From the time that at the river's bank she watched her infant brother's ark, through that long journey, where quails and manna mysteriously fed the wandering hosts, and water poured from the flinty rock to assuage their thirst, till the hour that entombed her in her sequestered grave, she proved herself a woman in all that was noble and pure and holy. And it was no unmeaning song of rejoicing that poured from her lips, when at the head of the Hebrew women, on the banks of the rapidly closing Red Sea, her clear, loud voice rang forth in notes of rejoicing and praise to God—

Sound the loud timbrel o'er Egypt's dark sea,
Jehovah has triumphed—his people are free.

But the history of these and others that we might name, whom the inspired penmen felt *must* be recorded to make their testimony perfect—such a record, taken in the aggregate, is a nobler testimony to woman, a worthier eulogy of her rank and honor than she can find in the histories of thousands of Earth's mightiest—of Elizabeth, of Cleopatra, of Catharine or Isabella. *Such* we do not cite for your emulation and imitation. But rather the record of those whom the Bible commends—who signalized their lives, not by bloody victories on fields of carnage and of death—not by despotic sway over a nation of millions—not by the meretricious charms of beauty—but by their zeal in doing good—in vindicating the true modesty and worth of woman's natural character—in pouring the oil of consolation into the wounds of the afflicted—in wispering words of sympathy in the ears of the heart-stricken.

Such, too, is woman's noblest work. It is a duty that angels might not, nay do not scorn to perform. It is that sphere in which your (*or* our) sex has gained its most unfading laurels. Nobly, right nobly, has she performed her mission. Poets have sung in glowing numbers of her constancy in hours of trial, of darkness, and of peril— of her labors at the bedside of the sick and afflicted— of her patient endurance of life's roughest lot when shared by those she loves. Wherever sorrow's cry is heard, wherever sickness lays its paralyzing hand —fellow, ladies, the innate sympathies of your nature. Wherever the hardships of adversity fall the heaviest upon those about you be it yours as far as possible to soften the blow. Wherever misery can be ameliorated or keen anguish assuaged, remember that you are women; and if further promptings to duty could be needed, remember the solemn obligation you have this night voluntarily taken, and write upon the tablet of your hearts that Golden Rule—"Whatsoever ye would that others should do unto you, do ye even so unto them."

While we shall expect the prompt and cheerful performance of these duties by those now affiliated with our Order as you are, we pledge to you duty in return. The benefits of our Order are not confined to our own members, nor to time, place, or circumstance. Its pleasant associations greet us smilingly when in the enjoyment of health and prosperity, its ministrations cheer us when the hand of sickness and disease is laid upon us, and when death, the fell destroyer, tears asunder the dearest ties of love, its highest excellence is manifested.

> We seek to dry the widow's gushing tears,
> We seek to calm the trembling orphan's fears,
> We seek to raise humanity above
> The ills of life by ministries of Love;
> And when the tale is told, and man resigns his trust,
> We seek, in Friendship's name, to monument his dust.

But we need not add more. We have alluded to some of the duties enjoined by Odd Fellowship. It *is* strange in a cold, calculating world like ours, where so many walk through life with ears hermetically sealed against the calls of humanity, encased in a frozen garb that repulses all approach—petrifying what little heart and soul they own—we say it is *odd*, to see a society like ours, banded together for the benevolent duties we have bound ourselves to perform. Hence we are ODD FELLOWS. To-night you have entered with us into a closer bond than ever before—you have assumed a part of our obligations— you are become of us and with us. Learn then, in conclusion, that to rectify, to correct this besetting sin of selfishness is one of the highest aims and objects of our Order. It teaches us that there is but one family—the whole human race—and that we are sent here together—the rich and the poor—the haughty and the humble—not as cumberers of the Earth, but as sharers of each others burdens. It teaches us that, wherever we hear the sigh of sorrow, the moan of the heart-broken, the appeal of the destitute, or the wail of the miserable, we should be quick in our ministrations of mercy, not passing by on the other side, but flying to relieve. It teaches us that we are sent here to labor for our fellow-men, for our age, for our country. That, when we shall have passed away into the stern realities of the Hereafter, we may leave behind us a name; honored and beloved for the good we have sought to accomplish—for the happiness we have striven to create—for the misery we have labored to ameliorate—a history more valuable in the sight of Him above than that of Chieftain, Warrior, or Sage.

Teaching such lessons within its walls—built on these immutable corner-stones, Friendship, Love and Truth, the mighty fabric of Odd Fellowship rears its stately form toward the skies; and though the storms of opposition may beat around its base, and the surges of prejudice strive to engulf it in the billows that they hurl upon it, its stately and majestic form will still remain unharmed amid the contending tempests, and crumble into atoms only when the Earth upon which it stands yields in the wreck of matter and the crash of worlds. There it will stand

> As some tall cliff that lifts its mighty form,
> Swells from the vale, and midway leaves the storm;
> Though round its breast the rolling clouds may spread,
> Eternal sunshine settles on its head.

Past Noble Grand. [*To the ladies.*] You will now

rise. The Conductor will present the ladies to the Noble Grand for final instruction in this lodge.

[The Conductor conducts the ladies around the room until he arrives in front of the Noble Grand's chair, and facing that officer.]

Conductor. Noble Grand, I now present to you these sisters, who have just listened to the beautiful teachings of our ritual, and now await the concluding instructions in this lodge.

Noble Grand. Ladies, having entered within our sacred circle and assumed with us obligations like those we have spoken of, it now becomes my duty in the closing ceremony of your initiation to confer on you the badge appropriate to this lodge. It is a pink and green ribbon, emblematic of steadfast Friendship and eternal Love, twisted or intertwined together like this; and this combination of colors may be thus worn, whenever you see fit to do so, as a bow, a collar, a bracelet, or on any part of the dress as a trimming. When you see this combination you may prove the wearer as has been stated to you.

[Here give the emblems and significations.]

Noble Grand. [*To the Conductor.*]   You will now present the ladies in turn, and by name.

[As each lady is presented she will advance in front of the chair of the Noble Grand, who will invest her with a badge or collar of pink and green ribbon, of about an inch in width.]

Sister ——— ———, receive this collar as the Token of the **Daughters of Rebekah** lodge, to which in the name and by the authority of the Independent Order of Odd Fellows, I now declare you admitted. Faithful to your own obligations, you will ever find us faithful to ours. Fail not—falter not—weary not in well-doing.

[Regular Lodges of the Daughters of Rebekah close, when the business of the evening is concluded, in the regular form.]

Chapter XIX.

CLOSING CEREMONIES.

Noble Grand. [*Standing.*] Officers and Members, our business being concluded, you will please be standing and assist in the performance of the closing ceremonies. [Two raps, all rise.]

CLOSING ODE.

Good night! a truthful, kind adieu;
"May joy be with you all,"
Who here the social bond renew,
And love our sacred hall.

Good night! Our Order's triple chain,
Keep ever strong and bright;
Each evil act and thought restrain,
Adeiu! Good night! Good night!

Noble Grand. Our worthy Chaplain will please perform the duties of his office. [Chaplain prays.]

[The following may be used]

Almighty Father, we pray thee to bless whatever of good we have accomplished at this time, and forgive what we have done amiss. We now commend ourselves to Thy care and protection. The Lord bless us, and keep us. The Lord lift up his fatherly countenance upon us, and give us peace now and evermore. AMEN.

Noble Grand. Warden, you will please declare this Lodge of the Daughters of Rebekah, closed.

Warden. By order of the Noble Grand, I declare this Lodge of the Daughters of Rebekah, closed.

Noble Grand. Officers and members, so be it.

Members. So be it-

[Noble Grand gives one rap]

ANALYSIS REBEKAH DEGREE.

It is difficult to analyze this degree without indigna-
tion and disgust. It is a degree which is not a degree,
but an excrescence. It inducts women into a secret order, intended and named only for men *(see p. 236)*, and
kept to its masculine gender from its origin to the year
of grace 1851. It is a woman's degree, practiced in the
night, in which men, known and unknown to the initiates, may be a majority of ten to one *(see note, p. 236)*,
while women, as before, are excluded from the Order itself; and, while the degree itself is an organized temptation, by its formal and flimsy guards against pollution
it suggests the very evil against which it affects to
guard.

With the customary formalities of an oath, with her
right hand on the Bible *(p. 244)*, the deluded woman is
pledged to conceal—not, indeed, the secrets of Odd-fellowship, of which she is permitted to know nothing,

but to conceal the secrets of her single degree; and she is solemnly enjoined to see that her husband is punctual in paying his *"dues,"* as her standing in this outside degree depends on his punctual payments within. *(Pp. 236, 247.)*

The motives which caused the adoption of this degree, stated by Mr. Colfax himself, are the following:

1. "It will tend to increase the resources of the Subordinate Lodges," and "to induce them (members) to progress upward in the Order"; *i. e.,* pay for more degrees.

2. Save the trouble of "wives' and widows' cards."

3. "Lessen and ultimately destroy the prejudice felt against the Order by many of the fairer sex," which "prevents accessions of members." *(Pp. 233, 234.)* In a word, *we shall get more money by it.*

This summary of selfish, money-making motives, remember, is given by the inventor of the degree. They were the motives by which he carried it. And when we remember that the Grand Lodge statistics show that the Order receives three dollars in dues to one paid back in benefits—taking these avowed motives and this published practice together the Order must, on its own authority, be regarded as a gigantic swindle. And nothing but the wide reputation of Mr. Colfax, and the success and popularity of the imposition, prevents its being handled by the law like mock-auctions, lotteries, and other swindling practices. And the benefits, such as they are, being paid indiscriminately to rich and poor, proves its perpetually repeated boast of being "a ministry of love," "drying the widows' tears," etc. etc., to be bald hypocrisy and wicked pretense.

All this in a world where, alas! corruption is so common, would not justify a national appeal against it, were not this secret order, like the others, a false religion, as is shown abundantly in the Analyses of the Order proper. Even the poor Rebekah-ite, after being bedrabbled through her weak degree, is told that she is now "*within our* SACRED CIRCLE," and receives a pink and green ribbon as an "*emblem of* ETERNAL LOVE."(!) *(See p. 254.)* The Bible is quoted abundantly to make the farce solemn, and the most fulsome adulation of woman, merely as a sex, is poured into the ears of the initiate throughout the lecture of the degree. Whoever reads and ponders the degree itself will see that its wicked and hateful nature is not and cannot be overstated.

The Philippian damsel who *"brought her masters much gain by soothsaying" (Acts 16: 16),* is a type of the condition of women in all false religions, ancient and modern.

A missionary of the A. B. C. F. M. informed the writer that no females were educated by the pagans in his part of Asia but a few brilliant and beautiful girls for the uses of the temple and companionship of the priests. Two thousand such were kept in the single Temple of Diana at Ephesus, which was 220 years in building, at the expense of all Asia Minor. The priests were pimps and panderers to the prostitution of these unfortunates, and gained untold wealth by renting their persons. The poor Pythian damsel at Delphi was placed upon a tripod over the exhilarating gas, when "she immediately began to swell and foam at the mouth, tearing her hair and cutting her flesh." Her masters took her ravings, while in this state, for oracles, and interpreted them for money. Such are some of the

Greek " Mysteries " from which Masonic and Odd-fel-lowship writers boast their orders descended! And women in Freemasons' and Odd-fellows' side-lodges are as near the condition of women in the old lodges of paganism as a Christian country will allow. They are under " masters."   Every lodge of females was finally obliged to be adopted by, and under the guardianship of, some regular Masonic lodge *(Mackey's Lexicon, p. 22);* and " a banquet and a ball," says Clavel, " are inseparable from a lodge of adoption, and are, in fact, the real design of its organization." *(Lexicon, p. 26.)* I passed through the Masonic Temple, Boston, on the morning after such a pagan debauch, while the vast dining halls and unremoved tables were in the condition in which the night revel had left them. The Boston Journal, next morning, in four solid columns, informed its readers that there were women of Boston and vicinity who danced with strange men from all parts of the country until 4 o'clock in the morning,—their secret worships having closed at ten. Every such " temple," as were those of old, is a spiritual, and doubtless also a literal brothel.

CHAPTER XX.

In the Subordinate Lodge the Entersign consists of one rap, or one pull at the bell if there be one, at the outer door, and three raps at the inner door.

THE COUNTERSIGN

has three motions: *First,* with the thumb of the right hand in the palm thereof, place the four fingers perpendicularly across the mouth, the back of the hand outward. *Second,* place the last three fingers upon the thumb in the palm of the hand, the index or fore finger being extended; carry it to the outer corner of the right eye, the back of the hand being outward, forming a right angle with the nose. *Third,* let the hand drop toward the ground and open, palm outward, the thumb nearly parallel with the fingers and the hand about six inches from the body.

Explanation of the Countersign.—The first motion signifies silence, and reminds us that we are bound to keep inviolate the secrets of the Order. The second motion signifies omniscience, and reminds us that the all-seeing eye of God is continually watching over our actions. The third motion signifies fraternity, and reminds us that the hand of an Odd-fellow should always be open to a brother.

INITIATORY GRIP.

With the first two fingers of the right hand seize and link with the first two fingers of the brother's right hand; with the thumb (your own) touch each of the two fingers (your own) and thus form the link. No shaking hands in making the grip.

SIGN OF DISTRESS.

Place the open right hand, palm downward, on the top of the head, raise the hand upward about nine inches, drop the hand to the head; this do three times; the hand after being placed on the head is to be raised and replaced on the head three times; then drop the hand to the side.

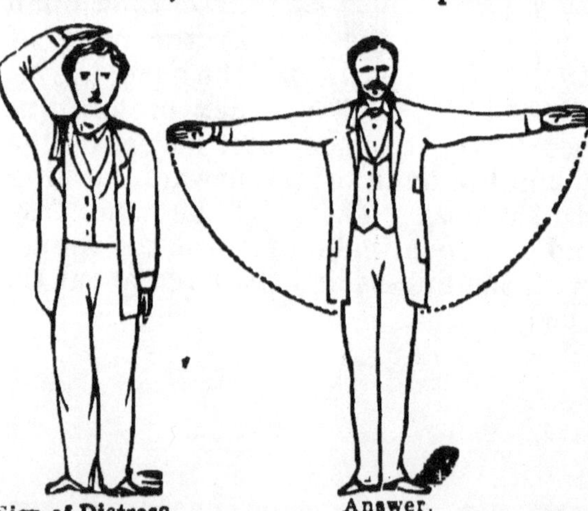

Sign of Distress   Answer.

Answer.—Extend the hands at arm's length off from the sides and at right angles to the body, palms outward; pause a moment and drop the hands to the side. This is not repeated.

Explanation—The Sign of Distress gives information to a brother at a distance that a brother of the Order is in want of assistance.   The answer is given by a brother who shall observe and recognize the Sign and denotes a readiness to give the requisite assistance.   When this Sign cannot be observed the brother in distress may use the words "*Give ear, O ye Heavens!*" which words must be pronounced in full and not the initials thereof.

THE SIGN OF RECOGNITION.

Sign of Recognition.   Answer.

First—When a brother shall desire to be recognized as an Odd-fellow by a member of the Order, he shall grasp with his right hand the lapel of his coat, the hand being placed over the right nipple, the thumb extended upward.   *Second*—An Odd-fellow observing this Sign shall recognize and answer the same by taking hold of the right lapel of his coat with his left hand, the same being also placed over the right nipple, thumb concealed beneath the coat   *Third*—When the brother who made the Sign shall observe the answer he shall advance to the person making the answer and extend to him his right hand, which the person (if he be an Odd-fellow) shall accept and shake with his right hand and at the same time shall ask, Are you looking for me?   when the other shall respond, For you.

If either of the brothers should be at the time without a coat he shall place his hand on his person in the same position, the challenging brother with his fingers turned under, the brother answering with his thumb concealed in the palm of his hand.

Voting Sign—The right hand uplifted.

In the use of the gavel, one blow calls the lodge to order, or seats it when standing; three blows call up the lodge.

DEGREE OF FRIENDSHIP.

THE ALARM at the inner door is three raps.

THE PASSWORD is QUIVER to be lettered at all times when used for working purposes, working into a lodge or in examination prior to opening. In communicating this word, either to the Inside Guardian or to the Warden the brother must give the letters Q-U-I, and if required by the Inside Guardian or Warden, he must give the remainder of the word V-E-R—lettered as before. The Inside Guardian and Warden must be satisfied.

Sign Degree of Friendship.

SIGN. DEGREE OF FRIENDSHIP.

The Sign is made as follows—extend the fingers of the right hand; place the thumb inside of, and parallel with, the first finger; carry the hand to the brow, with the thumb resting on the left temple; draw a line across the forehead (fingers touching) until the end of the thumb reaches the right temple describing a bow, then drop the hand.

ANSWER, DEGREE OF FRIENDSHIP.

Grasp the root of the left ear with the fore finger and thumb of the right hand, fingers below, thumb above the root of the ear.

THE MEMENTO

Is a bundle of sticks, to represent the strength of union; united cannot be broken; a single stick to represent that separated each may be easily broken.

Answer.

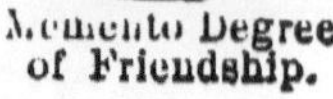

Memento Degree of Friendship.

WARNING SIGN.

Close the fingers of each hand, with the thumb in front of the first finger; place each elbow by the side of the body; extend each arm and closed hand horizontally.

Warning Sign.

SIGN OF SAFETY.

The hands and arms being in the same position as in the Warning Sign, extend the index finger of the right hand, with which point to and just touch the second or knuckle joint of the thumb of the left hand.

SIGN OF DANGER.

Elbows same as before described, place the wrist of the right hand on the second or knuckle joint of the thumb of the left hand; extend the index finger and point towards the ground.

Sign of Safety.

GRIP, DEGREE OF FRIENDSHIP

Form a link with the thumbs of the right hand; clasp hands, enclosing it, (Link of thumbs.)

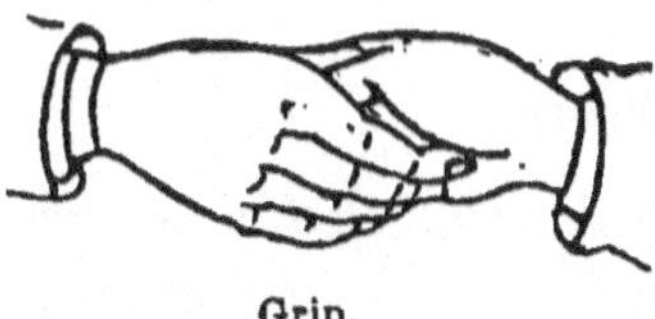

Grip.

Sign of Danger.

TOKEN—The rainbow.

THE PASSWORD is MOSES (M–O–S—ES), to be lettered at all times when used for working purposes. In communicating the Password give the letters M–O–S, and if required the remainder—E–S—lettered as before.

Sign 2d Degree.

SIGN.

The right hand is placed across the left hand, palms touching; clasp the hands both by fingers and thumbs, thumbs meeting. The answer is the same as the sign.

TOKEN—The Token is Moses' Rod.

GRIP.

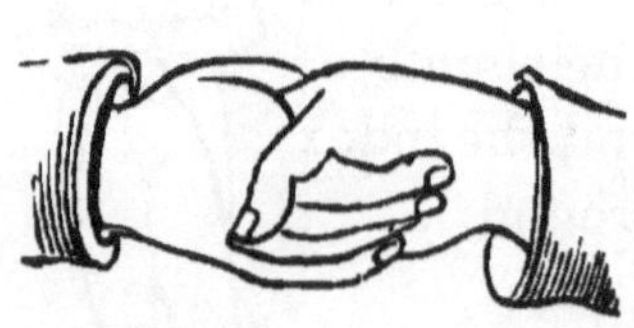

Clasp the right hands with the thumbs pressing the third or knuckle joint of the second finger. No shaking hands in making the Grip.

DEGREE OF TRUTH.

PASSWORD—The Password is AARON to be lettered at all times when used for working purposes; working into a lodge or in examination prior to opening. In communicating this word either to the Inside Guardian or to the Warden the brother must give the letters A-A and if required by the Inside Guardian or Warden he must give the remainder of the word, R-O-N, lettered as before. The Inside Guardian and Warden must be satisfied.

Working Sign.

WORKING SIGN, DEGREE OF TRUTH.

The sign is made as follows: Close the right hand except the index finger which is extended, thumb over fingers; press the centre of the forehead with the point of the index finger.

ANSWER.

Place the open right hand over the mouth, the fingers to conform to the face looking the brother addressing earnestly in the face.

Explanation.—Think before you speak.

Answer.

Principal Sign.

PRINCIPAL SIGN, DEGREE OF TRUTH.

Place the thumb of the right hand on the right nipple; using it as a pivot, make a span down with the little finger, then make a span across the breast with the forefinger.

GRIP, DEGREE OF TRUTH.

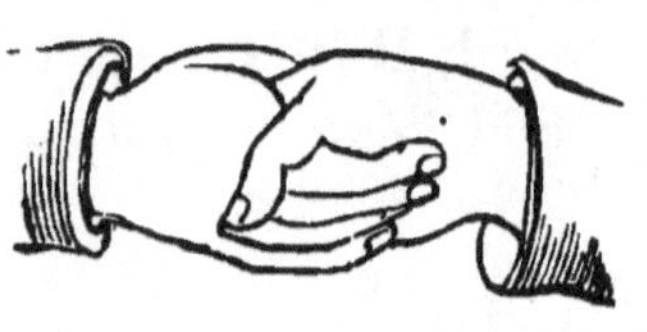

Clasp the right hands; with the thumbs press hard on the third or knuckle joint of the third finger. No shaking hands in making the Grip.

PATRIARCHAL DEGREE.

In the Encampment the Alarm at the inner door, or Entersign, is *two* raps.

PASSWORD OF PATRIARCHAL DEGREE, ADAM (A-D—A-M): to be divided at all times when used for working purposes when in an Encampment, or in examination prior to opening, in communicating the Password to Inside Sentinel or to the Junior Warden.

CHECK SIGN, PATRIARCHAL DEGREE.

Place the right hand, open, on the left breast, thumb parallel with the fingers; withdraw the hand and extend it nearly to a line off from the side, palm outward and the thumb parallel with the fingers; let the arm drop to the side. The Answer is the same with the left hand.

SIGN, PATRIARCHAL DEGREE.

Place the fingers of the right hand in and across the left hand, palm upward; grasp the fingers of the right hand with the last three fingers of the left hand; elevate the two thumbs and the index finger of the left hand so as to form three pillars. The Answer is the same as the Sign.

Sign of Patri
archal Degree.

GRIP, PATRIARCHAL DEGREE.

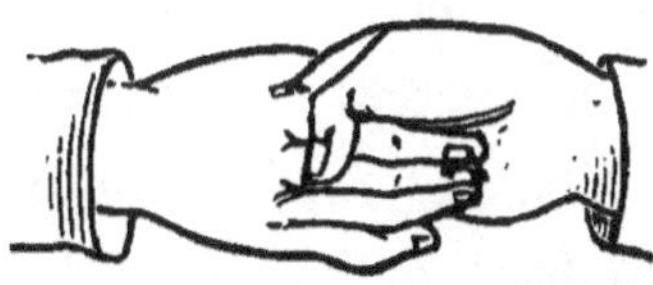

Grasp the fingers of the Patriarch's right hand with your right hand; press the same with the thumb, which must be across the fingers below the knuckle joint. No shaking hands in making the Grip.

GOLDEN RULE DEGREE.

THE ALARM at the inner door is two raps.

THE PASSWORD is A. M., to be lettered at all times when used for working purposes, whether in an Encampment or in examination prior to opening. The Explanation of the Password is Gold a Metal, given in full, but not used for working purposes.

The CHECK SIGN and Answer are made the same as in the Patriarchal Degree.

Sign of Golden
Rule Degree.

SIGN, GOLDEN RULE DEGREE.

Press the elbow of the right arm to the side, close the right hand, thumb over fingers; extend the index finger; when extended raise the arm from the elbow in a perpendicular direction; drop the arm in front, the index finger pointing to the ground. The Answer is the same as the Sign.

GRIP, GOLDEN RULE DEGREE.

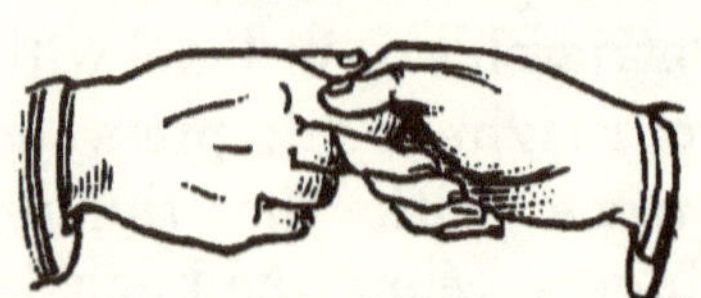

With the index finger of the right hand form a link at the second joint, and with the ball of the thumb press the back of the index finger of the Patriarch forming the link with you, between the knuckle and second joint. No shaking hands in making the Grip.

ROYAL PURPLE DEGREE.

In this degree there is an Alarm at the inner door, or Entersign, a Password, an Explanation of the Password, and Interpretation of the Password, a Check Sign and Answer to the Check Sign and a Grip.

THE ALARM at the inner door is two raps.

THE PASSWORD is M. K., to be lettered at all times when used for working purposes; working into an Encampment or in examination prior to opening. In communicating this password either to the Inside Sentinel or Junior Warden, the Patriarch must give the letter M, and if required by the Inside Sentinel or Junior Warden he must give the remaining letter K. The Inside Sentinel and Junior Warden must be satisfied. The Explanation of the Password is K. S. The Interpretation is Melchizedek, King of Salem, both given in full, but not used for working purposes.

The CHECK SIGN and Answer are made the same as in the former Encampment degrees.

SIGN, ROYAL PURPLE DEGREE.

Conceal the last two fingers of the right hand in the palm thereof; place the first two fingers and thumb together, ends touching, and with them trace a line from the left side of the brow to the centre of the forehead; then drop the hand to the side.

Answer.—With the left hand arranged as in Sign, trace a similar line from the right side of the brow to the centre of the forehead, then drop the hand to the side.

Sign of Royal Purple Degree.

GRIP, ROYAL PURPLE DEGREE.

Each Patriarch will grasp the index finger of the other's right hand, with the ball of the thumb across the knuckle joint on the back of the hand. No shaking hands in making the Grip.

THE TEST OR TRIAL SIGN for a sister, is made by placing the index or fore finger of the right hand, nail outward, perpendicularly to the right corner of the mouth; that portion of the fore finger beneath the nail resting on the corner indicated, the other three fingers being closed, with the thumb closed over them.

Signification. Are you of the Degree or Rebekah?

Sister's Trial Sign.

THE ANSWER TO THE TEST OR TRIAL SIGN is made by closing the last three fingers and thumb of the right hand as just described and place the fore finger thereof perpendicularly on the chin, resting the end of said finger, with the nail outward, about the center of the chin.

Answer to Trial Sign.

THE COUNTERSIGN for recognizing brothers, is made by placing the first three fingers of the right hand, extended but closely touching each other (thumb and little finger concealed) on a table, a chair or any other object; or by placing them on a book, recticule hankerchief, or other object held in the left hand.

THE ANSWER TO THE COUNTERSIGN is made the same as the Trial Sign for a sister.

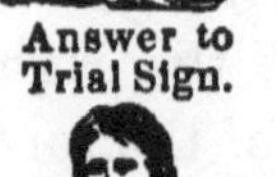

Countersign.

Patriarchs Militant Illustrated.

The Complete Ritual

With Eighteen Military Diagrams

AS ADOPTED AND PROMULGATED BY THE

SOVEREIGN GRAND LODGE

OF THE

Independent Order of Odd-Fellows,

AT BALTIMORE, MARYLAND, SEPT. 24TH, 1885.

COMPILED AND ARRANGED BY JOHN C. UNDERWOOD, LIEUTENANT GENERAL,

—WITH THE—

Unwritten or Secret Work Added,

—ALSO AN—

HISTORICAL SKETCH AND INTRODUCTION

By Pres't. J. Blanchard of Wheaton College.

* * *

CHICAGO, ILLINOIS.
EZRA A. COOK, PUBLISHER,
1886.

This Ritual, and the Forms and Ceremonies annexed, etc., for the DEGREE OF PATRIARCHS MILITANT, I. O. O. F., was adopted by a unanimous vote of the Sovereign Grand Lodge of the Independent Order of Odd Fellows, at the city of Baltimore, in the State of Maryland. on the 24th day of September, 1885, and of the Order the sixty-seventh year.

Officers of the Sovereign Grand Lodge.

HENRY F. GAREY,...Grand Sire.
JOHN H. WHITE,...Dep. G. Sire.
THEO. A. ROSS.....G. Secretary.
ISAAC A. SHEPPARD..G. Treas.
ALLEN JENCKES..Ass't. G. Sec.

REV. J. W. VENABLE..G. Chaplin.
JOHN T. JAKES........G. Marshal.
J. R. HARWELL.......G. Guardian.
E. H. WHITNEY.......G. Messenger.

Representatives of Grand Lodge.

OLIVER J. SEMMES.Alabama.
WM. H HOMER .... "
M. T. HERZOG.......Arizona.
SAM'L. W. MALLORY.Arkansas.
W. A. JETT,............ "
JOHN N. E. WILSON..California.
H. T. DORRANCE .... "
ALBERT E. GIPSON..Colorado.
CHAS. E. WALDO... . "
WM. H. STEVENSON Connecticut
LUCIUS P. DEMING.. "
A. E. CLOUGH........Dakota.
RALPH R. BRIGGS... "
E. W. COOPER ....Delaware
JNO. J. GALLAGHER. "
J. THOMAS PETTY..Dist. Colum.
M. D. BRAINARD... "
CHAS. C. PEARCE..Florida.
CHAS. H. DORSETT .Georgia.
JOHN B. GOODWIN. "
MONTIE B. GWINN.Idaho.
AUG. W. BERGGREN.Illinois.
ALF. ORENDORFF.... "
H. McCOY.............Indiana.
S. P. OYLER .... "
J. VAN VALKENBURG.Iowa.
GEORGE WHIPPLE..... "
CHAS. H. KREBS......Kansas.
ISAAC SHARP......... "
J. C. UNDERWOOD....Kentucky.
WM. W. MORRIS...... "
JACOB HOTH ....Louisiana.
ROBERT HOCKIN.. L. P., B.N.A.
ANDRE CUSHING... " "
EDW. W. CONANT...Maine
J. H. CROCKETT.... "
C. D. ANDERSON...Manitoba.
WM. H. RUBY.......Maryland.
JOHN M. JONES.... "
HENRY K. BRALEY.Mass.
SAMUEL COCHRAN "
LAW. N. BURKE...Michigan.
HARRISON SOULE. "
C. C. HURD........Minnesota.
WALTER G. DYE.. "
ISAAC T. HART....Mississippi.

G. W. TRIMBLE.......Mississippi.
HENRY CADLE.......Missouri.
CHAS. D. LUCAS....... "
ISAAC MARKS . .....Montana.
W. H CURTIS..........Nebraska.
J. T. HEDRICK........ "
GEO. HENNING........Nevada.
A. M. McCABE......... "
JAS. W. ODLIN........N. Hamp're.
L. F. McKINNEY...... "
WM. H. ISZARD.......N. Jersey.
JAS. S. KIGER......... "
JNO. W. STEBBINS....New York.
GEO. W. DILKS........ "
JNO. E. WOODARD....N. Carolina.
J. F. PAYNE......... .. "
E. K. WILCOX.........Ohio.
HENRY C. HEDGES.... "
CL. T. CAMPBELL.....Ontario.
JAMES WOODYATT... "
W. T. WILLIAMSON...Oregon.
T. O. BARKER......... "
FRANCIS M. REA.....Pennsylvania.
SAM'L. F. GWINNER.. "
H. A. JACKSON........Quebec.
GILB. F. ROBBINS.... Rhode Island
LESTER S. HILL ...... "
JOHN HEESEMANN...S. Carolina.
RUDOLPH WEBER....Switzerland.
GEO. B. BOYLES.......Tennessee.
WM. A. BARRY .... "
W. K. MAKEMSON.....Texas.
C R. GIBSON... ...... "
GEO ARBOGAST......Utah.
WM. W. HENRY.......Vermont.
H. M. CURRIER .... "
JAS. B. BLANKS...... Virginia.
MARION COLBERT.... "
JOHN M. SWAN........Washington.
W. G. ALBAN........... "
J. T. HOKE.............W. Virginia.
PHINEAS GANO........ "
JOHN G. CLARK. ......Wisconsin.
VAN S. BENNETT...... "
W. L. KUYKENDALL...Wyoming.

Representatives of Grand Encampments.

WM. A. SHIELDS....Alabama.
J. B. FRIEDHEIM...Arkansas.
CHAS. H. RANDALL.California.
L. L. ALEXANDER...   "
A. J. WOODBURY.....Colorado.
HIRAM FRANCIS . Connecticut
O. WOODHOUSE.....   "
ZINA RICHEY.......Dakota.
EDWIN HIRST.......Delaware.
OLIVER DUFOUR...Dist Colum
L. M. MERRITT ....Florida.
CHAS. A. ROBBE....Georgia.
WALTER E. CARLIN.Illinois.
WM. SCHUCHERT,...   "
ED. S. PORTER.....Indiana.
W. H. JACKS ....   "
HERMAN BLOCK... Iowa.
JAS. K. POWERS......   "
S. H. KELSEY........Kansas.
C. C. FURLEY........   "
WM. REINECKE... ..Kentucky.
T. J. ATKINS.........   "
JOSEPH VOEGTLE...Louisiana.
HENRY P. COX .....Maine.
CHAS. H. FRENCH...   "
JOSEPH THOMPSON..Maryland.
JOHN E. McCAHAN...   "
C. N. ALEXANDER...Mass.
JOHN U. PERKINS ...   "
SIMEON S. FRENCH..Michigan.
ALFRED MILNES ...   "
ED. A. STEVENS.....Minnesota
THOMAS RILEY,......   "

W. J. BRADSHAW.....Mississippi.
A. J. BLACKFORD,....Missouri.
C. F. VOGEL...........   "
JACOB LOEB, ... Montana.
ED. G. RYLEY.........Nebraska.
R. R. BIGELOW,.......Nevada.
JOHN GILLIS ... .N. Hamp're.
JOHN H. ALBIN........   "
LEWIS PARKER,.......New Jersey.
AARON B. CRANE,....   "
ENOCH JACOBS ...   .New York.
WM. I. CORNWELL...   "
CHAS. M. BUSBEE.....N. Carolina.
J B SHERIDAN,...... . Ohio.
JNO. N. VAN DEMAN... "
JOSEPH OLIVER.........Ontario.
FRANCIS RAE............   "
J. F. BACKENSTO,......Oregon.
M. R. MUCKLE ....Pennsyl'na.
ALFRED SLACK.........   "
LIND ANDERSON.......Rhode Is'd.
WM. S JOHNSON,.......   "
A. G. MAGRATH, Jr,....S. Carolina.
MARCUS JONES.........Tennessee.
FRED CARLETON,.......Texas.
LEO. J. RETTING,.......Vermont.
A. L. HILL...............Virginia.
J. T. BROWN.............Washing'n
JACOB MORRIS,..........W. Virg'n
P. VAN VECHTEN, Jr....Wisconsin.
CHAS. L. DERING,.......   "
LOUIS MILLER,...........,Wyoming.

Past Grand Sires of the Sovereign Grand Lodge.

JAS. B. NICHOLSON..Penns'va.
JAS P. SANDERS   .New York
MILTON J. DURHAM..Kentucky

JOHN W. STOKES....Pennsylv'nia
ERIE J. LEECH.......Iowa

COMMITTEE ON REVISION.

John H. Albin, P. G. M., New Hampshire.
Jno. C. Underwood, P. G. M., Kentucky.
Edward A. Stevens, P. G. M., Minnesota.

(Grand Rep. Underwood, having been elected Lieutenant-General, resigned from the committee, and the vacancy was filled by the appointment of John U. Perkins, Grand Rep., of Massachusetts.)

NEW COMMITTEE.

John H. Albin, P. G. M., New Hampshire.
John U. Perkins, P. G. M., Massachusetts.
Edward A. Stevens, P. G. M., Minnesota.

RESOLUTION RAISING COMMITTEE OF REVISION, ETC.

Rep. Albin, of New Hampshire, from the Committee on the Patriarchal Branch of the Order, made the following report, which was adopted.

To the Sovereign Grand Lodge of the Independent Order of Odd Fellows:

Your committee, to whom was referred the resolution of Rep. Furley, of Kansas, relating to additional legislation for the government of Uniformed Degree Camps, and also that changes be made in the secret working of the degree, so that the same may be made more effective and interesting to the candidate, beg leave to report that a large number of memorials, petitions, and resolutions, coming from very many jurisdictions, have been presented at this session and referred to your committee, relating in various ways to legislation for the degree, as well as for the government of the Camps themselves, thereby showing an imperative demand for a degree and the necessary legislation for the government and the successful working of the various Camps instituted in accordance therewith, that shall meet with the demands and necessities of the fraternity at large.

The session of this Grand Lodge is too short, and the work committed to its committee is too large, to enable us to give so important a matter the careful consideration and attention that it deserves, either at this or any other session.

We believe that, in order to make the degree what it should be, and to give it that position and importance by way of legislation for its government, which the large membership demands, the whole subject-matter should be referred to a committee of three, with instructions to ascertain what the demands of the fraternity require, as

thoroughly as they may be able, and that they be clothed
with the fullest power to make such changes and alterations in the ritual, and frame such legislation as may be
necessary for the successful working and government of
the Uniformed Degree, and report the same for the consideration of this Grand Lodge at its next session, therefore,

Resolved, That a committee of three be appointed by
the Grand Sire; with instructions to give the Uniformed
Degree, and all of the legislation heretofore adopted in
relation thereto, careful consideration, ascertain what
changes, revisions, alterations, amendments, and legislation may be necessary in order to make the degree as
satisfactory and effective as possible, and report the same
at the next session of this Grand Body for its consideration.

Respectfully submitted,

J. H. ALBIN,	H. T. DORRANCE,	FRANCIS JEWETT,
A. J. WOODBURY,	H. O. HEICHERT.	M. COLBERT,
JOHN HEESEMANN,	ISAAC F. CLARK.	

The Chair named as the committee:

Reps. Albin, of New Hampshire; Underwood, of
Kentucky; Stevens, of Minnesota.

(Proceedings of the Sov. Grand Lodge, I. O. O. F.,
session at Minneapolis, Minn., September 1884. *Journal*,
9778, 9813.)

THE PATRIARCHS MILITANT DEGREE.

HISTORICAL AND INTRODUCTORY.

This is a new degree in Odd-fellowship. It is an important event, at least to the five or six hundred thousand Odd-fellows; and to all thoughtful Americans who concern themselves about the destiny of the United States and that of the world as affected by our destiny.

I propose to consider: *1st. The History. 2nd. Motives. 3rd. Nature, and 4th. Relations* of this degree.

The history of Odd-fellowship as given in "Revised Odd-fellowship Illustrated* Chapter I, (from Standard writers; particularly from *Grosh*) with the ritual, now used in many Odd-fellow lodges, and the accompanying notes from their highest standard authorities put the whole system of Odd-fellowship; its origin, nature and history, under a shower of sunbeams.

The order thus (Revised Odd-fellowship pp. 21–30,) appears to have sprung up from old English clubs of immemorial usage, such as still exist in the back streets and blind alleys of London. There amid beer-mugs, on dirty dealboard tables, the poorer class of mechanics,

---

*Several months before the Lodges and Encampments of the Order had received their "*Charge Books*" from the Sovereign Grand Lodge, the publisher Ezra A. Cook had made a contract for copies of the Charge Books with the "unwritten work" added, so Lodges and Encampments instead of paying the Sovereign Grand Lodge $2.50 for the Lodge and $2.50 for the Encampment Ritual without the "unwritten" or Secret Work in, now get the exact ritual copied from the Charge Books, with the unwritten work added and illustrated for 50 cents in paper or $1.00 in cloth binding.

and their wives, even with babes at their bosoms: (I
have seen them) sit and drink, and listen to such songs
as

> In comes the jolly blacksmith, the prince of good fellows;
> He stands at the anvil while his man blows the bellows.

From this low origin has sprung the whole secret
lodge system.   Witness the four old masonic lodges in
four little Inns in London viz: "*The Goose and Grid-
iron*, "*Crown and Anchor;*" "Rummer and Grapes;"
and "Appletree Tavern" in 1717.   These four formed
the first Grand Lodge.   Satan, "the god of this world,"
kindles the fires of false religion at the bottom of the
human grate.   Ninety five years after these low Inn
Clubs formed the first devil worshiping Grand Lodge in
London, the same sort of drinking-clubs formed the first
Odd-fellows Lodge in Manchester, England.   The name
they chose, Odd-fellows, shows their vulgar and rowdy
origin.   This was in 1812; only seven years later, (1819)
Thos. Wildey, inoculated the United States, with this
religious epidemic, in a Baltimore tavern and it spread
like small pox.   Wildey's substitute for Christianity
was "to improve and elevate the character of man."
(*Grosh's Man. p. 31*, by making able bodied white men,
above 21 years of age "*Odd-fellows;*" stealing from the
Bible, but omitting Christ; while believing in a "Supreme
Being."–(*White's Dig. p. 48.*)

FIRST:—HISTORY OF THIS DEGREE.

A few years since, as Odd-fellowship was getting
familiar and stale, observing that the war had made the
false "Grand Army," and Knights Templar popular;
some Odd-fellows invented a Uniformed Odd-fellowship
which they called *The Patriarchal Circle*, and initiated
some who were not Odd-fellows.   The thing took and
the Circle set up for independence of the Sovereign

Grand Lodge This *Circle* charged $30 for its charters and $10 for four copies of its ritual and was doing a thriving business, which, of course, cut into the revenues of the Odd-fellows, and war at once arose between the Sovereign Grand Lodge and the "Supreme Temple."

Some Encampment Odd-fellows, in the "Patriarchal" degree of which system the candidate represents Isaac and his attempted sacrifice by Abraham on Mount Moriah, met in Wisconsin to contrive a Uniform like the Knights Templar. Learning that some Rhode Island and New Hampshire Patriarchs had already invented one, they sent for and adopted it; this was in 1868. Two Grand Sires of the Odd-fellows forbid, by proclamation, wearing that uniform. Grand Sire Stuart went to Providence to abolish the uniform. The Grand Patriarch and Scribe of Rhode Island, met the Grand Sire of the *Lodge of the World* at a tavern, doubtless took something to drink; and got him into an open carriage and the Patriarchs, with the brave uniform which he had forbidden them to wear, marched before him through the City and back to his Hotel. "Well" boys said Grand Sire Stuart, "it is fine, but you must not do it." Seeing the cap, plume and gauntlets were to be the rage, and the *Circle* would beat the Grand Lodge, Odd-fellows, who were also in the Patriarchal Circle, attempted to merge the Circle in this new degree which the Odd-fellows were getting up, called "The Patriarchs Militant," to swallow up the "Supreme Temple" of the Circle in the Sovereign Grand Lodge of the Odd-fellows. This attempt to merge the Circle in the lodge was made at a special session of the Supreme Temple in Chicago, November 1885. It was defeated by Ayes, 25; Noes, 37.—So the Sovereign Grand Lodge and Supreme Temple are still (1886) running head and head.   The Supreme Temple meets this year (July 14th, 1886) in Grand Rapids, Michigan, and though somewhat depleted by secessions to the Odd-fellows Grand Lodge, boast that but one in fifteen of the young men of America, are yet drawn into these lodges, and they are confident their swindle is to succeed.

Thus this degree of Patriarchs Militant is a fly-trap degree, to catch and bring back Odd-fellows who have wandered into the Patriarchal Circle.

This military degree was completed and its guns mounted against the Patriarchal Circle by the Sovereign Grand Lodge at its meeting in Baltimore, September 1885.   This was "the principal business" of the session and this is from the report adopted:

"SPECIAL COMMITTEE ON PATRIARCHAL ORDER.

"The principal business before this committee was the revision of the Uniform Degree Ritual.   The report which was adopted provides for a military system, something similar to the army regulations.   The name of the Degree is changed to "Patriarchs Militant," and the name of Canton substituted for Uniform Camp, as a unit of organization.   The Grand Sire is ex-officio Commander-in-chief, a Lieutenant-General who is the active Commander of the forces, a Captain-General, a Major-General, a Brigadier, a Colonel, a Lieutenant-Colonel, a Major, a Captain, a Lieutenant, an Ensign. These constitute the commissioned officers.

"The non-commissioned officers are a Sergeant-Major, a Quartermaster-Sergeant, a Commissary-Sergeant, a Color-Sergeant, an Equipment-Sergeant, a Hospital-Sergeant, a Trumpeter, a Standard Bearer, a special aid to the Lieutenant-General, with the rank of Lieutenant-Colonel for each State or Territorial department.

"There are to be Cantons and Grand Cantons, and the Sovereign Grand Lodge is the Supreme Canton, from which all authority emanates.   Members are to be addressed as Chevaliers.   Warrants and outfits are to be provided by the Sovereign Grand Lodge.   An outfit is composed of 3 Degree Books, proclamation, military blanks, etc., at a cost of $20.   The same outfit however is to be furnished bodies already organized, who have attained the Royal Purple Degree and who desire to be merged into a Canton of Patriarchs Militant, at actual cost, $12.00.

"A banner, 36 inches wide by 54 inches long, of scarlet silk, trimmed with gold lace fringe and tassels.   A flag, 40 inches wide by 60 inches long, composed of three vertical stripes—purple, white and scarlet, with guidons 24x36

Inches, half white and half scarlet, were adopted.   Also, a jewel composed of the escutcheon shields of the banner.

"The uniform is a full dress coat, undress, a black broad cloth military sacque, white vest, black cloth pants.   The Chapeau the same as now used, except that two white and one purple feather are used.   Shoulder knots are worn.   The baldric is changed and is worn by all Officers and Chevaliers over the left shoulder and under the right arm, so that the pouch or dispatch box will be above the belt.   The pouch is made of patent leather, with gilt ends and binding, and have a raised gilt crown enclosed on cover, with appropriate buckles and ornaments.   The belt of Russia leather, and the sword the same as now in use.

"The report is very lengthy, too much so to be presented in full in this number.   The ritual and laws governing the Degree will be issued as soon as they can be printed, and will at once go into effect.

"John C. Underwood, of Kentucky, was elected Lieutenant-General. The adoption of the new Degree is not compulsory."

This is the official report on this degree, adopted by the Sovereign Grand Lodge, and published in The Companion and American Odd-fellow, Columbus, Ohio, October 1885.

Mormons, Knights Templar, Grand Army of the Republic, Armed Secret Socialists and Dynamiters, The Patriarchal Circle; and now this Patriarchs degree, resting on half a million of Odd-fellows, are turning these United States into a nation of Secret Guerrilla bands, armed and drilling nightly, sworn to obey orders and waiting for something to do!   And while this writing proceeds, news comes of a new Secret Order of "Minute Men," started by a preacher, Edmonston of Sedalia, Mo., professedly to swear the friends of "law and order" in the United States, to aid in suppressing "Strikes and Boycotts" by armed secrecy, oaths, signs and grips, and, in a few weeks this new secret order reports seventeen thousand members.   As the daily papers inform us that large numbers of Knights of Labor, Freemasons and Odd-fellows have joined this new order and as it is given out that the order proposes to investigate the causes of strikes and boycotts, and oppose them if they are unwarranted, there is no reasonable doubt but the real purpose is to organize an armed force to sustain Strikes and Boycotts, while professing their object to be to regulate them. Another secret order against Strikes is just started in Chicago, called "*Conservators of Order*," to concentrate and aid in suppressing laborers' strikes wherever they may occur. Of course they must be armed.

Now these secret "law and order" bands, the Sovereign Grand Lodge of Odd-fellows included, exist in violation of the laws, which forbid bands of men to uniform, drill and parade, unless they belong to our open, organized Militia, and when their work is completed, "law and order" are at an end. Is not this Military outburst the flaming sword which spanned the heavens of the Hebrew Commonwealth before it fell? We have only to suppose some miscount in a Presidental Election; some Mormon outbreak and secret league with a political party such as Joe Smith attempted, and partly accomplished with Stephen A. Douglas, or some spark from the laborer's anvil, to ignite these magazines of political and military dynamite, and we shall have a war of internal factions, such as made the blood run ankle deep from the principal gate of Jerusalem; and such as kept the French guilotine wet, and the rivers of France red in the reign of terror under Robespierre, Couthon and St. Just.

Not counting Christians outside; if American church members, or one half of them, can be enlightened and brought to "vote as they pray," for God, the Sabbath and the Bible; impenitent and ungodly men cannot and will-not rule this Country:—Oaths will again become sacred and jurors honest. Our Presidental Campaigns will be-come, like the campaign of John Knox in Scotland, which overturned Popery without shedding a drop of

blood. Liquor will be prohibited; not licensed; the
earth will open her mouth and swallow up this flood of
darkness and crime which now issues from the mouth
of the dragon and the promised and predicted reign of
Peace, (not war) will come.

SECOND:—THE MOTIVES.

The prime motive of this new Odd-fellows degree, as
seen above, is to win back its military wanderers by
adopting cap, plume and gauntlets; and so out-strip and
swallow up the Patriarchal Circle. But swindlers, like
conquerors, must go on; and secretists are swindlers.
There must be new degrees to get more money:—To
prevent disgust by familiarity with the old degrees:—
To diminish the number at the top who divide and share
the funds and to amuse and bewilder those half sincere
souls who float in the "troubled sea" of imposture, by a
perpetual mirage of new inventions. So was it in France.
So is it here.

THIRD:—ITS NATURE.

The Patriarchal Degree scares its candidate by making
believe to sacrifice him, as Isaac. The Pariarchs Militant
play mustering in the candidates to fight Chedorlaomer
and rescue Lot, Abraham's Nephew. This perpetual
borrowing from the Bible, a trick practiced by the devil
before Christ; has the double effect of giving seeming
sanctity to the lodge, while it weakens faith in the Scriptures. The scene is the Plain of Mamre; the members
Abraham's "trained servants:"—the moral to intimidate
traitors to Odd-fellowship; and the whole drama to
substitute lying legends for divine truth; to sanctify
fraud; to seize on the popular taste for military music,

marching and parade; and keep the multitude from coming to Christ by consuming their time and means in the service of the Devil.

FOURTH:—ITS RELATIONS

It is allied to the whole dark family of Spiritual antogonisms to God and goodness. In it are the elements of Mesmerism, Charming, Spirit Worship, Sorcery, Animal Magnetism, Lodgery and every force, natural, spiritual and social; by which Satan finds access through the animal passions, to confuse the understanding, weaken the conscience and enslave the human will. As planets, approaching the sun, gain light, heat, expansion and life; so the soul of man gains elevation, growth and goodness in worshiping God. This coming to God, by worship through Christ, but for the fall, was our normal condition; forever to drink in glory, growth and goodness from God, as flowers get strength, colors and fragrance by opening to the sun. Satan's object is to stop that process by by substituting something else; for worship, wonder; for joy, giddiness; for the Holy Spirit, himself. And thus every lodge, mesmeric or Spirit circle; every dance of dervishes, shakers, Bondoo or Purrow in Africa, or among our own Indians, is a devil's waltz, in which the head swims, the brain reels, conscience slumbers; mind grows weak and the passions strong. Worship is the mightest effort of mind. To know God in Christ, is "life eternal." Worship, without Christ, is to wander from the way of understanding and remain in the congregation of the dead. To open one's house to thieves is harmless, to opening one's worship to devils. Look in the faces of a crowd coming out of a mormon temple, a masonic hall, a spirit dance or a brothel, and you are struck with the same weird mesmeric expression in them all. They all worship devils. I have seen mediums and false prophets who could pass into the cataleptic state at will; and in that state exhibit tokens of super-human and supernatural power.

Dr. Samuel Collins told me he had seen snakes, in his father's pasture in Indiana, crawl up upon stumps and charm birds on summer afternoons. It is said that charmed creatures, men or animals, see beautiful rainbow colors which entrance them and experience strangely delicious sensations, which enslave their wills, as liquor enslaves drunkards.

The newspapers, once in a while, give an uncontradicted account of a girl pining away. who went daily to a jungle and sat down on a rock, from which an adder crawled and coiled himself upon her lap, whose eyes held hers in a fixed gaze till the spell was over. Her father watched his child, shot the snake, and the girl recovered.

Rev. J. R. Baird also who had taken seventeen degrees, addressing our Pittsburgh Convention (1868) said; "You ask: "why did you go on to seventeen degrees of such stuff after you knew what it was? I answer, we go on in those degrees, as a charmed frog goes into a snake's mouth!" The story of his escape on the night of a revival, was thrilling in the extreme. An otherwise respectable neighbor, in Wheaton, Illinois, has said he was never conscious of such full and perfect satisfaction and delight as while going through with the masonic ritual in a lodge at night. Yet, to some outsiders, nothing seems more loathsome and disgusting. But we need not particularize. The inspired writers from Moses to Paul, nay from Genesis to the Apocalypse, set before us legions of devils who tempted Christ, entered Judas, sifted Peter, possessed demoniacs, helped sorcerers and wrought miracles to *"deceive the Kings of the Earth and the whole world."*

This is New Testament teaching, while in the Old, the same fallen spirits everywhere appear, receiving the worship of Gentile nations, withstanding God's Prophets, overturning dynasties; instituting false religions without law, gospel or mediator, and in their chosen character of "unclean spirits," setting up temples to impurity and divorcing souls from the true bridegroom Christ, who is the source and fountain of moral goodness, and enslaving those to

"Gods partial, changeful, passionate, unjust,
Whose attributes, were rage, revenge and lust."

Such is the family to which this new Patriarchs degree of Odd-fellowship belongs. Does any believer of the the Bible suppose these evil spirits are less active now than formerly? Now that their time is short, and as we prove by *reductio ad absurdum* that the shortest line is straight, because between two points there can be no other; so we know that devils run these lodges, because, within the scope of finite intelligence, or the revelation of the infinite mind to ours, there is no order or class of creatures who ever did or could induce men to practice the degrading mummeries of idolatry but these. And if the facts and reasonings here given are correct, the dusky broods of secretism now, weekly pouring in upon the Christian nations, are locusts from the "bottomless pit" whose smoke now "darkens the sun and the air." The Masonic Lodge sits chief and owns the large temples in which she shelters her dusky brood; and they together form one system whose law is despotism, whose religion is heathenism, and its end blood. Never since Mahomet, did an armed false religion end otherwise.

And if history repeats itself, if rejecting Christ from their religion sunk the Hebrew Common-wealth, this sudden burst of night drilling lodges, Mormons, Grand Army, Knights Templar, Patriarchal Circle, and this degree of Patriarchs Militant; with a reserve corps of Secret Dynamiters behind, swearing the same obedience to they know not whom:—these are not only facts but precursors.   They are the cohorts which Josephus tells us were seen in the clouds above Judea and the flaming sword which hung over Jerusalem before Titus burned their temple; and that wonderful nation went down by "rapine, murder, famine and pestilence within; and fire, sword and all the terrors of war without," (Jos. p. 557.) When "the people fed on one another, and even ladies broiled their sucking infants and ate them."

Just fifty years ago when the white haired Dr. Lyman Beecher taught us that the terrible predictions of Christ and his Apostles would be fulfilled on American soil; his words seemed to us harmless vaticination.   But a brief quarter of a century passed and Julia Ward Howe's "Battle Hymn of the Republic" showed these prophetic pictures turned to real life and set them to music whose echoes still live:

Mine eyes have seen tho glory of the coming of the Lord,
He is treading out his vintage where the grapes of wrath are stored.

Yet how few of the million who have sung those words saw in them the literal fulfilment of the prophecy of John, (Rev. 14, 20.)   When the Angel cast "the vine of the earth into the great wine press of the wrath of God, and blood came out of the wine press."

There is but one preventive of a repetition of these horrors; that is the repentance, fasting and prayer which saved Nineveh. This will save us. The Hebrews never turned from their idol vanities, to the altars where Christ was worshipped as their Messiah, but their enemies made peace with them; their Common-wealth was restored and the hills and valleys of Judea rang with the joyous anthems of that "happy people whose God is the Lord."

QUALIFICATIONS FOR MEMBERSHIP, ETC.

This Military Degree shall be open to Patriarchs of
the Royal Purple Degree everywhere, the condition requisite for receiving or retaining membership being good
standing in a regular Encampment of the Order, without
reference to jurisdiction.   Thus an applicant for enrollment on the roster of a Canton shall furnish only a
certificate of membership and good standing in his Encampment, and make application in the form prescribed
by law, and it shall be received and considered, regard-
less of the jurisdiction from which he hails; but it shall
require a three-fourths ($\frac{3}{4}$) ball vote of the members present at the time the ballot is taken to elect.

HEADQUARTERS

Patriarchs * Militant,

I. O. O. F.

OFFICE OF THE LIEUTENANT-GENERAL.

GENERAL ORDER No I.

Covington, Ky., November, 1885.

To the rank and file of the Army of Patriarchs Militant:

Pursuant to enactment of the Sovereign Grand Lodge, I. O. O. F., September 24, 1885, the following Ritual and Ceremonies for the Patriarchs Militant Degree are promulgated for the guidance and government of Cantons and Chevaliers. All organized Bodies and Chevaliers comprising the rank and file ot the Army of Patriarchs Militant, are hereby ordered to observe and obey the forms and requirements herein set forth, under penalty of the law.

By command of

Jno C Underwood

Lieutenant-General Commanding.

Official:

O J Hemms

Adjutant-General.

INSTRUCTIONS.

The word to be given at the outer door is the Countersign, selected annually by the grand Sire and promulgated by the Lieutenant General.

When the Commandant of a Canton is absent, the Lieutenant will assume command and take the Captain's tent; the Ensign will take the Lieutenant's station; and the acting Commandant will appoint a temporary Officer of the Guard, etc.

When the Commandant of a Grand Canton is absent, the next Field Officer in rank, or the senior Captain present, will assume command, and take the Commandant's tent, etc.

Should all the commissioned officers be absent, the senior *retired* officer present will take the Commandant's tent, etc.

In floor work by a Grand Canton, the officer next in rank to the Commandant will take the Lieutenant's tent, and the next in rank the Ensign's station; and all be addressed by their proper military titles.

The uniform to be worn in this degree must conform to the regulations adopted by the Sovereign Grand Lodge of the I. O. O. F., and the floor movements must be executed after the manner of ritualistic requirements.

When the Canton is open and at work, it will be necessary for each Chevalier present to be clothed in the stipulated uniform, or as may be modified by provisions of law.

In petitioning a Canton for membership, it is necessary to annex to the application for membership, a certificate from the Encampment of which the applicant is a member, setting forth the fact that he is a Patriarch of the Royal Purple Degree in good standing.

The elective officers of a Canton are a Captain, a Lieutenant, and an Ensign, commissioned; and a Clerk and an Accountant, non-commissioned. They hold office for one year, and until their successors shall be mustered and installed.

The appointed officers are a Standard-Bearer, a Guard, a Sentinel, and a Picket, who rank in the Canton in the order named. They are appointed by and hold their positions at the will of the Commandant.

The quorum for a Canton is nine (9) Chevaliers present.

Balloting on applications for membership shall be by ball ballot.

The manner of voting (except upon an application for membership) shall be Yes or No.

There should be a circular tent at the stations of Captain and Lieutenant.

(For other and detailed law, see Organization, regulations, etc.)

(In the arrangement of this work, founded upon the narrative contained in the fourteenth chapter of Genesis of the Old Testament, the Ritualistic charges, lectures, obligations, etc., were prepared by John H. Albin, Grand Rep. from New Hampshire; the Military features, including Plates showing floor manœuvres, etc., Forms for opening and closing a Canton, for the installation of officers, for mustering a Canton into service, for the burial of a Chevalier, etc., were prepared by Jno. C. Underwood, Grand Rep. from Kentucky.)

NOTE—In all the military manœuvres that I have prepared, I have adopted the movement by "threes" instead of by "fours," as the number of files to be made the ordinary unit for breaking into column. Not that I prefer such file unit, where numbers are unlimited, but with a small command a much greater display can thereby be made. Thus; 24 file will break from line into column of 8 sets of "threes," or 6 sets of "fours." Now the casual observer will never notice the slight difference in the width of the column, but will very likely count the number of "threes" as they pass; and, consequently, the display is practically one-fourth greater.

In order to make the greatest possible display with the fewest men, I have dispensed with the "file closers," and place the Lieutenant and Ensign on the right and left of the line, and use them, if necessary, as guides. Also, that the Canton may always appear to advantage in public, I have designated 24 file and 3 officers, 27 in all, as the minimum number to be allowed to turn out and parade as a Canton on display occasions.

In the arrangement of special military movements for display purposes in a hall, some license should be allowed in the formation of bodies, position of officers, and in distances. Where double ranks are used in the following ritual manœuvres, the distances have been extended for floor effect (see Diagrams 4, 5, 6 and 8;) however, the single rank movements (Diagram 7) are easier and equally handsome.

In the Tactics, approved and promulgated, the Chevaliers FALL IN with swords at a "Carry;" but in the floor manœuvres, I desire the effect of the display derived from the *flash of steel*, obtained by drawing the swords simultaneously. Hence the command to Draw—Swords, and return—Swords, given to Canton in line.

To execute the movements hereinafter described, the Canton should be counted off by sixes. For formations of Canton (except in *special* movements and positions of Officers and Chevaliers, hereinafter explained by text or diagrams,) and plate representations of Officers, etc., see Diagram 1.

J. C. U.

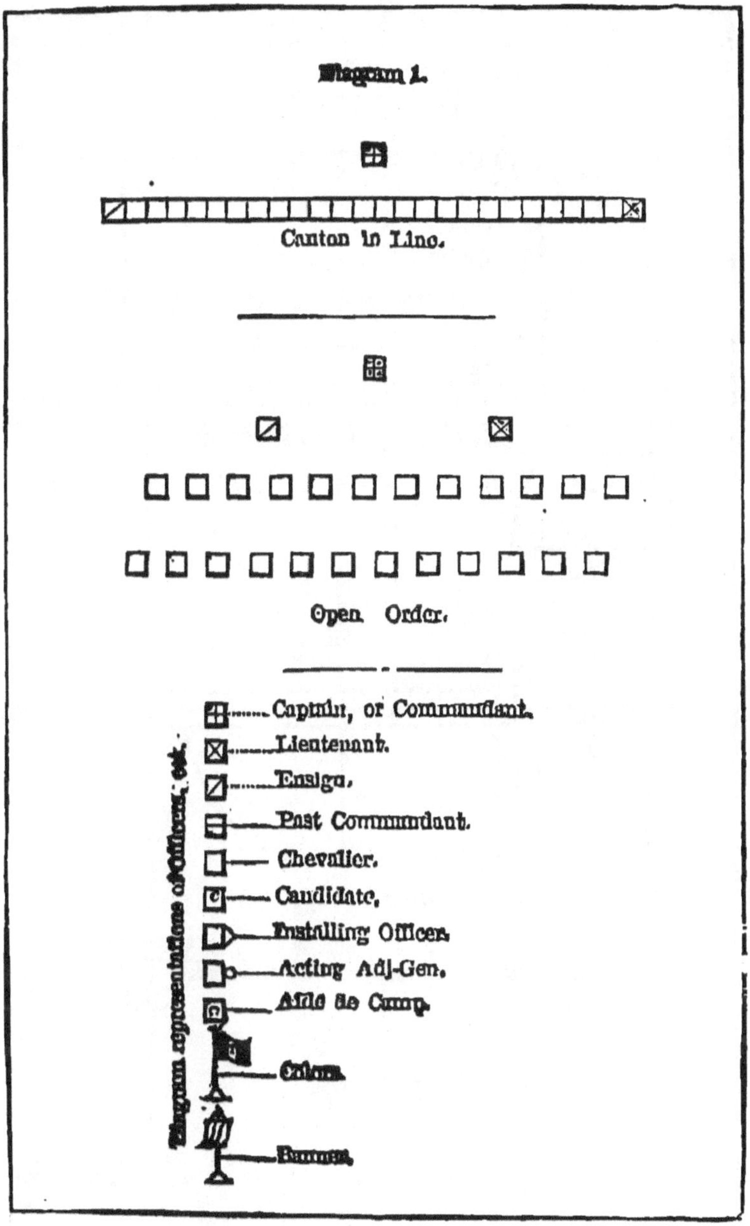
Diagram 1.
Canton in Line.
Open Order.
Captain, or Commandant.
Lieutenant.
Ensign.
Past Commandant.
Chevalier.
Candidate.
Installing Officer.
Acting Adj-Gen.
Aide de Camp.
Colors.
Banner.
Diagram representations of Officers, etc.

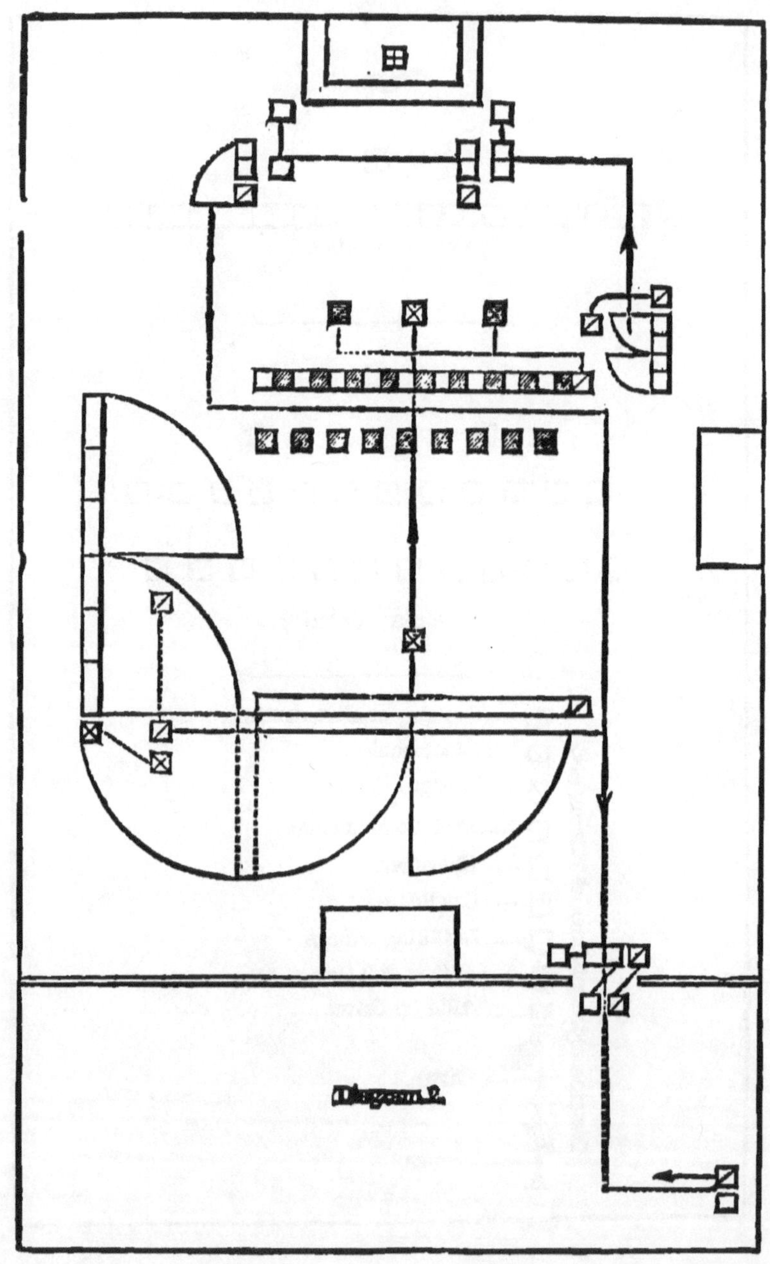

Diagram 2.

FORM FOR OPENING A CANTON.

[The Captain (the Commandant) is in front of his tent. At the time for opening, the Ensign will station the Guard on the left of the tent, the Standard-Bearer on the right of the tent, the Sentinel at the inner door, and the Picket at the outer door. (See Diagram 2.) He will informally require the countersign and Department check of each of the above officers, as he places them on duty; and will communicate to the Sentinel the Canton pass; after which he will report to the Lieutenant, who has formed the Chevaliers in line, at a "*carry*" and then take his position in front of the second platoon; the Lieutenant will then command·]

Lieutenant—Continue the march, Platoon, Right wheel—MARCH; Forward, Column left—MARCH; Guide left; Continue the march, Left into line wheel—MARCH; Forward—MARCH; Guide right; Canton—HALT; Right —DRESS; FRONT; Present—SWORDS.

[See Diagram 2. In wheeling Platoons, the Chief of each Platoon gives the proper sub-command. (See Tactics.*) The Lieutenant will About FACE, salute the Commandant, and report as follows:]

Lieutenant—Sir, the Sentinel and Guards are at their stations, the Canton pass has been communicated, the banner has been unfurled, and the lines are formed.

[The Commandant salutes the Lieutenant with hand, and commands:]

Commandant—Examine—CANTON; and Prepare for —INSPECTION.

Lieutenant—Carry—SWORDS; Rear open order— MARCH; FRONT. [See Diagram 2.] (Addressing Ensign.) Sir, you will ascertain if all Chevaliers in rear rank are in possession of the countersign and Department check.

[The Lieutenant takes position in front of the right file in the front rank, and the Ensign takes position in front of the right file in the rear rank, both officers facing their respective ranks.]

Lieutenant—(Addressing the first Chevalier in front rank.) Give countersign and Department check— ADVANCE.

---

*Note—Upton's work on Military Tactics has been adopted as the standard for this degree.

Ensign—(Addressing the first Chevalier in rear rank.) Give countersign and Department check—ADVANCE.

[The Chevaliers come to position of "Swords—PORT;" advance one step with left foot, and communicate the words in a whisper to the officers respectively. The officers will say "Correct," when the Chevaliers will come to a "carry;" "About—FACE;" march forward two steps "About—FACE:" advance and resume positions in line. Each officer, with sword at a "carry," will then pass to the front of the next Chevalier, and so on down the line, receiving the countersign and Department check in like manner from every Chevalier in the ranks. As soon as either officer completes the examination of his rank, he will take position opposite to and in front of the center of his platoon, both two paces in front of the front rank. When the last officer has completed his examination, and has taken his position, the Ensign will face and address the Lieutenant:]

Ensign—Lieutenant.   (Whereupon that officer will face the ensign, who salutes and reports:)   Sir, all correct in rear rank.

[The Lieutenant and Ensign then face the Commandant, and both officers saluting, the Lieutenant reports:]

Lieutenant—Sir, all Chevaliers are in possession of the countersign and Department check.

Commandant—(Addressing the officers.)   Gentlemen, you will accompany me in the inspection.

[The Lieutenant faces the Canton and gives the order:]

Lieutenant—Inspection—SWORDS.

[And with the Ensign, accompanies the Commandant in the inspection. They pass in front and rear of each line, and make such examination of the Chevaliers and arms as the Commandant deems sufficient. The officers return to their positions, and, with the Commandant standing in front of the tent, the Lieutenant commands, carry—SWORDS; Close order—MARCH; and the canton passes in review. (See Tactics.) After review, the body will be moved to a proper position in line, facing the Commandant:]

Lieutenant-Present—SWORDS; (and, saluting, reports:) Sir, the Canton awaits orders.

Commandant—Canton, Carry—SWORDS; Return—SWORDS; Right—FACE; Break ranks—MARCH.

[The Chevaliers will take seats, the officers take their chairs and stands, and the business will proceed,]

[At the time of opening, Chevaliers present from other Departments shall not be required to give the Department check.]

[The Commandant will rank as a Captain; and in Grand Cantons may be a Captain or a Field Officer and rank as a Major, Lieutenant Colonel, or Colonel, according to the size of the Grand Canton.]

ORDER OF BUSINESS.

1. Call roster of officers.

2. Read minutes of the last Cantonment; which must be declared approved unless objections are made, in which case, errors (if any) must be corrected, and then the minutes must be approved and signed.

3. Consideration of reports upon previous applications for membership.

4. Candidates admitted and mustered into service.

5. Proposals for membership received and referred.

6. Unfinished business.

7. New business.

8. Has any Chevalier anything to offer for the good of the Canton?

9. Closing ceremony.

[A Canton may adopt such Order of Business as it deems necessary; but the above form must be used when no other has been provided.]

(Patriarchal Proclamation.)

A ROUGHLY
DESIGNED
ANCIENT SEAL.

Lot, my brother's son, has been taken prisoner by Chedorlaomer, King of Elam, and carried away into captivity. Now, therefore, I do command all of my trained servants, born in my own house, to report without delay, at my tent beneath the Oak of Mamre, near

Hebron; there to be enrolled and supplied with weapons of war, and march at once in pursuit of the enemy; recapture my brother's son at all hazards, and bring him back to his home.

ABRAM,
Patriarch.

AN OUTLINE

OF A

WILD BOAR'S HEAD.

[The foregoing Proclamation shall be of ancient design, and be issued by the Sovereign Grand Lodge as supplies. It shall be printed in red ink, in imitation of the blood of a wild boar, the type to be large, and so made that the proclamation will appear to have been rudely lettered with a stick, dipped in blood to make a mark, on imitation of old hand-beaten paper (made by the ancients out of the inner bark of the papyrus, spread upon and beat into the porous mummy-cloth) or a dressed hide, and a copy thereof shall be placed in a conspicuous position near the Ensign's station, during Part First of the initiation.]

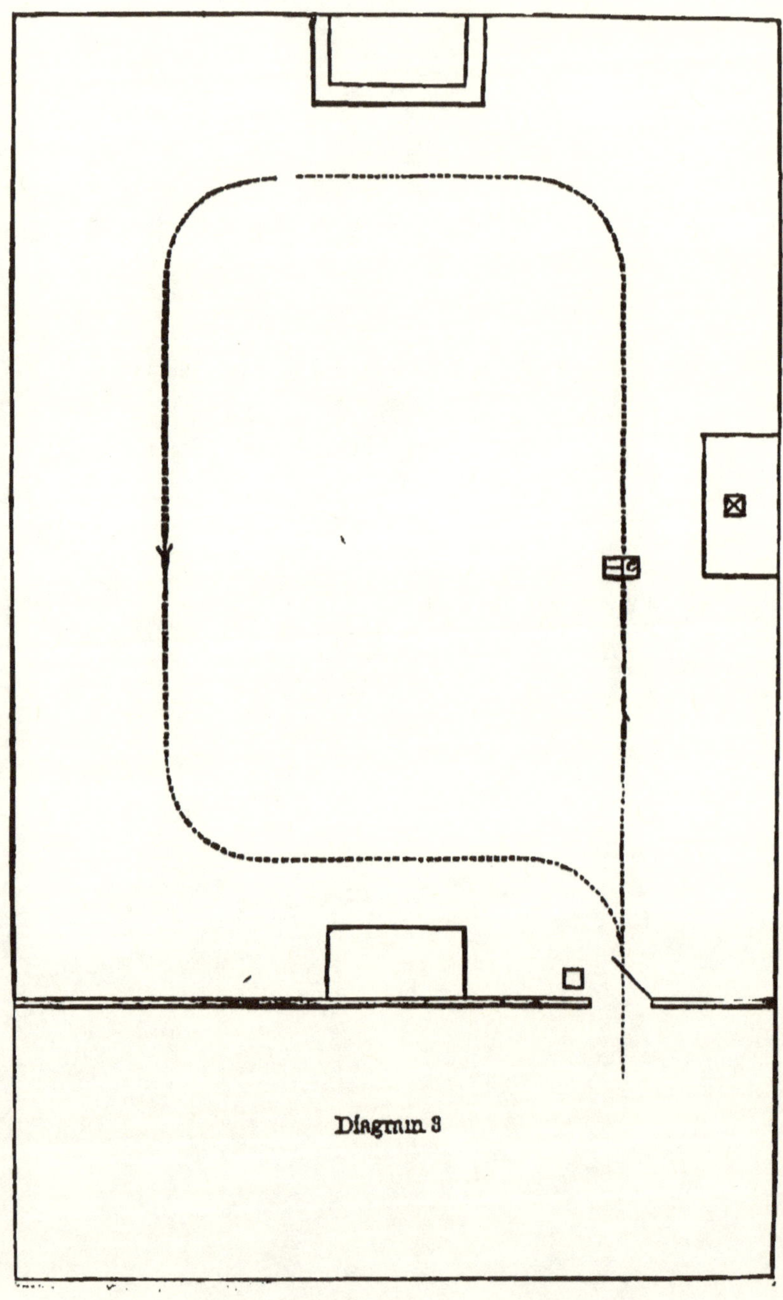

Diagram 3

DEGREE

OF

PATRIARCHS MILITANT.

PART FIRST.

[Scene supposed to be on the Plain of Mamre, near the tent of Lieutenant commanding outpost. The members are seated about the room in undress uniforms; the Lieutenant is the only officer at his station. (See Diagram 3.) The candidate, with shepherd's crook in his hand and accompanied by the Past Commandant, enters the room without form and passes in front of the Lieutenant's Station. As they reach the Lieutenant's station, that officer salutes the Past Commandant, who with the candidate halt, and the Lieutenant addresses him as follows:]

Lieutenant—Welcome, my friend.

Past Commandant—Hail, worthy Patriarch. This stranger, whom I now present to you, has read the proclamation of Patriarch Abram; and, in obedience to his command, is hastening to the tent beneath the Oak of Mamre, near Hebron.

[The Lieutenant advances to the candidate, shakes hands with him, and proceeds as follows:]

Lieutenant—Welcome, my friend. I now recall that we have met in the past. I well remember the many perils and dangers through which you passed on your way to the tent of the excellent High Priest. Abram the Patriarch, is sore distressed. A terrible battle has been fought in the V. 'e of Siddim, in which the King of Elam and his associates were victorious. Thereupon, the victors took all of the goods of Sodom and Gomorrah, and all of their victuals, and went their way; and took also Lot, Abram's brother's son, who dwelt in Sodom, and all of his goods, and departed. And there came one, who had escaped, and told Abram all of these things; and when he heard that his brother's son was taken captive, he issued a Patriarchal proclamation to all of his trained servants, born in his own house, of whom there were three hundred and eighteen in number, to report immediately at his tent at the Oak of Mamre, near Hebron, in order that they might become duly enrolled, armed, and equipped to redress the wrong. You will, therefore, proceed to the Plain of Mamre, where you will find the army of Patriarch Abram securely intrenched, with picket lines thrown out, and guards stationed at every point. The utmost precautions are everywhere taken to prevent the admission of enemies or spies within the lines or ranks; hence you must expect to be subjected to many inconveniences during your progress to the tent. I shall meet you again in camp and on the march; side by side we will render valiant service in the cause of our good Patriarch Abram. Farewell.

[The Past Commandant and candidate proceed on their way around the room, past the stations of the Commandant, Past Commandant, and Officer of the Guard, and thence into the anteroom. (See Diagram 3) As they leave the station of the Lieutenant, that officer stands looking after them until they have proceeded a short distance, and then, as if soliloquizing, proceeds as follows:]

Lieutenant—Alas, what a strange contrast to the usually quiet life of a Patriarch, this state of things presents. In "peace or war" he is equally ready and earnest in the discharge of his duties. In times of peace, his attention is taken up with his flocks and herds; he is then thoroughly engrossed in rural pursuits, and in doing good among his fellow-men. His sheep know his voice and seek his presence. The needy and distressed reverence him. He mingles with them in their joys, sympathizes with them in their sorrows, and never allows them to go empty-handed from his tent. But in times of war all is changed. The Patriarch then becomes thoroughly armed and equipped; he submits to and aids in enforcing the most rigid military discipline. He never resorts to arms for purposes of mere personal aggrandizement. His conflicts are always waged for the redress of injustice, or for the establishment of some high moral principle; and at the termination of the contest, he quietly returns to his flocks and herds, and resumes the life of the noble Patriarch. His crowning motto is "Universal Justice."

PART SECOND.

[The Commandant is in his tent, the Ensign (Officer of the Guard) is drilling 6 or 12 Guards in the use of the sword (see Diagram 4 or 7,) and the members are scattered about the Canton in fatigue uniform. The candidate and Past Commandant arrive at the inner door on their way to the tent, where the Past Commandant gives the entersign, and in reply is challenged by the Sentinel as follows:]

Sentinel—Halt. Who comes there?

Past Commandant—A servant and kinsman of Patriarch Abram, who desires an interview with the Commandant.

[They are admitted. Sentinel, turning to the Officer of the Guard, and, after he has completed one or two movements in the manual, ending with a "carry," says:]

Sentinel—Ensign.

[The Officer of the Guard turns toward the Sentinel, who reports:]

Sentinel—Sir, I have here one who desires to communicate with the Commandant.

Officer of the Guard—(Facing and addressing the candidate.) Who are you?

Past Commandant—(Replying for candidate.) I am a servant of Abram, born in his own house.

Officer of the Guard—How old art thou?

Past Commandant—I am of lawful age.

Officer of the Guard—Whence came you?

Past Commandant—From the flocks and herds committed to my care.

Officer of the Guard—Your answers are satisfactory. You may pass through the lines, under guard, to the tent of our commandant, upon the strict condition that you pledge your sacred honor that you are not an enemy nor a spy, and that you will not disclose anything that you may discover during your stay within our lines. Are you willing to bind yourself by such an obligation?

Candidate—I am.

Officer of the Guard—Raise your right hand and repeat after me the following obligation: (and, turning to the Guard, commands:) With swords—CHARGE. (See Diagram 4 or 7.)

[The candidate, standing just within the inner door, which has been closed behind him, raises his right hand and repeats the following obligation after the Officer of the Guard:]

FIRST OBLIGATION PATRIARCHS MILITANT.

I,............., do solemnly declare that I am of the Patriarchal Order; that I am a friend to the cause which this army is endeavoring to vindicate; that I am actuated by honest and worthy motives, and am not an enemy seeking to pass through these lines for hostile or unworthy purposes. I will never improperly disclose anything that I may learn while within this Canton. All this I promise upon my honor as a Patriarch of the Royal Purple Degree.

Officer of the Guard—If you are what you claim to be, you have nothing to fear. I will escort you under strict guard, to the tent of the Commandant: (and, facing Guard, commands:) Carry—SWORDS; Right forward, Threes right—MARCH; Guard—HALT. [See Diagram 4 or 7.] (And, placing candidate between the middle "threes" of column, at extended or wheeling distance, commands:) Forward—MARCH; Column right—MARCH; Column right—MARCH; Threes left—MARCH; Guard—HALT. [See Diagram 4 or 7.]

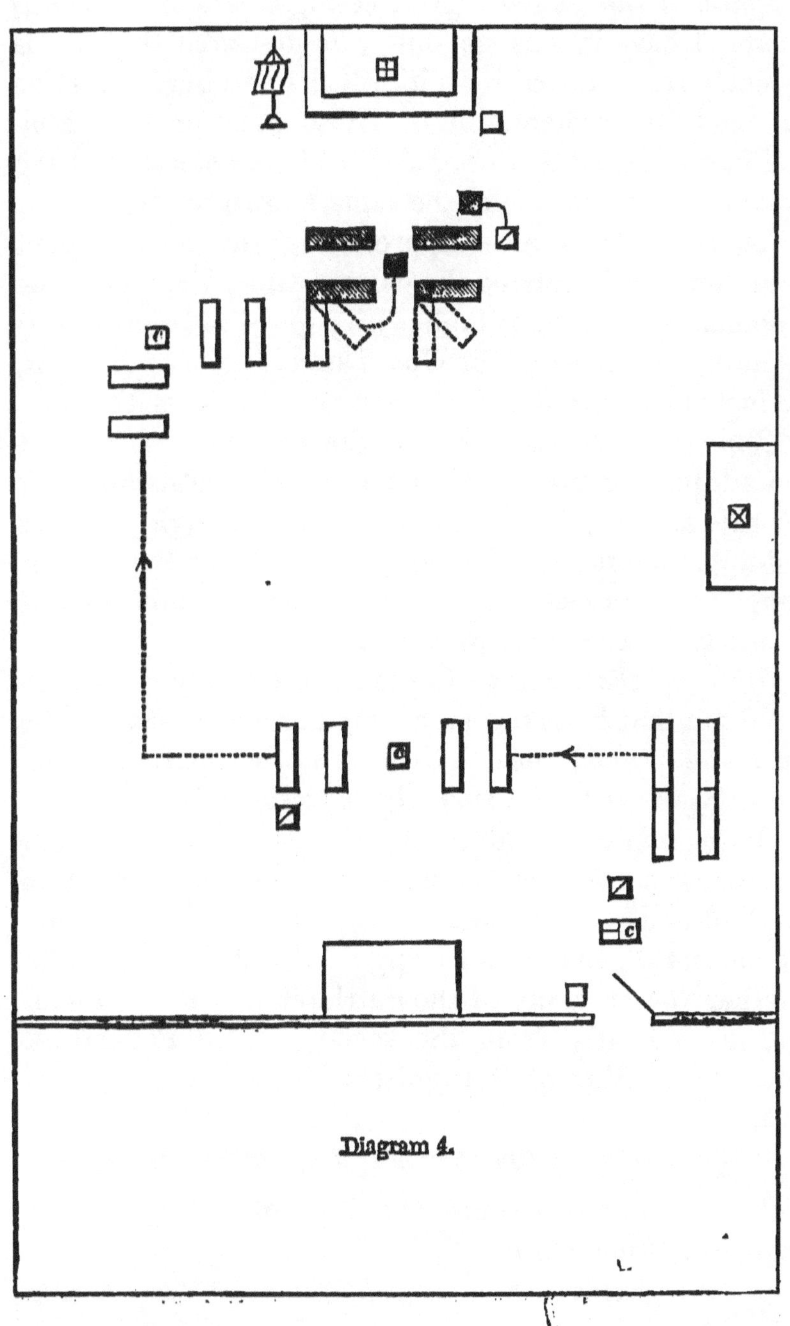

Diagram 4.

Officer of the Guard—(Addressing Guard of the Tent.)
Guard, I have in charge one who declares that he is
recently from the care of his flocks and herds; that he
has read the proclamation of Abram, and presents himself in obedience thereto.   Ascertain the pleasure of the
Commandant, and make the same known to me.

Guard of the Tent—(Approaching the Commandant
in his tent, and drawing the curtain aside, displaying the
Commandant sitting at table with papers, addresses him:)
Captain, the Officer of the Guard stands before your tent,
having in custody one who desires to confer with you.

Commandant—(Coming to the entrance of his tent
and addressing the officer of the Guard.)   Ensign, why
has this stranger been allowed to pass through our lines
and approach my tent?   Do you not know that in our
camps every precaution must be taken to admit no one
who may be an enemy or a spy?

Officer of the Guard—Captain, this stranger has assured me that he is not an enemy nor a spy, but that he
has come in obedience to Abram's proclamation, to enroll himself with the army which you so ably command.

Commandant –(Addressing the candidate.)   Your
purpose, if sincere, is commendable; but you cannot be
enrolled under our banner until I am certain that you
are neither an enemy nor a spy.   I must first ascertain
whether you are truly of the Patriarchal Order, of lawful
age, and recently from the society of the Patriarchs.
Advance the Sign of Recognition in the Initiatory Degree.

[Candidate gives the sign as on page 67 of *Revised Odd Fellowship
Illustrated.*]

Commandant—Advance the Sign of Safety in the
Degree of Friendship.

[Candidate gives the sign as on page 97 of *Revised Odd Fellowship
Illustrated.*]

Commandant—What is the Token of the Degree or Brotherly Love?

[Candidate gives the token as on page 110 of *Revised Odd Fellowship Illustrated*.]

Commandant—Advance the Principal Sign of the Degree of Truth.

[Candidate gives the sign as on page 139 of *Revised Odd Fellowship Illustrated*.]

[If the candidate answers the foregoing questions correctly, the Commandant will call for other proofs in any of the Subordinate Lodge or Encampment degrees. and must by some means cause him to fail or hesitate. As soon as the candidate fails or hesitates to answer any question that he may put, the Commandant will proceed as follows:]

Commandant—Now I know that you are an enemy and a spy. Ensign, why did you allow this person to pass through our lines without some pledge as to the truth of his statement?

Officer of the Guard—Captain, I did require of him a solemn pledge that he was neither an enemy nor a spy, but a true and honest Patriarch.

Commandant—Can it be possible that he is so base, so devoid of honor? Drive this man beyond the lines, and inflict the punishment merited for his perfidy.

Officer of the Guard—Threes right, double time—MARCH; Column right—MARCH. (See Diagram 5 or 7.)

[In compliance with the command of the Commandant, the prisoner is being forced out at "double time," when the movement is arrested by the Lieutenant, by whose station the Guard is passing.]

Lieutenant—Hold.

Officer of the Guard—Guard—HALT. (See Diagram 5 or 7.)

Lieutenant—(Addressing Ensign, the Officer of the Guard.) Sir, why this outrage to my friend?

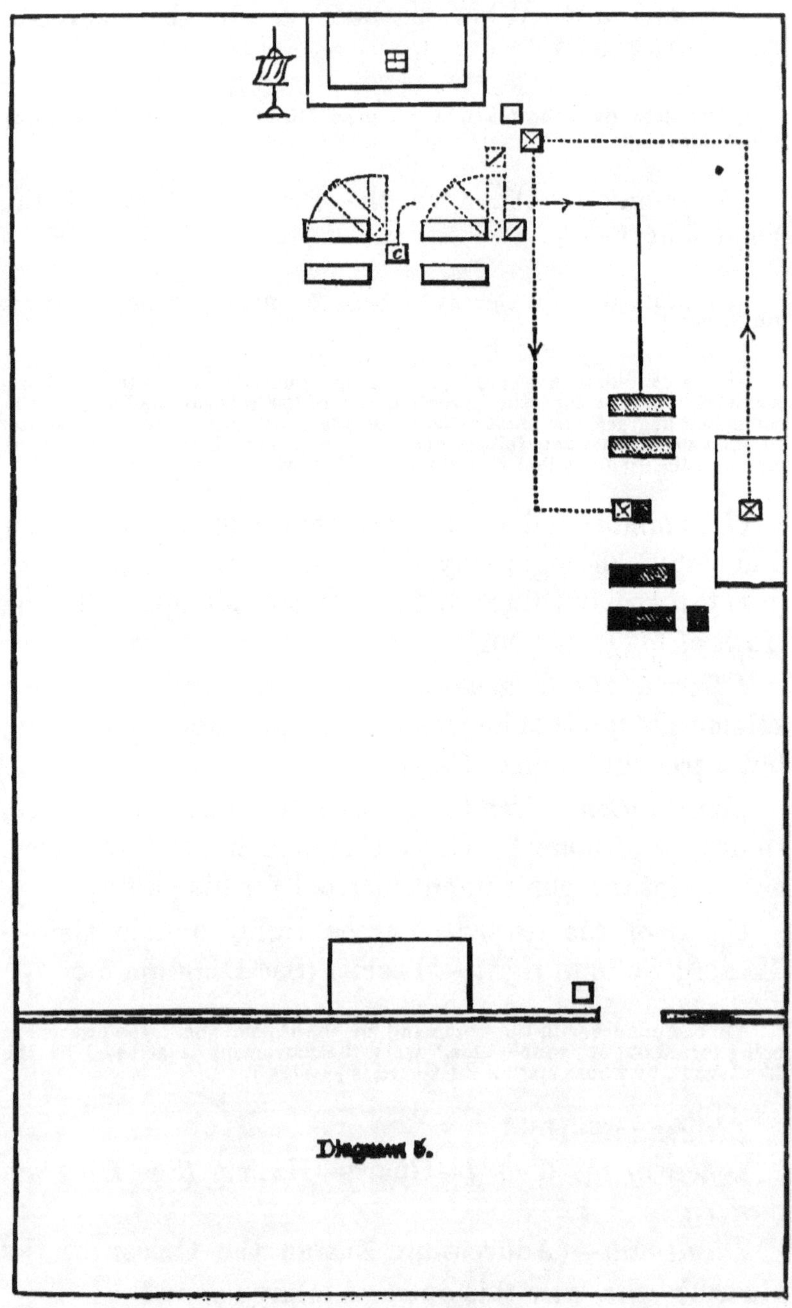

Diagram 5.

Officer of the Guard—Lieutenant, this man cannot be your friend. He came here as a Patriarch, and asked to be enrolled into our ranks; yet, out of his own mouth has he been condemned. The Commandant has ordered that he be immediately driven beyond the lines, there to receive merited punishment for his perfidy.

Lieutenant—He is neither enemy nor spy. I know him well. Halt here, while I proceed to the tent and confer with the Commandant.

[The Lieutenant proceeds rapidly to a position in front of the Commandant's tent, and addresses the Guard of the Tent.]

Lieutenant—Guard, is the Commandant at leisure? I would confer with him upon a matter of pressing importance.

Guard of the Tent—(Approaching the entrance of the tent, and drawing the curtain aside, says:) Captain, the Lieutenant stands without, and desires to confer with you upon a matter of pressing importance.

Commandant—(Coming to the entrance of the tent.) Lieutenant, what do you desire?

Lieutenant—Captain, a deserving friend of mine presented himself before your tent, desiring to be enrolled under our banner; he was not allowed to do so; but is being driven beyond the lines in disgrace, and is to receive punishment. I saw him, recognized his deplorable condition, and commanded the Guard to halt. I pray you that he may be returned to your tent, and his request be complied with.

Commandant—Permit him to be enrolled under our banner? Impossible! We admit neither enemy nor spy within our ranks.

Lieutenant—Captain, he is neither an enemy nor a spy, but a true and honest Patriarch.

Commandant—How do you know all this?

Lieutenant—I have known him long and well. I first saw him sitting at the feet of "age and experience," patiently learning that in the practice of friendship, love, and truth would be found the best safeguards against the ills of life; after this, I observed him at the "Stone Ezel," where he devoutly studied the beautiful truths taught by the Degree of Friendship; I next met him "traveling from Jerusalem to Jericho on a mission of humanity;" afterward, I saw him with those of the Priestly Order inculcating the principles of the Degree of Truth; later I sat with him in the High Priest's tent, where he partook of refreshments; thence he went out to impress upon the different nations of the earth the important doctrine of toleration; and, before to-day, I last saw him pursuing his weary way past the four Watches in the wilderness, determined to "go on," until, at last, I saw him presented as a weary and worn pilgrim at the tent of the High Priest, and surrounded by the Patriarchs.

Commandant—Can this be so? If it be true, he is neither an enemy nor a spy, but worthy to be enrolled under our banner. Command the officer of the Guard to return him to my presence, at once, that I may examine him further.

[The Lieutenant returns to the Guard, and, placing himself by the side of the prisoner (see Diagram 5 or 7,) says:]

Lieutenant—Ensign, the Commandant directs that you immediately return this my friend to his presence.

[And, retaining position alongside of candidate, accompanies him to the Commandant.]

Officer of the Guard—Forward—March; Column right—March; Column right—March; Column right—March; Threes left—March; Guard—Halt. (Ad-

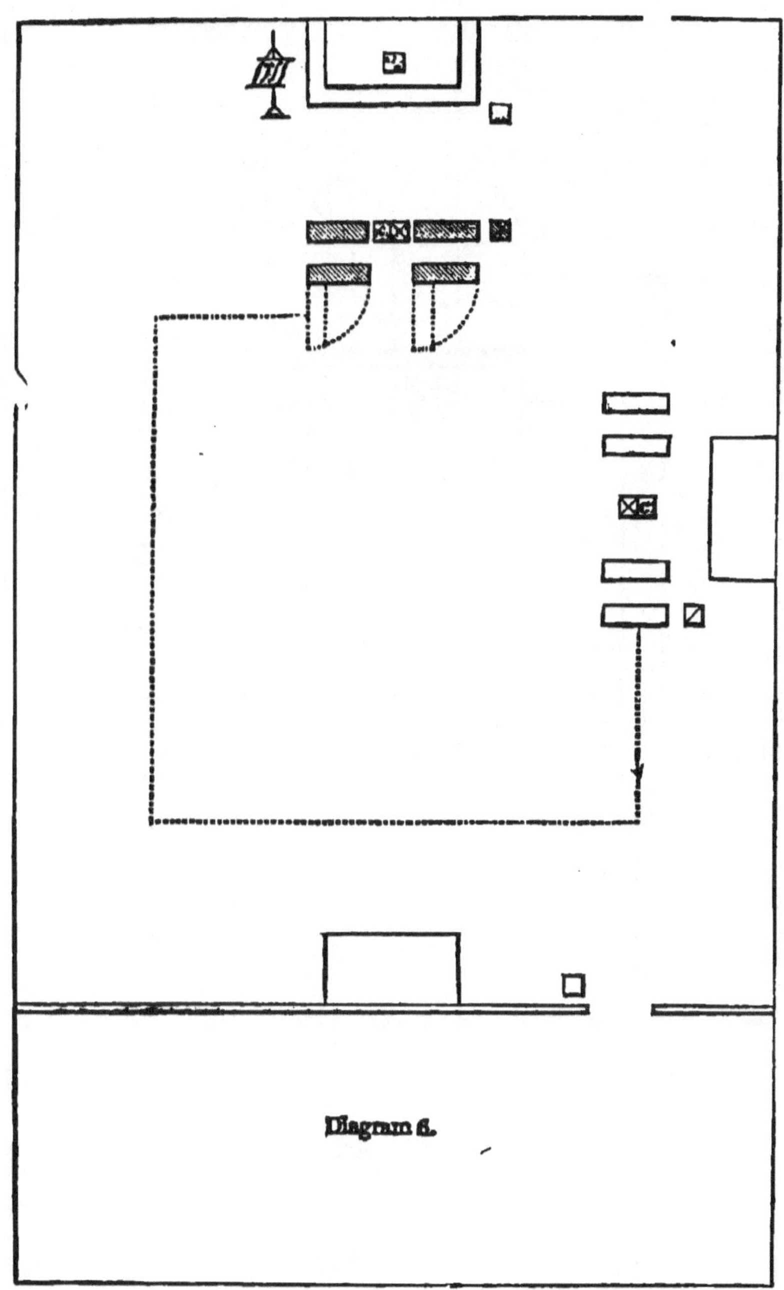

Diagram 6.

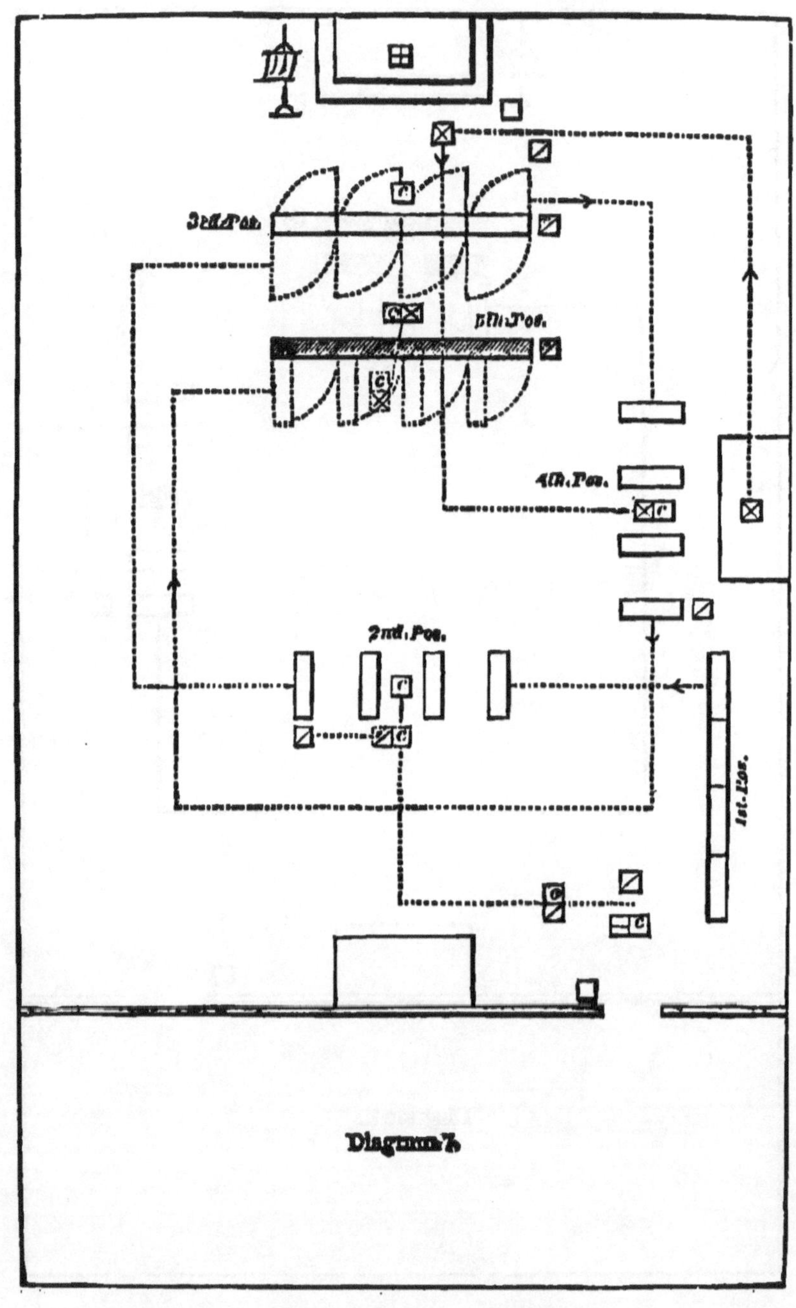

Diagram 7.

dressing Captain, who is standing in front of tent watching for them.) Sir, in obedience to, orders, I return prisoner. (See Diagram 6 or 7.)

Commandant—Stranger, the Lieutenant has spoken in your behalf; at his earnest entreaty, I am inclined to examine you further and ascertain whether you are what you profess. How did you first come into the society of the Patriarchs?

Lieutenant—(Answering for the candidate.) I came through the wilderness, passed the four Watches; at one time I was beset by wild beasts; at another, the clash of arms sounded in my ears; then, again, I heard the voice of mirth and revelry; over rough roads and dangerous ways my path lay; the flood-gates of heaven opened upon me, and I sought the shelter of a friendly oak; at last there appeared in the heavens above me the bright "Rain-bow of Promise," reminding me that ours is a covenant-keeping Father; soon the sweet music of the Patriarchs greeted my ears, and under its sublime influence I found my way to the tent of the excellent High Priest, and was safe.

Commandant—Had you a word in mind to cheer you while upon that dismal journey?

Lieutenant—I had such a word; ay, it was my countersign.

Commandant—What was it?

Lieutenant—"Go on."

Commandant—It was a good word. Your zeal and determination to reach my tent betokens how well you have lived up to the injunction so solemnly given to you before you entered the wilderness. Lieutenant, prepare to enroll your friend beneath our banner.

Lieutenant—(Addressing Standard-Bearer, and desig-
nating with sword the center of the room as the place,
commands:) Chevalier, With banner—ADVANCE. (Addressing Ensign.) Sir, About Standard; Form—CROWN.

[He then conducts candidate to the center of the room, and all take positions shown on diagram 8.]

Ensign-Threes right—MARCH; Column right-MARCH;
Column right-MARCH; Take wheeling distance-MARCH.*
Reserves—FALL IN; Column left—MARCH.

[On command "Reserves—FALL IN," the right file of the Reserves will
command "Threes right—MARCH;" and as the column turns to the left, the
Reserves close up on left of column.]

Threes left—MARCH; Canton—HALT; Right—DRESS;
FRONT; Form—CROWN; Right forward, Threes right—
MARCH; Right by file—MARCH.

[And, if the Canton is small, commands: Take double distance—MARCH;
and taking position on the left of the leading file, and giving necessary num
ber of commands (Column half left—MARCH,) conducts line in a circle about
the Standard, as center for the Crown, and, when the Crown is formed, com
mands:]

Canton—HALT; Left—FACE. (See Diagram 8.)

[The candidate will prepare to take the obligation by kneeling upon left
knee, on a cushion, with right hand on left breast, and left hand grasping the
naked blade of the Lieutenant's sword; which being done, the Lieutenant
commands:]

Parade—REST; Canton—KNEEL; Rest on SWORDS.

[Or, if the Canton is very large, the command to take double distance—
MARCH, should be omitted, and after the circle has been formed and the Canton faced to the left, the Lieutenant will command:]

Front open files—MARCH; (whereupon the odd numbers step forward;) HALT; Parade—REST; Front rank
(or Canton)—KNEEL; Rest on—SWORDS. (See Diagram 9.)

Lieutenant—Repeat after me;

[*If Guard has been formed in single rank, this command is unnecessary
and should be omitted.]

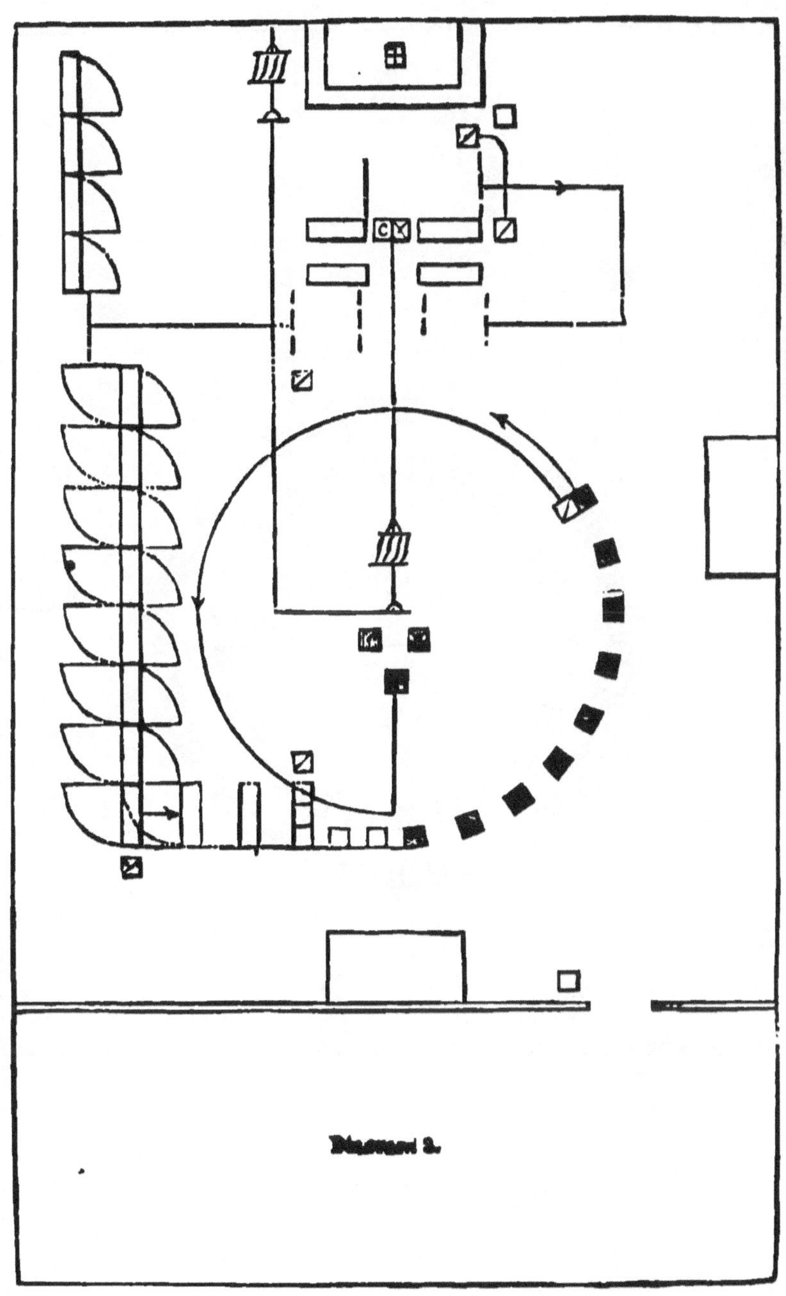

Diagram 2.

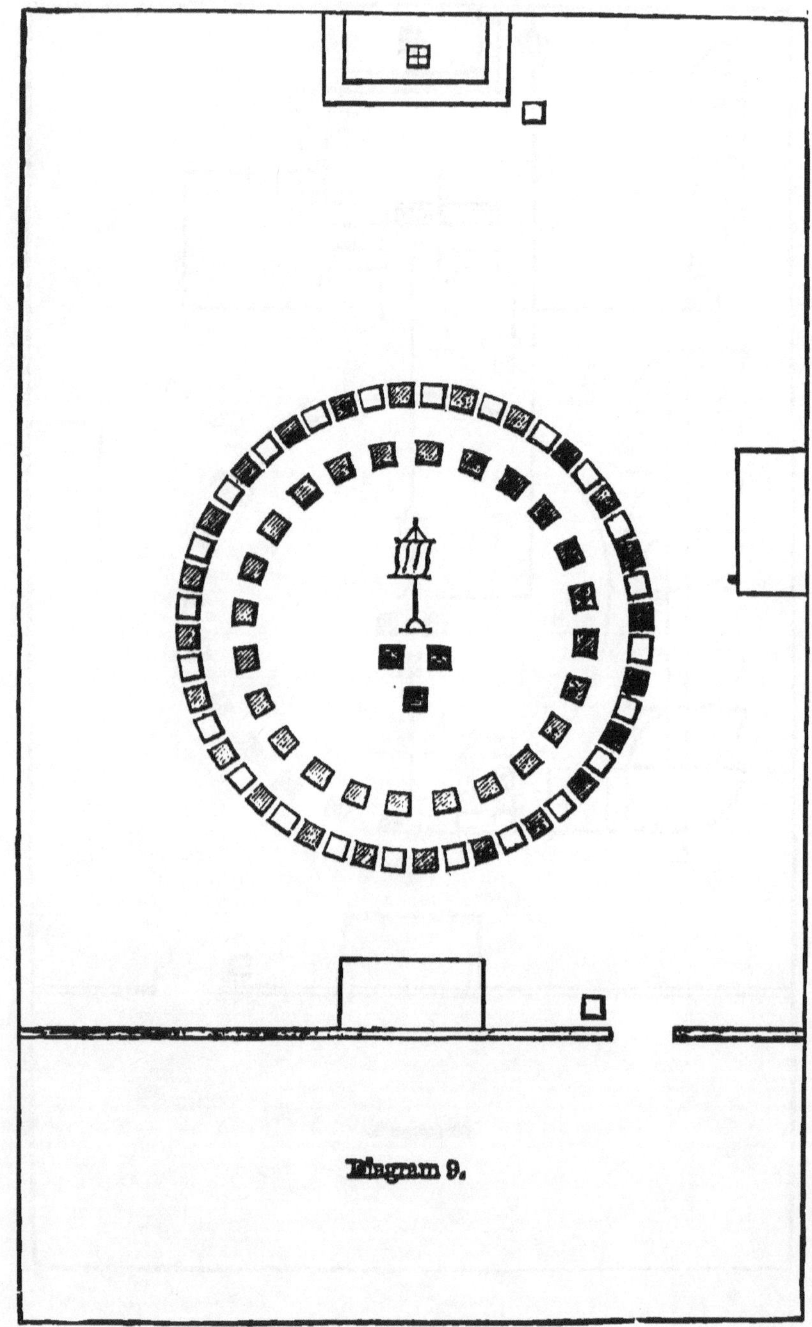

Diagram 9.

SECOND OBLIGATION PATRIARCHS MILITANT.

I,..........., kneeling within this Crown, formed of living witnesses, do solemnly promise, declare and avow, that I will never, in any manner whatever, communicate, or cause to be communicated, any of the signs, secrets, mysteries, rites, written or unwritten work of the Patriarchs Militant, to any person or persons whomsoever, unless he or they be legally entitled to receive the same from me; that I will promptly and cheerfully obey the commands of my superior officers in this or any other Canton to which I may be attached; and will at all times render to them that respect which their official position entitles them to receive at my hands; that I will constantly use my best endeavors to promote harmony, peace, and concord within the ranks, always avoiding discord and strife. For the faithful performance of all these obligations, I pledge my sacred honor as a Patriarch of the Royal Purple Degree, as well as whatever military rank or preferment I may hereafter receive through the medium of this degree.

[If it is desired to increase the martial effect, the roll of a kettle-drum may be here   troduced, and, if used, the roll should commence immediately after the obligation, and continue until the Canton is in line]

[After the candidate has arisen, under the direction of the Lieutenant, the Ensign commands:]

Ensign—Canton—Rise. (The Chevaliers execute command, leaving sword at "Order.") Carry—Swords; Right—Face; Form—Threes; Left oblique—March.

[At command "Form—Threes; Left oblique—March," Nos 1 and 4 stand fast, Nos. 2 ... 5 march obliquely and form on the left of Nos. 1 and 4 respectively, and Nos. 3 and 6 on the left of Nos. 2 and 5 respective y.]

Forward—March; Column left—March; Column left —March; Column left—March; Threes left—March; Canton—Halt, Right—Dress; Front; Parade—Rest. (See Diagram 10.)

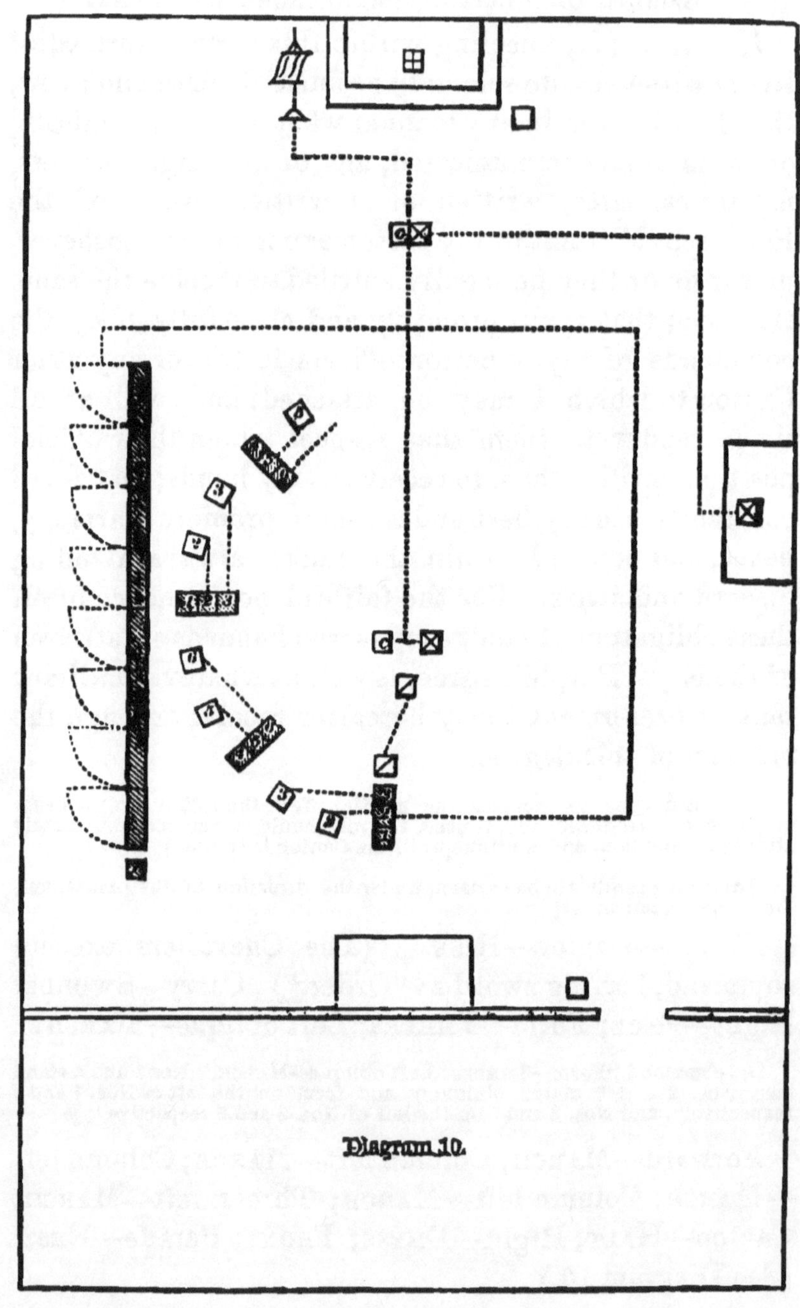

Diagram 10.

Lieutenant—Standard—STATION.

[The Standard-Bearer, with banner, returns to his position at right of tent, and the Lieutenant conducts the candidate to a position in front of the Commandant, and then returns to his station in the room. The Commandant now instructs the candidate in the unwritten work, and, after giving the secret work, continues:]

Commandant—When desirous of being admitted into a Canton, you will give [any] the alarm, [which will be attended to] at the outer door. The Picket will thereupon open the wicket, and require of you the countersign, [Justitia] which is given in full. If correct, he will admit you to the ante-room. You will then clothe yourself with a fatigue cap, belt, and sword. You will then advance at a "carry" to the inner door, and give the signal, [which is four raps.] The Sentinel will respond by giving four raps, and will then open the wicket and receive from you your name, rank, the name and number of your Canton, and the Department to which you are attached, and the Department check of the Canton visited. [The Department check is the check pass-word of the subordinate encampment which is changed yearly.] (If you are not in possession of the Department check, or belong to a Canton in another Department, you may be admitted on the order of the Commandant on satisfactory evidence of your membership.) The Sentinel will then close the wicket, open the door, and you will enter, make the entersign [which is "sword's port"] and give the test to Sentinel, [which is Corona, lettered at all times. When used for working purposes, give the letters C.·.O.·.R.·.O.·. and if the Sentinel is not satisfied, he requires you to give the balance of the word lettered as before N.·.A.] If correct, you will advance at a "carry" to the center of the room, face the Commandant's tent, and make the sign of the degree; [Bring the sword to a "present;" remain in that position until the Commandant acknowledges you as a Chevalier by making the answer to the sign, which is a "full hand salute."   You will then complete the sign by making a "salute swords."]   He will acknowledge you as a Chevalier of this degree by making the answer to the sign of the degree; after which, you will salute with sword, come to the position of a "carry," Right (or left)—FACE, march to a seat and Return—SWORD.

On leaving the Canton before it is closed, you will come to the position of a "carry," march to the center of the floor, face the Commandant, and make the retiring sign; [Bring the sword to a "present," remain in that position until the Commandant acknowledges you as a Chevalier by making the answer to the sign which is a "full hand salute."   You will then complete the sign by making a "salute swords," which he will acknowledge by making the answer to the retiring sign.   You will resume a "carry," and advance to the Officer of the Guard, salute him, and receive from him the Canton pass (a word given by the Officer of the Guard at opening of Canton, and used the same as the pass-word of the evening in the Subordinate Lodge,) which you must give to the Sentinel before he will allow you to retire.

You will always salute when addressed by or addressing a superior in rank.

[After the instruction in the unwritten work, the candidate is conducted to the ante-room by the Past Commandant, and by order of the Ensign, the Canton comes to a "Carry," Return—SWORDS, "Break ranks," and dresses in full dress uniform; and is re-formed in line, with swords at a "carry."   The candidate in ante-room puts on a fatigue cap and belt, after which he is returned before the Commandant's tent, and the Commandant proceeds as follows:]

Commandant—Sir, you have now attained the highest and most exalted rank in Odd Fellowship. Step by step you have been deservedly advanced to this high and honorable distinction, and I am gratified that you have

been found worthy to be enrolled as one of our number.
The true soldier, engaged in a just warfare, presses forward and strikes valiantly against the stronghold of the
adversary, never yielding until that adversary capitulates.
He is not easily turned aside; he fears no danger, he heeds
no voice excepting that of his commander; and when
the conflict is ended, he is equally ready to grant quarter and regard the rights of those who can no longer
protect themselves.

So you, as a soldier in our cause, must always earnestly contend for those reforms best calculated to promote
the moral welfare and advance the condition of mankind.
Upon all questions affecting the good and well-being of
the community in which you live, you must have an
opinion of your own, which you should fearlessly ex-
press whenever occasion may require; yet at all times
bearing in mind that others have an equal right to entertain honest opinions of their own.

On taking the obligation, you were required to kneel,
in token of obedience to those in authority, and of proper humility; you were required to place your right hand
over your heart, to indicate the sincerity of your purpose
to faithfully adhere to your sacred pledge of honor; and
your left hand was made to grasp the naked blade of
the sword, in order to teach you that justice will sooner
or later overtake you, should you disregard your obligations.

Your inability to satisfactorily prove yourself a Patriarch would have prevented your admission to our
ranks, and might have resulted in disgraceful consequences to yourself, had it not been for the timely inter-
ference of a friend who interceded for you.

Learn from this, that you should condemn no one
hastily; strive rather, by kindly words, to correct and

counteract the influence of errors.   Do all in your power to restore those who are worthy to the confidence and respect of their associates, never forgetting that "Universal Justice" is the first principle of soldierly manhood, to be carried into effect, first, by means of peace, but the right of every cause should be enforced, even to the waging of war.

Such is the lesson that we inculcate at this time, and trust that its influence shall not be without good effect upon your future life.   (Addressing Ensign,) Sir, form Arc of the Covenant.

Ensign—Right forward, Threes right–MARCH; Threes left—MARCH; Guide right; By the right flank—MARCH; Column left—MARCH; Form—RAINBOW; Column half left—MARCH.

[And placing himself on the left of the leading file, and giving the necessary number of commands (Column half left—MARCH,) conducts him along the line of a circular arc, until the rainbow is properly shaped, when he commands:]

Canton—HALT; Left—FACE; Rear open files—MARCH; HALT.   (See Diagram 7.)

[On command "Rear open files—MARCH," each even number steps backward and opposite his place in line.   When the movement is completed by halting the files one or two paces to the rear, the Ensign salutes the Commandant, and says:]

Ensign—Sir, the arc is formed.

Commandant—Prepare for enrollment; Standards—POST.

[Whereupon the Commandant passes around the right of the command, and takes position in front of the center of the Canton; the Standard-Bearer takes position on the right, one pace from first file in front rank with unfurled banner; the Lieutenant takes position on the left, two paces from last file in front rank, with colors to the wind; and the Clerk, with drum, and Ensign form on line of candidate and Past Commandant—all as shown on Diagram 11. The movement having been completed, the Commandant commands:]

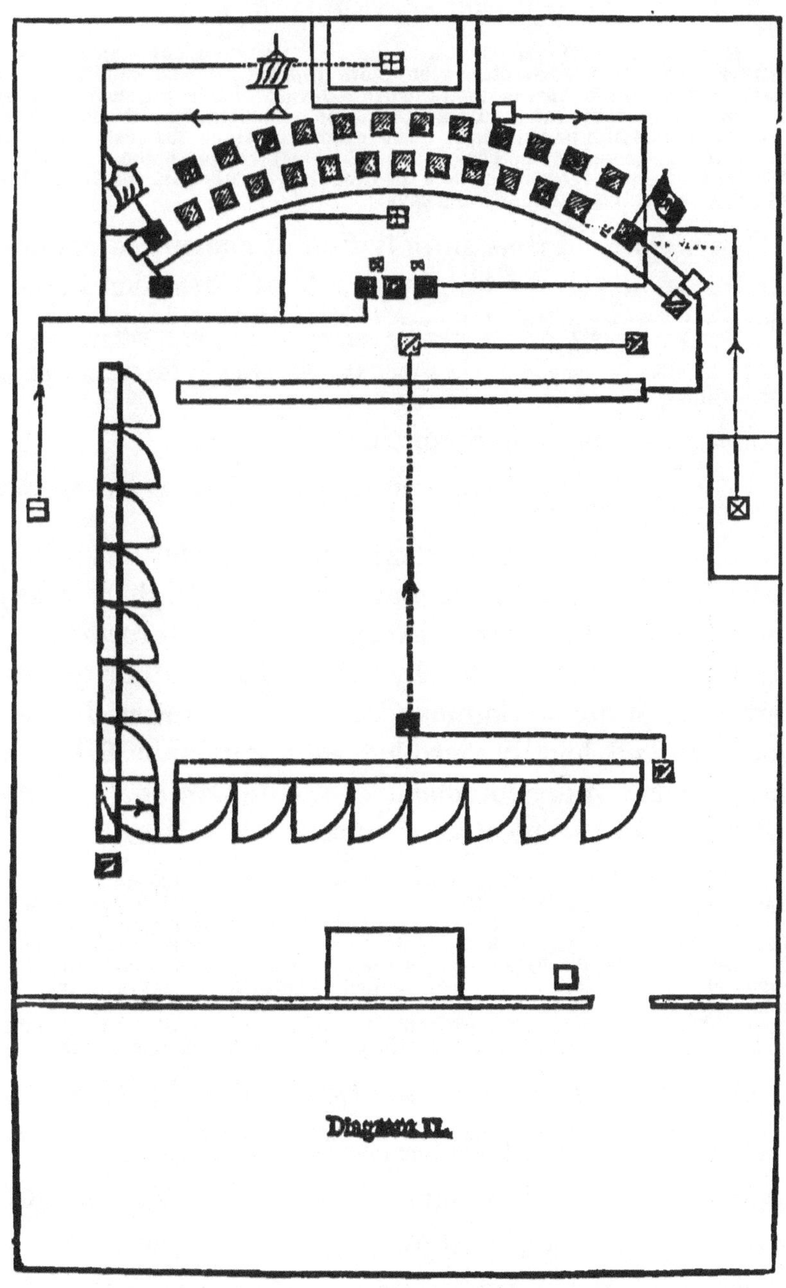

Diagram IX.

Commandant—Enroll—CANDIDATE.

[Hearing the command, the Clerk and Past Commandant step one pace in advance and face each other; the Clerk presents to the candidate the roster of the Canton, spread upon the drum-head, which he places in front of him on a camp-stool; the candidate kneels, on a cushion, and the Past Commandant hands him pen and ink. The candidate signs the roster, and his signature is attested by the Past Commandant; which being done, the Commandant, stepping forward, strikes the candidate lightly with the flat of his sword between the shoulders, and says:]

Commandant–I thus, in imitation of ancient ceremony, confer upon you the knightly rank of Chevalier in the army of Patriarchs Militant. Arise, Sir Knight.

[And when the candidate has arisen, at a sign given by the Commandant, the Ensign commands:]

Ensign—Present—SWORDS.

[Whereupon the Commandant, with sword in hand, (given him by Past Commandant,) addresses candidate:]

Commandant—Noble comrade, Chevalier.........., receive this sword as the mark of your knightly rank; let it never be drawn except in the enforcement of necessary justice. I now, by virtue of the authority conferred upon me as Commandant of this Canton, declare you duly and legally enrolled as a Patriarch Militant, and member of my command. (Facing Canton.) Trumpeter, herald the additon of another Chevalier.

[The Trumpeter steps from center of front rank and blows a suitable blast, in acknowledgement of the addition to the ranks. This can be dispensed with, or it may be increased by appropriately beating kettle-drums. The Commandant now faces about and congratulates the newly-made Chevalier, and takes position by his side, facing the Canton. The Lieutenant then hands the colors to the nearest file, and, advancing, also congratulates the new member, and then returns to his position on the left of the Canton; after which the Ensign comes forward and welcomes the Chevalier to the ranks, and returns to his position; the Commandant then commands:]

Commandant—Officers and Standards—STATION.

[Whereupon the Commandant, the Lieutenant, and Standard-Bearer return to their stations in the room, and the Ensign commands:]

Ensign—Carry—SWORDS; Close order—MARCH; Return—SWORDS; Right—FACE; Break ranks—MARCH.

[And the Chevaliers surround and congratulate the new member, and welcome him as a Chevalier and soldier companion]

FORM FOR CLOSING A CANTON.

Commandant—Lieutenant.

[That officer faces the Commandant and salutes.]

Sir, form the lines and announce that the Canton will now be dismissed until the next regular Cantonment, unless sooner assembled by special order.

Lieutenant—FALL IN; Left—FACE; Right—DRESS; FRONT; Draw—SWORDS. Chevaliers, it is the order of the Commandant that the Canton be now dismissed until the next regular Cantonment, unless sooner assembled by special order.

[The Lieutenant then faces about, and, saluting the Commandant, says:]

Lieutenant—Sir, your orders are published.

Commandant—(Addressing Canton.) Chevaliers remember your vows to promote harmony, peace, and concord, avoiding discord and strife.

Lieutenant--Return—SWORDS; Right—FACE; Break ranks—MARCH.

[The Chevaliers retire without further ceremony.]

FORM FOR THE
INSTALLATION OF OFFICERS.

[The Installing Officer, acting for and representing the Lieutenant-General, with Acting Adjutant-General, and Aid de Camp, (which staff may be increased for effect, where the installation is public) appear at the inner door and give signal.]

Sentinel—Who comes there?

Installing Officer—The representative of the Commander and Staff, with countersign.

[The Sentinel reports the same to the Commandant, who causes the Canton to be drawn up in line, with swords at a "carry," and officers to the front, as shown by first position on Diagram 12. He then commands the Sentinel to admit the General's Lieutenant and Staff if "correct." Whereupon the Sentinel opens the door, and standing in front of it with drawn sword, says:]

Sentinel—Advance one, and communicate the countersign.

[The Aid will bring sword to "port," advance, and give it in a whisper:]

Sentinel—Correct. Pass, Chevaliers.

[The Sentinel will step aside, face and salute the officers as they pass him, and when they have entered the room he will close the door, and resume his proper station. The Installing Officer and Staff will march to the center of the floor, and salute the Commandant, who will arise, return salute, and command:]

Commandant—Canton, Extend—HONORS.

Lieutenant—Present—SWORDS.

[The Installing Officer will then step to the front, and, addressing the Commandant, says:]

Installing Officer—Sir, we are here for the purpose of installing the officers of this Canton, and bear with us their commissions issued by the Commander as the Lieutenant of the Grand Sire. Are they present?

Commandant—They are.

Installing Officer—Sir, you will surrender your chair to me.

[Whereupon the Commandant vacates, and the Installing Officer occupies the stand, and the Staff take positions shown on diagram. As the transfer is being made, the Lieutenant commands:]

Lieutenant—Carry—SWORDS; Left wheel—MARCH; Canton—HALT; Right—DRESS; FRONT.

[He then takes position in front of the first platoon, and the Ensign, upon whom the wheel has been made, retakes position in front of the second platoon, and the Commandant comes forward and takes position in advance of the Lieutenant and Ensign, opposite the center of the Canton. (See Diagram 12, 2d position.) The command, thus formed, will await instructions.]

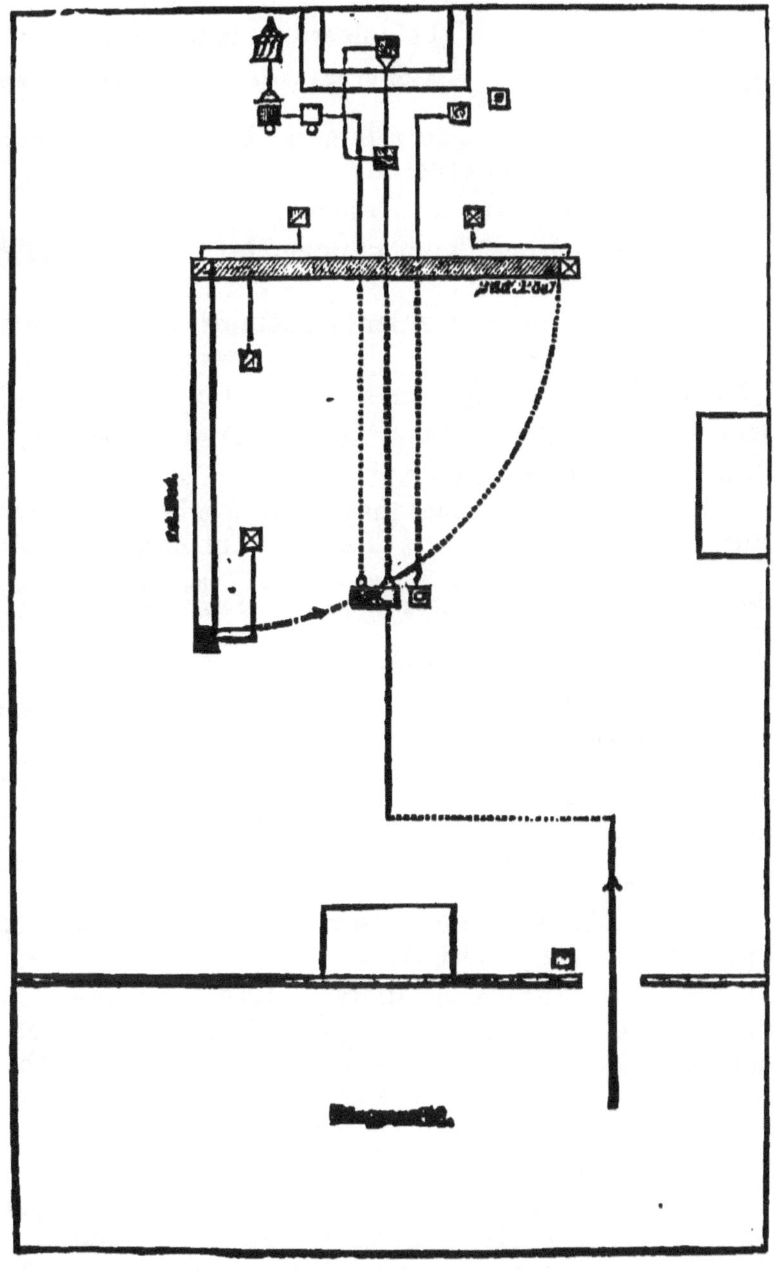

Installing Officer—(Addressing A. A. G.) Sir, you will read the names of the officers elect to the Canton.

[The A. A. G., will then advance to and in front of the Standard, and read the roster of officers elect.]

Installing Officer—Chevaliers, is the report correct? Shall the installation proceed?

Rank and File—It is. Proceed.

Installing Officer—(To Commandant.) Sir, dismiss your command.

Commandant—(Facing Canton, commands:) Officers, To place in line—MARCH.

[The Lieutenant and Ensign form on right and left of line respectively.]

Return—SWORDS; Right—FACE; Break ranks—MARCH.

Installing Officer—(To Aid.) Sir, you will retire with the officers elect. See that they are properly attired, and return and present them to this Chair for installation.

[The Aid retires with the officers, and they clothe themselves in the undress uniform of a Chevalier, without sword. Returning, the Aid gives the signal:]

Sentinel—Who comes there?

Aid—The General's Aid de Camp and officers elect for installation.

[The Sentinel so reports to the Installing Officer, who will instruct him to "admit them." The A. A. G., will form Canton as in first position on Diagram 13, command "Draw—SWORDS," and take position on the right; and the Aid and officers elect, being admitted, form as shown by Diagram 13, and march once around the room to a point in front of the Installing Officer, and the Aid, addressing him, says:]

Aid—Sir, I have the honor to present the officers elect of this Canton for installation.

Installing Officer—Chevaliers, before installing you into office you must take upon yourselves a solemn obligation to faithfully perform the duties incident to the offices you are about to assume. Are you willing to take such obligation?

Officers Elect—We are.

Acting Adjutant-General—Right forward, threes right —MARCH; Threes left—MARCH; Guide right; Canton— HALT; Right—DRESS; FRONT; With Swords—CHARGE. (See Diagram 13.)

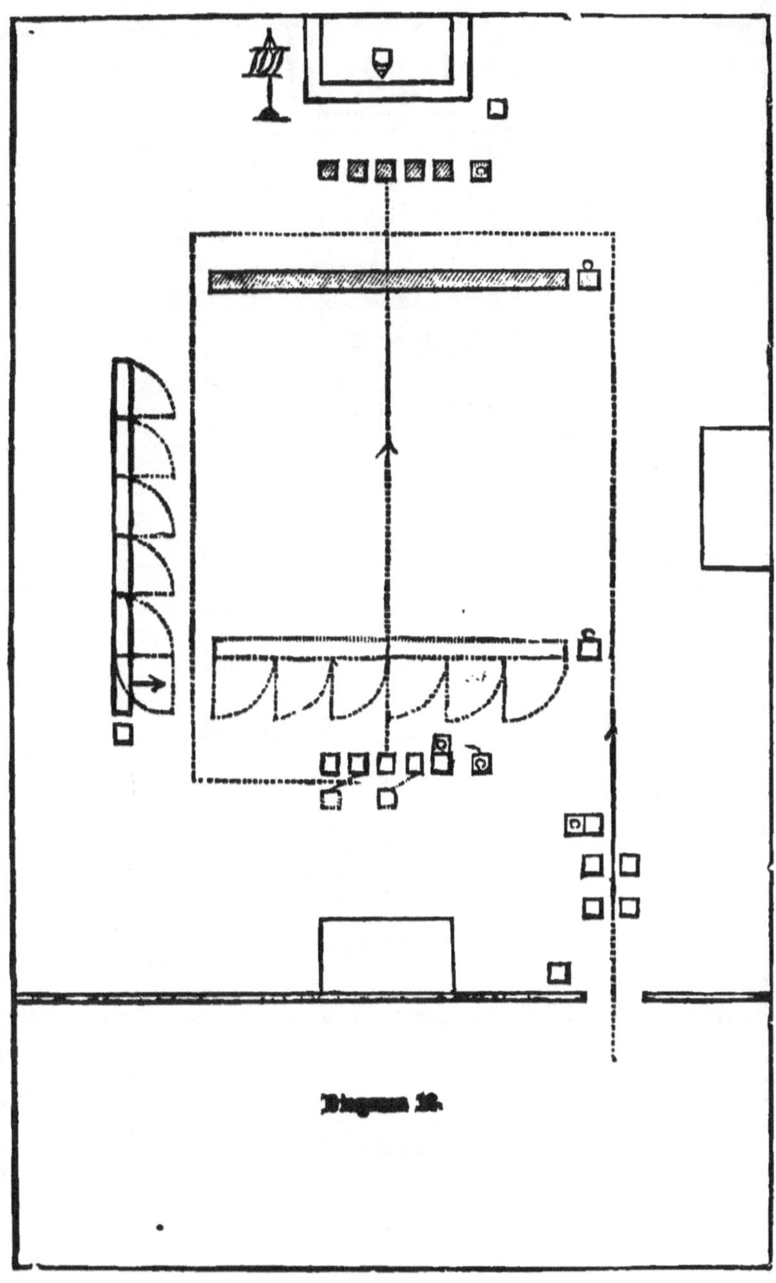

Diagram 12.

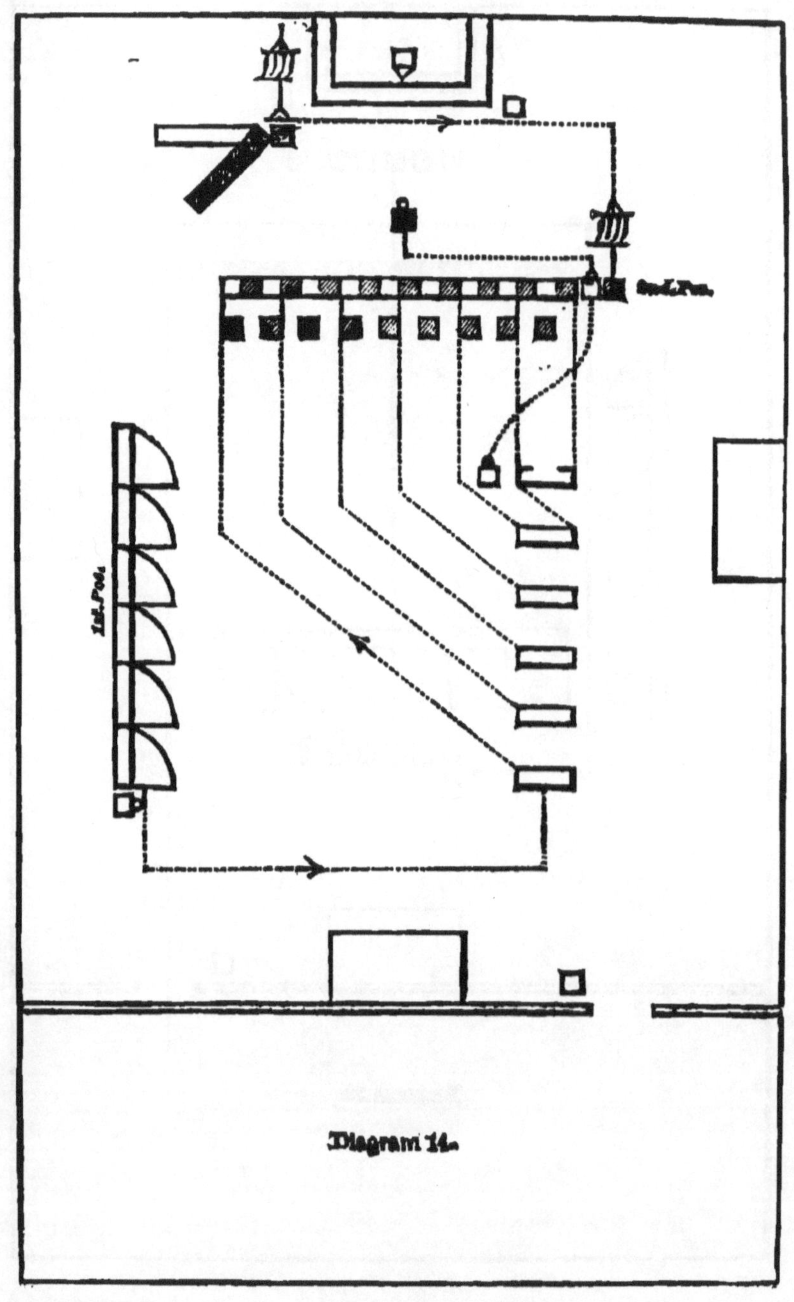

Diagram 14.

Aid—(Addressing officers elect.)   Officers—KNEEL; UNCOVER.

Installing Officer—You will each raise your left hand and repeat after me: I,............do solemnly promise that I will perform all of the duties of the office to which I have been elected, to the best of my ability; that I will obey all orders that may be issued by my superiors in command; and that I will not wrong this Canton, nor any Chevalier thereof, to the value of anything.   To the faithful performance of all which, I pledge my sacred honor.

Aid—(Addressing officers elect.)   Officers—COVER; RISE.

Acting Adjutant-General—Carry—SWORDS; Return—SWORDS; Right—FACE; Break ranks—MARCH.

Installing Officer—(Addressing Aid.)   Sir, you will retire with the officers elect to the ante-room, where they will clothe themselves in the uniform of their respective grades, and return them, thus attired, before me.

[The Aid and officers elect march into the ante-room; the officers elect dress as instructed; they form in two ranks, and the Aid gives the signal at the inner door.]

Sentinel—Who comes there?

Aid—The Aid to the General, with the officers elect of this Canton.

[The Sentinel reports as in previous instances, and upon receiving instructions, admits them. On being admitted, the Aid conducts the officers elect to the right of the Installing Officer, and forms them in line, facing the line of Canton extended. The A. A. G., forms the Canton as in the beginning, and takes position on the right. See first position on Diagram 14.]

Acting Adjutant-General—Draw—SWORDS;   Threes right—MARCH; Column left—MARCH; Column left—MARCH; Left, front into line—MARCH; Canton—HALT; Right—DRESS; FRONT.

[See second position, Diagram 14, and advancing to a point two paces in front of the center of the line, will face and salute the Installing Officer and report the presence of the Canton. The Installing Officer returns the salute, and Commands:]

Installing Officer—Sir, prepare to publish commissions.

Acting Adjutant-General—Rear, open order—MARCH;
FRONT; Parade—REST; Banner—POST.

[And taking position three paces in front of the Canton, facing Installing
Officer, will salute. The Standard-Bearer takes position on right of line, and
one pace from the first file. See second position on Diagram 14.]

Installing Officer—(Addressing A. A. G.) Sir, Commissions—PUBLISH.

[Whereupon the A. A. G. faces the Canton, and the Aid, addressing the
officers elect, who have been previously formed in line, facing the line of the
Canton extended, commands:]

Aid—Officers, Left half wheel—MARCH; HALT.

[See Diagram 14. Or he may wheel them to suit the relative positions of
Canton and officers elect. The A. A. G. then reads the commissions, and
when he has finished, faces about, and, addressing the Installing Officer,
says:]   .

Acting Adjutant-General—Sir, the commissions are
published.

Installing Officer—Sir, form line to receive officers.

Acting Adjutant-General—Carry—SWORDS; Close order—MARCH; Present—SWORDS.

[At the command MARCH, the A. A. G. re-takes position on the right, two
paces from Standard-Bearer, and the Installing Officer, addressing officers
elect, commands:]

Installing Officer—Officers, To your posts—MARCH.

Aid—Officers, Right half wheel—MARCH; Forward—
MARCH.

[The commissioned officers take their proper places, and the Clerk and
Accountant form on the left of the line. See Diagram 15.]

Installing Officer—Canton, Carry—SWORDS; Captain
(that officer salutes.)

[If Commandant is of a Grand Canton, he should be addressed by his
proper military title.]

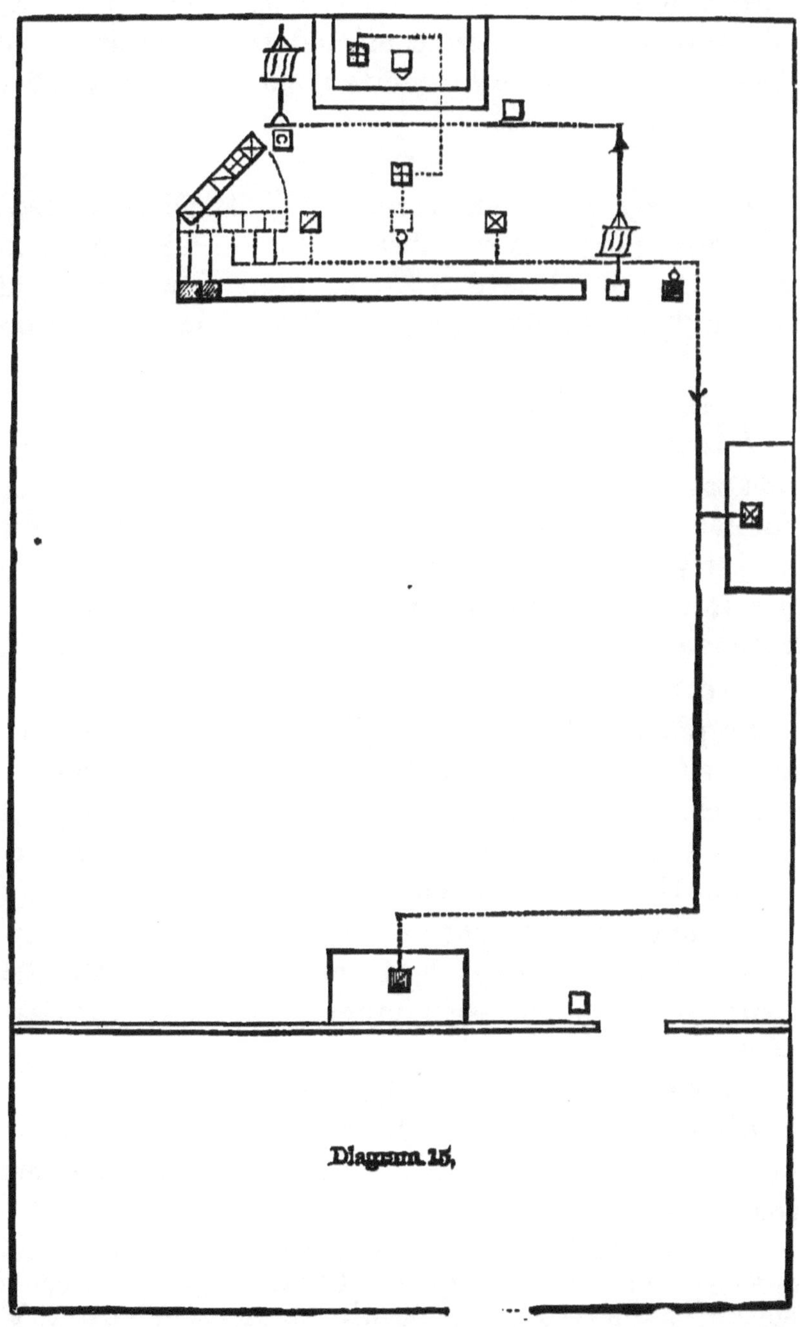

Diagram. 15.

Installing Officer—Sir, I congratulate you upon your elevation to the highest command in this Canton, and feel confident you will perform the duties of your office in a faithful manner.

[The Captain comes to a "carry."]

Installing Officer—Lieutenant.   (That officer salutes.) Sir, when the Captain is absent, you will take command of the Canton.   It is therefore important that you should be familiar with his duties, as well as those of your own office.

[The Lieutenant comes to a "carry,"]

Installing Officer—Ensign.   (That officer salutes.) Sir, you are third in command in this Canton.   It is your special duty to see that the outposts of the Canton are properly guarded, and it will be expected of you 'to promptly execute the orders of your superior officers in command.

[The Ensign comes to a "carry."]

Installing Officer—Clerk.   (That officer steps one pace in advance of the line and salutes.)   Chevalier, you have been elected and elevated to a responsible position.   It will be your duty to keep a correct account of the transactions of this Canton; to collect all moneys due, and pay the same to the Accountant, taking a receipt therefor. Subject to the orders of the Commandant, you will take charge of the minute book, order book, roster and seal of the Canton.

[The Clerk comes to a "carry," and retakes position in line.]

Installing Officer—Has the bond of the Accountant been approved?   (Upon receiving an affirmative answer, continues:)

Installing Officer—Accountant.   (That officer advances one step from line and salutes.) Chevalier, you have been elected to the responsible position of Accountant to this

Canton. It will be your duty to receive, receipt for, and hold all the funds belonging to it; to keep a regular and correct account of the same; and pay out such amounts only, as may be called for by the warrant of your Captain or Commandant, when directed to do so by the vote of the Canton. You will be expected to account for, and pay over to your successor, any balance in your hands at the time of his installation.

[The Accountant comes to a "carry," and resumes his position in line.]

Installing Officer—The officers will now take their stations in the room, and assume their duties. Return—STANDARD.

[See Diagram 15. All of which having been done, the A. A. G. commands:]

Acting Adjutant-General—Present—SWORDS.

Installing Officer—Now, by the authority of the Lieutenant-General Commanding, I proclaim the officers of Canton........., No...., Patriarchs Militant, of the Independent Order of Odd Fellows, in the Department of........, to be legally mustered and installed for and during the current term of their commissions, and until the installation of their successors. (Addressing A. A. G.:) Sir, dismiss the command.

Acting Adjutant-General—Canton, Carry—SWORDS; Return—SWORDS; Right—FACE; Break ranks—MARCH.

[The Installing Officer and Staff signify their intention of retiring, and the Ensign will form Canton in line, as in the beginning.]

Ensign—FALL IN; Left—FACE; Right—DRESS; FRONT; Draw—SWORDS; Present—SWORDS.

[The Installing Officer and Staff will salute the Commandant, and being saluted in return, will march along the line and pass out, the Sentinel saluting as they pass. The Ensign will then command:]

Ensign—Carry—SWORDS; Return—SWORDS; Right—FACE; Break ranks—MARCH.

[And the Canton will proceed with business.]

FORM FOR

MUSTERING A CANTON.

[Applicants for warrant. if an organized body, must appear in full dress uniform; if R, P. Degree Patriarchs only, they may appear in fatigue cap, belt, and sword   The Mustering Officer, representing the Commander, his Acting Adjutant-General, Aid de Camp, and Chaplain, being present, the Mustering Officer will take the principal chair, and the Staff will take positions near by.   The Mustering Officer will appoint a temporary Sentinel, communicate to him the "Canton pass," and instruct him to close and guard the door, and cause all present to be properly examined, so as to protect the Degree.   The Sentinel having taken position and closed the door, the Mustering Officer will announce the object of the assemblage, and if the applicants for the warrant are Royal Purple Degree Patriarchs only, he will confer upon them the Degree of Patriarchs Militant, which should be done in ritualistic form, if he has present a sufficient and properly drilled command to execute the floor work of the degree—otherwise he must informally administer the obligations and charges.   Thereupon the Acting Adjutant-General, addressing the Mustering Officer, will say:]

Acting Adjutant General—Sir I have the pleasure to inform you that a number of Royal Purple Degree Patriarchs, Chevaliers Militant, duly conversant with the principles of "Universal Justice," and actuated by a desire to promote the interests of our beloved Order, have applied to our Commander for a warrant to establish a Canton of Patriarchs Militant of the Independent Order of Odd Fellows; which warrant has been duly granted, and the Chevaliers are here convened for the purpose of being regularly mustered into the service as a Canton; and of electing officers and having them commissioned, mustered, and installed conformably to the usages of the degree and the Order.

Mustering Officer—(Addressing Aid.) You will present the applicants for the warrant.

[The Aid will form the applicants in front of and facing the Mustering Officer, and commands:]

Aid—Draw—Swords; Present—Swords. Sir, I present these applicants for warrant.

Mustering Officer—Carry—Swords. (Addressing applicants.) Worthy Patriarchs and Chevaliers, it is with great satisfaction that I appear before you as the bearer of the legal instrument which conveys to you, as a body all the rights, privileges, and immunities that are conferred on a Canton of Patriarchs Militant of the Independent Order of Odd Fellows. Acting by authority of the Commander, the Lieutenant of the Grand Sire, it becomes my duty, previous to presenting you with this warrant, to ascertain whether you are the Chevaliers who applied for the same. (Addressing A. A. G.) Sir, you will call the roster of applicants.

[The A. A. G. reads the names, and each applicant answers to his name as it is called. Upon the completion of the roll-call of applicants, and all being found correct, the Mustering Officer proceeds:]

Mustering Officer—(Addressing A. A. G.) Sir, read the warrant.

[Whereupon the Aid commands. Present—Swords, and the A. A. G. will read the warrant aloud to the applicants; which being completed, the Aid commands: Carry—Swords, and the Mustering Officer continues, addressing applicants.]

Mustering Officer—Chevaliers, previous to delivering this instrument into your possession, it is proper that you should enter into an obligation, for which purpose you will place yourselves in proper attitude, and repeat after me, as follows:

Aid—Parade—Rest; (Calling name)—Kneel; Uncover.

We, each for himself, in the presence of these noble witnesses, do solemnly and sincerely promise and declare, that the warrant for a Canton of Patriarchs Militant, read in our hearing, was applied for in good faith; and that it shall not be used for any other purpose than that

for which it has been granted. To the faithful performance   of which, we pledge our Patriarchal and Military
honor.

Aid—(Addressing Body by name, commands—COVER;
RISE; Carry—SWORDS.

Mustering Officer—Worthy Chevaliers, by virtue of the
high power vested in me, I do hereby institute and proclaim you a lawfully constituted body, regularly mustered
into the service under the style and title of Canton.....,
No...., of Patriarchs Militant of the Independent Order of Odd Fellows, in the Department of.....; and do
authorize and empower you henceforth to do and perform all such things as may of right belong to a regularly constituted Canton of Patriarchs Militant. In all your
transactions you must faithfully conform to the landmarks of the Order, obey the commands of your officers,
observe the requirements of the Military Council, and
maintain and abide by the mandates and laws of the
Sovereign Grand Lodge of the Independent Order of
Odd Fellows; and may all your acts be governed and
directed by the principles of "Universal Justice," Love,
and Truth. (Addressing the Chaplain.) Sir, invoke a
blessing.

Aid—Parade—REST; UNCOVER; Bow.

Chaplain—Most holy and Gracious Father, Supreme
Ruler of the Universe, with reverence and humility we
invoke and implore Thy blessing and protection for this
Canton. We humbly beseech Thee to inspire its members with principles of "Universal Justice," with love
for each other, and with fear of offending Thee. In Thy
great mercy pardon all our transgressions; be with
and direct us along the paths of righteousness; and teach
us to be grateful to Thee for the manifold blessings we
receive. Amen,

Aid—Cover; Carry—Swords.

Mustering Officer—(Addressing the Staff.) Gentle-men, prepare for the election of officers.

Aid—Return—Swords; Right—Face; Break ranks—March.

[The A. A. G. will prepare ballots, which the Aid will distribute and col-lect when the vote is ready.]

Mustering Officer—Chevaliers, nominations for Cap-tain are now in order.

[After nominations are made, the vote will be taken, and the result an-nounced by the Mustering Officer; and so on throughout the various grades of offices to be filled, until all the officers are elected, when the A. A. G. will fill out commissions (which he must have in blank.) When all is in readiness, the Mustering Officer will proceed with the installation of the officers, com-mencing at the point of such ceremony where the Aid is instructed and or-dered to "retire with the officers elect, see that they are properly attired, and return and present them" for installation. See Form of Installation.]

[In installing the officers of newly instituted Cantons, the Mustering Officer must exercise judgment, and may omit the ceremony where it cannot be properly executed by an undisciplined and undrilled command.]

FUNERAL ESCORT.

AND

BURIAL OF A CHEVALIER.

———

[The Ritual must not be taken to the grave; this form for Burial for a Chevalier is in Tactics.]

[Upon all funeral occasions the Canton shall turn out in full dress uniform, with sword hilts, standard, and guidons appropriately trimmed with crape. The Commandant of the Canton must appoint six pall-bearers, and at the appointed hour have his command at the residence of the deceased, etc., where it shall be formed in line facing the entrance. The pall-bearers must then be detached and ordered to report for duty within the house. The command will come to a "Parade—REST," and await the completion of the civic ceremonies within the dwelling, or church, etc. When the pall-bearers approach with the corpse, the Captain will command:]

Captain—Attention, Carry—SWORDS; Present—SWORDS.

[After the coffin has been placed within the hearse, the Captain will command:]

Captain—Carry—SWORDS; Reverse—SWORDS; Threes left—MARCH; Column left—MARCH; Column left—MARCH.

[And marching, the Canton, left in front, will take position immediately in front of the hearse, and conduct the column and procession to the place of interment. The pall-bearers will take position along each side of the hearse; two opposite the front wheels, two opposite the rear wheels, and two opposite the center, midway between 1 and 3 on each side. They will march with reversed swords, and move with such cadence as will keep pace with the hearse. On approaching' and at a suitable distance from the grave, with the grave to either side of the line of the column extended, the Captain will command:]

Captain—Carry—SWORDS; Threes right—MARCH; Canton—HALT; Left—DRESS; FRONT; Rear open order —MARCH; Front rank, About—FACE; With Swords Form —ARCH. (See Diagram 16.)

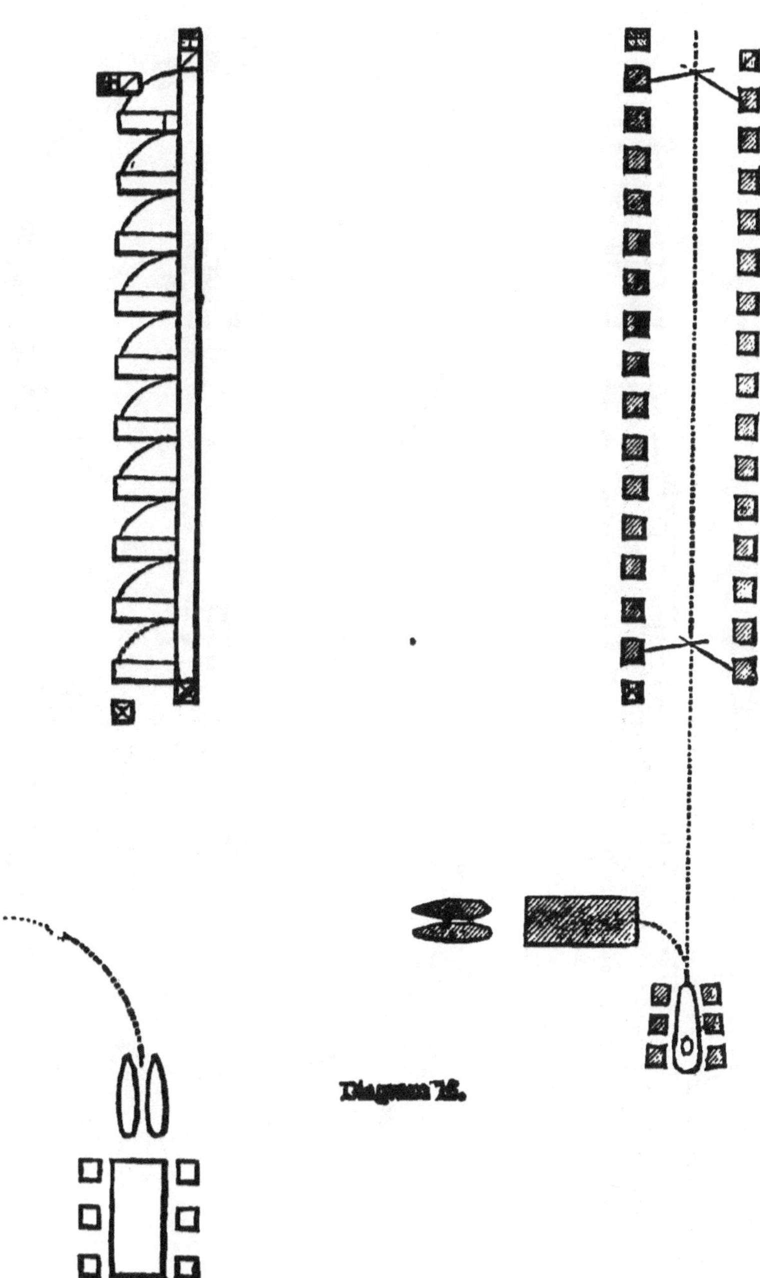

Diagram 76.

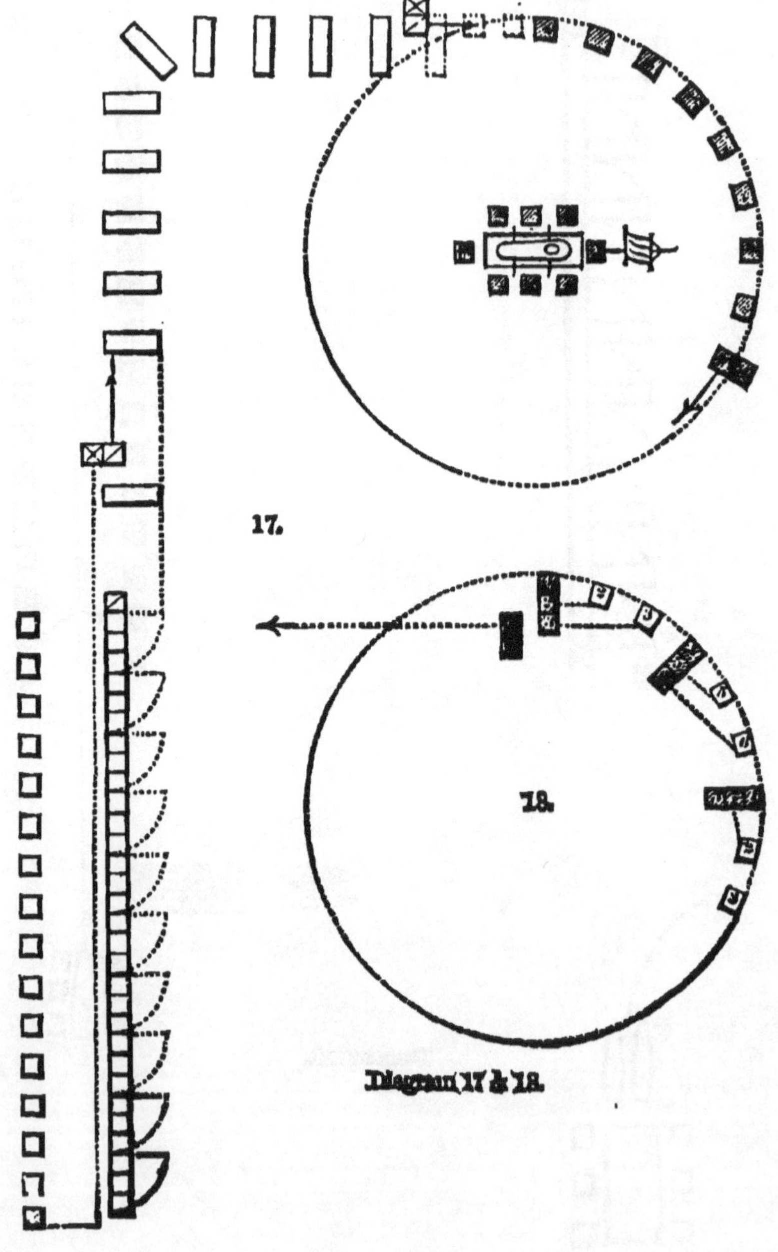

17.
18.
Diagram 17 & 18.

[The pall-bearers must pass under this arch of steel, bearing the corpse to the grave. When the Canton is halted, the hearse will be turned to the right (or left,) as may be most convenient, and stopped. The coffin will then be withdrawn and placed foot foremost, opposite the space between the right files of the Canton, drawn up in open order. When these movements have been completed, and the corpse borne past the left of the line, the Captain and Standard-Bearer (with banner) will follow, and take position at the foot and head of the grave, respectively. The Lieutenant, assuming charge of the Canton, will command:]

Lieutenant—Carry—Swords; Front rank, About— Face; Close order—March; Threes left—March.

[And moving the Canton in column of threes to a suitable position, according to the location of the grave, commands:]

Lieutenant—Column right (or left)—March; Form— Crown; Left (or right) by file—March (and, if necessary;) Take double distance—March.

[And, placing himself by the side of the leading file, and giving the necessary number of commands (Column half left—March,) will conduct him in a circle around the grave; and when the circle (or crown) is formed, commands:]

Lieutenant—Canton—Halt; Right (or left)—Face; Parade—Rest; Uncover; Bow.   (See Diagram 17.)

[The Captain, observing that the crown has been formed, will proceed:]

Captain—Chevaliers, we are here to render the last rite the living may minister to the dead.   Man is born to die.   The coffin, the grave, the sepulcher, speak in silent language of human mortality.   Youth, manhood, age, weakness, vigor, strength; poverty, affluence, riches; humility, pride, arrogance; influence, power, greatness; are all leveled by the immutable hand of death.

The handiwork of the Creator constantly displays the unerring certainty of the end and decay of all things. The beautiful and exquisite plant creation, from the glories of the Tropics, to the ever agreeable verdure of the North, alike, fade, wither, and die.   So it is with the human family; the living of to-day become the dead of to-morrow; and we, mortals, can but bow in recognition of the Divine law, which inevitably brings man to mother earth. He who now speaks to you, may, ere he moves from this sepulcher, be called to enter eternity; for all in time must occupy the silent tomb. The strong and mighty may, in a moment, be swept into the un-fathomable void between the living and the dead.

As we behold the remains of our departed companion, let us, as "Patriarchs Militant," inwardly vow to throw the cloak of charity over the errors of the deceased Chevalier, and bury them from recollection under an arch of steel, as we bury the body in this grave; and let us monument the memory of his noble worth by herald-ing the good, great, and knightly deeds only of his honorable life.

[The pall-bearers lower the coffin into the grave.]

Captain---The dust has returned to the earth, the spirit has gone to God who gave it. Have mercy on it, O Lord.

[The Chevaliers respond:]

Chevaliers---Mercy, have mercy, O Lord.

[At this point, the Captain will deposit in the grave a crown made of evergreens, saying:]

Captain---We place this crown within the grave as an emblem of the Order; and as the evergreen is a token of immortality, so let our remembrance be undying. Chevaliers, you will now inspect the tomb, and deposit your last tribute.

[Whereupon, the Lieutenant, Ensign, and Chevaliers, beginning at the left, will come to a "carry," and one at a time advance to the grave, Present—Swords, and deposit a sprig of evergreen; salute, and come to a "carry," return to place in line, at Parade—Rest; uncovered, with head bowed. This movement having been completed, the grave will be filled with earth; the Lieutenant, when necessary, detailing Chevaliers for such service, and frequently relieving the shoveling parties by new details. As each party is relieved, it will resume position in line. The grave having been filled, and the mound properly shaped by the undertaker, the Lieutenant will com-mand:]

Lieutenant---Canton----COVER; Carry----SWORDS; Present----SWORDS.

[Whereupon, the Chaplain will advance and take position under the banner at the head of the grave, and offer prayer. When the Chaplain has taken position, the Lieutenant will command:]

Lieutenant----Carry---SWORDS; Parade---REST; Canton---KNEEL; Rest on----SWORDS.

[The above movements having been executed, the Chaplain will offer prayer as follows:]

Chaplain----Our Father, who art the great creator of all things, who in Thy wise providence does dispense Universal Justice, we beseech Thee to hear the voice of Thy creatures here assembled in humble supplication. O God, the Almighty Ruler of the universe, we implore Thee, in our entire helplessness, to bless and comfort those whom it has pleased Thee to add to the number of the disconsolate; bear them up under their great affliction, and sustain them against despondency.

O Heavenly Father, imbue us with the conviction of the uncertainty of life, and of the certainty of death; and we pray Thee to bless the brethren here prepared to commit the remains of a companion to their last resting-place on earth. Constantly remind them of their obligations and duties as men and brethren through the various walks of life; and grant Thy Holy Spirit to those whom Thou hath spared, and confirm their faith in Thee forever. Great Commander of Heaven and Earth, preserve the principles and purposes of our beloved Order, and defend it in the right; guard it against doing or countenancing evil, and lead its members along the paths of virtue and righteousness. Amen.

Captain---Chevaliers, we have administered the last rite to our departed friend, the Chevalier............, and as the Supreme Judge extends mercy to our deceased comrade, so let us hope that He will to us, in turn, mercy show.

[The Chevaliers respond:]

Chevaliers—Mercy show, O Lord. To us mercy show.
Chaplain and Captain----Amen.

[The Lieutenant, rising, will command so as to form column of "threes" from right.]

Lieutenant----Canton----RISE; Carry---SWORDS; Right (or Left)---FACE; Form---THREES; Left (or Right) oblique ---MARCH; Forward----MARCH.

[See Diagram 18, and move the Canton at option, according to surroundings at the grave, so as to form line facing either side of the grave, and several paces from it. This being done, he will command:]

Lieutenant----Present---SWORDS (and, saluting and addressing the Captain, says:)   Sir the line is formed.
Captain---Banner----POST.

[Whereupon the Standard-Bearer, Pall-Bearers, and Chaplain will take place in line, and the Captain, assuming command, will move the Canton from the grave at will.]

[Unless necessary, the Canton will not be required to fill the grave; in which event, it may be filled up by the Sexton after the conclusion of the ceremony.]

Judge Whitney's Defense before the Grand Lodge of Illinois.

JUDGE DANIEL H. WHITNEY was Master of the Lodge when S. L. Keith, a member of his lodge, murdered Ellen Slade. Judge Whitney, by attempting to bring Keith to justice, brought on himself the vengeance of the Lodge, but he boldly replied to the charges against him, and afterwards renounced Masonry. 15 cents each.

Reminiscences of Morgan Times.

BY ELDER DAVID BERNARD, Author of Bernard's Light on Masonry. This is a thrilling narrative of the incidents connected with the Revelation of Freemasonry and the publication of his book, and showing the indisputable fact that it is a reliable revelation of Freemasonry prepared by the highest Masonic authorities. 10 cents each.

Minutes of the Syracuse Convention.

CONTAINING ADDRESSES by Rev. B. T. Roberts, Chas. D. Greene, Esq., Prof. C. A. Blanchard, Rev. D. P. Rathbun, Rev. D. S. Caldwell, Mrs. M. E. Gage, Elder J. R. Baird and others. Unpublished Reminiscences of the Morgan Times, by Elder David Bernard; Recollections of the Morgan Trials, as related by Victory Birdseye, Esq., and presented by his daughter, Mrs. C. B. Miller; Secretary's Report; Roll of Delegates; Songs of Mr. G. W. Clark; Paper by Enoch Honeywell; Constitution N. C. A.; Reports of Committees and a Report of the Political meeting. 25 cents each.

Proceedings of the Pittsburgh Convention.

CONTAINING OFFICIAL REPORTS; Addresses by Rev. D. R. Kerr, D. D., Rev. B. T. Roberts, Rev. G. T. R. Meiser, Prof. R. W. G. Sloane, D. D., Pres't. J. Blanchard, Rev. A. M. Milligan, D. D., Rev. Woodruff Post, Rev. Henry Cogswell, Prof. C. A. Blanchard and Rev. W. E. Coquillette; also Report of the Political Mass Convention, with Platform and Candidates for the Presidential Campaign of 1876. 25 cents each.

Masonry a Work of Darkness.

ADVERSE TO CHRISTIANITY, AND INIMICAL TO A REPUBLICAN GOVERNMENT. By Rev. Lebbeus Armstrong, (Presbyterian,) a Seceding Mason of 21 Degrees. This is a very telling work and no honest man that reads it will think of joining the lodge. 15 cents each.

History National Christian Association.

ITS origin, objects, what it has done and aims to do, and the best means to accomplish the end sought; the Articles of Incorporation, Constitution and By-laws of the Association, Condition of the Carpenter Donation with Engraving of building donated by Mr. Carpenter; Tables showing the number of Pastors and communicants in churches that exclude members of Secret Societies, Tabular view of Local, County, State and National Conventions, and list of organizations, Auxiliary to the National Christian Association; Brief opinions of Eminent men on Secret Societies, and Testimonies of Religious Bodies against them. This book will be found invaluable by all who wish to know the character of this reform and how they may do the most to further its object. It should be in the hands of every Anti-mason. 25 cents each.